MYSTERY BALL '58

A Season-Long Whodunit

JEFF POLMAN

Grassy Gutter Press
Culver City, CA

Front cover design by Bethany Heck

Back cover photo courtesy of Shaping San Francisco
Title page photo courtesy of Sporting News Collection Archive
Bronx Bugle photos from Google Images
Author page photo by Larry Fryer

≈ *Beforewords* ≈

This is not your average baseball murder mystery.

I have this odd compulsion, you see, to replay entire old seasons using the Strat-O-Matic tabletop baseball game—then take them a fictional step further. This time I chose 1958, the year the Giants and Dodgers first played out West, and fashioned a baseball whodunit (or *whowunit*), a pulpy tale smothered in fish smells and fog, beats and barrios, all wrapped around a fun pennant chase featuring Willie Mays, Hank Aaron, Mickey Mantle, Stan Musial, Ernie Banks, and plenty of other late '50s greats.

Our hero and narrator, Snappy Drake, is an usher at Seals Stadium, the San Francisco ballpark the Giants initially played in, a single-decked treasure wedged into four corners of the Mission District, a site now occupied by a giant parking lot and Petco store. Thankfully, I've been able to mine my imagination to recreate what it must have been like in that first exciting year of major league ball by the Bay. Raised in New England, I now live in L.A., but have always loved San Francisco and the rich history and culture enveloping it.

As was the case with my two previous book "fictionalizations"—*1924 and You Are There!* and *Ball Nuts*—the results of my '58 replay are a bit skewed from what actually happened, and often dictate the direction of the narrative. On the other hand, this being a murder mystery, the killer's identity and climax were always known far in advance.

How Snappy and the characters he meets eventually *get* to this climax is where the real fun of *Mystery Ball '58* lies. So come on in, pal, take off those penny loafers and have a cool glass of ball-noir on me...

—*J.P., Culver City, CA*

For my dad, who turned me on to
Stan Getz and Lawrence Block

≈ *Unsafe at Home* ≈

April 15th

Tough to make out a dead body when it's covered in peanut shells and Royal Crown Cola. But there it was. Head wedged under the wooden seats of row D, section 16, third base side.

My section of Seals Stadium.

Bad enough they wanted me and the other ushers and usherettes here two hours before Johnny Antonelli's first pitch to Jim Gilliam, it being the first big league game ever played in this state, but I had to spend the whole afternoon babysitting San Francisco fat cats and skinny weasels who probably never saw one Pacific Coast League game in their lives.

And now this. Some poor sap who either had a stroke from the Giants edging the Dodgers 7-6 in the 9th inning chiller, or got trampled in the post-game exit stampede. At least that's what I thought. Until I crouched, brushed the peanut shells off him and saw the pearl white handle of a switchblade stuck in his lower back.

Guess I better introduce myself. Snappy Drake here. You can call me by my birth name if it floats your rubber duck, which happens to be Milton. Just don't expect any flowers and wine from me if you don't go with Snappy. See, every Seals Stadium ush called me Snappy because of my famous curve ball. Threw it two years for the Oakland Oaks and one for the Seattle Rainiers before the thing stopped snapping altogether and hung there like an executed prisoner waiting for hitters to club it to death. Which is why I'd been showing Seals fans to their seats since 1951.

Of course that PCL gig is history now. In case you were in Alcatraz or drinking too many rusty nails down at Lefty O'Doul's, the big news in the Bay the past eight months was that the New York Giants moved out here over the winter, along with the Brooklyn Dodgers down L.A. way. Hell, I don't think the town was this hot and bubbly since the Gold Rush, and that was a couple of my grandpas ago.

So yeah, I was planning to dust off those third base boxes and rake in quarter tips at 16th and Bryant all summer. And soon as I was done getting questioned by the law I figured to be back again with some inside dope about this poor murdered bastard in row D, section 16.

Wished I had more dope to share on the shiny new baseball year. Milwaukee and their killer Aaron-Mathews-Spahn-Burdette combo took all of baseball's beans last season, but big whoop. I had to figure the Giants and Dodgers to thrive in their new joints in front of packed crowds. Besides, I'd already put 600 clams down on the local boys taking the N.L. flag with Chumpo over at the Double Play. So you know where I stood.

Perfume at Midnight

April 17th

Totals for our opening series with the Dodgers: three knuckle-chewing one-run games, 68 combined hits, 52 suckers left on base, two wins, one loss and one corpse with a knife in its back. I would've passed out right then if I had a choice in the matter.

Spent at least an hour with the cops after that opener. One of them was built like Gorgeous George Wagner but his suit was too small. The older one who asked all the questions actually was named Malarkey, smelled like scallions and probably hadn't smiled since before the Depression. They had nothing on me but you wouldn't know from their attitude. They didn't know the stiff's name because his wallet was gone and no one had come looking for him yet. Not one person in the stands saw what happened. All the cops found was a piece of paper in his pocket that said *"A band on…"*

with the rest of the sentence or whatever the expression was torn off.

Afterwards I was so annoyed I tipped a few more Hamm drafts than usual across the street at the Double Play. Chumpo poured me a free one when I told him the story, and then Reggie Fleming and Bob Stuckey arrived. Reggie and Bob were my partners in inebriation after Seals games. Reggie was in construction. Bob sold nine-inch screws, and if they didn't start a lame-brained argument on a given day then that day was ruined. This one was about Horace Stoneham, the Giants owner, supposedly making a land deal to build a brand new park for the team the next few years. Bob didn't believe it because he was sure they were going to double-deck Seals. Reggie did because he had ears in the land-grab trade, and so they were off.

Twenty-four hours and our first night game victory later, Reggie and Bob were still at it. I got bored. Paid my tab and hiked down the hill to my walk-up at 15th and Van Ness. The usual clammy fog was rolling in from South Bay. The thick kind that makes even mailboxes look spooky. I hiked to the top of my creaky wooden steps and stopped.

A woman stood there in the shadows. I couldn't see her face but the perfume she was wearing convinced me she had to be a looker. What I could see was a cloud of cigarette smoke blowing toward my face from where her head must have been, and a smart navy skirt that showed enough leg to keep my shoes stapled to the porch step.

"Mr…Drake?"

"You could say that."

"I hear you found that body after the game yesterday."

"Yeah? Says who?"

"It was in the papers."

"Too bad I don't read 'em. Can I help you?"

She dropped her cigarette, pulverized it with a high red heel, and emerged from the shadow.

I was dead right. She was blonde, late 20s. With a sweet, farm-raised face that made you want to whinny and a gait to match. She held out a slender, very white hand for me. It was holding a business card. I read her name out loud the way it looked.

"Liz…Du-mass. *Los Angeles Herald Examiner?*"

"Yes, I'm one of their crime reporters. I was hoping to get an exclusive interview with you. And 'Dumas' is pronounced 'Doo-mah' by the way. It's French."

"Well, I'm pretty damn tired and need to sleep. The finale tomorrow is a day game, you know."

"Oh I know. I just—"

"So good night."

I took out my key, stepped past her to the door. Her hand found my shoulder.

"Please. The police were no help at all. You must have something more—"

"Hey, lady. I don't know you. The guy had a knife in his back, okay? For all I know he was a Dodgers fan."

"Was he? Because that's—

"Forget it, okay? I don't know any more than the cops right now. Not to mention, Miss Doo-miss, that my feet are about to fall off."

She stood there with a sweet, pathetic pout. Like a lost school girl. I felt bad all of a sudden.

"Hey. I don't mean to be a jerk. You just caught me on a bad night. Besides…you haven't even told me what that perfume is you're wearing."

She smiled a little. It was a nice smile. "Dioissimo…By Christian Dior."

"Mmm. Ten bucks says I remember that." I unlocked my door and stepped inside. Stood there and waited for her high heels to make it to the bottom of the steps. Then I killed the outside light.

◆ ◆ ◆

After the last game, another mad house of runners all over the map and this time an extra-inning loss, I went under the stands to the usher's room to change my clothes. Johnny Heep, one of the clubhouse boys, walked up behind me and handed me a sealed envelope. Said this "actress-looking" girl just gave it to him outside.

I opened the thing. Read the piece of paper first, which said "PLEASE COME. LIZ." Inside the paper was a ticket to tomorrow's Giants-Dodgers opener at the Memorial Coliseum— and a plane ticket to Los Angeles.

City of Angles

April 18th

Nice seat, lady.

I knew the Dodgers were opening the season at the L.A. Coliseum instead of the Trojans, but the deep right grandstand really was a football field away. No kidding. The place had more people in it than the city of Bakersfield. The blinding sun was playing chopsticks on my temple, me stupidly without any shades, and when the Dodgers scored four in the 1st off Stu Miller I thought my ears would slide off my head.

For starters, the flight down this morning was a doozy. Wind gusts over the San Joaquin wrestled my stomach to the mat. I swear I heard the propellers cry for mercy. Hadn't been down to L.A. since our Rainiers swung through to play the Stars and Angels years back, but that trip was by bus. You know, on one of those roads.

Liz never said where she'd meet me, but that's what seat numbers are for, and she sure knew *mine*. Plopped down beside my aisle chair around the bottom of the 3rd. She seemed flustered, but in sunshine looked no less fetching than she did in foggy darkness. Wore a creamy blouse and tangerine skirt that begged for ogling, and it even matched her press pin. She'd already made reservations for dinner at Tam O'Shanter on Los Feliz, and on a couch at her place for my sleeping. Meaning except for the fact that the Giants were behind most of the game, there wasn't much I could squawk about.

Then the game went into extras again. Damn these teams. I used the opportunity to walk the massive stands, transistor radios all around me creating a weird Vin Scully echo chamber. Also got a good look at the tall screen and jai alai court they call left field here. Turned and peered up at the press box a few times but didn't see any sign of Liz.

She met me an hour later under the columns at the far exit, after the Dodgers had blown yet another one to us. Her mood was rotten. She drove us across town in her white T-Bird convertible, more quiet and reckless than I cared for.

Everyone parking cars and seating tables at Tam O'Shanter seemed to know her. Walt Disney apparently ate at this place all the time, but he wasn't there. Neither was Mickey. Liz ordered English Goose and I had a steak that was perfectly tender and bloody. It went down even better with my tumbler of Glenfiddich.

"So," she began, waiting for me to light her cigarette after mine, "Anything new?"

"I don't know. Besides you?"

"I meant about the case, silly. The body."

I said no, but did tell her about the torn-off note the cops found in the stiff's jacket. It got her mind dancing.

"A band on...the radio? A band on...the run? Wait! How about a band on stage somewhere? Like a local club! This guy must be a musician somewhere, right?"

"For a crime reporter, you sure jump to daffy conclusions."

Her pout returned. She speared a brussel sprout. I leaned in. "Must be making a damn good wage at that paper to spring for my airline ticket and all this. What's your angle, Liz?"

"What do you mean?"

"You know what I mean. All I am is a lousy stadium usher and you're glommin' on to me like I saw the Lindbergh baby get snatched."

"But you did find a stabbed body in a ballpark. Isn't that a good story?"

"Not especially. What if our locker room kid Johnny Heep found him? Would *he* be sitting here?"

"If he was as cute as you…maybe."

The Glenfiddich blended nicely with my sudden body warmth. I winked and finished off my steak. Liz paid the gaudy bill and we drove across Los Feliz to Franklin and into the Hollywood Hills. Nat King Cole was on her T-Bird radio. The balmy night air teased her blonde mane around.

But something bugged me, and I asked her to pull over at a late-night market so I could buy more smokes. There was a pay phone in back. I dialed the *Herald Examiner* and asked for the crime desk. Got some gravelly night editor who sounded like he had a stack of felony reports in his in-box he would rather be leafing through than talking to me..

And he didn't know anyone named Liz Dumas.

Well La La De Da

April 19th

I didn't say a peep to Liz about that weird phone call. Not even when she poured us brandies in her bungalow later and tried to get chummy with me. I may not be Robert Mitchum but I'm sure as hell no pigeon. Too bad that when I passed on the cuddle business she stopped talking to me for the night.

It was a tiny place, clean and functional with turquoise kitchen cabinets and a Kelvinator Food-O-Rama. All perched on a steep slope like someone's twisted version of a tree house. I curled up on her dinky living room couch and slept badly. Between the crickets and the howls of coyotes before they tore apart some neighbor's cat, I wished I was back in my clammy and quiet hovel.

Breakfast was more of the same between us. It didn't help that her coffee tasted like something that poured out of a rain gutter. I waited till she started in again with the fishing for info nonsense, then told her about the phone call I had with the *Herald*.

She crumbled like an undercooked cobbler. "Okay," she started, "I lied a little bit. I do write for the *Herald*— you saw my press pin, right?—but it's um…for the show biz section."

I said nothing. She let out an exasperated sigh that puffed up the front of her hair. " 'Gaddy's Gadabouts.' Ever read the column? Movie and TV gossip mostly, who's dating who, who was seen at which hotel, eating what dish. Gaddy's in a wheelchair now and I help write up celebrity sightings for him."

"O-kay…So why the hell did you—"

"Because I WANT to write about crime, okay? City desk cronies won't even give me the time of day. Why do you think that guy you got on the line never heard of me?" She spooned out a hunk of grapefruit, chewed it up. "So there I am at Seals Stadium on Opening Day to look for celebrities, and this murder just…happened to happen. Get it?"

"Sure…One juicy scoop about something like that and maybe you're in the big boys' room. Cute. Well, you could've been nice about it and told me the truth."

"I know. And I'm sorry. Guess I thought you'd slam the door in my face."

"Kind of did that anyway, didn't I?" Her school girl smile reappeared. I took my half-drunk cup of mud to her sink. "Well Liz, you sure got some gumption."

"Got more coffee too, if you want a refill."

"Naw, that's okay."

She then told me about her upbringing in Iowa. How she took a bus to L.A. in '53 to be an actress and got nowhere fast. Well-off Daddy set her up in the hills anyway and made a few calls to old friends to get her a spot on the *Herald*. Her first regular gig was scouting the stands at Gilmore Field, home of the Pacific Coast League's Hollywood Stars, and on our way back to the Coliseum for the Saturday game, she took the long way to Beverly and Fairfax. Gilmore Field was supposedly a week or two away from the wrecking ball, and Liz gazed at the decaying, fenced-in grandstand with a pained face.

"Had a two-week thing with Red Munger once—the year he won 23 games—but that was about the only perk."

From Gilmore it was back to the south central part of town. The Dodgers lost another very winnable game to the Giants. Four out of five of those now, by my count. This time we just went out to a pizza joint on LaBrea afterwards where we could have some beers and not have to worry about being polite.

We sure weren't. Back up in the hills she kissed like a champ. Right when things were about to take a turn for the saucy, though, I heard something.

A creak on the outside deck. I slowly raised my eyes from the curve of her neck…up over the living room couch…

…and saw a human shadow duck away from the window.

Something Askew

April 20th

I was off the couch and onto Liz's outside deck like Jack Sprat. Whoever the dark shadow belonged to was gone. Thought I heard some crackling twigs somewhere down the hill but wasn't sure. I looked around. No telltale cigarette butts or matchbook. Not even another torn-off note.

Liz was spooked much more than me. I sat in a chair by her bed most of the night holding a pretty sharp steak knife while she tossed. We went to a waffle place in the morning, took in the last game with the Giants in the afternoon. It was their sixth straight hell-raiser and one that finally put the lady in a better mood.

Monday would be a day off for the Giants, then it was back to Section 16 for me against St. Louis on Tuesday. I was ready to get out of L.A. by 5 p.m. Sunday, though. Didn't feel good about leaving Liz at her place all alone and talked her into staying with some of Daddy's friends down in El Segundo.

She dropped me at the airport on the way. Never been much for long goodbyes, so I smooched her in the car for a second and promised a phone call. She knew how to take it.

The plane ride north was calmer than the one south. I could tell because the Gordon's and tonic I drank worked like a charm. Got back to my apartment just after dark. Walked in, shut the door and looked around.

Something wasn't right. Maybe askew. But I couldn't put a finger on it. Maybe it was the window in the kitchen that was open a crack, the one I was sure I had left closed. Maybe it was the half-eaten apple in the fridge I was pretty sure I hadn't touched. Maybe the gin was just too strong.

Either way, I had just kicked off my shoes, lit up a Camel Filter and dropped *This is Sinatra!* on the turntable when I heard heavy footwear on the outside steps. Knuckles rapped on my door. I approached and asked who was there.

"Police."

I moved the curtain for a look. Saw Gorgeous George and Scallion-Breath standing there, the two cops who grilled me after Opening Day. I opened the door.

"Where you been, Snappy?"

"I don't know. Out."

"Yeah. For the whole weekend, it seems."

"If you already know, why are you asking?"

"Don't get smart, pal. We got a late tip from a fan who saw you poking through the stiff's pockets right after you found his body."

"Well, that fan's a liar. Who was it?"

"Mind if we come in?"

"Kind of. I just got back, and you're making me miss 'I've Got the World on a String' here."

"Got back from where?"

"None of your business."

"Open the damn door, Drake."

What the hell. I could enjoy "Three Coins in the Fountain" now while they dug around and found nothing.

Except they didn't. Scallion-Breath walked over to a little table next to my couch that had a butt-filled ashtray on it. Next to the ashtray was a wallet. The wallet was a brown alligator number, not in too bad shape. And definitely not mine.

"John Martin Blaziecsky Jr.," said the cop, reading a driver license inside it. "That you, by any chance?"

"Someone broke in here. That window in the kitchen? They planted the thing. I'm telling you, it's the first time—"

"Yeah, and Blaziecsky was the stiff's name, so shut up."

Gorgeous George already had his cuffs out, and they were finding my wrists.

Not My Idea of a Day Off

April 21st

Can't say it was my first jail cell. About seven years ago, I didn't like what a Vancouver Mountie fan was saying to me one night. So after the game I served him an open knuckle sandwich with gravy and a couple of sides. At least the Canadian jail was clean.

The one at the Mission District precinct could've used an Ajax attack. It stank like six-month-old body odor, and the lowlifes across from me hadn't even peed their pants yet. The thing I hated the most was that the smell distracted me from my real quandary: figuring out who the rat bastard was that set me up.

The stiff in the grandstand was one thing; this was another. Somebody went to a lot of trouble to break in my place, leave that wallet and tip off the cops. Once I proved I was down in L.A. about ten different ways, though, they had nothing on me. My one phone call had been to my mother, thinking I might need some bail money, and Dorothy Gladys Drake used the opportunity to invite me out to the East Bay for dinner. Lucky me. Hadn't seen Mom since the last anniversary of Dad's bus accident, and it was too cold and wet that day to even visit his grave.

"You look like hell, Milton," she said, the moment I stepped on her Oakland porch.

"I was in jail all night, Mom. Remember?"

Dinner at Mom's always involved me cooking, since anything more than a piece of buttered wheat toast was too much of a challenge for her now. She had read about the body in the *Tribune*, and after I told her the rest of my tale she started lobbing theories at me while the spaghetti cooked.

"What about someone from your playing days?"

"Well, I thought about that guy in Vancouver, but that was so long ago. Plus he's Canadian."

"No old war fellows? Agatha likes to use those." Mom had little to do all day but watch *The Guiding Light* and read mystery books. Agatha Christie had become a recent obsession.

"I wasn't in the war, Mom. Not even the Korean one."

"I know! An old flame!"

"Don't have any."

That was a lie, of course. I collected girlfriends like chewing gum packs. Every one lost her flavor pretty quick, and Liz was one she didn't need to know about yet. I poured us something warm and red from Sonoma and we sat down to eat. Her dining table was like one you'd find in a kid's playhouse, and I had to squirm to get my bad knee under it.

"That leg still bothering you? I told you to go see someone, Milton."

"I manage."

She had already gulped down her first glass of wine. I poured her another. "How'd you get that, anyway?" she asked, "I forget."

So had I. And as I sat there twirling the pasta on my fork, an old name came back and hit me like a snapping twig in my face.

"Paulie Suggs has a beef with me. I bet on Seals game with him all last year. Did pretty damn well at his expense, too..."

"So?

"So I think maybe I'll pay Mr. Paulie Suggs a visit."

Steep Droppings

April 22nd

Lieutenant Scallion-Breath called me this morning right before I went out for a ride. Seemed that this John Blaziecsky Jr., the Opening Day stiff, was a vacuum salesman from San Jose who was at the game by himself. Normal family guy. In other words no reason for anyone to shish-ka-bob him. I said I didn't know the man and hung up. But I sure did know Paulie Suggs.

Paulie lived on a hill. Like, who doesn't in this city? But this one was Bradford Street in Bernal Heights, an incredibly steep incline that took me an hour and a full set of brake pads to find. My '53 Coronet was gasping for air before I was halfway up the thing, and I patted her rusty nose after exiting it for the sidewalk.

Paulie would have been gasping for air soon himself, except the bum wasn't even home. On vacation in Atlantic City said his neighbor, who had no idea when he skipped town. It seemed pretty clear he wasn't around the day someone broke in my place, so I stuck a mental pin in him for a future gab.

Nobody was gabbing in the Seals' usher room, that's for sure. At least not to me. Word had spread that the law held me overnight, so there were a lot of cool nods and evading eyeballs. Most of the guys stuck in the lousier sections of the park hated me anyway for having one of the prime ones, so this was a great excuse to close ranks.

It was still nice to be back on the job, though. The game with the Cards was another close and weird one that we somehow pulled out, and I was nicer than I usually am to the snottier box seat holders.

The trouble came when a pack of hooky-playing urchins snuck into a row of seats next to the field and interfered with two straight balls, one fair and the other falling into Jim Davenport's glove. I kicked them out of the section, but afterwards my darling of a boss Pence Murphy let me have it for letting the kids even get in the park. I let Pence have it right back in so many four-letter words, which was a big mistake.

"I don't like your mouth, Drake." he barked, a handful of ushies grinning in the background, "So how about we give your section to old McGee for a few days? I got something more politeness-building for ya."

It was a beauty, alright. Swirling seagulls paint Seals' outfield fences routinely with their white gooey droppings, and I was now elected to clean it off for two hours every morning.

Don't have to tell you I wasn't spinning like a top over this. To not celebrate, I tipped a half dozen draft Hamms at the Double Play later with Reggie and Bob. The place was electrified, everyone toasting the Giants being tied for first with Cincy. I said it probably wouldn't last because our wins seemed to be sprinkled with leprechaun dust, and this Willie Mays hadn't done anything yet to make me forget Joe DiMaggio. Bob didn't exactly agree.

"They're 5-2 and you gotta piss on our party? What the hell's wrong with you, Snappy?"

"And Mays now?" piped in Reggie, "You sound like one of those Negro-hater meatheads who wouldn't sell him and his wife a house. I think Bob's right. What the hell is wrong with you?"

"Well, the last thing I am is a Negro-hater. But let's see…I find a body at my feet, get grilled by two idiot cops, get lured to L.A. by a cute slinky broad who really wants to hang around at murder sites, end up with the dead guy's wallet planted in my broken-in apartment, get grilled again by the same idiot cops, and today get a new job cleaning up seagull crap. How's that for starters?"

Bob and Reggie didn't squawk again, and after another couple Hamms I didn't hear much of anything. Last I remember Chumpo was tucking me into a back booth. Draped one of his bar towels over my head to keep out the light. I passed out talking to myself, and before long found myself stumbling around the Irish countryside. A pack of leprechauns chased me into a dark forest, and I climbed up a slippery stone staircase where a tall blonde woman was waiting for me at the top. She had the face of a seagull.

Eggs on Plate, Tomato on Phone

April 23th

"Snappy! Phone for you!"

It was Chumpo, back behind the bar in a clean shirt the next morning. Couldn't say the same for myself. A mirror would've been afraid to look at me.

Chumpo locked me in for the night like this once in a while. The Double Play didn't open for another hour, but he'd already gotten the cook to make me some eggs. Poured me a tall tomato juice and slid over the bar phone.

"Yeah."

"Hey! It's Liz!"

"Oh. Hi…"

"Tried you at home a few times and got nowhere, so…Are you okay?"

"Just talk."

"Okay, listen to this! Daddy got me in touch with the editor of *Ellery Queen's Mystery Magazine*. Ever hear of that?"

"Uhh…nope."

"Well, it's only the best of its kind. I lobbed them a short story idea based on the Opening Day murder and he LOVED it! So guess what?"

"You're quitting journalism."

"Hardy har. No, I'm coming up there to research and write the short story! Thought maybe you could help me find a a place to stay, show me around. You know, at least when the Giants are out of town."

My eggs arrived. Three over easy with Chumpo's wonderful greasy home fries. "Sure, I guess…Except the Giants don't leave town until after Mother's Day. Think the league was counting on horrible spring weather back east or something."

"I promise I'll stay out of your hair."

Actually, I didn't mind at all having her in my hair. But no sense giving in too quick to a dame, and there was a touch of desperation in her voice.

"Creepy shadows outside your window again?"

"What's that supposed to mean?"

"Nothing. Just that I worry about you."

"Baloney. Doesn't even sound like you want me up there."

"Oh give me a break, Liz. I just woke up."

"Fine then. Take a sip of coffee and tell me you'd like to see me."

"I happen to be drinking tomato juice."

"Yeah, probably with vodka in it. Talk to you some other time."

She hung up. So did I. Chumpo refilled the juice and I pulled out my last Camel.

◆ ◆ ◆

Hosing seagull crap and wiping it off a fence with a giant sponge at the end of a long mop was one thing. Getting it off the Seals Stadium scoreboard was another. Milwaukee was pounding Cincy all afternoon, the only out-of-town game everyone was following, but it was hard to see the actual score with dried hunks of white poop all over it. I ended up watching us beat St. Louis again from the grounds crew alley, and the view was awful. When Mays doubled into the left corner off Mizell to set up the winning rally in the 3rd, all I saw was him swing and tear around the first base bag. I guess that's exciting enough by itself, but the last thing I wanted to do was crane my neck out more and catch a glimpse of Old Mc-Gee working my grandstand section and farting it up.

Maybe I should've been nicer to Liz on the phone. It's tough to fake your mood, though. My local team was 6-2, had first place all to themselves, the city was doing somersaults, and I was a big puddle of mess.

The Thing That Dropped From the Sky

April 24th

And then there's days of wild magic. Days that drop out of the sky, tap you on the shoulder, spin you around and kiss you with good luck just when you're ready to quit on life. This one sure didn't start that way. A fresh batch of seagull juice was waiting for me on the fence, and I hosed it off pretty quick. The Cards were in for another matinee, meaning I had the place to myself at 8 a.m. and could smoke my Camels and hum Frankie as loud as I wanted. A couple times

it felt like someone was watching me, but every time I turned the grandstand looked cold and empty.

The stadium filled up earlier this time, the Giants being in first and all. Cards skipper Fred Hutchinson was trying something new, starting lefty Irv Noren in place of Del Ennis in the lineup. The grounds crew guys didn't think it would do them much good and predicted a sweep, so I bet a fiver on the road boys.

Fortune hugged me right off the bat, as St. Louis plated five in the 1st on a bunch of walks and singles and a horrible dropped fly by the Say Why Kid.

Our clubhouse boy Johnny Heep tracked me down around then, said some guy was on the phone. I ducked under the stands to take the call. It was a cigar-choked voice I didn't recognize.

"Snappy Drake? Phil Todd here. You free for dinner?"

"I don't know. Depends on who Phil Todd is."

"Sorry. I do that all the time. Assume things. Bobby Bragan sent me down to talk to you about pitching for the Spokane Indians."

I froze. Waiting for the clown horn to blow. Or Tinker Bell to fly by. "You mean in the Pacific Coast League?"

"Yeah, we're having a bad start with lots of injuries. Could use a little fresh arm meat. Bobby says you got a real nasty curve."

"Had one, anyway…"

"Tell ya what, think about it, call me

at the 7th inning stretch at the Hotel Stewart, room 42, okay?"

I hardly remember walking back up the grandstand tunnel. Meanwhile, this young St. Louis pitcher wearing specs named Jim Brosnan was throwing like Walter Johnson, and the first 12 Giants went out. We were losing 6-0 but that kind of thing hadn't been a problem for us yet. The Cards were still putting guys on against Stu Miller but had stopped scoring them. Almost like they couldn't wait to get Brosnan back on the mound.

We went 1-2-3 in the 5th and 6th. The fans had been quiet but now they were buzzing and blabbing. Every grounds crew man was perched on the rail. Even my seagull pals had stopped circling and were perched in a row atop the scoreboard. Numbers unsoiled for the moment.

But I had to call Phil Todd back at the stretch, and Wagner, Rodgers, and Mays were due up! It's not like I had real thinking to do. If a team was willing to pay me to pitch again you're damn right I was going to do it, even for the crummy Spokane Indians.

Superstition is a flaw of mine, though. Can't wear the same color socks two days in a row. Won't order anything with sauce on a Sunday. And if I left my spot again Brosnan would lose his perfect game.

So I waited until Willie Mays flied out for the third time, then bolted back to the telephone. Set up dinner at an Italian joint I liked in North Beach and ran right back.

Just in time to see Brosnan walk Jackie Brandt with two gone in the 8th. But a Cards no-hitter was still in the cards. Valmy Thomas lined to Ruben Amaro at short to start our 9th. Kirkland pinch-hit and grounded out easy to second. It was up to Leon Wagner. No one could breathe, especially me. I had never seen a no-hitter in I can't tell you how many PCL games.

Wagner took two balls, then a strike. It was a cool late afternoon but Brosnan was sweating; I could see it on his neck. He paused to wipe off his glasses and looked back in to Katt for the sign. Threw a heater and Wags pulled it to the right. Blasingame snatched the ball before it hit the outfield grass. Whirled, threw to Musial and Brosnan had done it! Seals Stadium exploded. Sure we lost, but how often do you get to see one of those?

After getting home from some great chicken parmigiana with Phil Todd I sat outside on my top step. Watched the last wink of sunset and smoked the fat Por Larrañga Perfecto cigar Phil gave me. It was sweet.

So to hell with my job, and to the murder of John Blaziecsky and all the grief attached to it. I could disappear faster than a Jim Brosnan fastball, and if his game today and Phil's phone call weren't signs for me, then I didn't know what were. Tomorrow before our night game with the Cubs I would tell my boss I was going out for a cup of coffee—and jump on a plane for Spokane.

Goose Egg of Doom

April 25th

How do you pack up your life in five hours?

The baseball stuff was easy. Old Susan, the trusty Rawlings glove I'd been using since high school, was the first thing to slide off my closet shelf and into the open suitcase. Next came Breezy, my lucky practice ball I finished a one-hit, 12-whiff shutout against Portland with back in '49. Superstitions travel well.

I called my landlord, told him to look for a new renter. The plan was to get to Seals Stadium in early afternoon, hose off the seagull crap, then tell the boss I was "stepping out for a few minutes." Already had my plane ticket to Spokane from Phil Todd, a rooming house lined up, and my brain in a better location. I'd call or write Liz as soon as I got there. Maybe even invite her up if she could stand seeing me for a few days without talking about murder.

I tossed an extra bag of Camels into the bag and zipped it shut. Halfway up the hill to the ballpark, though, I walked into a fog bank that would scare Moby Dick. Couldn't even see the traffic lights at each corner. The Seals field was a spooky, hopeless moor that seemed to end somewhere just past the pitcher's mound. I wasn't even sure the game would be played.

I uncoiled the hose from the shed anyway, dragged it out in the assumed direction of center field. The grass crunched lightly under my shoes and seemed to be the only sound on Earth. I was peering into the fog for the scoreboard, always the worst part of the job, and made two wrong turns before I saw its dark mass looming above me.

Except there was another shape attached to it.

"Those damn kids…"

There was a whole gang of neighborhood brats I had run-ins with for sneaking into the park, and now they'd gotten me back by defacing the scoreboard somehow. But what *was* that thing? I dropped the hose, hauled myself over the fence and climbed a hunk of scaffolding. Some kid's shoes, apparently. Sticking out of the vacant number hole for the Giants' first inning.

Except there was something attached to the shoes. I climbed higher. Caught my breath in my throat.

It was a man's body. Head, shoulders, and the top of his torso crammed sickeningly into the scoreboard hole. Blood still dripping down from the slot where an innocent goose egg should have rightfully gone. Dark green corduroy slacks that looked vaguely familiar, but not with that much blood on them. I grabbed hold of his legs and yanked him out of the thing with three tugs.

Masking tape was sloppily wrapped around his mouth, blood-smeared hair, and much of his mashed-in face. A note was stuck to his shirt with a smaller piece of tape. The words, scrawled with a leaky blue pen, read "OUTTA HERE!!"

I shouted something vile I don't even remember shouting, then quickly hushed myself.

Low voices. A gate opening nearby. *Uh-uh, you sick bastard. You're not gonna finger me for this one.* Shoved the body back into the scoreboard the best I could, hopped the hell down, and started running.

The Recovery Room

April 27th

Yeah, so maybe I was a creep. A coward. Call me whatever you want for leaving the scene, then put yourself in my white bucks for an hour.

I just mysteriously "found" another murdered guy. It was so foggy on that Seals Stadium field that I was positive no one saw me there. I also had a chance to take a break from a dead-end job, rekindle an old dream and pitch ball again. So hello Spokane.

After slipping a note under Pence Murphy's office door about my "leave of absence" from ushering to go pitch in the PCL, I grabbed an earlier flight. Tried to relax with a Camel and highball, though mainly gazed out at the clouds and thought about the mess I had tumbled into.

If this killer didn't know me, he was sure going out of his way to convince me otherwise. The cops showed me the first body's note at the station, and this one was definitely in the same handwriting. Even though "*a band on*" and "*outta her*e!" didn't exactly fit together.

Either way, I was suddenly worried. Placed a call to Chumpo the second I landed in Spokane, told him about my new gig and asked him and the other guys to watch out for anyone suspicious asking about me. He didn't know about any body yet, but I stayed mum, thinking it would be better to let them all find out about the stiff naturally.

Although that didn't sit well with me either. Crossing the Monroe Street Bridge in a taxi, I suddenly remembered I'd pulled the body out of the scoreboard and got my fingerprints all over it. It was only a matter of time before I got yanked off the mound and taken into custody in front of my Spokane teammates. Some I hadn't even had a chance to drink with yet.

Most of them seemed like nice guys. After checking in at my rooming house I went straight to Avista Stadium in time for our night game with Salt Lake City. Everyone was already in the dugout. I threw on my uniform with the number 93 and joined them on the bench for some handshaking. Like Phil had told me, they were struggling so far, but they were the

Triple-A farm team for the Dodgers, so there was certainly some talent. Jim Gentile was a slugger-looking first baseman. Norm and Larry Sherry were a funny pair of brothers. Norm caught and Larry pitched. And there was this little guy that could run like the dickens named Maury Wills.

Bobby Bragan managed, and he wasn't as friendly but said he'd get me into a game as soon as he could. The main thing I had to do was get my old arm in shape and quick. No easy thing. Right then I wished I'd been a peanut bag thrower at Seals instead of an usher all those years.

The Bees had a hitter named Jimmie McDaniel who had three homers off Connie Grob by the 6th inning. We were getting trounced. I'd been tossing warmups pretty steadily to Ron Bottler in the bullpen, and my arm was already sore. Ron flipped me something he called "illegal cream" and it worked pretty well on my shoulder.

Believe it or not, the bullpen gate opened in the 8th and in I came to mop up the 14-2 Salt Lake wipeout. There were maybe 1,000 people when the game started, and it had whittled down to a couple hundred. Fine with me. My curve was snapping pretty well in the warmups, but this day had been so nuts I was happy not to have a big audience.

They announced my name and a couple of folks clapped. Most likely old-timers who saw me pitch once. Or maybe just liked my nickname. A first baseman who couldn't hit named George Schmees stood in there, and my first pitch went to the backstop screen. The second one bounced two feet in front of the plate. The third and fourth were no improvement, and Schmees walked to first.

Bragan came out to talk to me. I said I was fine, and looked in at Sammy Miley. Another wild pitch, and then I knew the problem. I couldn't focus on the catcher's mitt because I couldn't even see it. The only thing in front of me—and the only thing in my brain—was the mangled face of that scoreboard victim.

The Bronx Bugle Sporting Life

Stengel to Shake and Shimmy Yank Lineup

by Archie Stripes
American League Beat

After an exhausting week-end in Baltimore that saw the Bombers earn a split with the Orioles thanks to a surprise win by Duke Maas, they're resting up on this off-day for a long stretch in the Bronx against the four western clubs—no spring pushovers in the bunch.

The Yanks struggle to win every game because they either get no hitting or no pitching, depending on their mood. After going with a set lineup the first two weeks, Casey Stengel has decided to put his platooning skills into effect for the homestand.

"Mantle don't move, because no sense moving trees. Siebern and Carey can either flip or flop first or second, and I'm gettin' Slaughter in there too so watch what happens. Bauer ain't being

used enough so more of him, Howard up there for the lefties, sometimes righties, but not in the field when I can. Kubek's too young for lefties so if you see Richardson shovin' over McDougald, don't scream about it. If you don't use all your nuts then some of your bolts fall off every time and if I didn't think that I wouldn't believe it."

New York's first western foes will be Al Kaline, Frank Lary and the Bengals of Detroit.

TED WILLIAMS MAKES 2 OUTS
Details in next edition

No Games Today: East-West Matchups Are Next

Following this baseball-wide travel day, Here are the pickings for the first round of "cross-country" play:

TIGERS at YANKEES (Hoeft vs. Ditmar)
A'S at RED SOX (Garver vs. Monboquette)
WHITE SOX at ORIOLES (Wilson vs. Portocarrero)
INDIANS at SENATORS (Woodeshick vs. Clevenger)

CARDS at REDS (Mizell vs. Purkey)
BRAVES at CUBS (Willey vs. Hillman)
PIRATES at DODGERS (Kline vs. Koufax)
PHILLIES at GIANTS (Roberts vs. Gomez)

≈ *Dark, Starry Road* ≈

April 29th

Before our next drubbing I used the clubhouse phone and made a long distance call to Chumpo at the Double Play. He was jollier than ever, which threw me. I asked him if he'd mentioned my last call to Reggie and Bob and he said just Bob, because he thought Reggie was out of town on some construction job.

And obviously, still no news of the found body, which was beyond strange. I hung up and got nervous all over again. There was still a half hour till game time so I left the park, jogged a few blocks to Frenchy's News and checked a few out-of-town papers. Nothing in the *Chronicle* or *Examiner* on a second body found at Seals Stadium. Not even in the sports section.

"Pay up, Drake!" yelled journeyman outfielder Glen Gorbous the second I got back to the clubhouse in a sweaty, confused state. During warmups I had stupidly taken him up on a bet that he couldn't throw a resin bag farther than me. Not knowing, of course, that he was in the damn *Guinness Record Book* for throwing a baseball over 445 feet once. So there was 25 bucks gone, plus another full night of shoulder ache.

Thankfully Bragan didn't stick me in the game this time, but I still wasn't in the mood to pour into town for drinks with the other players. Instead I sat in the whirlpool a good half hour, washcloth on my face, until my fingers were all pruny, my head groggy, and I couldn't feel my shoulder anymore.

The players' lot was empty and all 1,500 or so fans had gone home. The stadium lights were off. A chilly night breeze was blowing through from one of the surrounding national forests. I walked out to the road and readied my thumb.

A handful of cars blew by. Maybe I should've kept my uniform on instead of just my Spokane Indians cap. I kept walking west, stars came out, and the darkness seemed to get darker. I heard the roar of a bigger oncoming vehicle and spun around.

It was a clanky, medium-sized white bus with green trim. Maybe about fifteen years old. A round decal on the side said "Washington Motor Coach". The driver slowed down and threw open the door for me. I hopped on board.

The thing was filled with young ballplayers. I mean, they weren't in uniform but I know ballplayers when

I see them, and these were chewing, spitting and smoking like players always do. Some even had gloves and hats in their laps. I told the driver I was heading into town in search of a late dinner and he nodded, motioned to a tiny open seat right behind his.

What was weird about these players was there wasn't the typical amount of ribbing, swearing and card playing going on. Actually, most weren't even talking, just chewing their whatevers and staring at me with spooky eyes. They made me jumpy.

"You guys just play a game?" I asked the nearest one.

"Uh-uh. Goin' to one."

"Really? This late?"

He didn't answer. A scrawnier player next to him asked my name. I told him, and he said "I'm Vic."

"I'm Mel," said his buddy.

"Robert," said a guy a couple rows back.

"George" said another.

And then they were all silent again. I shivered, turned to the bus driver, and asked him where they were headed.

"Bremerton" is all he said. I wasn't sure where the hell that was, but it sounded familiar. The bus made a lot of chugging and wheezing noises whenever it shifted gears. An old Bing Crosby song played on the radio. It was so cold on the bus I could see my breath.

Then the long railroad car shape and neon sign of Frank's Diner came up on the left. I tapped the driver's shoulder, asked him to stop.

He did, with a loud, hideous squeal of brakes. "Good luck guys!" I said to the players. A few nodded glumly. Most of them didn't move. I hopped off, waited for the bus to groan away and disappear around the bend, then shook off my willies and headed into the diner.

Meat loaf and two cups of coffee never tasted so good. While the waitress was adding up my check I mentioned the weird old white bus to her and her pen stopped in midair. Every person left in the place turned and stared at me.

"What'd I say?"

"Ballplayers on that bus?" asked one of the patrons.

"Yeah…not really friendly ones, either."

The waitress wasn't laughing. She led me over to a wall of framed pictures. People who had eaten at Frank's, people who had posed with Frank. Along with some news clippings of famous local events. She took her pen and pointed to one, a team photo of the 1946 Spokane Indians. Some of the faces looked weirdly familiar.

Because I had just seen them on that bus.

A black-framed clipping underneath was dated two days after the team photo, (and here it is atop the next page).

The waitress tapped my arm with her pen. "That's what you get for wearing that ball cap, fella."

Did I really ride on that bus? Naw.

Spokane Ball Team's Bus After Crash That Cost Lives of Eight

Eight members of the Spokane Indians baseball club lost their lives and seven others were injured when the chartered bus in which they were driving to Bremerton plunged off Snoqualmie pass highway Monday night. The machine tumbled 300 feet down an embankment and caught fire. The bus struck boulders in the foreground after tearing out guard rail. (AP wirephoto.)

It had to be the weird phone call to Chumpo, or the whirlpool I sat too long in that got my brain imagining things, mixed with bad memories of my dad dying in *his* bus accident.

All I know is that my bad San Francisco luck has followed me up here, and I'll be damned if I go on one road trip with this team.

(with a tip o' the cap to Red Sovine and Tom Waits)

National League thru Wednesday, April 30

Milwaukee	8	6	.571	—
Chicago	7	6	.538	0.5
Pittsburgh	8	7	.533	0.5
Los Angeles	7	7	.500	1
San Francisco	7	7	.500	1
St. Louis	6	7	.462	1.5
Cincinnati	6	7	.462	1.5
Philadelphia	5	7	.417	2

American League thru Wednesday, April 30

Baltimore	10	5	.857	—
Boston	10	5	.714	—
New York	10	6	.667	0.5
Chicago	9	6	.571	1
Detroit	7	9	.438	3.5
Cleveland	7	9	.438	3.5
Kansas City	5	10	.333	5
Washington	3	11	.214	6.5

The Last Spokane Show

April 30th

Spokane may be a very nice place to have dinner. Or raise a kid. Or pick wild blueberries. But four days up here was four days too long for me.

The Indians team I was occasionally pitching for was lousy, with a wage to match. The electric hot plate in my rented room never worked. Worst of all, things down in San Francisco were going from weird to nightmarish.

After breakfast at Frank's, three over easy with lousy home fries, I placed another call to Chumpo. As far as murder news goes, I had struck out with the morning papers again. This time, though, Chumpo's voice was slow and dark, like someone had forced him to drink motor oil. I asked him what was wrong.

"You didn't hear?"

"Hear what? Remember, I'm 1500 miles away—"

"They found Reggie."

I paused. To let the skin on my backbone ice over.

"Reggie Fleming? What do you mean 'found him'?"

"He's dead, Snappy! Someone killed him!"

I was mute. And then I remembered the dark green corduroys.

"That bastard..."

"What's that?"

"Nothing. I just...I just can't BE-LIEVE it!"

I only had to fake half of my shock. Meanwhile, Chumpo sounded like he might cry. I pictured him wiping his eyes with his filthy bar rag.

"Right across the street from here, too...Can you believe that?"

"I can believe anything these days. Russian satellites in space? Two bodies found in one ball park? Weird."

"Oh no. They found Reggie in *Franklin Square* Park. His face all mashed in."

I didn't know what to say.

"I mean, you'd think mugging a guy would be enough, right? But whoever did this must've used his head for batting practice! Son-of-a..."

I heard him drop the phone on the bar.

"Chumpo? You there?"

He picked it up again. Snorted back a sniffle. "Yeah...Had to go see Diane and the kids this morning. They're a wreck, Snappy. When are you coming back?"

"Sooner than I thought I would, that's for sure. There's something very smelly about this thing."

"How's that?"

"How's about I tell you when I'm back in town?"

There was a long pause. "You got something to do with this, Snappy?"

"What's that?"

"You were pretty strange on the phone the other day...kind of paranoid, if you know what I mean."

"Hey. Whatever you think you

might be thinking about, it isn't that. Talk to you soon."

I hung up. Let my brain go to work while I dressed for our homestand finale with the Bees. Who the hell moved Reggie's body across the street to the park? And a day later?

Bragan put me in for a longer relief stint this time, game tied 6-6 in the 5th. My curve was snapping a lot better. Whiffed .300 hitter Joe Christopher on three pitches, looking for a fastball each time. Gentile gave us the lead with a two-run shot, and I left after three innings of one-hit ball. Ducked into the clubhouse to hit the whirlpool again.

Found an envelope from Western Union taped to my locker. I ripped it open.

TO: SNAPPY DRAKE
NEEDED DOWN HERE ON URGENT MATTER. AIRLINE TICKET IN YOUR NAME AT SPOKANE AIRPORT. SPEAK TO NO ONE CONCERNING BODIES AND REPORT TO MY OFFICE ON ARRIVAL.
—HORACE STONEHAM
OWNER, S.F. GIANTS

The Office

May 1st

I took the night flight back to Frisco as dry as a preacher. Whatever mess I'd gotten myself into had just become thicker and stickier, and I needed my wits to start cleaning off the gunk.

I'd seen Horace Stoneham at his of-fice window a couple of times, peering down at the field. From what I'd heard, he wasn't much for socializing. Anyway, one of his flunkies drove me straight from the airport to Seals Stadium. The Giants had beaten the Phils again in exciting, late fashion earlier, and the place was dark except for the light coming from Stoneham's office.

He was sitting behind his big desk. Stocky, red-faced, hair thinning. Coddling half a glass of Glenlivet in his hand. As I entered he stood a bit wobbly, shook my hand with his free one.

"Thanks for coming, Mr. Drake. Sorry to have to do this."

"Don't be. Spokane wasn't paying me dirt anyway."

"Well, if you help me out, I can offer you a lot more than dirt. Have a seat and a drink."

He poured me a glass before I even bent my knees. I sipped it like a parakeet.

"Very unfortunate about your friend Reggie."

"Yeah…I heard."

He eyed me for a long, bloodshot second. "Did you hear some son-of-a-bitch shoved him into my new scoreboard?"

"Naw. You're not serious."

"Pence Murphy found him. Ten minutes before we opened the damn gates. Thank god he hid him in the equipment shed before I came up with the idea of re-locating him across the street."

"Pretty damn illegal there, Mr.

Stoneham."

"It's not as illegal when you're friends with the police. And I had my reasons, which I'll get to. It also might interest you to know that Pence Murphy thought you did it and ran away."

"Big atom bomb there. Did he tell you why I would want to kill one of my best friends?"

"Hey, I didn't even know who you were. When you run a club you don't really have time to meet the ushers. Or ushers who've been relegated to hosing off seagull turds. But it so happens I do know Phil Todd, who vouched for your Spokane 'promotion' right away."

"Why am I here, Mr. Stoneham?"

He set his glass on the desk. Pulled his stocky frame off the chair and strolled to the window. Looked out at the black field.

"This was a big move for me, you know…My father made the Giants an institution in New York. Hell, when I was a kid I'd sit and listen to John McGraw talk strategy with him in our living room. But I'm no social gaddabout like O'Malley is, and I don't like spending money on newspaper, radio and television ads. I'd rather build our new following here by winning ballgames."

"Might want to invest in some better relief pitchers then."

"Listen, Drake. I got a stake in keeping you on the payroll. Don't blow it."

"What kind of stake?"

He walked over, grabbed the Glenlivet and topped off my glass, spilling some on my fingers. "Like I said, until my new park's built out on Candlestick Point, the Giants need big crowds. Meaning I can't have some nut job leaving corpses in the stadium. Which is where you come in."

"Me."

"That's right. Someone seems to have a grudge against you, Drake. My pals on the police force sure think so, and they barely know who the guy in the scoreboard was." He leaned in, scotch-breezed my face. "The idea is to put you back in the grandstand ushering those seats at triple your old salary. With plainclothes cops all over the yard, waiting for the creep to make another move."

This time I drank half the glass in one swig. "You wanna throw me out there like bait?"

"More like a magnet. And don't worry, you'll have an assistant to help you out, organize things. This wasn't entirely my idea, you know."

He turned and nodded to his flunkie, who swung the door open to the hall.

In walked Liz Dumas. Pretty damn radiant for late at night.

"Hey there again…Snappy."

The Hunker Game

May 2nd

The idea was to get Liz as far away from Seals as I could, so we grabbed a cab uptown to The Saloon on Grant. I needed more than one cocktail after that shaky Stoneham meeting, and hunkering down in one of the few places here to survive the 1906 quake seemed fitting.

Turns out that Liz had called Chumpo looking for me again, heard about the stiff across the street, flew herself up to research this "crime story" of hers, and ended up sweet-talking her way into Stoneham's office by saying she was my "colleague". I had to hand it to her; the lady was a real pip. When I told her what I had discovered on that foggy morning, though, she was suddenly less pippish.

"Stoneham never said a word...I can't believe you found Reggie in the scoreboard."

"Yeah. One of the perks of my job."

She fingered the rim of her Tom Collins glass. "You should've snatched that note off his body. We could've studied it."

"C'mon, it was a simple piece of paper. Bad enough I left the scene in the first place."

"So Reggie being your friend pretty much rules out a coincidence here."

"Not really. The killer might not know me at all, and just latched on to me after I found the first body."

"Well, hopefully this new game plan of ours will shake him out of his creepy tree. Stoneham wants to kick it off during Sunday's doubleheader with the Pirates."

"Great. Now I can be a nervous wreck for five hours."

"You don't like the idea?

"I'd rather cliff dive off Point Diablo. But we have to try something. Where are you staying while you're here?"

She smirked a bit. Downed a big sip of her drink. "Oh, a nice little walk-up place a few blocks down from the ballpark. It went up for rent last week."

I stared at her. "You have to be kidding."

"Hey, if you stay nice to me, I'll let you use the couch."

"First you help organize Operation Cockamamie and now you take my place? Who do you think you are?"

"If you don't know who I am by now, Snappy..." She polished off the Tom Collins, "you never will."

We had two more rounds to make things friendlier, but on top of Stoneham's Glenlivet I was in no condition to even hail a cab. It was closing time when we left The Saloon, and there weren't many on the streets anyway. Liz dragged me onto the last bus heading back toward the Mission. We had a hard time not falling over each other on the turns, which wasn't a bad thing.

The bus dropped us just north of the ballpark. We still had a few blocks to walk. The trees of Franklin Square

Park loomed by on our left, and it was hard to even look at them.

"I'm gonna make you be nice to me yet, mister," Liz cooed into my ear, lightening the mood.

"Many have tried. Hate to tell ya that few have succ—"

"SSSH!"

She clutched my arm and I stopped. Leaned against a light pole to keep from falling.

"Whazzit?"

"Nothing…Thought I heard footsteps."

We were past Seals, heading down the hill into my neighborhood. The sidewalk was empty in both directions. Dripping with alleys and shadows.

"Come on." I sobered up quick and led her away, around a corner and up the back wooden steps to my just-vacated apartment. She had trouble with the key.

"Amateur." I moved her aside. Jiggled it in the lock my special way and the door opened. She poked my ribcage, walked in first.

All I wanted to do was collapse, but being in my mostly empty old place was strange, and the footsteps Liz thought she just heard bothered me even more. She threw her coat on the sheetless mattress, fell face first on it and was snoring in seconds. I found the one chair that was left, slid it over. Sat beside her and smoked the first of many Camels.

I woke up at the crack of dawn, still in my coat. Cigarette ash all over it. Liz was still comatose. I stood painfully, went to the door and opened it to suck in some fresh air.

A note was stuck to the door with masking tape. This time scrawled on a bar napkin from The Red Parrot Room:

"2 OF YOU MAKE IT MUCH WORSE"

The Mongo Room

May 3rd

"Let me see that again." Liz had to whisper the request because we were dressed in black, seated on a couch in Reggie Fleming's living room Saturday morning. The memorial service went okay, but the house in Daly City was stuffed with working handkerchiefs, and Reggie's wife and kids needed as much quiet as possible.

Liz turned the bar napkin every which way. All she was missing was a magnifying glass and big Sherlock pipe. "You been to this place?"

"Red Parrot? Nope. Heard of it, though. It's on Evans Avenue, down near Hunter's Point. Lots of Latin bands play there."

"Can you dance?"

"Now you're being ridiculous."

Reggie's wife Diane walked over at that point. I introduced Liz and gave the widow a comforting hug. She looked like she hadn't slept since Christmas. "Thanks so much for coming, Snappy…" she said, then broke down and I had to hug her again. Liz stood there helplessly.

"I just wish I knew who would do this…Everyone liked Reggie."

"He never said anything about someone, y'know, out to get him?"

"Oh no. No…He was just so looking forward to starting his new job, buying us a new car. Who would have ever thought he'd end up in that park…" Her voice evaporated on my shoulder. I wanted to tell her about the scoreboard, but what good would that have done?

Afterwards I drove Liz back into the city, giving us plenty of time to think.

"What was his next job?" she asked.

"Construction on the new park. Candlestick Point."

"Really? I think Seals is pretty nice. Why doesn't Stoneham just double deck that place and build a parking garage?"

"Don't get me started. Not sure of all the details but you can bet he got a sweetheart deal."

"Hmm. Might be worth looking into that deal."

"How come?"

"Maybe someone else likes Seals Stadium too. Someone who doesn't want to see it vacated. Someone who would kill to make that not happen."

"Then why wouldn't they go after Stoneham? I don't know, Liz…"

"Well, I still think we oughta check out this nightclub. Have a little tequila, ask around."

"Or we can just show this napkin to the cops and let them do it."

"That's no fun. Where did you say this Candlestick Point is?"

"I didn't. It's down near the airport on this little peninsula. Just south of…south of Hunter's Point."

We looked at each other. And just like that we had a post-game date.

◆ ◆ ◆

The Red Parrot was a kick. Mongo Santamaria and his Afro Cuban Drum Beaters were the headline, and the place was a spicy sardine can. A shiny wood dance floor was packed solid with couples feeling the salsa. The tables were full too, so Liz and I wedged into a spot near the bar. While we ordered margueritas, I quizzed the barkeep about any strange *hombres* he might have seen in the club lately. He told me to mind my own cheeseburgers in so many words.

Just as Mongo launched into "Pito Pito," smacking away on his congas, I spotted two guys in a prime booth at the edge of the dance floor. They both wore tropical shirts. One had a fedora and smoked a cigar. Waiters and assorted patrons paid a whole lot of attention to them. I inched closer for a better look, then retreated and nudged Liz.

"Hey. Guess who's here."

"If it isn't Harry Belafonte, I'm not interested."

"It's better. Orlando Cepeda and Ruben Gomez!"

"Who?"

"Cepeda's our rookie slugger. Not burning up the field yet but he did belt a couple winning homers. And

Gomez smoked the Phillies on the mound today, remember? When you're at the game you should check the scorecard once in a while."

I coaxed her over to the booth. Cepeda and Gomez had big blue drinks. Their eyes looked like bloodshot wading pools. But they were digging Mongo with a vengeance. Cepeda's giant torso was grinding to the rhythm beneath the table and making it bounce.

"Hey Ruben," I said to Gomez, "Great game this afternoon."

He nodded and grinned without looking at me. "Thanks a lot, man."

Then he looked up at Liz. So did Cepeda, who shoved Ruben over in the booth to make room for us.

"Have a seat, chiquitos! You two like to mambo?"

"Sure!" I said, earning a glare from Liz. "You guys come here a lot after games?"

"Not too much. But for the Mongo Man? Anytime!"

Gomez knocked some ash off his cigar, turned so he was directly facing Liz. "This friend of yours here...he show you the right moves?"

'What's that?"

"You gonna move wrong to the music, might as well not move, si?"

Liz was dumbstruck. A slower rumba called "A Ti No Mas" began. Ruben cocked his fedora, slid out of the booth. Came around, took Liz's hand and she followed him onto the dance floor without a peep of protest.

Cepeda just smiled and handed me a cigar. "So you some big Giants fan?"

"You can say that." A lighter appeared in his big hand, and I let him fire me up. "Actually...I'm also an usher at the park. People call me Snappy."

The lighter snapped shut. Cepeda's smile dropped through a trap door.

"You the one found that *hombre muerto*!"

"Excuse me?"

"The body! The one with the knife in him Opening Day!"

"Well, yeah...but that's why—"

He snatched the lit cigar out of my hand. "Go, man! Get away from me!"

"What's the problem?"

"YOU the problem! I got a .208 batting number so far and you wanna hex me some more? Adios!"

I tried to reason with him but a 300-pound door man was on me in seconds. Liz slid away from Gomez, came to my rescue. Seconds later we were in the parking lot.

"Well, that got us nowhere in a hurry," I said, fixing my manhandled shirt collar, "Enjoy your salsa lesson?"

"Shut up."

My Coronet was parked at a far, dark edge of the lot. A cold wind whipped off the bay, shook the bushes in front of its hood. As we neared the car, we both stopped talking. Looked around and listened. Our hearts pounding.

There was no new note taped to the door, no knife sticking out of a tire. Whoever this killer was, though, he was spooking us without even being there.

Double Indignity

May 4th

Before today's twinbill with Pittsburgh, I found myself stuck in a back room of the Seals clubhouse. Not that I minded the back room; I didn't need to see the other ushers and my boss Pence Murphy throwing me the evil eyes. But the gates opened in five minutes and there I was, getting a briefing from my old pal Scallion Breath. The flatfoot's real name was Lieutenant Malarkey, and both names were fitting.

"Do what I tell you to do, Drake, and this'll be real easy. I got five plainclothesmen in your section. Can't tell ya who they are because that could blow their cover. They'll be there for both games. See anyone that looks suspicious, all you gotta do is use this and we'll be on him in seconds." He handed me a silver whistle.

"Are you kidding? You guys all carry .38s and I have to fight this lunatic with a party favor? Maybe you should just give me a pinwheel hat to go with it."

"Like I said, Drake. If he makes a move we'll be on him like flies. Not to mention ten extra officers at the gates to watch the crowd coming in."

"Great. Do they have whistles, too?" Malarkey just glared at me. I asked him what Liz was going to do.

"Miss Dumas will be wearing an usherette uniform and working a first base section, with another set of of-ficers around HER. Mr. Stoneham wants this plan to succeed, Drake. From what I hear he's paying you a nice little chunk to try and help that happen. Don't throw it away."

And with that, I was back in the stands. Many of the Section 16 regulars were there, like the Jorgensens, a wealthy old Pacific Heights couple who had been attending Seals games here since the '30s. Like Johnny and Tony Muccio, two brothers who worked for the same concrete waste company, bet each other like crazy during the games and were the best tippers I had. It was close to a sellout, but kind of dizzying to show folks to seats while I stared at their faces or looked for objects in their hands.

The Pirates took a quick 2-0 lead on McCormick thanks to a Dick Stuart bleacher blast, but the home team strung five hits and a walk together for four runs off Ron Kline in the same first inning. From that point on, though, we were drawn and quartered, as the Bucs scored the last ten runs of Game One. Three different Pirates—Stuart, Frank Thomas and Hank Foiles—each homered twice, and the game was doubly awful because the fans who would have normally just left had to force themselves to stick around for Game Two.

There was a 20-minute break before Porterfield and Monzant took the hill, and I spent it smoking cigarettes with Liz in a tunnel. Her usherette outfit included a cute little skirt she wasn't thrilled with. It was the first time I saw most of her bare legs. They were whiter than I expected living down in L.A. and all, but otherwise perfect.

"Any strange characters in your section?" she asked.

"You didn't hear me whistling, did you? This whole thing is idiotic. Let's say you're a diabolical killer with an axe to grind against me or Giants fans or something. Why the hell would you try and knock someone off at the ballpark again after barely getting away with it the first time?"

'He might be diabolical but no one said he's a genius."

"If it's even a he."

She frowned. Crushed out a cigarette with her usherette sneaker. "Girls don't do those things. See you afterwards."

Game Two was more of the same. Except for Clemente, who went 0-for-10 on the long afternoon, they could've hauled the entire Pittsburgh lineup into custody for attempted murder. Catcher Bill Hall drove in six with a homer, triple and single, making that 11 RBIs on the day for their backstops, while Leon Wagner's late homer was our only damage against Porterfield.

This time the crowd was thinning out, so it was easier to scope the fans. A pack of teenagers snuck into the section and when I tried to boot them out, one who looked a little older spun around and flashed me his badge. A guy on the grounds crew was spending a little too much time sweeping off third base and glancing in my direction, blowing his cover all by himself.

The Muccio Brothers got tired of betting when the score became 9-1 and headed home. Then a fat little guy with peanut shell flakes on his muscle shirt sided up to me during the bottom of the 9th and gave me a nudge.

"What's the matter, Snappy? Pitching didn't work out for ya?"

"What's that?"

"I was at your first game up in Spokane last week. Pretty sad."

I looked him over. Sure didn't recognize him from my bygone PCL days.

"Not as sad as you feeling like you had to tell me this."

"Oh yeah? Maybe you should work on your snap instead of the clap."

My blood boiled. To hell with the whistle. My fist was in his gut before I knew it and he was tumbling backwards on the aisle steps. A nearby soda vendor dropped his entire tray of Royal Crowns, yanked a police revolver from his apron and was on the creep in seconds. Three "fans" and a "photographer" from the field joined in.

"He's not the killer, he's just a jerk!" I yelled a few times, but they didn't hear me and pushed me aside so they could handcuff him.

Valmy Thomas fouled out to end the game just then, and the rest of the crowd began to file out. I scanned the park. Could see Liz watching the commotion from the other side of the field and trying to squeeze through the crowd to join me.

Then I turned to the left field bleachers. They were almost empty, but one big guy was sitting there in the second row, paying no attention to the exiting people around him. As a matter of fact, he was staring bullets right at me.

As another matter of fact, it was the jerk I was looking for a week ago: Paulie Suggs.

Not Quite Fishy Enough

May 6th

I lost Paulie Suggs—or at least the sight of him. The cops brought me under the stands with the muscle-shirted moron after the second game, and I had to help straighten things out. Lt. Malarkey was more full of some than usual.

"What d'you mean you've never seen him?"

"Hey, I know they don't pay you much, Malarkey, but you can't afford a new set of ears? I told you. He's a Spokane Indians fan who's on vacation down here, okay? Let him go already!"

The moron fan may have been an idiot, but hardly deserved the Public Enemy No. 1 treatment they were giving him. He was relieved to get unhandcuffed and slapped with a peace-disturber warning. Malarkey didn't want to hear one word about Suggs, though.

"Sure, Drake. Send us on another goose chase. We already got one near-lawsuit on our hands today."

In a way I didn't blame him. It had been a long afternoon. But I couldn't get Suggs' staring eyes out of my mind.

Liz was even less sympathetic later. She had bad blisters on both feet from the tight usherette shoes, and soaked them in a hot tub of water all night while she drank Cabernet. There was hardly any furniture in her/our place now, so she gave me one half of the mattress and serenaded us to sleep with boozy snoring.

I was up at dawn's crack, threw some cold water in my face and carefully slipped outside. Two cops were in a sedan across the street staking the apartment, no doubt on Malarkey's orders. They were also dozing, so I climbed over the staircase rail. Dropped behind some bushes and used a back alley to escape.

Went by foot, bus, and cable car down to Fisherman's Wharf. I knew Suggs unloaded shrimp and crab boats six mornings a week. It was a decent job considering his brain size, and kept him active at the track and poker rooms. The wharf was fogged in as usual, packed with fishermen and boats. I was having a tough time finding him.

Then I heard a ghostly singing voice, coming from somewhere out on the water. It was a male falsetto, crooning the opening bars of Domenico Modugno's Italian hit "Nel bu Dipinto di Blu". In ancient Wharf days, singing was the way fishermen signaled each other in the fog, and some of them liked to carry on that tradition. Sure enough, seconds later I recognized Paulie Suggs' gruff baritone answering his colleague, clear as a foghorn:

"VOLLL-ARRRE!"

A crab boat materialized, loaded with fresh Dungeness, and docked at the wharf. Suggs boarded and started hauling off the beauties with five other guys. He was uglier than I remember, and I saw him less than 24 hours ago.

I watched them work from the other side of a nearby pylon. Waited until the catch was clear and Paulie was the last man on the boat. Slipped on board, snatched a free grappling hook. Snuck up behind him and shoved him through a galley door. Pressed the hook to his neck. He was much bigger than me, but I had the hook.

"Drake! What the hell—"

"Hell is right, Paulie. And it's where you're headed if you don't come clean."

"Come clean about what?"

"I saw you watching me yesterday from the bleachers. I wouldn't call it a friendly look, either."

"Whaddaya, nuts? The Giants just got their clocks cleaned twice! I lost fifty bucks! I was staring at the field!"

I felt a little stupid right then. It passed.

"Don't give me that. You're still sore about losing that dough to me last year, aren't you? I told you Sacramen-

to didn't have enough good starting pitchers and you were too cocky to listen. If you haven't been doing these murders you've been trying to pin 'em on me!"

"What murders?? I've been away in Vegas for a week! And why would I do anything to you?"

"You didn't follow me and my lady friend the other night? Stick a note on my door?"

His nervous face suddenly relaxed. Twisted into a smirk. Big hands grabbed me from behind, spun me around. Four crew members were leaning over me, and the nastiest one held a very sharp crab-splitting knife to my face.

"You better know the words to the second verse of 'Volare', you son-of-a-bitch."

I'm not much of a singer and I'm certainly not Italian, but tried to fake them anyway. Thirty seconds later I was swimming to shore.

Breakfast of Chumps

May 7th

"What's the matter? You can't make an egg?"

"Hey Snap, you're in *my* place now. And I already told you I'm no Donna Reed."

So began our Wednesday morning. I was still grumpy from being tossed in the bay, and Liz was dealing with her red wine and shopping hang-overs. She was at Ransohoff's all day yesterday and came home with three dresses, two skirts, and a lamp. But who was I to complain? She was put-ting me up rent-free for the time be-ing and all we'd done so far was neck. Her obsession with this murder case had a lot to do with that.

"So what's our next move?" she asked, dumping sugar into her black coffee.

"I don't know, but mine is to make myself some eggs. Interested?"

"I eat light for breakfast."

"Ha. I'd call a peach and two spoon-fuls of cottage cheese barely eating."

"You want to sleep on the porch to-night?"

"I just want to sleep. You got a saw-mill going in that mouth of yours."

She simmered while I fried up two eggs, home fries and some bacon. Then we got back to the murder busi-ness. We agreed that until the killer left another note or victim, we were kind of helpless. And if there's one thing I don't like, it's being helpless.

So we took the day off. I called Pence Murphy and Lt. Malarkey, cry-ing stomach flu. His stakeout goons were asleep at their wheel again, and we passed up an exciting Pirates win in the finale for a picnic lunch and walk in Golden Gate Park. The air was crisp. Spring flowers bloomed. Liz and I had sandwiches and cold pops on the grass by the De Young Museum.

"You know the way you called me 'Miss Doomis' the first night you met me?"

"Yeah."

"Well…Doomis is my real name. Not *Dumas*. Thought I'd lose a piece of my midwest corn pone when I got to L.A."

"Then I imagine you'll want your French name again this weekend with the Dodgers back in town. Lots of *Herald Examiner* pals in the press box to keep impressing."

"Aw, heck with them. I have a better chance becoming Nancy Drew than making their dumb crime beat."

We strolled through the botanical garden, then over to the Spreckels Temple of Music. Everyone basked in the sunshine. There was improvised theater, clown acts for kids, even a trio of mimes juggling frozen fish sticks.

There was also a protest of some sort that was drawing a small crowd.

"CANDLESTICK POINT AL-READY HAS A POINT!" yelled a thin, beatnik-type. He had a beret, goatee and earring and stood on a stool. "And that point is to exist the way it always has! As a sanctuary for seabirds and marsh grass! PRO-TECT THE POINT!!"

Liz chortled to herself. "Sure, go ahead. Disturb the peace here for ev-erybody."

"No, wait. Maybe we're on to some-thing here."

"On to what?"

"Paulie Suggs said something the other day when I had that hook to his neck that stuck with me. 'Why would

I do ANYTHING to you?'"

"Yeah?"

"Well, maybe we have to start with this killer's real motive. There has to be one, right?"

"Of course."

I pointed at the protestor. "Why not these 'Save the Point' fools? They

have a damn good one."

"I'm not following."

"Reggie had just gotten a construction job out there, remember? This new stadium has lots of enemies. Maybe one of these guys knows somebody who's a little more extreme about it."

"I don't know, Snap. Sounds a bit—"

The Bronx Bugle Sporting Life

BELIEVE IN IKE	Thursday Late Edition, May 8, 1958	DUCK AND COVER OFTEN

Turley Tames Tribe with Two Tainted Tallies

by Archie Stripes
American League Beat

How lethal are the Bombers right now? Let me count the ways. With workmanlike pitching and timely hitting, the Yanks swept the Indians out of their wigwams today with a fairly bloodless 6-2 matinee win in the Bronx.

"Turley ain't no Thanksgiving goose," said Casey Stengel after the game. "'Cause if he was or he wasn't I'd say so in the first place." Indeed, Bob pitched the stuffing out of the Tribe, allowing just two unearned runs after Norm Siebern dropped Preston Ward's sun-blocker in left. Norm and the Mick had given

us a 2-0 lead with solo homers off Mudcat Grant in the 1st, but no matter. An error, passed ball, and Slaughter's double in the 3rd put us back ahead, and four straight hits to open our 6th generated further abuse.

There's no denying this is the best the remaining New York club has looked in this young season. Baltimore is still a pesky bunch, but the White Sox have slipped and Red Sox just dropped six out of seven. The unchallenging Senators now visit for a 4-game weekend series. I expect one-sided boredom, and may spend my free time following the vibrant boys of the rival senior circuit.

CUBS BASH SEVEN HOMERS IN GAME AT WRIGLEY
Details on whether they won inside

No Leads Yet in S. F. Tragedies

SAN FRANCISCO(UPI)—The Giants' effort to secure a fan foothold in their new California city has been marred by the unfortunate deaths of two Seals Stadium fans the past few weeks.

According to local law enforcement, there are no definitive leads in the two incidents, one a stabbing victim on Opening Day, the other the apparent victim of a robbery, found in an adja-

cent park. "We've beefed up security big time," says team owner Horace Stoneham, "Trust me when I say that Seals Stadium is still a fun family place to watch a ball game."

"Far-fetched? Definitely. But it's better than the nothing we got right now. And I know a Haight-Ashbury couple who I can bet is in with this bunch."

"Think we can find them?"

"We can sure as hell try. Met them at the Double Play one night. One's named Chrissie and the other Chris."

"That's easy enough."

"Sure. And If you can figure out what sex they are you're smarter than me."

Beats Don't Fail Us Now

May 9th

It didn't take long for us to locate Chris and Chrissie's spiced tea shop on Haight Street. The only problem was that Chris and Chrissie hadn't owned the place for a year. The neighborhood was a dump, with boarded up storefronts and lots of vacant houses. My guess is that in ten years the whole area will be bulldozed for car dealerships and shopping centers.

The guy who ran the tea shop disappeared behind a curtain, came back with a slip of paper.

"They run Daddy-O's Records now, at Kearny and Columbus."

I stared at him. "Jesus…that's near Chinatown."

"North Beach, mister. Relax. Mostly beatniks and kids who THINK they're beatniks—"

"Yeah, yeah. Been there. Thanks."

◆ ◆ ◆

Actually, except for some recent drinks I had with Liz at The Saloon, North Beach wasn't a place I stuck around long in. Since the literary and poetry scene exploded there the last few years it's been overrun by a whole raft of turtle-necked punks in glasses who like to hang out on corners and question the universe. I gave up questioning mine a long time ago.

Daddy-O's was stuffed with these well-educated vagrants. Political leaflets of every stripe were taped to one wall, including a few for the SAVE THE POINT COMMITTEE. Cigarette smoke and Cal Tjader jazz music filled the room, and Liz and I had to squeeze down an aisle of record bins toward the back counter.

"Ten bucks says we see Cepeda and Gomez here," I said.

"Isn't there a day game today? They're probably doing warmups with their cigars."

"They're playing tonight. And don't make fun of Latin players. Wouldn't be surprised if Cubans end up taking over the game."

I recognized Chris and Chrissie at the counter. They both had hoop earrings and matching fuzz on their chins. God only knew which was which.

"Remember me? Snappy Drake?"

"Vaguely," said one of them.

"Double Play Bar and Grill, maybe a year ago. We talked about tea. I was an usher at the Seals games."

"Oh yes!" cried the other, "you left with that boozed-up redhead!"

Liz shot me a look. I smirked.

"Um, this is my friend Liz. We're kind of interested in Saving the Point."

"Wonderful!"

"Not like *you* mean, though," piped in Liz. "We're looking for someone."

"Someone who might be a little angry about the new ball park getting built there."

"Well," said the first one, "that could be any of us."

"Yeah, but I'm thinking of someone who's so angry they might, y'know... kill to stop it."

Chris or Chrissie exchanged a worried look with Chris or Chrissie. Then turned back to us.

"We don't appreciate your sinister thoughts in our shop, Mr. Snappy. Are you working for the police now?"

"Nope. Just a ball park usher trying to get a killer off his back. And you're telling me no one you know fits this bill?"

They shook their heads. Eyed Liz up and down for more devilish reasons. The first one spoke.

"You two are awful amusing, though. I should tell you there's a big poetry reading late tonight at Co-Existence Bagel. Lots of Save the Pointers will be there. You can scope out the scene. Isn't scoping what a lot of you amateur ball park detectives do?'

I wanted to haul back right then and put a fist through his or her cheek, but kept my cool.

◆ ◆ ◆

The first game of the Dodgers series that night was amazing. The park was so electric that if the killer was there he would've been too gripped by the action to squeeze a gnat. Liz and I changed out of our usher outfits the second it ended. Made it back across town to Co-Existence Bagel for the 11 p.m. reading.

This joint made Daddy-O's look like a sewing circle. Tables had been removed, and people stood and sat wherever possible. Someone passed a jug of red wine around that Liz and I both sipped from. Somebody else passed me a hand-rolled cigarette. I said I already had my Camels but he insisted I try his, so I grabbed a few puffs and found it a little sweet and strong for my taste.

A raised platform was at one end with a chair and microphone set up. The master of poetry ceremonies, an old guy with wild white hair, bow tie and rumpled tweed sport coat, appeared. Read one of his short ones first. The crowd cheered after the last line, even though I found it impossible to understand and Liz applauded to be polite.

After the third or fourth of these things, my head started to swim. Damn cheap Napa wine. Liz nudged me, said I should get up there between poems and say something about Saving the Point. "Y'know, to see which creepy-looking worms pop out of the woodwork."

So I did. After this overbearing guy

named Ginsberg read and the crowd went bonkers again, I slipped my way through the mob and onto the platform.

"Hi folks…" I looked out at the sea of turtlenecks and horn-rimmed glasses and went completely blank for a second.

"Who ARE you?" yelled some guy with a strong, deep voice from the shadows.

"Umm…Milton Drake?"

"Read your poem, man!"

"Well, I don't really have a poem. See—"

"Sure you do. It's in your face!!"

What was in my face was a visible afterglow from the game earlier at Seals Stadium. And either the wine or that weird tobacco was doing something funny to my thoughts. Because I grabbed the microphone and just started to ramble.

"Drysdale and Gomez, Dodgers and Giants
No big deal, neither team would win,
Mays with a bomb, a cannonball, a missle!
Shooting into the Mission night, two to nothing us
Snider, Snider, the Duke of Flatbush
Old and slower and migrated west
Puts one into orbit"

"YEAH, MAN!" yelled the same guy again.

"Hail Kirkland, and Valmy Thomas
Exploding their balls into bleacher

hands
5-1 us but oh no, oh no
Fairly and Rodgers and Zimmer aboard
And the Duke launches another
But Wagner and Mays and Cepeda strike back
And 8-6 for the locals now!"

"GO, MAN, GO!!"

"Cold Hamms and hot franks fatten the crowd
Big hits dizzy the minds
Furillo out of the park for 8-7
And Grissom for the rescue!
Except 24,000 desires dissolve
Like seagull prints on sand
At high tide
Under a Pismo Beach sky
On Snider, Furillo and Fairly singles
Last gasp we say, down 9-8
Willie at the plate, Ed Roebuck ain't great
Dreams of a Bay Area nation all noosed
A grounder to Gilliam,
And all of us die
Like Doubleday dogs
Lost to American fate on this cool Friday night…"

I stopped. Wobbled. There was a slight pause and the bagel shop exploded. People I would never bother to talk to glad-handed me, pounded my back. Liz just gazed in my direction from the center of the room, dumbfounded.

Then a handsome, chiseled guy in a T-shirt with little curl of wavy black hair on his sweaty forehead walked up. I knew right away it was the guy who had coaxed me on.

"You were gone, man. Real…plain… gone." He gripped my hand with one of his meaty ones. "Jack Kerouac. And it's a damn pleasure."

The Dharma Cats

May 10th

The Dodge bounced down Route 82 the next afternoon like a squeaky supernova. Liz was half turned next to me, getting an earful of Kerouac from the back seat and sharing his bottle of cheap Chablis. I did all the driving because as Jack put it, "I'd rather watch someone at the wheel than use one." Either way, we were off to find the "it" of our murder case.

"I can tell you things and show you things," Kerouac told us last night after the Co-Existence Bagel poetry party. He was jazzed about helping us with the murders, but downright bebopped over my made-up baseball poem. It made sense. Jack was a huge baseball fan, and a few years ago created a whole fantasy game using hand-drawn cards and fictitious teams. I know this because he pulled a set out of his coat and showed them to us while we were driving. "I'm partial to the Boston Fords, but I think the New York Chevvies will edge out the Philly Pontiacs for the pennant," he said. Now a made-up fantasy baseball game has to be the nuttiest thing

I've ever heard of, but Jack could sure write so I cut him some slack.

Liz didn't have that much interest in the cards, goo-goo-eyeing him the whole way and purring over and over how much she dug *On the Road*.

"Got a new one coming out this October," he said. "Not sure what I'm calling it yet, but I kind of like *The Dharma Cats*." Liz then made the mistake of asking what dharma was, making the next 20 miles a traveling Kerouac seminar on all things Buddhist. I finally interrupted to ask where the hell we were exactly going.

"Faith in time, brother. Faith in time." He handed me the last wine glug, told me to stop at the next liquor store we saw. I wasn't too keen on that, said as much, and he sulked a bit until we got onto Highway 101.

"Yeah! All be humble now. We're on royalty!"

"We're on what?"

"El Camino Royal! The Royal Road. Connects every mission from Sonoma all the way down San Diego way. Didn't you see the sign with the little bell over it? Used to be over 450 of those ding-dongs."

"Again…Where are we going?"

"See the way I sauce it, your killerman's gotta be wack-crazy, right? Definitely not cool enough for 'Frisco."

"Trust me, Jack," said Liz, "There's plenty of crazies in that city."

"Friendly ones, maybe. Ones without beds, without coins, without food, happy to lay under the Dippers surrounded by gutter piss and drink their lives down the toilet, all the time wishing they'd done that thing, that supreme thing that could've saved them, saved them from watery soup and holy garments of stink, saved them from—"

"HEY!" I shouted, "Where. The hell. Are we going?"

He looked at me with a blank face for a moment, then just shrugged, waved a hand at the windshield. "Down 101 about 60 miles. Got a feeling about a place." He winked and grinned at Liz, who I was convinced would follow him to Death Valley and under the sand if he asked her.

◆ ◆ ◆

We got off Highway 101 past Redwood City. Headed up a twisty mountain road in the direction of the Pacific. "He's an isolated guy, right?" continued Kerouac, "Has to be. Probably likes it. Makes me think he's up in the wild here."

"Oh," spoke up Liz, looking a little green on the narrow road. "So you're saying we're going to wherever, just because you have a hunch."

"My hunches are always worth it, baby."

We stopped for early dinner at a mountain eatery that served buffalo burgers. Kerouac gobbled down two. Liz and I ate chicken sandwiches real slow to settle our innards, and then we hit the road again. It was getting dark. After another 45 minutes of hairpin turns Jack finally said we should stop at the next trail sign.

"The answer's up here. It's always up here."

"So you've been on this trail?"

"Hell no."

I'm about as comfortable in the woods as a lobster in a pot, but the route to the top of this peak was certainly a nice change from the smell of the sidewalks. Besides, it was Liz's crackbrained idea to take Kerouac up on this little day trip in the first place. Meaning at least I could blame it on her later.

The sun had just set when we reached the top. Our new friend pointed out Half Moon Bay off to the north, slightly covered in evening fog. Stars were filling the sky overhead, an absolute planetarium just for us. Kerouac was ecstatic. Pulled a bottle of Hiram Walker out of his back jean pocket we didn't even know he had. took a big sip, handed it off to Liz and lit a cigarette.

"Figure it out yet?"

"Huh?"

"Your baseball-killer. Know how to get him?"

I couldn't believe what I was hearing.

"We thought you were showing us where he was, Jack. We thought you knew something, maybe even a Save the Pointer. You sure as hell told us as much."

"No sir I didn't. I said I know things. And I do know things. I've been to more places on this heavenly continent than the two of you could ever dream of. I know what makes men cry and wail and bleed and screw and yeah, even kill. It's the darkest of dark places and there's always a reason, Snappy. Always a reason. Feel that dark soul of his the way this sky and these stars and that ocean down there's feeling you, brother. Crawl inside that evil skin of his and find that evil reason and you got him stone cold, yes sir you do… Okay! Let's head back."

He pocketed the brandy, started back down the trail. Liz and I wanted to put on our evil skins and kill him right there.

A half hour later, we took a wrong turn and got hopelessly lost. The fog poured over the mountain, making the trail all but vanish. We had to find a shallow cave to spend the night freezing and cursing in. Kerouac just slept like a baby, cradling his brandy bottle.

"Look at it this way," said Liz, her teeth chattering. "If we make it down the mountain alive, I'll have a hell of a story for the *Examiner*."

All Dressed Up for Mom

May 11th

Somehow we found our way out of the de-fogged mountains the next morning. Kerouac whistled the whole way while we growled. He sprung for eggs and coffee at a San Bruno diner, which was damn nice and necessary of him. Liz's hair looked like it had been put through a washboard, and she certainly wasn't making plans to

go hot-rodding with free-spirited novelists anymore.

"Look at us," she said, poking at her omelette, glancing around at the better-dressed crowd, "A bunch of bums sitting here."

"That's IT!" said Kerouac, snapping a finger at her, "*The Dharma Bums*. Much better title. Thanks, doll."

So at least he got something out of this little trip. We had diddly-nothing until we dropped him off at Ginsberg's place in Berkeley, where Jack was shacking up. "Y'know," he said, toying with the car's door handle, "I ran across a guy who works for the city this month named Henry you might wanna look up. Can't remember what the hell he does, though."

"Well that's a big help."

"No, seriously. He was in City Lights Bookstore one night. Cat was in a heated talk with the owner about a land swindle involving the new Giants' ball park. Spoke a real good swindle-ese if you know what I mean."

"Not really."

"I mean he was plugged into the wall, man. In the know. Anyway, good luck with it." He gave Liz a final wink. "You too."

Liz uttered a charmed little squeak and looked away. Kerouac climbed out, headed across the street for Ginsberg's bungalow. The bulge of his empty brandy bottle still in his back pocket.

"You gonna be in town long?" I yelled.

"Doubt it! Miles to go before I weep!"

And then he was gone.

◆ ◆ ◆

Mother's Day game with the Dodgers at Seals Stadium. Yahoo. Liz stayed at the apartment and slept. I ignored Pence, the other ushers, even little pre-game pep talks from Stoneham and Malarkey and just worked my section. Until just like I figured, my mother showed up.

The only games she ever went to were on Mother's Day. She was pooped from the many buses, street and cable cars she had to take, and I felt like an absolute heel for not swinging by her place in the East Bay to pick her up. Probably would have if I wasn't stuck on a mountain all night and forgotten it was even Mother's Day. Anyway, she bought one of the last grandstand tickets for what must have been the last empty seat in my section to seat her in.

"Get me a glass of wine would you, honey?" was her first inane request, somewhere around the third inning with Stan Williams and Stu Miller still throwing goose eggs.

"They have soda pop, Mom. Coffee, too. But no wine. And they also have vendors, remember."

"I don't want a vendor, I want a drink from you."

"I'm trying to work, Mom."

"People are seated already! I don't care how dressed up you look in those smart usher clothes, Milton, you're just idling around."

And so it went for most of the game. On the field, things were worse. With Dodger third sacker Dick Gray still out, Ron Fairly blasted one deep to left center with two aboard in the 4th. Wagner and Mays ran for the ball, smashed into each other and lay there on the outfield grass while Fairly circled the bases. Willie recovered enough to hit a solo shot in the 8th, but pitcher Williams had also gone deep for them by that point, and snuffed us out on just five hits. Hard for me to understand why our hitting has been so weak with all the fence-busters we have. If I can ever stop thinking about these murders maybe I'll put on my baseball thinking cap soon.

When the game ended I had to shake Mom awake so I could drive her home and buy her some flowers on the way. Cruising over the Bay Bridge while she babbled on endlessly, the only thing in my mind was the name Henry...

Dizzy Miss Liz

May 13th

No time for eggs this time, barely any for coffee. Liz had me pack a bag and fly with her to L.A. for the last two Giants-Dodgers games of this home and road series.

It was also the start of a mammoth, 21-game road trip for the Seals men that would take them through St. Louis, Chicago, Cincy, Milwaukee,

Pittsburgh, Philly and St. Louis again before getting home on June 2nd. This meant I'd be scrapping around for free dinners here and there, running up my tab at the Double Play. Chumpo did offer me a small job behind the bar with ushering unavailable, but L.A. was the first thing on my mind today.

Liz had bungalow issues to resolve with her landlord, and for good reason, not being too eager to dump her lease yet. She also wanted to put in a couple more days of celebrity gossip research at the Coliseum for the *Herald*, because she felt she "owed it" to old Gaddy. Never said the girl wasn't a masochist.

The Giants spent Monday what they did down here last time: whacking the tar out of the ball. Al Worthington stymied the Dodger sticks while the 'Gints rolled up 16 hits and 11 runs on Erskine, Kipp, McDevitt, Giallombardo, and the peanut guy from the left field bleachers. That's where my lousy seat was this time, behind the high cockamamie home run screen. But I didn't much care. The sun was glorious, and I even stripped down to my undershirt at one point to tan my ghost arms.

Liz was tired and a little less charming afterwards, as you'd expect. She said she might have a big surprise for me for the Tuesday game, then held it back from me over dinner like a ham bone in front of a terrier. She wanted something, and I didn't have to be Sam Spade to figure it out.

"I like doing things with you," she said when we finally got back to her bungalow Monday night, opened some wine and put on a stack of Perry Como albums.

"Same here."

"So what d'ya think?" She was wearing a loose green blouse that threatened to get looser.

"About what?"

"Y'know...about you and me."

"I'm not a house and kids kind of guy, Liz. Thought I mentioned that."

"Whoa, Tex. We haven't even got big time chummy yet." She twirled a finger into my hair.

"Yeah...But you know what they say: beer leads to vodka, diapers and a mortgage."

"Who said that?"

"Never mind. I just like to take things super slow, lady."

She moved closer on the couch. "How slow?"

"Slower than this."

"Come on, Snap...Just for one night, don't think about dead bodies...and ushering...and Paulie Suggs...and the Spokane Indians...and whoever the hell this Henry is....just think about all of little me..."

The next Perry Como platter dropped: "You'll Always Be My Lifetime Sweetheart". I was helpless. Her warm, tobacco-tasting mouth found mine, and a long night of carnal bliss and endurance began.

♦ ♦ ♦

She was all smiles and giggles on Tuesday. Partly because she thought she had me locked up, partly because of the big surprise she revealed in the morning. I'd be able to join her in a private Coliseum box with Rock Hudson and Doris Day that afternoon. Wasn't exactly zinger news for me, but she insisted that Doris was a huge baseball fan so I played along.

Unfortunately, Liz was one of about 17 other L.A. reporters and gossip hounds who'd been invited into the box. It was so stuffed in there I could barely reach the shrimp cocktail table. Doris was more friendly and freckled in person than she was in her movies. Rock was kind of a stiff and kept eyeing me for some reason, and with the Dodgers way ahead by the 5th on four home runs, I excused myself to sit in the sunny stands and breathe again.

There was more hay-rolling that night, thankfully less Perry Como, and I was actually contemplating taking a three-week vacation there with the Giants on the road.

Until something crashed on Liz's outside porch at two in the morning. "What was THAT??" she cried, bundling herself in sheets.

"Stay here."

I threw on my pants, stepped out on the porch. There was a light breeze in the foothills, but nothing that would have toppled over and smashed the vase of tall flowers she had next to her bedroom window.

The porch creaked behind me. I heard breathing. Slowly turned like I was heading back inside, then leaped at something crouched in the shadows.

Yanked out a thin, handsome guy in a Riviera Country Club polo shirt. He was in his late 20s, and trying to babble.

"Don't hurt me, okay??"

Liz stepped out in her nightgown, put a hand to her open mouth in shock.

"Randy!!!"

Farewell, My Nookie

May 14th

I gripped the punk's polo shirt in my left hand, readied my right fist to sock out his lights.

"Who the hell is Randy?" I asked Liz over my shoulder.

"Please, mister..." he squeaked, "I just run a pro shop at the club. Met her at a junior dance there one—"

"Shut up, Junior, before I make your dentist rich." Turned to Liz. "Again. Who's Randy?"

"Let him go, okay? He's nothing. I mean, we went out to the movies once. The Bowl maybe. And he sent me some letters."

"LOTS of letters!" he blurted, "And you didn't answer a single one—"

I let go of his shirt. Squeezed his mouth instead. "Didn't I tell you to shut up? Ladies don't answer letters from creeps. Or peeping toms."

"I wasn't peeping, I swear—"

"Baloney. Two out of four nights I've been up here you've been outside her window. What do you call that?"

"LOVE!!"

I stared at Randy for a long unfathomable second. Jerked him to his sneakered feet and marched him straight off the porch. "Don't hurt him!" yelled Liz behind me. I ignored her. Walked him down the twisting driveway toward the road.

"She's my dark angel, mister! Don't you see? I gotta have her!"

"Sorry, pal. Looks to me like you cast a vote and lost the damn election."

"She told me what to do! Real nasty! I like that—"

"Hey! If I wanna hear sick things from sick minds, I'll go home and watch *Naked City*."

I grabbed the front of his polo emblem again, pulled him up to my face. "Meantime...if I ever catch you bothering her again I'll mash every one of your potatoes and make you eat them. Got it?"

Shoved him onto the road. He slipped and took a tumble. Recovered, stood up again, backed away. "She'll drive YOU crazy, too...Just wait... She's got an evil side to her, mister! EVIL!!"

And then he was gone, his words echoing down the hill and through my brain.

◆ ◆ ◆

Liz was standing in the living room when I returned. She had donned a robe and lit a cigarette. All I could do was stare at her.

"Randy?"

"I told you. He's nothing."

"A junior dance?"

"It's an old country club filled with fuddyduds. Anyone under thirty is considered a junior."

"So how come you were there?"

She shrugged. "There was a good chance I'd see Humphrey Bogart playing cards."

"Oh. But instead you got Randy. Creepy, perverted Randy."

"He's not a pervert, Snap! Just a little bit...young. Needy. Kind of the way you're being."

"Don't flip-flop this thing, doll. You're the one who invited me down here to make nookie glue, remember?"

She took what she thought was a hint and moved toward me. Her robe loosened. "I know...and I so liked that nookie glue."

I squirmed away. Walked into the bedroom to get my overnight bag. Started filling it.

"Where are you going?"

"Where do you think? The airport. Probably no flights until 6 a.m., but heel-cooling's my specialty."

"Please, Snap. You're being a child. Why can't you just believe me about Randy?"

"I never said I didn't. But how many other Randys are out there, Liz? How many Mikeys and Biffs I haven't met yet?"

"That isn't fair."

"Yeah, well, neither was not telling me about this dweezil. You knew he might have been outside the other time I was here, right?"

She looked past me and mutely smoked her cigarette.

"All I'm saying, baby, is that when I spring for a tasty dish I just like to know all the ingredients first."

"Did you forget about our murder case?"

"Nope. Doesn't change a thing. We can still work together, trade ideas, go snooping. You can win a damn Pulitzer writing about it for all I care. I'll pay the rent on my old place again if you want, but feel free to come up and visit anytime. Let's just keep everything the way it was before, okay? Nice and friendly."

I zipped the bag and walked out the door.

A fat tangerine moon was setting. Not many cabs came up into the hills, but I would walk until I found one. About twenty yards from Liz's place I nearly turned around. Afraid to see either her tear-stained or evil face at the window, I didn't.

Dispatch from the Eastern Front

May 15th

Liz was right. About my need to relax, at least. So after informing Malarkey's stake-out goons that I had been out of town on none of their business, I took in a full evening of baseball-following over Chumpo's

drafts at the good old Double Play.

Back in St. Louis, the Giants absolutely flattened the Cards earlier in the day, belting seven balls out of Sportsman's Park—two by Say Hey Willie—and the entire bar stunk of cigars and crazy pennant talk.

I didn't partake. The Seals won 101 games last year in their swan song for the Pacific Coast League, and they didn't even have any playoffs, so it's been hard for me to get too thrilled about players like Valmy Thomas and Andre Rodgers. Still, I let Bob go on and on about various Giant feats of skill, because we all missed Reggie. He certainly would've been right at the bar with us, dishing it out and lapping it up.

The fun part of the night was when I helped Chumpo bus tables and found a sports section from the Wilmington (Delaware) *News Journal* sitting in an empty booth. Someone had probably bought it at the nearby out-of-town newsstand and used it to dump peanut shells on while reading the box scores. Anyway, that baseball columnist I like who covered the Yankees was in Philly to write about the big first-place matchup with Milwaukee, and I enjoyed every word.

This morning, after the beer cleared my head, I tracked down his next story in the *News Journal* morning edition, because Thursday afternoon's game was one hell of a doozy. Here ya go, folks:

PHILS FOILED IN FIGHT FOR FIRST, FOLD IN FOURTEEN

By Archie Stripes
The Bronx Bugler
Special to the *News Journal*

PHILADELPHIA—Could they do it again? These Wheez Kids, these overachieving underachievers, this most fun collection of ball-rippers that has taken Brotherly Loveville and most of the country by storm in the first month and a half: could they sweep the World Champs with a matinee win?

They're sure taking ME by storm. Gave up the last two games of the Oriole-Yankee series in the Bronx just to train it down here and see for myself. Series hero Lew Burdette was on the Milwaukee slab, Jack Sanford for the home gang. The unlikely swatting firm of Bowman, Anderson, and Philley all singled with two gone in the 1st for the first run of the game, but two walks and a flubbed grounder to the mound equalized things the next inning.

Then the Braves got busy. Filling in for injured Bruton, Felix Mantilla singled to open the 3rd. One out later, Hammerin' Aaron yanked one into the left field upper deck, and after two singles and a walk and Red Schoendienst sac pop to right, the Phils were down 4-1.

Never say the word "down" to THIS bunch, though. Sanford got his rhythm back, while Burdette began handing out hits like Sugar Babies on Halloween. By the time Philly plated one in the 3rd and three in the 6th, they had ten singles and a double to brag about, the fans swayed with glee and visions of Dick Sisler danced in their heads. They led 5-4, the Braves were reeling and first place could be theirs in less than an hour.

Juan Pizarro had come in to calm down the locals, but the Braves had stopped doing a blessed thing at the dish. Leadoff slugger Wes Covington was zero-for-four going to the 9th, and after Adcock pinch-hit a single with one out, Wes rolled one out to Hamner. Granny moved like his sweet old namesake, though, missed the bag at second and pinch-runner Casey Wise was in a scoring spot. Mantilla came through like no one dreamed he would, rifled a single into left as Wise skipped home and tied the game 6-6!

The Great Humberto then took the hill for the Braves, and I speak of ace reliever Robinson, of course. He mesmerized Phillie bats for the next four innings, whiffing five and giving a hit to no one. Turk Farrell had given up the tying run, and he was equally fine, but the unlucky 13th proved his undoing.

Crandall boomed a one-out double. Logan walked. Schoendienst singled in Del. Jim Hearn took over and Mel Roach crawled out of a crack in the dugout to single in two more off him. The game couldn't have been more over.

Except nobody left the park. Because they knew. Even with two outs, the occasionally surly Philadelphians roared with glee as Eddie Mathews—having a meaningless day with the bat—botched his second grounder of the day. New hurler Don McMahon was miffed enough to boot Bowman's ball seconds later. Harry Anderson, of course, singled in a run to make it 8-6.

Pancho Herrera had gone in earlier at first base against the lefty Pizarro, and there he was, the pride of Santiago de

Cuba, flanking the plate as the possible winning run.

McMahon looked in, peachy afternoon light dusting his uniform. Stared in, got the sign for the 3-2 pitch and threw. Pancho missed. Connie Mack Stadium deflated like 30,000 balloons and the Braves shook hands with each other, exiting quickly to make their cloud hopper to Cincy.

The winning team was outhit in all three games, and the champions lost two of them. But as this Band of Phillie Brothers learned, first place is a hard-earned treasure that's rarely shared for long.

National League thru Thursday, May 15

Milwaukee	15	12	.556	—
Philadelphia	14	13	.519	1
Chicago	15	14	.517	1
San Francisco	15	14	.517	1
Pittsburgh	15	15	.500	1.5
Los Angeles	14	15	.483	2
Cincinnati	12	14	.462	2.5
St. Louis	12	15	.444	3

American League thru Thursday, May 15

New York	23	7	.767	—
Baltimore	18	12	.600	5
Chicago	16	13	.552	6.5
Detroit	15	15	.500	8
Cleveland	15	17	.469	9
Boston	14	16	.467	9
Kansas City	11	18	.379	11.5
Washington	8	22	.267	15

≈ *Regarding This Henry* ≈

May 16th

The guy behind the counter at City Lights Books had grey hair, old lady glasses and a bushy beard that apparently swallowed his mouth.

"Umm, excuse me?" It was the third time I had to say that. He was deeply into a small book of Chinese poems.

"Yes?"

"Jack Kerouac said he met a guy here recently named Henry. Talking with the owner about some land swindle at Candlestick Point?"

He lowered the book, scratched a chin somewhere inside the beard. I wasn't sure if I'd ever see his fingers again.

"Seem to remember that...The owner would be Mr. Ferlinghetti, but I am Woodrow."

"Fine. So you were here that night?"

"I would have been. It was our Thursday Prose and Bread Raising Night. We have another on the 28th, you know."

He reached for a flyer and I stopped him.

"Please. I'm kind of in a hurry. Kerouac said this guy's name was Henry, but I need a last name."

"I'm sorry. I think Jack's off to Mexico with a friend. But his name's Neal, not Henry—"

"Hey, pal. Lay off the reefer and listen to me. The Henry who was here. In the bookstore. Talking about a land swin—"

"Oh, him. Henry North."

He went back into his book. I was a second away from putting my Zippo to the bottom of his beard.

"Henry North? Okay. Great. And who's he?"

Woodrow shrugged, produced a grimy tissue and wiped his nose. "City guy, I think. Runs some kind of jury. Frankly I found him boring, and he never bought a book."

"Is Mr. Ferlinghetti around?"

"No, in New York. Looks like you'll need a local phone directory. They sell those across the street."

I thanked him for his minimal help. The phone book had twelve Henry Norths and about 25 H. Norths. To hopefully save work I trudged over to the nearest paper, The *San Francisco News-Call Bulletin,* and asked to see a city editor. He didn't have a beard, but had a lot less time.

"Right. Henry North is the foreman of the city's grand jury. Used to work for Metropolitan Life. What swindle are you talking about?"

"I don't know, exactly. That's why I wanted to talk to him."

"You a tipster?"

"No, kind of a…private eye. If you know where I could find him, it would help a lot."

"Not a clue. And the jury office is closed for the weekend by now. I can tell you for sure, though, that there's no land swindle whatsoever going on with Candlestick Point, and you'd be wasting your time looking into it. Don't you read the paper? That new ballpark's going to be a gold mine for this city. Tell you what…" He plucked a business card out of his vest pocket. "Give me a ring if you ever hear something worthwhile I'd want to write about."

He disappeared into a smoky newsroom. I grabbed one of their papers on the way out. It was owned by Hearst, and sure enough, had a blocky Hearstian headline across the bottom of the front page:

ALL SYSTEMS STILL "GO" FOR NEW GIANTS PLEASURE PALACE

I trashed the paper and headed up the street. Got halfway home when it suddenly occurred to me:

All I said to the editor was the word "swindle". I never even mentioned Candlestick Point.

State of the Union Club

May 17th

Metropolitan Life Insurance wasn't open for business on Saturday, but their lobby had a guard sitting at a desk. Even better, he wasn't new on the job.

"Sorry sir, but Mr. North hasn't worked in this building since he retired. Years ago. You got a better chance of finding the crown jewels in Coit Tower."

"What was this North guy like?"

"Oh, I didn't know him all that well. Seemed nice enough. Tipped me a few times just for holding the elevator. Gotta figure the folks up at the P.U. Club feel the same way."

"The what club?"

"The Pacific Union Club. Top of Nob Hill. If he's retired you can bet he's still having his fancy lunches and drinks there."

I thanked the guard very much—and tipped him.

◆ ◆ ◆

An hour later, the California Street cable car dropped me off in front of a stunning and melancholy brownstone mansion. A wealthy cat named James Flood built the place in 1886 for his family, and it became the Pacific Union Club a little later when the Pacific Club and Union Club merged.

Can't say I've ever been inside, though; you have to be white, male, rich, Republican, and invited for that to happen. So instead I bided my time. Parked myself at the foot of the front steps, lit a Camel and watched the routine. It was close to lunch time, and a parade of cabs and town cars rolled up to deliver members and a few guests. Nearly all of them were long in the tooth and deep in the wallet, and had to ring the imposing front door to be admitted.

A younger businessman showed up on foot. He was nervous, winded, as if late for a bridge game. I got in his way as he approached the front walk.

"Hey. I'm trying to get a message to Henry North in there. You know him?"

"Sorry. I can't—"

"You can't do it, or you can't tell me if you know him? I'm pretty sure he's a member. And it's kind of an emergency."

The guy was flustered. Confused. I pulled out the business card the *Call-Bulletin* editor had given me.

"I need to quote him for a big story. If you can get me inside somehow there's fifty bucks in it for you."

He smacked me with a haughty laugh. "Are you serious? The Pacific Union Club never lets the working press inside. Good day, sir."

Plan B involved cutting around the left side of the building on Cushman Street. I found an open gate where delivery trucks were parked and slipped around the corner of the wall. Finished my Camel. Waited for someone to roll a stack of vodka cartons through the open door and snuck into the basement of the club.

The kitchen was down there. An army of waiters and cooks. I had zero chance of mingling with them, but did find a storage closet with an unused white apron on a hook. I exchanged my coat for it. If anything, it would buy me a minute or two until I could find a staircase.

I found the stairs, and a silver pitcher of water to carry with me. The first floor was magnificent. High ceilings and chandeliers overhead, with live chamber music echoing from a nearby room. Liz would have loved it, assuming she put on a fake moustache, mutton chops, and tuxedo before approaching the front door.

I stopped a waiter hurrying my way. "Mr. North wanted some more water. Which room is he in again?"

The waiter stared at me in bafflement. Then at my hands in horror.

"Your gloves!"

"Huh?"

"Your white gloves, man! Where are your gloves?" He had an annoying British accent that could have been phony.

"Oh, I um…left them—"

"Who the devil are you?"

"Rumswell. Rumswell Hocking. I started today—"

"Nonsense. I oversee all the new service."

He turned to flag someone down. I emptied the ice water on his trousers. He gasped, crumbled. I dropped the pitcher and bolted down a hallway.

Opened the first brass door handle I saw.

Found myself in a nearly empty room of mahogany lockers. A steam room door opened around the corner and a fat old man in a towel waddled out. I hid behind a row of lockers. Heard a commotion in the hall. They were definitely hunting me down.

Got a new idea. Quickly shed all my clothes, piled them in a dark corner. Grabbed a giant towel with a Pacific Union emblem and ducked into the steam room.

A handful of men sat in there. Steam obscured everyone's faces, and thankfully mine. I found a spot in the corner, nodded to someone nearby I could barely see. I think he nodded back.

"I don't care how you try to hide it, George. It isn't good business." It was the voice of a tired, angry man sitting with someone.

"Who's hiding anything?" said his smooth colleague, "Stadium, Inc. is a lawful, non-profit corporation."

"Well, we'll have to see about that..."

A third club member somewhere in the mist piped up. "No business arguments in the club, gentlemen."

"We're sorry," said the tired man.

"Actually," said his colleague, "I don't think my Mr. North really is."

My ears perked up.

"George! How dare you?"

"Listen to yourself, Henry. First you insult club members by bring-ing a couple Jews to lunch, and now you're insulting me. I think we should put off Monday's squash re-match for now."

The colleague stood up, walked past me to the door. The mist cleared for a second or two, long enough for us to stare at each other.

No doubt about it. Henry North's squash partner was a distinguished guy with thick eyebrows and a prominent Greek nose I'd recognize anywhere.

It was George Christopher—the Mayor of San Francisco.

Salads on a Wet Afternoon

May 18th

I followed Henry. How could I not? It took some doing, as in throwing on my clothes, retrieving my coat downstairs without being seen, and exiting the Pacific Union Club in time to catch him walking out the front door.

He started to hail a cab. None were stopping, so he headed for the nearest corner. I was right behind him.

"Henry North?" He stopped and turned, naturally wary. I stuck out a hand. "Milton Drake, *Sacramento Bee.*"

He refused to shake it, kept walking. "Sorry, I cannot talk to you about the Club."

"The hell with the Club. Tell me

about the Candlestick Point land swindle."

He stopped a second time. His face brightened. Hope crawled into his eyes. "I know plenty of reporters, but I've never heard of you. Why is that?"

"Probably because I just started this week. Trying to break in with a juicy scoop, and someone over at City Lights suggested this. And mentioned you."

A cab finally rolled up. He opened the back door, climbed inside. I had to be quick.

"How about a cup of coffee? On me."

He shut the door, then rolled down the window. "I don't think so...Instead, come to my home for noon Sunday lunch. 2223 Scott Street. Did you hear that, driver?" The cab drove away.

◆ ◆ ◆

It was pouring rain on Sunday. Lunch was in the drawing room of his narrow, museum-like Victorian home, right across the street from Alta Plaza Park in Pacific Heights. His wife, an attractive lady with social event written all over her, brought in Waldorf salads and slid the doors closed on the way out, a dash of concern on her face. My salad was delicious, but it would've been nice to have the Giants' double-header in Chicago on in the background.

"City Lights is not my kind of shop," began North, washing down a couple of pills with his club soda and lime before taking his first bite. "I was hoping to find a book on the history of that area by the bay. The library wasn't too helpful."

After agreeing I would not use him in my story—which wouldn't be hard because I wasn't going to write a single word—he filled my ear for the next half hour with one labyrinth of a real estate tale. Seems that Elmer Robinson, the mayor five years ago, asked his board of supervisors to approve a $5 million bond proposal to build a new stadium and attract a major league team. Seals Stadium, as much as everyone loved it, was just too small and didn't have good parking. But when the supervisors visited Horace Stoneham in New York to try and lure the Giants, Stoneham said it would take at least double that amount to woo him. So back they went to San Francisco, and created a "dummy company" called Stadium, Inc. to bypass the city charter.

"So where does Mayor Christopher fit in?" I asked.

Henry didn't answer right away. Munched on a lettuce leaf.

"You play squash with him, right?"

"George cares very much about this city. But his campaign to make this stadium a bonanza is a little too... self-serving."

"How's that?"

This time he looked right at me. "He was on the original Board of Supervisors. And he's the one who pushed for Stadium, Inc. to take advantage of Charles Harney's land."

"Who?"

"Mr Harney's the man who first bought the Candlestick Point land. In 1953. For just $2,100 an acre."

"That's dirt cheap."

"Exactly. But through Stadium, Inc., he sold it back to the city for over $65,000 an acre."

"That's baloney."

"Worse. It's criminal."

"You should do something."

"Oh, I am. I've been preparing a report on the transactions for months. Care for some tea?"

"No thanks. I'm a coffee man, remember?" The only sound for about ten seconds was the ticking of a grandfather clock. "You wouldn't happen to have a TV or radio around—"

Mrs. North walked in just then with two perfect chocolate eclairs. Henry took a moment to grip her hand, waited for her to leave again.

"I've worked with all kinds of businessmen and city officials on all kinds of contracts. But this one just smelled rancid. I do hope whatever you write will help my cause."

"I'll try. And if you can steer me to some other people who want to stop this park from being built, I'd sure like to meet them."

Henry's face darkened. "I would tread lightly, young man. These people say they have the best interest of the city at heart, but they don't. They are a sinister band of selfish cutthroats."

With that in mind, I wolfed down my eclair and stood up. "Mind if I contact you again?"

"If you must. And the next time I'm in Sacramento, perhaps I'll come visit you at the *Bee*."

"Umm…sure. Call me at home first. You know, to make sure I'm going to be at the office."

I scribbled my number for him and got out of there quick. I had a lot to think about, and the raindrops hitting my head weren't helping.

Long Road Ahead

May 19th

I spent late Monday afternoon sitting under the tree in Franklin Square Park where Reggie's body was "found." Trying to glue the pieces of this strange puzzle together.

Let's see…Two Giants fans have been killed, one a good friend of mine, the other left for me to find in my Seals Stadium section, with the victim's wallet "left" at my place. That sure seems personal. But then there's these shady shenanigans going on with Candlestick Point. The city grand jury foreman is trying to mess things up for Horace Stoneham and Mayor Christopher, and who knows how many dangerous pinko sympathizers may be helping HIM? But if that's what this is all about, then what's their beef with me?

At least the Giants were having a less-confounding day off, on their way to Cincy for a quick two-game show-down with the red-hot Redlegs. I had picked up the out-of-town *Bugle* on the way over to the park, to bone up on the standings and let my old pal Archie lighten the mood...

The Bronx Bugle Sporting Life

| EAT YOUR WHEATIES | Monday Late Edition, May 19, 1958 | FRENCH KISSING LEADS TO MARXISM |

Stengel Stumps on the Streak

by Archie Stripes
American League Beat

The trip began with the inevitable floor-mopping of the lowly Seantors in our Nation's Capitol, but now the trail ahead for our Yankee wagon train could be fraught with Chicago ruts, Detroit fallen logs, Cleveland Indian attacks, and Kansas City poison ivy. If they emerge with their winning streak at 22, get those record books ready for etching, boys, because this drama-less race may be closing its curtain early.

How to explain these 13 straight victories? Certainly not with just a few small twists of the lineup card. Yet maybe Old Professor Casey is more of a born scholar than we thought. On his way to the Windy City, I was able to scribble down his short answer:

"There comes a time in a man's life, and I've had plenty of 'em. What I mean is you don't cry all night when you lose your shirt and you don't beer it up when you get a lucky roll. I'm keepin' there boys even-headed, some of these wins have been close and you don't get to play Washington all year, that's how the masterminds figured it. Top of that, Bauer, Slaughter, Mantle, Skowron, Berra, Howard and McDougal take turns with the big hits every day and the starters are so good the bullpen's out there clipping fingernails. First week or two we couldn't spit in a washtub and now we're walkin' across the lake. So if that don't explain what you can't explain, nothing I say's gonna reverse all that for no one."

Redlegs Sweep Luckless Braves Out of Town

CINCINNATI (UPI)— Warren Spahn was given a 4-0 lead, and it still didn't help. Riding two three-run innings in the 6th and 7th, capped by a 3-run homer by the unstoppable Jerry Lynch, the Redlegs finished a 4-game sweep of the World Champions, 7-4, and have closed to within half a game of the league-leading Giants despite being in last place a mere week ago. After Aaron struck a 2-run homer off winner Nuxhall in the 5th, the Braves were not heard from again.

NEXT NL MATCHUPS
Giants at Reds • Cards at Phillies • Cubs at Pirates • Dodgers at Braves

The Pounding of Pavement

May 20th

I tried like hell to see Horace Stoneham at his stadium office this morning, but he was both out and about. I could have waited around for three hours, except with more denials and whiskey being the only likely outcome, I went down to City Hall instead.

Mayor Christopher's secretary was a middle-aged tart named Mrs. Bluebottom, and she was right out of library school. Even kept a sharp pencil lodged in her hair bun. Her first lie came in the first five seconds, when she said the Mayor was out to lunch, even though I could clearly see him through the crack of his open office door. Then she lied and said he was "back from lunch but in a meeting now," when I could hear him yelling at a travel agent on the phone.

So I borrowed a pen and piece of paper and scribbled out a note for him:

Dear Mayor Christopher,
Rumor has it you're involved with this Candlestick land "deal." The recent Seals Stadium tragedies may be connected. Please call me when you can. Maybe I can help.

Milton "Snappy" Drake
RO-74922

I folded the note, scotch taped it shut, and handed it to Mrs. Bluebottom.

"Please give this to the Mayor when you see him, okay?"

"Sometimes he's out the entire day after a meeting."

"I don't care if he's sailing the Orient. Just give him the note when you see him."

"He doesn't have time to read every note."

"Believe me, he'll read this one."

"I wouldn't presume things, Mr…"

"Drake. And I'm not presuming anything. Except maybe that you got this job because you're related to someone, and won't lose it no matter how many visitors' palms you slap with your nun's ruler."

Her nose crinkled. "I'll do the best I can, sir."

"I look forward to seeing what that is."

◆ ◆ ◆

I took a long walk home to flush out my annoyance. Buses, autos, streetcars and cable cars jockeyed for space with workers flooding out of their offices. The weather was cooling down quick, the city braced for another dinnertime fog cloud. I found myself walking up steep Webster to Broadway. The slow climb put my lungs and heart through the ringer, but it felt good.

Broadway was noisy, and I ducked into a quiet alley behind some apartments. Paused to crouch and tie one of my shoelaces.

Heard heavy footsteps a few yards

back. I peered over my shoulder. No one was there. Stood back up and kept walking.

Footsteps again, practically pounding the pavement. I whipped around again. Still no one there. A couple of fog fingers were groping into the far end of the alley.

"Hello?"

No answer. No sounds. I picked up my pace, rejoined the traffic on Buchanan and started heading back. Hopped a bus stopped at the first corner and repeatedly glanced at the mysterious alley until we rolled away and it disappeared in the fog.

Not surprisingly, the Mayor never called later. I dialed Chumpo for the Giants score (they lost in Cincy, damn it), poured myself a stiff gin and tonic, and knocked off early by listening to every creak—even when there weren't any.

Flatfooted

May 21st

Enough already. I hopped down the stairs first thing in the morning, rapped on the driver's side window of Malarkey's goonmobile.

"Wake up, boys! You're taking me in."

"Why?" said the yawning driver. "What'd you do?"

"Nothing at all. Same as you. But I miss your boss, so how about a ride?"

◆ ◆ ◆

Fifteen minutes later, I sat in a room across from Malarkey and his sidekicks. To no one's surprise, Malarkey was eating scallions and eggs.

"Gotta admit, Drake," he said between mouthfuls, "Keeping tabs on you may be the dullest beat we've ever had."

"So pack it up. It's been almost three weeks since the last killing, and the Giants don't get back until early June. Pretty obvious that Murder Man's lost interest in me."

"Mr. Stoneham isn't too sure."

"Oh really. Hmm. So the owner of a ball team is now running this case?"

Malarkey munched away and didn't even look up. I slid my chair closer.

"Let me tell you something, mac. I've drummed up more info in the last 48 hours than you deadbeats have in a week. Ever hear of Henry North?"

One of the cops behind Malarkey scratched his pimply chin. "Wait... Wasn't he the guy in that Steinbeck movie about grapes?"

"That's Henry Fonda, numbskull," said his partner.

"I'll spare you any more thinking," I said. "North is Mr. Grand Jury in this town, and he thinks the Mayor and some other characters are fleecing the city for that new ballpark out on the Point."

Malarkey laughed to himself. "The Mayor, huh? You been hittin' the peach brandy, Drake?"

"I'm a gin man. And the Mayor's definitely in on it. I heard him arguing with North in a steam bath."

"Steam bath?" barked the film scholar, "What are you, some kind of a fairy now?"

"Calm down, Griff," said Malarkey, "Our friend here just fancies himself as an amateur little Hercules Poirot. Despite the fact that city hall shenanigans have absolutely nothing to do with two dead bodies at Seals Stadium."

"You sure about that? After I tried to see the Mayor yesterday, someone was on my tail pretty damn quick. And it wasn't either of you sleepy buzzards, that's for sure."

Malarkey finished his breakfast, shoved his plate aside. "Listen, Drake. I happen to like the Mayor. He's good to the police and cares a lot about this town. If I were you I'd stay home for a while. Follow the Giants' road trip in the papers. Hell, I'll even call off my hound dogs here and you can invite that tomato of a girlfriend over for a noodle and meatballs night. But most of all…" He leaned forward, scallions wafting into my face, "keep your snoopy, snappy nose out of places it ain't invited."

"Even steam baths?"

"ESPECIALLY STEAM BATHS!" yelled Griff.

Attack of the 50-Second Phone Call

May 22nd

I wasn't in the mood to do a damn thing today. My visit to the S.F.P.D. was a frustrating waste of time, like I figured it might be. Bought a quart of milk, a loaf of Wonder Bread and some tuna fish for my empty kitchen, then parked myself on the porch steps for most of the afternoon with a fresh pack of Camels and read the newspaper.

Not much going on. Some guy rode a "water-braked rocket sled" at Holloman Air Force Base in New Mexico the other day at a record 82.6 G. If I were ever to go that fast I'd sure want more than 0.4 seconds of glory. A new science fiction movie called *Attack of the 50-Foot Woman* had just come out, and I made a note to catch that one.

Otherwise, dullsville. And no ball games till night time. I swept the floors, made things a little more homey. Plugged in a radio and listened to some fine Nat Cole music on KJBS. Still felt pretty empty, though, so headed over to the Double Play for an early burger and some drafts around five o'clock.

The Giants were kicking off a three-gamer in Milwaukee, first time they've played the World Champs this season, and Chumpo had Russ Hodges' call piped in loud at the bar. Eddie Mathews took Stu Miller out of the park in the very first inning, and the more we couldn't do a thing off Bob Rush, the more Hamms I drank. Finally Miller singled in our first run to tie the game in the 5th, and the place whooped it up some.

"I don't get this team," said Chumpo, "First two weeks of the year no one can get them out, and now getting runs is like yanking teeth."

"That's baseball."

"No, that's a bunch of malarkey!"

I wish Chumpo had used a different word. I hadn't thought about those cop clowns for 24 hours, and now it all came back again. Especially Malarkey's comments about Liz being a tomato.

When Schoendienst walked, Mel Roach hit a pinch-double, and Covington drove in the Braves' 2-1 winner with a single in front of Kirkland, the beers did their work on my manhood and I found myself missing her. I asked Chumpo to slide over the bar phone, dialed Liz's long distance number.

"Hello?" She sounded like she was at the bottom of a well.

"Hey. Guess who."

"Well my my. Didn't think I'd hear from you for a while. Sounds pretty noisy at the Double Play."

"Good guess...You're smart. That's what I like about you, Liz."

"Oh. As opposed to my shoes? Or...my shapely figure?"

"Like that too..."

"Snap? How drunk are you?"

"Whaddya mean?"

"What I mean is I can smell the booze with my ear."

Chumpo gave me a quizzical look. I rolled my eyes and he got the message.

"Okay, so I had a couple. Nothing to do with why I'm calling though—"

"So why are you calling?"

"'Cause I'm havin' a tough week here. Lookin' into this Candlestick land mess involving Henry North and the Mayor, and no one's around, and I even swept our place today and I miss you, Liz. Yeah, that's it. I really miss you."

There was a very long pause at the end of the line.

"You're talking about Mayor Christopher?"

"Yeah, yeah. Good old George the Greek...Anyway, let's get together again, okay? I'll drive down and we can go to Tijuana. Or maybe even halfway, like meet in San Luis Obispo. We can visit a winery and drink for a while."

"I think you've been drinking enough as it is, Snap. Let me call you this weekend—"

"Somethin' wrong? Hey...You got a new guy over there?"

"Sure, Snap. Every night."

CLICK. I let the receiver drop on the bar. Chumpo walked back over to take the phone and I snatched up the receiver again. Stared at it in my hand for a good second or two.

"She's not inside of this anymore..."

VapoRub of Doom

May 24th

This was no hangover. It was like having one half of a washing machine on my head and the other half churning my guts. My coughing fits were scaring the neighborhood dogs and my nose needed a full-time plumber.

Coffee was out of the question. I was so weak all I could do was pave myself a highway between the bed and the toilet. Tried to tune my radio in to the Giants game in Milwaukee, but kept getting the same episode of *Ranger Bill*. At one point I did drag myself to the telephone to call my mother, asked if she'd heard about an influenza or smallpox epidemic on the news. All that did was get her over to my place late in the day to lay cold washcloths on my face and spoon feed me some egg drop soup she picked up in Chinatown.

But that wasn't all. She disappeared for a while, returned with a bag from a nearby pharmacy. Grabbed a small towel from my linen closet and I knew what was about to happen.

"Oh no. Not that crap again."

Too late. She had the jar of Vicks VapoRub out of the bag, and was already coating the towel with it.

"Be quiet. Atomic scientists are swearing by it now. I saw it in *Family Circle* the other day."

"Yeah, well I've been swearing about it since I was five."

"You have a better remedy for this, Milton?"

"How about a fifth of scotch? At least I'll be too drunk to feel my nose exploding."

She stuffed the entire Vicks-ified towel inside my sweat-drenched T-shirt and tucked it under my neck.

"There. Now get some sleep. A lot of it."

"You try sleeping without breathing—"

"Use your mouth then. I'll call you tomorrow after church."

♦ ♦ ♦

The Vicks worked its way through my sinus cavity like a minty enema. I was exhausted. Delirious. Before long was standing on a ball field's pitching rubber in the middle of a patch of woods. The field seemed familiar, but I couldn't place it. It was hot and humid and sunny, and crickets were chirping like crazy. There was a clean baseball in my right hand. I heard a small crowd of people cheering me on, but couldn't see anyone. Not even a batter.

"Hang in there, baby…"

This was Liz's voice, and she was suddenly leaning over to kiss my sweaty forehead. Was she really in the room? Seconds later she wasn't, neighborhood dogs were barking again, and I was back on the ball field. It was night, under a full moon, but the crickets had vanished.

The ball in my hand felt wet. I turned it over, held it up in the moonlight. It wasn't made of cowhide anymore but human skin. And the stitches sewn into it were leaking blood…

Sloppy Sunday at Bob's House

May 25th

Good old Mom and her VapoRub. I might not have been feeling like a million bucks this morning, but a few thousand were definitely in play. And when Bob invited me down to his place on lower 3rd Street to watch the Giants' twinbill in Pittsburgh, I jumped at the chance to rejoin the living.

Bob didn't make great money selling his 9-inch screws, but it was nice enough to buy himself a homey little bungalow on the edge of China Basin, where a lot of his factory folks were. Being almost a mile away from the bay, his street didn't even smell like dead crabs.

If it did, it may not have mattered. Bob had a pot of his famous Sloppy Joes simmering on the stove, and the meat-pepper-onion aroma filled the place. My gut wasn't recovered enough for a big helping, but he'd also stocked up on bottled lagers, so I was grateful enough to try his latest batch out. Bob is what you'd call a Sloppyphile, an expert on the recipe, which as I learned from him once, was invented in 1930 by a cook named Joe in a Sioux City, Iowa diner. Bob's additions of paprika, brown sugar and Worcestershire sauce gave it a killer flavor, along with the fact he buttered the insides of the buns.

Anyway, Gomez was on the hill for us in the opener against Friend, and for the first part of the game I thought I was still delirious, because the Giants were hitting and scoring like escaped convicts at Mardi Gras. It was 12-2 after three innings, and the more they scored, the more glum I got. "Watch this," I said. "Fifteen runs this game, zippety-doo-dah the next. Baseball does this all the time." The final was 17-5, and all we had to do was beat Bob Porterfield in the nightcap to make it back to .500.

It was a rare thing to have the second half of a Sunday doubleheader on television, and by the 5th inning, the three camera angles were starting to make my eyes swim. So were the Giants. Ramon Monzant was pitching as well as he possibly could for us, but it was a losing battle.

When Roy Face whiffed Ed Bressoud with the bases loaded to end the 2-1 loss, I cursed at the top of my lungs. An Oriental next-door neighbor yelled something back that sounded much nastier. I marched over to Bob's open window to fire a volley back, but my friend jumped up from his recliner and blocked me.

"Forget it, Snappy. It's China Basin."

Instead, I let my fourth bottle of beer calm me down. After a piece of chocolate cream pie, Bob escorted me to the door.

"So you liked those Sloppy Joes?"

"Always. Thanks. Next time maybe you can add some ballpark food, too. Y'know, hot dogs. Peanuts…"

He paused abruptly on the carpet. His face darkened. "Naw. Not those things."

"What things?"

"Peanuts…They found an open bag of them on the seat of Reggie's car. Far as I know he didn't even eat them."

I stared at him. "He was parked near the stadium?"

"Yeah. You didn't know that? I fig-ured he bought 'em at the Double Play that night, but Chumpo doesn't carry Salty Dog Nuts."

And then I stared some more, thinking. And I remembered the Opening Day body I found in section 16, covered in peanut shells. And my favorite out-of-town paper left in the booth at the Double Play—covered in peanut shells.

And I suddenly had the chills…

The Bronx Bugle Sporting Life

SMOKE KOOLS   Monday Late Edition, May 26, 1958   DON'T BEFRIEND RUSSKIES

National Chills Beat American Yawns

by Archie Stripes
American League Beat

Has there ever been, or will there ever be again, as close a pennant race as that which the Senior Circuit has offered this first month and a half? With today's nerve-stretching, hair-ripping, and finger-nail-chewing 9-6 Dodgers win in Philadelphia, matched an hour later by the Cubs' third straight one-run victory in cold Milwaukee, the eight clubs find themselves separated by the thinnest of seven toothpicks.

L.A. bashed five home runs in Brotherly Lovetown, two by the former Duke of Flatbush, and still nearly lost the affair after Granny Hamner poled a 3-run poke off Fred Kipp in the 9th.

The Cubs took their brilliant Dave Hillman/Carl Willey matchup 2-1 on a 9th inning homer by reserve out-fielder Chuck Tanner, to complete the unlikely three-game sweep at County stadium.

But how unlikely was it? None of these teams have a clear edge in hitting, pitching or fielding, meaning day in and day out, baseball can count on four games with a completely unpredictable outcome.

As much as this reporter follows the fortunes of the Bronx Bombers, it only makes we New Yorkers pine for the grand old Dodger and Giant days even more.

Orioles Peck Athletics to Death, 14-0

KANSAS CITY (UPI)— In the only American League "contest" of the day, Baltimore made it two straight on the other western frontier with a bloody trouncing of the upstart A's.

"Worst game I've ever seen played, no doubt about it," said Orioles skipper Paul Richards, "I usually hold my tongue when discussing the other team, but boy oh boy, peeeuw!"

Kansas City made four infield errors, each time lead-ing to big Oriole rallies. Gus Triandos and Jim Marshall both knocked in four runs in Baltimore's 15-hit attack. The 7th place A's will now try to rebound by "welcoming" the Yanks to town for two.

≈ *Just Plain Nuts* ≈

May 27th

I spent all Monday and most of today trying to reach Liz. First to apologize for calling her when I was drunk last week, second to fill her in on the peanuts revelation. Whoever this murdering bastard was, he seemed to have a fetish for salted-in-the-shells. A call to Reggie's wife confirmed that her poor husband not only never ate the things, he was allergic to them.

Anyway, Liz wasn't answering her phone in L.A., so I gave up and went to the Double Play late in the afternoon to see Chumpo and catch the start of the Giants game in first place Philly. As I mentioned last time, Chumpo didn't carry Salty Dog Nuts. He hadn't even heard of them. But while I sat there, drank a Hamm's and rooted for Mike McCormick to keep the damn ball in the park for a change, Chumpo dialed one of his peanut wholesaler friends and left a message to try and get more info.

"Can't say I remember Reggie talking to anyone here the night he bought it," he said, wiping the bar down, "and nobody eating from their own bag of nuts, neither."

"How about the day I cleaned the newspaper and those peanut shells out of that booth?"

"That neither too."

Then the bar phone rang, and he grabbed the receiver. Said "Yup… Yup…Yup…Okay" and hung it up.

"So?"

"So the Salty Dog Nut factory's in Ohio. You can buy 'em as far west as Colorado, but nowhere on the west coast."

"Well, that's interesting."

"It is?"

"Sure. Our killer could be a traveling salesman."

◆ ◆ ◆

After the Giants were done looking terrible again and I had four beers in me, I wobbled back to my place. Paused on the outside steps.

The living room light was on. I heard the floor creak. Climbed carefully to the door and burst inside.

Liz sat at a typewriter in a robe, cigarette in mouth and hair up in a towel. Shrieked like I had stabbed her.

"Damn it, Snappy! Can't you knock??"

"I don't knock on my own place."

"You mean OURS. Oh, who cares…" She started pounding on the keys. A legal pad filled with scribbles sat next to the typewriter. "I need to have this draft finished tonight, so don't bug me."

"A draft of what?"

"What do you think? My exclusive for the *Herald*! Y'know, on the Mayor

Christopher Candlestick swindle. Thank you so much for that tip, by the way—" She popped up for a second to smooch my cheek, dropped back down. "You're a doll."

I had no clue what to say. While thinking of something, I headed for my gin bottle.

Sorry, Not the Wrong Number

May 28th

While Liz was up all night typing, I was down with a pillow over my head.

Found her slumped over her typewriter in the morning, and when I shook her she was out the door with her pages in a minute flat. The editor at the *Herald* was expecting them by special delivery sometime after lunch, and when you're trying like hell to get hired somewhere, being late isn't the best idea.

What this did was give me a chance to take her out for a late breakfast and sell her on my peanut theory. She wasn't buying it.

"So big deal, the guy likes Salty Dog nuts. Doesn't mean he travels to get them. Maybe he buys them by the gross, right from the company, and lives across the street from you."

"Don't make fun of me, Liz. It's the first break I've had since Opening Day."

"I'd hardly call it a break. And I'd

think twice before bothering the cops with this."

"So what do YOU think? That this land deal is behind the murders?"

"Why not? People kill over money every day. You can set your alarm clock to it."

I was done arguing, and suggested we take another walk in Golden Gate Park. It was sprinkling rain, so we headed to a movie theatre instead. Shared a big bag of popcorn and watched *Attack of the 50-Foot Woman*. Liz thought it was dumb and I thought it was a riot.

Afterward she called her editor from a pay phone and couldn't reach him, which put her on edge for the next two hours. I calmed her down with beer and burgers at the Double Play, though hearing the Giants get hammered 10-0 in Philly got me all upset.

The phone was ringing when we got back to the apartment. I snatched the receiver so hard I almost yanked the cord out.

"Yeah."

No answer.

"Hello?"

"Is it the *Herald*?" asked Liz behind me.

"Shh!…Hello?"

Nothing. I hung up the receiver.

"Why'd you do that??"

"Why do you think? It was a wrong number."

"How do you know? Maybe it was my editor trying to call. I left him this number—"

It rang again. This time I let her grab it.

"Hello, Liz Doo-mah."

She stood there in silence. Listening a few seconds. Her face slightly contorted. Then she shrieked, dropped the receiver on the floor and grabbed me.

"Someone's there!"

I carefully picked it up and listened. The person was outside, but I distinctly heard breathing. Male breathing.

"Say something, you bastard."

He hung up.

Remember This...

May 30th

I don't carry a knife or a gun, but I do have Triples Trevor, a 38-ounce, Joe DiMaggio model wooden bat my dad got for me once that I keep under my bed in case of emergency.

After that creepy call Wednesday night, Trevor slept all night with us. Liz found a way to tuck her entire head and most of her body against my left arm, Trevor's scratchy handle secure in my right. But the only noises all night were the occasional passing siren and a pair of cooing, cuddling doves in the rain gutter at daybreak.

The entire major leagues had Thursday off, teams getting ready for Friday's holiday doubleheaders, but Liz had a full schedule of obsessing over her newspaper article to do. She called her editor first thing. He loved the story, and after assuring her he wasn't the one who was breathing into our phone, said it would run in the Friday morning edition. Liz was worried it would be buried by the Memorial Day coverage, but he said no, he'd make room for it in the left feature column.

So Liz spent the day with me walking on nervous air. It was gorgeous out, and we took a boat ride that went under both bridges, circled Alcatraz, and even passed by the U.S. missle launching pad on Angel Island. I've always thought protecting San Francisco Bay from a Soviet invasion was a little paranoid on our part, but Liz didn't trust them Russkies, and convinced me to be nice and grateful on the eve of our national holiday.

As for her article, she was already planning what to say when she accepted the Pulitzer Prize. When we got back she let me read it, and I was pretty impressed. She managed to raise all the right questions, get some choice quotes from Henry North, get even less from City Hall than I did, but write it up in a catchy style without even using my name once. I took her out for a nice seafood dinner that night, and unplugged the phone later so we could get romantic.

Then Memorial Day happened. Like a Howitzer shell landing on our heads. We skipped the annual parade at the Presidio and ran to the out-of-town newsstand to get the morning Herald. Not only was Liz's story missing from the front page, it was nowhere to be found in the entire paper.

Liz called them in a rage. The editor wasn't there so she called his house. Barked a blue streak at him, then listened with her face turning from red to white. Then she hung up. I stared at her.

"What happened?"

It took her half a minute to actually speak. "They killed it…Christopher threatened to sue the paper and they wet their pants."

"Why? You had quotes from North, and—"

"Yeah, but someone pretending to know North called them and said I made them up. That I couldn't be trusted. That all I'm doing is protecting my boyfriend!"

"That's ridiculous!"

"Of course it is! But they're cowards and sissies, and now they don't want me writing for them anymore!!"

She stood there shaking for a second, then drifted out of the room like a beautiful piece of floating wood.

♦ ♦ ♦

I was at the Double Play all afternoon, drinking and barely able to enjoy the Giants' shocking doubleheader sweep in St. Louis. Liz had left earlier for L.A. again, shell-shocked. I guess it was better than her barging into City Hall with a gun or Triples Trevor, but my attempts to console her had done absolutely no good.

One thing was clear, though. Whether the Candlestick Point deal was related to the murders or not, someone sure didn't want the public to know about it.

Eight Ball, Too Many Pockets

May 31st

Horace Stoneham wanted to see me again, but I wasn't in the mood to hear a lecture about my snoopy girlfriend. I told him I was sick and tried to go see Henry North instead, but Henry and his wife were on a holiday weekend road trip up the coast. Chumpo was around and boring as usual, but he did say something that nudged my ears.

"If you got peanuts on the brain, maybe you should trade jobs with Duffy Dieter for a month."

Duffy Dieter was the peanut vendor in section 16. Had been chucking bags so long at Seals Stadium most people thought he was born there. His other home was Break Shot Billiards on Kearny Street, so I headed down there for a little best-of-three in Eight-Ball.

Most of the Seals ushers didn't socialize with the food vendors, but Duffy had friends in all places. He was also King of the Break Shot, and had the beard, six-foot-five bulk and trophies on the wall to prove it.

"Not sure I oughta play with you, Drake," he said as we chalked up, "People you know been turning up dead lately."

"Yeah? Well, I didn't know the dead guy on Opening Day. Anyone buy five or ten bags of peanuts from you that day?"

He paused a long moment to line up his thought, then broke the rack like a human pile driver, sinking two stripes. "Can't say I remember, because I don't. Why you asking?"

"Because the guy's body was covered in shells. My guess is they were out-of-town shells."

He dropped four more striped balls before I took a crack at an easy 5-ball shot and drubbed it. "It was crowded as hell that day, Drake. You know that. Everyone and their mother-in-law wanted to be there for the first west coast game. Chances are if the jerk bought half my tray I wouldn't have even remembered him. Wanna break this time?"

I looked at the table, which he had already cleaned up. I broke for Game 2, which was a better match. I won my five dollar bill back by sinking three easy shots at the end and nailing a lucky bank job on the 8-ball. Game

3 looked like a certain Duffy shutout. I had a half dozen decent-looking stripe balls to play and never got to hit one. As he prepared to hit his game-ending 8-ball dagger, he paused and fixed a stare on me.

"Y'know, dealing with Stoneham and these other fools are gettin' you nowhere. If I were you, Drake, I'd stop ruffling feathers and start burning 'em."

"What do you mean?"

"I mean do something you really shouldn't and watch what happens. Something they won't see comin'. Corner pocket."

He fired. The cue ball clacked the 8-ball, but the 8 sideswiped one of mine and it shanked into a side pocket for the shocking defeat.

"Yeah…" I said, "Something nobody would see coming. Thanks for the tip and free demonstration, Duff." I grabbed his five and walked out the door to think of whatever the hell that something would be.

National League thru Saturday, May 31

Philadelphia	23	19	.548	—
Los Angeles	24	21	.533	0.5
Chicago	23	23	.500	2
Pittsburgh	23	23	.500	2.5
St. Louis	21	22	.488	2.5
Cincinnati	20	21	.488	2.5
Milwaukee	21	23	.477	3
San Francisco	21	24	.467	3.5

American League thru Saturday, May 31

New York	31	14	.689	—
Chicago	27	18	.600	4
Baltimore	26	19	.578	5
Boston	25	20	.556	6
Cleveland	23	25	.479	9.5
Detroit	21	24	.467	10
Kansas City	16	28	.364	14.5
Washington	12	33	.267	19

Incident After the 13th Inning

June 1st

"Hit the damn ball, Willie!" Bob and me were Hamming it up at the Double Play, watching the Giants suffer through extra innings in St. Louis. It was the finale of their first road trip—one that saw them go 10-11—and I was actually eager to get back to ushering in a few days to distract myself from thinking too much.

I had thought about Duffy Dieter's idea to do something outrageous to upset the Mayor's apple, orange and horse carts, but it just wasn't coming to me. By the time the Cards' Bob Mabe coughed up an early 4-0 lead they had taken on Gomez, I was already happily skunked and not feeling compelled to be anywhere but two feet away from Chumpo's tap.

We were up 6-4 in the last half of the 8th. Rigney stuck Andre Rodgers in at short and moved Daryl Spencer to second. Spence had had a killer game—two doubles and a triple—and he rewarded his fans right away by letting a Hobie Landrith roller bounce off his face for an error. Joe Cunningham slammed the next pitch into the pavilion in right for the 6-6 tie, and extra frames.

The Cards had their chances to score off Gordon Jones, but couldn't cash in. So we did. Two walks and a single off Phil Paine loaded the sacks, Felipe Alou worked a fourth walk for the go-ahead run. After Willie finally hit the ball but lined into a DP, Boyer, Musial, and Moon went out 1-2-3 and the saloon exploded.

I was in a feisty mood afterwards. It was a nice warm evening, and for some strange reason really felt like the first day in June. I asked Bob if he wanted to take a spin down to Monterey and fish for a couple of unattached tomatoes. He wasn't too keen on that, so instead I fired up the Coronet, found a radio station playing Bobby Darin and gave myself a nice long motor tour. Headed over the Golden Gate to Sausalito, circled around through Berkeley and back over the Bay Bridge by the time it got dark.

Stopped at a tavern on the other side of the bridge for a few nightcaps, and that was when The Idea came to me. Just dropped in my darn lap. First I found a nearby hardware store that was still open and bought a few items. Then I drove out to Candlestick Point.

The construction site was easy to find, a big long pile of dirt carved out of a tall hillside. There was a wire fence around the whole thing and a night watchman's shack at one end. I killed my headlights, parked on a dirt road around the side and climbed out.

A frigid wind whipped off the bay and just about iced my eyebrows. Whoever thought this was a good spot to build a ball park was definitely out of his mind. I opened the back door and took out my supplies: a blank sign on a post, a fat felt-tipped pen, and a hammer. Found a spot along the fence that looked easy to climb over. Tossed the stuff over the top and scaled the fence.

The wind here was ferocious. I had to put my arm over my face to keep the dirt from blowing in my eyes. At one point I thought I heard footsteps but no one was behind me. The guard was still in his shack. I could see his shadow moving in its lit window.

I uncapped the pen, scrawled my message on the sign and hammered it into the ground at the edge of the dirt pile. Stood back to admire my work:

THIS SITE MAY
BE ILLEGAL!
FOR INFO,
CONTACT HENRY NORTH,
S.F. GRAND JURY

I grinned, all liquor-wobbly, and imagined the morning workers showing up and seeing the sign. Just getting the Mayor to sleep a little less was enough for me.

Then I heard the footsteps again. Quickening. Turned a second too late and a beefy arm was around my neck. Whoever it was held me fast, his mouth close to my ear. His breathing was labored. I distinctly smelled peanuts.

"You're a bad boy, Milton..." he said in a low, polished accent I had a tough time placing. "Makes me think...you ought to be punished."

It was hard for me to talk, but I managed to squeak out "the Mayor sent you?"

"Uh-uh...Never met...this mayor. Afraid it's just you against me, Milton. All...season...long."

I tried to raise a hand, hoping to nail his face. He kicked out one of my legs and dropped on top of me. He may not have been tall but he was solid. Pressed my face into the dirt.

"Seals is sure a nice park. Plenty big enough for...hide and seek, don't you think? All I can say is, you better... play along."

Then his arm jerked once under my neck and everything went black.

❖ ❖ ❖

A worker slapped me awake first thing in the morning. "Get the hell up, you son-of-a-bitch."

Before I had a chance to spit the dirt out of my mouth, two more workers appeared to drag me across the site. My sign was lying next to me, already smashed into kindling wood.

"See you in San Quentin, you sick bastard."

"What the hell are you talking about?"

They dragged me the rest of the way to the guard shack, dumped me on the ground. I could hear police sirens in the distance. Getting closer.

"Pick up a little nylon rope when you were at the hardware store, moron-face?" When I didn't answer right away I got kicked in the ribs, and rolled over. Looked into the sky above me.

The dead night watchman swayed from a light pole next to the shack. Nylon rope tied around his snapped neck.

A bag of Salty Dog nuts sticking out of his back pocket.

A Whole Bunch of Malarkey

June 3rd

For my one phone call I tried Liz, but she wasn't home. Neither was Henry North. My mother was, but seeing my name in the morning paper had put her on a bloody mary kick, and she had nothing to offer but a lot of slurry hysteria.

Like with the first two killings, the cops had nothing on me except a lot of circumstantial weirdness—but boy had it ever gotten circumstantially weird. A dead night watchman now. Found in the same place where I'd hopped the fence in a drunken stupor to pound a smart-aleck sign into the ground. Even weirder, the nylon cord used to hang the guy was from the same hardware store I bought the sign.

"Got an answer for that one, Drake?" Malarkey and his muscle-headed minions had me in the precinct's upstairs interrogation room the whole day, barricaded from a pack of ravenous press wolves down the hall.

"Nope. Maybe you should talk to the guy at the hardware store."

"We did already. All he remembered was you."

"Well, it's pretty clear I was being followed. So maybe he lifted the cord right after I left the place."

"The only thing clear to me, Drake, is that either you're the one doing these crimes, or you've had more bad luck than a blind man at a blackjack table. You still expect us to believe this baloney about somebody framing you?"

"I would. Especially with your clown car staking me out for over a month and coming up with less than poodle poop."

"HEY!" It was Griff, the idiot from

my last time at the precinct. Ugly as ever. "Watch your mouth there, Melvin."

"It's Milton, jerko. The papers had it wrong, too. Actually, I'm kind of surprised you knew how to read them."

Steam came out of his bull nose.

Malarkey casually stepped between us.

"Nobody was at the construction site but you and Vincent Grosso, Drake. Don't make this difficult."

"You're the one doing that. I told you, the guy was all over me, and he

---

The Bronx Bugle Sporting Life

Scorching Hot Pale Hose Invade Stadium

by Archie Stripes
American League Beat

They single you to death, they homer in extra innings, they can beat you 1-0 or 14-1, depending on their mood. Their relief corps is thin but their bench is deeper than a Roman cistern, and their starting arms can shut you down before you've done your deep knee bends.

The White Sox are back in town, riding their South Side steam roller, and Casey's army had better be prepared because the season has entered its serious time. With Chicago going 11-2 since snapping the Bomb-

ers' 13-game win streak out at Comiskey Park recently, the gap between the foes has been sliced to three games.

To make matters more nervous, Mickey Mantle will be

out for all three games with a bruised knee.

Whitey Ford will get the first ball against Dick Donovan, with Don Larsen facing Early Wynn and Art Ditmar matching with Jim Wilson to round out the series. Expect throngs.

May was a hugely winning month for the Bronx Boys, but June is already busting out as a far bigger challenge.

SENATORS LOSE TO ORIOLES,
FEW NOTICE
Details unavailable

Usher Nabbed Following Third S.F. Murder

SAN FRANCISCO (UPI)— A 37-year-old Seals Stadium usher has been detained for questioning about a series of recent "Giants-related" killings that has startled this city.

Melvin "Snappy" Drake, an ex-journeyman minor league pitcher, was arrested at the

Candlestick Point construction site for the team's new ball park this morning, hours after night guard Vincent Grosso, 43, was found hung by his neck from a nearby light pole.

Grosso's body was the third to be found in the club's first

month and a half in the city. Mr. Drake was at the scene of all three crimes, and personally knew the second victim, making local authorities eager to question him.

Giants owner Horace Stoneham could not be reached for comment.

smelled like the peanuts in Grosso's pocket. Didn't you see his footprints?"

"Are you kidding? The wind was blasting so hard all night we didn't even see your prints."

"Then this is just crazy. What the hell motivation would I have to string someone up, let alone knife a guy on Opening Day and beat one of my best friends to death in a park?"

"You tell me. I know some baseball fans who react pretty strange when their team's been losing."

"That's real funny, Malarkey. How about I just pay the 30-dollar trespassing fine now so I can go home and get some sleep?"

Griff snorted at me. "This fine's about ten grand more than that. Looks like your seat-dusting and butt cheek-kissing job ain't exactly gonna cover it...Melvin."

I looked at his oafish face one more second, then sprung from my chair and took a swing at it. My fist grazed the side of his head, knocked him back. Was able to lunge again before they had their arms around me.

"Malarkey! Chief wants ya!"

Another cop stood in the doorway. Malarkey disappeared for half a minute, leaving me with my cheery friends. I shook them off, did my best to pretend they weren't there, which made them even more crazy. When Malarkey returned, his face

was flushed.

"You're a luckier bastard than you have any right to be, Drake. Some big shot just paid your entire bail, plus the sixty dollars we just milked out of him for your 'special' trespassing fine."

"Well gad and zooks. Was it the Mayor?"

"Nope. Someone bigger than him... lately. Now collect your crap and get out of my sight so we can start tailing you again. And this time you can bet it'll be half the force!"

◆ ◆ ◆

Griff's sidekick took me down a back staircase ten minutes later to avoid the reporters. Popped open a door to a dark back alley and stuck an envelope in my hand.

"From your angel of mercy, whoever he was. Don't leave town and stay the hell out of trouble, Drake, would ya? I got a vacation coming up."

He left me in the alley, and I started walking. It was going to be pretty hard to stay out of trouble if my personal tormentor was always trying to keep me in it. I waited till I was two blocks from the station, then ripped open the envelope. There was a note inside:

Mr. Drake—

We have a 1 p.m. matinee with the Braves tomorrow. Come up and watch the game with me.

—H. Stoneham

≈ *Private Boxing* ≈

June 4th

Hot dogs, peanuts, and cold pop were nowhere to be found high up in the owner's box. Horace Stoneham had his girl bring out baked chicken breasts smothered in herbs, candied carrots and tall glasses of raspberry lemonade, each one crowned with a mint leaf. And the Giants owner didn't have gin in his yet.

"About time we started hitting, don't you think?" he said, trying to keep the air easy.

"This Antonelli has to get his head on straight," I replied. "Long as we're pitching, we don't need to hit too much. Look what the Orioles are doing."

Down on the field, Stu Miller plunked Johnny Logan with a bases loaded pitch to make it 2-0 Braves in the 1st. Warren Spahn was pitching for Milwaukee, but he'd been knocked around a lot lately, so I wasn't too worried.

"You're a pretty sharp fellah, Snappy. What the hell are you ushering for?"

"Like being around the games, I guess. And my pitching career still isn't panning out."

"Come on, you're no old man. Walter Johnson pitched until he was forty."

"Right. But he was Walter Johnson."

He sliced open his chicken breast with a shiny steak knife. "Any of those newshounds bother you last night?"

"A couple tried. Put my shades down, the radio up, and drank myself to sleep."

"Hmm. Usually works for me...So I'm going to be frank again here: Who the hell is doing this crap? Who's got an axe to grind with you? We've still got over fifty home games left, and I'll be damned if I'm going to lose one fan over this."

"Listen, if I knew who it was I would've killed him myself by now. I still say this Henry North business—"

"Nothing to do with this, and none of your business, understand?" He speared a candied carrot, threatened me with it. "The Candlestick deal is just your typical big time big city business, and the only thing getting hurt is a few wallets. This maniac is hanging around here, and we're going to catch him."

"Well, that decoy idea didn't exactly—"

"I seem to remember that being your idea."

"It was. And it might have worked if the damn team didn't have to leave town. Or maybe the cops and city officials you've been paying off should look a little less into me, and more into people addicted to Salty Dog Nuts."

Stoneham frowned a moment. "So that's your tip? Start selling those here and see who buys the most bags?"

"I can think of a worse idea. But actually…" I watched a nearby usher leading a late-arriving couple to their seats. "Making me live bait on that last home stand wasn't entirely wrong." I turned to Stoneham. "We just *did* it wrong."

"What do you mean?"

"Okay. Malarkey put plainclothes cops all over the park, but this killer is no dope. He could sniff those guys out. I say ditch the cops and use the army you already got working for you."

"Oh really. And what army is that?"

I grinned. Stood and whistled down at the usher. "Hey Butch!"

Butch was bulky, big-faced, with a flat-topped marine haircut. Saw me and worked his way up the aisle to the edge of the private box. Tipped his cap to the team owner.

"Afternoon, Mr. Stoneham. Taking care of our new local celebrity, I see."

"Butch," I asked, "Do you like your job?"

"Guess so, yeah. Pays the rent. You know, lots of fresh air."

"What if you got paid a little more, and the job suddenly got kind of… exciting?"

"Gee Snappy, that sounds like it could be pretty swell. Exciting how?"

I glanced at Stoneham, and he gave me a resigned look back. Because he already knew what the answer was.

House of Ushers

June 5th

They were all there: Butch and his pal Dominic, Rudy Krupp, old McGee, Cheesesteak Sid (our east coast transplant), Stan Lowsack and his real deep baritone, Gus and Russ Nicholson, colored identical twins who used to porter on the same California Zephyr train and confuse the passengers, and even Tall Tom Tupper, who was so old I think he once showed Mark Twain to his seat.

Our boss Pence Murphy had let me call this meeting of Seals ushers, a half hour after today's afternoon finale with the Braves, and space was tight in our bite-sized changing room. It was about to get tighter.

"First off," I began, "I know there's been a lot of creepy trash in the papers about me. But don't believe a damn word of it."

"Aw, don't worry," said Rudy, "That was about some guy named Melvin."

The room broke up, and then Butch piped in. "And we already knew you were a murderin' degenerate!"

The room exploded. It helped me relax, but not by much.

"Okay, guys. Listen. This killer—the one who attacked me the other night and knocked me out—hinted pretty strongly he was going to kill again, 'all season long' as he put it. So why make it easy for him? Putting plainclothes cops in the park got us nowhere, so this time Mr. Stoneham has agreed to give each and every one of you a two hundred dollar bonus to become undercover usher cops for this home stand. With a bigger reward for someone who actually nabs him.

"Count me in," said Gus Nicholson.

"Sign me up," said Russ Nicholson.

"Do we get to beat him to death?" asked Dominic.

"Don't think you'll need to. Starting tomorrow night against the Reds, you'll all be given one of these…" I motioned to clubhouse boy Johnny Heep in the corner, who carried over a big carton and ripped open the top. Inside were a dozen or so hand-held radio boxes, like what our soldiers used at the Battle of the Bulge. A few of the ushers grabbed one. "They're Motorola 'Handy-Talkies'. They were good enough for World War II, so they're good enough for us. See anybody who even looks suspicious, especially around my Section 16, talk to each other, and talk to me. But do NOT push the red button unless you're just about positive you have the killer."

"Why? Does it explode the joint?" asked Cheesesteak Sid.

"No, but it will buzz a room under the stands that's filled with cops ready to make the arrest."

"So what's this meathead look like?" asked Sid.

"How do you turn this thing on?" asked Tall Tom.

"Right now we can narrow it down to a muscular guy with a bit of a stutter who seems to like peanuts."

"Oh good," said Dominic, "That's only half the damn park."

Then Stan Lowsack got to his feet. The room quieted down, braced itself.

"Tell me something" he began, his depth charge of a voice rattling the lockers around us, "How do you know this murderer isn't one of us?"

He was dead serious. There were a few nervous squeaks of laughter, a lot of quick, suspicious eye glances. I crossed my arms.

"Because I've been working with you bozos here for years. I know your voices, I know what's on your breath and it usually isn't peanuts. And I know you wouldn't risk being able to usher major league ball games for anything."

The room cheered. Even Stan grinned. I knew they were all on board.

And then three possible mutineers swung open the changing room door.

"Okay. We want in on this *Dragnet* stuff."

It was Dot, Lindee, and Veronica— our fetching usherettes.

D-Day, as in Dames

June 6th

Dot wore her knee-length skirt, light orange blouse, red curls exploding out from under her cap with lipstick to match. She'd more or less assigned herself to my section for the first game of Operation Handy-Talkie, and because she was pleasant to look at I put up with her motor mouth.

"Don't worry, Snappy. If we meet up with this maniac he'll be no match for a big strong guy like you!

"Did I tell you about my sister's divorce? Married just one year and he started cheating on her. When she found out later he was actually fooling around a week after their honeymoon, she tried to divorce him twice."

That sort of thing.

It took a good three innings for the Giants' bats to wake up against Nuxhall, and at least that long for the ushers to get their talkies working right. Tall Tom never did figure out how to turn his on, then ten minutes before game time remembered he had meant to take the day off for the 14-year anniversary of the Normandy Invasion so just plain left. I could see Veronica trying to work with Gus and Russ out in the bleachers. They appeared to be abandoning her. Butch and Dominic were in the section behind home plate, finding suspicious things about as many male fans as possible. And letting me know about it.

"Come in Snappy! Fat man in 12 just bought three peanut bags!"

"I never said he was fat, Butch. I said muscular!"

"Should I push the red button?"

"NO! Don't push any buttons!"

Dot shook my sleeve. "Did the killer seem like someone who liked girls?"

Boy, did I ever miss Liz's brain right about then. "Honestly? I didn't have time to ask him."

She dusted off a few seats for some late-arriving old couples. Paused to sneeze. "Actually…what do you think he might do to a girl like me?"

"Dot. Either watch the game or work it, okay?"

She put a hand on her hip, was about to sass me back when a loud WHOCK came from home plate. Hank Sauer had just put a Nuxhall fast ball deep into the left field bleachers with two on base, and we went up 3-1. Two innings and about twelve Dot-ecdotes later, Sauer hit another one with Mays aboard, Cepeda followed with a blast and we were up for good.

Between innings, a mother and her little boy came down some aisle steps toward me with fresh boxes of popcorn. I tipped my cap and moved sideways to let them by. The mother stopped in her tracks and gave me a funny look.

"You're the one in the newspaper, aren't you? The one the police suspected!"

"Ma'm, it's really been a big misunderstanding—"

"Well of course you'd say that. To save your own skin." Her kid held out a fistful of popcorn for me and she yanked him away. "Get away from him, Davey. We're going to another section. Miss?"

She waved Dot over. Dot was more speechless than me, but walked them back up the aisle to a row of empty seats in the adjacent section. I shook my head, turned to head back down.

A dozen or so fans were turned around in their seats, gazing warily at me. Like I was about to run them off the road.

I had not counted on this.

Report from the Peanut Gallery

June 7th

"Drake! You're in the left field bleachers!" Pence Murphy was in no mood to smile or negotiate.

"How come? where's Sid going?"

"Where you were yesterday. Scaring the fans away."

I kind of saw the reasoning. On Saturdays the left field bleachers was mostly a babysitting job, for the parents who dropped their rascals at the ballpark gate or stuck them on a bus or streetcar. The seats weren't assigned, so I didn't need to be showing anybody to any of them. In Stoneham and Murphy's eyes, it was a much better place to station me because I was a lot less likely to be recognized in the stands.

I borrowed a pair of dark glasses from Pence just in case I crossed paths with another eagle-eyed mom, and got out to left field as the snot-nosers flooded in. From a few past experiences and talking to Cheesesteak Sid (who was saddled with motormouth Dot for the afternoon), it made no sense to even try to keep the kids in their seats. I parked myself in the middle of the section, leaned against the outfield wall and took in the field. I had Leon Wagner and Frank Robinson catching flies right in front of me, the sun was out, and for the moment things seemed just fine.

The other ushers were using their Handy-Talkies less, now that the novelty had worn off. The cops had found a room under my bleachers to hide out in, but even they had to figure the killer wouldn't try anything with all the young 'uns around.

"Hey Mister! I can't see!"

"Me neither!"

I moved a few feet to the left, closer to centerfield. Mays darted past me on the grass below like a ball-hungry antelope, snagging leadoff hitter Johnny Temple's fly to start the game. Willie Kirkland put us ahead with a solo shot down the right field line in the second, but George Crowe's sacrifice fly out to Mays tied it in the 3rd.

"Hey Mister!"

I turned. The same kid, in his boy scout uniform, had sticky candy apple all over his mouth and hands.

"What's that thing in your back pocket?"

"It's um…a radio."

"Can you listen to Russ Hodges on it?"

"No, not that kind of radio. It's for talking to other ushers."

"What do you talk about?"

"Oh y'know…Which fans are troublemakers and have to get kicked out. Stuff like that. You're not going to be a troublemaker, right?"

He shook his head violently and stopped asking me questions, so that worked.

On the field, Bob Purkey and Al Worthington were dealing, and it was still 1-1 into the last of the 7th.

"WE WANT A HIT! WE WANT A HIT!"

The chant started in the left corner of the bleachers, spread like measles through the entire section and picked up somewhere in the right field bleachers before fading away.

"CINCINNATI STINKS!! CINCINNATI STINKS!!"

The little natives were restless. Empty popcorn boxes were starting to fly. One fell over the railing onto the warning track and I had to address the horde.

"No more throwing boxes, okay kids?"

"What about soda cups?"

A flattened one whizzed past me. I suddenly felt like Skipper Stu, a kiddie TV show host up in Sacramento.

"Didn't you hear me? You wanna get booted out??"

Something hard dropped from the sky, smacked the side of my head. I looked down.

A bag of Salty Dog nuts lay at my feet. The impact had split the bag open. I spun around, suddenly frantic.

"Who threw that??"

"PURKEY IS A TURKEY!! PURKEY IS A TURKEY!!"

The bag came from pretty high up, maybe even from someone who threw it a long way. I raced up the ten-row aisle to glance over the back wall. Saw no one outside the park that looked suspicious, or was running away.

Suddenly Malarkey and his boys were exiting their room, charging up into the bleachers. There was a blip in the field action as the rest of the stadium no doubt stared.

"Where is he?" yelled Malarkey, out of breath.

"I don't know!"

"Why'd you push the button then?"

"What??"

I felt in my back pocket for my Handie-Talkie radio. Gone. turned and saw it sitting in the sticky hands of my boy scout friend. I showed Malarkey the open Salty Dog peanut bag.

"You kidding me? That again?"

If the killer threw it, he was long gone by now. And after our third-string catcher Bob Speake threw a dribbler down the line to kick-start the Reds' winning rally in the 9th and the hours of kid-screaming had my head crying uncle, I helped myself to a couple extra drafts at the Double Play.

The Case of the Bloody Bullpen

June 8, 1958

I needed an ushering break. Actually, a week in Honolulu would've done the trick, but Malarkey had other ideas.

"Sit in the stands like an average

Joe, in your average Joe clothes. Enjoy the game and a hot dog and I'll have a guy sitting one row behind to make sure you enjoy your game and your hot dog."

Fair enough. A full day of Dot-chatter and another in Kiddie World had me ready to scream. I threw on a tee-shirt and an old fishing hat I had left in my closet to complete my lei-surely "disguise" and sank into a per-fect seat behind the Giants' first base dugout that Stoneham had left for me. We were battling the Reds and Pirates to stay out of last place, but Brooks Lawrence was going against his sketchy equal Mike McCormick, so it seemed like a fun afternoon.

Fun wasn't in the cards quite yet. Temple singled, Lynch doubled and Walt Dropo, this big lug who just ar-rived from the White Sox, sacrifice popped out to Kirkland, and we were behind 1-zip. Cepeda, Kirkland and Davenport all reached in our 2nd, Spencer pop flied a run home, but Bob Speake, an outfielder forced to catch because of injuries to Thomas and Schmidt, lined into a killing DP.

There was a lot of killing and a lot of bodies on the bases today. For them, Frank Robinson doubled and was left to rot. Dropo, Whisenant and Bilko all singled to fill 'em up but Gram-mas grounded into a DP. The Giants stranded two in the 3rd, went up 2-1 but double played themselves out of that one. After Cincy tied it 2-2 we got singles from Mays, Cepeda and Kirkland to finish off Lawrence, but

Tom Acker weasled out of the inning leaving 'em loaded.

Somehow we were ahead 4-2. Then it got creepy. A fog bank rolled up the hill and poured into the park. Gordon Jones took the slab from McCormick and doused it with petrol. Thurman, Temple, Lynch, and Dropo all got hits and we were scorched and sprawled in the gutter at 5-4. A Bressoud double and Kirkland single tied it 5-5. Spen-cer led with an 8th inning triple but three straight Giants left him to die. I was on my fourth beer and a stinking mess.

For the next four innings Tebbets and Rigney emptied their bullpens and benches like crazed generals at Verdun. Ghastly walks, screaming errors, painful double plays filled the Seals trench. Ramon Monzant issued a bases-loaded pass to Gus Bell to put the Reds ahead 6-5 in the 12th, but Alex Kellner, who'd retired all six Giants he'd faced, picked the wrong time to explode. Brandt, Mays and Cepeda all singled to tie it 6-6, but Johnny Klippstein burst in. Whiffed Kirkland in his tracks and got Daven-port to—you guessed it—smack into another twin killing.

Monzant was spent, but the only sap left in the pen was Ray Crone. I had an urge to cold-cock Ramon, steal his uniform and get out there myself. If I wasn't shivering from the fog I might have. Instead I sat bound and gagged, gaped in terror as Big Frank Robinson sliced a two-run single in the 13th, Lynch cracked one halfway to Salinas and Crone finally came in to mop up the entrails.

We went out 1-2-3 like condemned men. Against a team missing four guys in their lineup we'd given them 21 hits. We stunk like dead fish and deserved to be in the cellar and I was angry. If one person looked at me sideways that night...

And Miles to Go Before I Creep

June 9th

The marathon Giants game wore me out. I couldn't look at the newspaper in the morning. Eating a meal didn't even thrill me.

This "usher sting" was getting us nowhere. The Peanut Killer seemed to be wise to every move, and now he was just playing with me. Maybe I'd crossed a few people and punched a few faces in my journeyman travels, but what did I ever do to deserve this mental case shadowing me? I almost wished he would knock on my door with a club or switchblade or noose in his hand so we could have it out once and for all.

Bob and Chumpo were good pals, but they hadn't been much help. The remedy was obvious: I needed to talk to Liz. I spent the morning re-dialing her home number in L.A. No answer. An editor at the *Herald* hung up when I mentioned her name. I tried her at home two more times, got no answer, and then got worried.

After calling in sick—a good move because Awful Antonelli and the Giants ended up sleepwalking through another loss to the Reds—I got out to my car unseen. Stopped at the bank for some cash, loaded up on petrol and jumped on the 101 highway south.

Nothing irons out your headache better than a gorgeous, gently curving road and the hope of a matching dame at the end. I wasn't sure Liz would even talk to me, but I didn't have to be back until 7 p.m. on Tuesday, more than enough time to find out. Misty mountains and valleys on my left, ocean somewhere on my right, fresh fruit every ten miles and good diner coffee in San Luis Obispo and Ventura to fill in the gaps.

It was early evening when I hit Los Angeles. Somehow I remembered the way to Liz's canyon, and parked at the foot of her sloping driveway. The house was dark. I crept up the drive to peer in the windows but couldn't see much. Returned to my car, uncapped a fifth of Hiram Walker I'd bought on the way, cracked open the window and began to wait.

The brandy was peachy and smooth. I thought I heard a phone ringing, but wasn't sure which house it was from. I thought about going back up and knocking or camping on her front step, but I didn't want to get accidentally shot. After a while, the long drive, the brandy, and a chamber orchestra of canyon crickets put me out...

◆ ◆ ◆

BAM-BAM!! Not gun shots. The knuckles of a Japanese gardner on my window. It was morning. I sat up groggily, rolled it down.

"You seeing house?"

"What's that?"

"Suppose to clean bushes. No seeing house until I clean bushes."

"Why would I see the house?" Where's Liz?" He stared at me blankly. "The lady who lives here?"

"Oh no. Nobody live here."

This time I stared at *him*. Climbed out, hiked back up the driveway. Pressed my face to a window.

The house was cleaned out.

"Wait! Let me clean bushes!" He started clipping away behind me with his giant shears. I turned and grabbed his arms.

"Where'd she go? The lady!"

"Don't know! Nobody know….One day lady here, then she gone!"

Rockabilly Guy

June 10th

I took a long drive through the Hollywood hills while the gardener finished up his work and left. Circled back down to Liz's place and jimmied open a window on the side.

She'd left a few items behind. A hair clip. Empty nail polish bottle. Red lipsticked cigarette butt in the toilet. Nothing that told me where she was.

Then the telephone rang in the kitchen. Strange. She was in such a rush she hadn't bothered to disconnect the line. I picked it up on the fourth ring. Some guy with ants in his pants.

"Liz around?"

"Who's this?"

"Billy Frack. Frack Automotive. Can you put her on?"

"I would if she was here. If she hadn't flown her damn coop."

He whistled. "Well, how do ya like that?…"

"What's this about?"

"Oh, just a repair bill of 60 bucks she stiffed me for. You her cat?"

"Her what?"

"Her cat. Her honey. Her daddy-o. As in, 'Fix my car quick, Billy, so I can run away from this cat and stiff you on the repair.'"

"I think we better talk."

"Sure. And bring along my sixty bucks, Pops."

"Keep dreaming, friend."

◆ ◆ ◆

Frack Automotive was a one-bay garage wedged into a baking hot alley off teeming Ventura Boulevard in the San Fernando Valley. And Billy Frack had the perfect look for the tight space: rail-thin, slicked-up pompadour atop greasy jeans and a black tee-shirt. Tattoos of a viper on one arm, half-naked damsel on the other.

He also had auto repairs pouring out of his pant cuffs, and from what I could see, ran the whole operation himself. He rolled out from under a Buick, gave me a wink when I introduced myself.

"Need brake work on that Coronet?" He instantly knew the Dodge parked among nine other cars in the alley was mine. "Got a special this month."

"No thanks. So you know Liz pretty well?"

"Like my left collarbone." He popped a giant pink gum bubble as the phone rang in the garage. "Gotta get that, Pops."

So it went for most of the day—me slipping in Liz questions between his phone calls and customer chats. Most of the answers I got were quick, meaningless crumbs, but I did learn he'd been working on her T-Bird for years, probably even dated her a few times. This guy was no Randy, though. He had rockabilly 45s stacked up on his tool bench record player, twangy guitar chords bouncing off the garage walls and drawing in one saucy girl with a flat tire or broken hose after another.

The problem was getting more than a minute of Billy's attention. "Liz was jumpy like a bean, that's for sure" he'd say, and then "Stick around and I'll tell ya more." By the time he closed up shop at 5, my plan for getting back up to Seals for that night's game was shot. After calling a teed-off Pence long distance to whine about my two-day flu, I followed Billy's weaving hot rod to a bar in Santa Monica. Found the Dodgers game against Philly on my car radio, and really enjoyed Vin Scully's call as I drove. Scully hadn't been announcing Dodger games for too

long, but it wouldn't have shocked me if he stuck around another few years.

The Hideout Lounge on West Channel used to be a speakeasy during the '30s and had a killer juke box, which quickly became Billy's next distraction.

"Got some dimes?" I filled his hand and he was over there in seconds. "Roll Over Beethoven" started up and he shook and shimmied his way back to me. "The King might be a king, but Chuck Berry is the Lord!"

"So why do you think Liz was scared?"

"I said jumpy, not scared. Big difference, Pops. Pretty clear she wanted to split town in a hurry, but a dish like her? Could have been all sorts of reasons. Stick around and I'll tell ya more."

A busty brunette a foot taller than him was making eyes from the juke box. He swigged half his draft beer in one gulp, began to slide off the stool again and I stopped him.

"There's a guy up north they're calling the Peanut Killer. Maybe you've heard about him." Billy drew a blank. "Anyway, my fear is he might have something to do with this."

Billy's face darkened. He set his beer on the bar, unwrapped a fresh stick of Bazooka and shoved it in his mouth. "Got any smokes?"

"Yeah."

"Well come out back and have a smoke with me."

I followed him through a back door. The second we hit the lot he spun on a booted heel and slammed me against the wall.

"You're making this up, right?"

"Huh?? Why would I do that?"

"I lied, okay? She did seem scared. Matter of fact her cage was flat-out rattled. Made me think someone creepy might've been after her. Someone like you."

"You're crazy."

"Think so? How come you know so much about this Peanut Man?"

"Because I've stumbled over every damn body he's left, that's why. Why do you care so much about Liz? If you need the sixty bucks that bad I'll take care of it!"

He shook me loose. Paced around in a small circle.

"It ain't the money, Pops…

"Okay. So what the hell is—"

"She's my everlovin' SISTER! Alright??"

Meg's Waffles and Other Pickles

June 11th

Thankfully Billy had a couch for me. Though by the time we got to his rat trap of an apartment in the Silverlake area and talked, drank and smoked for another two hours, I could have nodded off on hot coals.

Billy was Liz's younger brother by four years, and as black a sheep as a family could have. "Daddy Doomis" had a career in banking carved out for him since he started high school, so Billy spent the next ten years rebelling, escaped to L.A. to become either a mechanic or rhythm guitarist and changed his last name in the process. He and Liz wrote and saw each other occasionally, but there were long stretches they didn't talk at all.

I bought Billy breakfast in the morning at Meg's, a loud, wonderfully greasy pancake and eggporium on Cahuenga, where I ordered Meg's Cheese Waffles (don't ask) and listened to a little more Liz lore.

"I worry because her taste in guys can be pretty rank—sorry, old man. Jumps into love pools when she oughta be perched on the diving board a while, y'know?"

"And she didn't tell you where she was driving?"

"Big nope. Not like I didn't ask her nine times. She's got a new mood every day and when she ain't talking the best thing I can do is back off."

"Where might she go, if someone was after her?"

Billy's breakfast arrived: country steak, hash browns, three eggs and two giant pickles. I had no clue where in his body he was intending to put it all.

"Well…she always liked the desert. Y'know, Palm Springs, Thousand Palms…Whatever-Palm-You-Feel-Like…'Course if someone was on my tail the last place I'd go would be the big Wide Open."

"What would be the first place?"

He wolfed down some potatoes, crunched into his first pickle. "Mom and Dad's. Instinct, right? She sure got enough repair work from me to get her to the midwest. I don't know, though…"

"You don't know what?"

"Why she'd even bother with them crazy fossils."

"Hey, c',mon. They're your mom and dad."

"Tell ya what—"

He dug a handful of change out of his pocket, slid it over. Plucked a miniature pencil out of the side of his pompadour I didn't even know was in there and scribbled a phone number on a napkin. "Call Mommy and Daddy Doomis on that pay phone in the corner. Ask if Liz is there, or on her way there. Just don't say I didn't warn ya, and don't use my name."

First my eggs were scrambled, now my mind. I dropped my fork, grabbed the change and headed for the phone. A long distance operator got me through after two failed attempts. An older woman with a soft, brittle voice picked up.

"Hi, ma'm. Are you Mrs. Doomis?"

"Yes…"

"I'm Sid Crawford, a friend of your daughter Liz on the west coast?… Anyway, I have a possible writing job for her and I've been trying to reach her."

"Lizzie lives in Los Angeles, sir. How did you get our number?"

"Umm…from another friend. It doesn't matter. Is she there now or is she supposed to be coming there? I heard she might be—"

"Not to my knowledge, sir. And I don't appreciate you calling us. Is she in some kind of trouble again?"

"No, no. I just…What do you mean by 'again'?"

Suddenly the phone was snatched out of her hand by a guy with a voice harder than concrete.

"What about our daughter? Who IS this??"

"Max Crawford, Mr. Doomis. Nothing's wrong, I was just trying to reach her. Sorry I—"

"Reach her for what?"

"Never mind, sir. Thought maybe she was visiting, that's all."

"Is she missing again??"

"Umm…no. Well, sort of. She packed up and left from L.A., and I didn't know how—"

"SHE WHAT??"

"Forget it, Mr. Doomis. Maybe I'll try back another time—"

"WHO ARE YOU??"

I hung up and retreated to our booth, shaken. Billy's plate was almost wiped clean.

"Enjoy that?" he asked.

"Not especially. But according to them, Liz has been in trouble and missing before."

He sighed. Leaked out a long, slow burp. "Yeah, well…parents like to exaggerate. 'Course, Liz's goofy moods make her do some goofy things."

To thank me for buying his breakfast, Billy gave my Coronet a free hour-long tune-up at his shop before I hit the road. We exchanged phone numbers, vowed to stay in touch about Liz. I liked the kid.

And now my Dodge purred and raced like an eight-month old kitten. I took my time heading north. Stopped for a Mexican lunch in Santa Barbara, a glass of wine in San Luis Obispo. Tried to tune in the Giants' afternoon game on my radio but could only get preachers, Pat Boone and scratchy fiddles. It was dark and I was beat when I finally got to my neighborhood. Trudged up the apartment steps and paused.

The window next to the door was open. I carefully stepped inside, saw a few magazines knocked on the floor, my bedroom in slight disarray.

Someone had broken in again.

Fall of the House of Ushers

June 12th

Nothing seemed to be missing from my place, and the only thing the intruder left was a safety pin under the windowsill. Maybe he tried to open the door lock with it. What I really wanted to do was take Triples Trevor to work with me that day, but that may have looked a bit strange.

It was strange enough just walking into the usher's changing room. Everyone looked at me like I had leprosy.

"Sniffles all clear up, Snappy?" asked Cheesesteak Sid.

"We were really hoping to catch the guy while you were gone," said Dominic, "and a few of us was hoping it was you."

Stan Lowsack stepped between us before anything escalated. "No picking on Snappy, got that?" After the room stopped shaking, everyone went back to their business and headed out to the stands. Pence decided to pair me with Tall Tom for the finale with the Pirates, the best move he could have made. Tom worked the lower first base boxes over the Giants dugout, land of the richer season ticket holders and serious ball fans. He knew every one by name, where they went to school, and as long as I was with him (in my "sunglasses disguise" again), they barely noticed I was there. The price, of course, was having to endure Tall Tom's nine innings of anecdotes. Such as…

"Hollywood Stars were up here in '46, and Bogey sat in my section. Bet me twenty bucks they'd beat the Seals and when they went extra innings and didn't, he tried to slip me fifteen due to the Stars' 'extra effort'. Great actor, but a real cheapskate."

And…

"Should have heard this kid. Twelve years old with a mouth like a drunken wife-beater. Calling the home plate ump a blind rotten so-and-so from the first inning to the seventh. Finally I grab his collar, haul him down to a vacated front row seat behind home and tell him to try cursing from there.

The ump turns, stares right at him and the kid just about floods his trousers."

After another dozen tall tales, I barely noticed we'd scored three runs in the 7th off Ron Kline to snap a 2-2 tie and send us to a three-game sweep of the Bucs. Tall Tom may have been a motor mouth, but he sure made the games go quicker.

Unfortunately, for the third straight day there was also no action on our Handy-talkies. The ushers were getting annoyed with the whole scheme and I still got the silent treatment later. It was a nice late afternoon when I left the park and looked forward to my short stroll home.

"Hey Snappy!"

Some guy in his late 20s with shirtsleeves, tie and a little notebook in his hand was coming up behind me on the sidewalk.

"If you got a few minutes I got a few questions."

"Who the hell are you?"

"I'm uh…from the *Tribune*?"

"Prove it."

He fished in his slacks, pulled out a press badge reading

EUGENE BUZZBEE
OAKLAND TRIBUNE

When I saw the unused hole on top of the badge I suddenly knew more about this guy than he thought I did.

"Why should I even talk to you?"

"Because I'll get the story right."

"What story? Nothing's happened since the last body."

"Oh really? Is that why you split town for a few days?"

I took a menacing step, backed him against a lamp post. "The only thing I'm going to split right now is your head. Tell me Eugene, they pay you well at that paper for your stories? Or do you bill them for a little after-hours snooping?"

"I don't know what you're talking about."

"The hell you don't!" I dug into his pocket and yanked out the press badge again. "Missing a little safety pin, I see. The one you left in my place yesterday?"

"That wasn't me. I swear—"

"Don't lie to me, weasel. I got enough freaks on my tail right now to last me a lifetime, and I don't mind one bit putting one out of commission."

"Okay, okay… I didn't mean nothing by it. There's a lot of reporters lookin' for leads on this story and I thought maybe if I dug around some I could get an edge."

"Oh. I see. Digging around includes breaking and entering?"

I took his badge, tossed it into a nearby storm drain. "Go dig for that. And if I catch you anywhere near my place again I'll sic Malarkey's police dogs on your rookie rump."

I let him go so he could scramble after his badge in the gutter. Went home, slammed the door and made friends with my gin bottle.

≈ *The Voice at the Other End* ≈

June 13th

Friday the 13th. The Phillies were in town, and Tall Tom decided not to show up. Perfect. Flag Day wasn't until tomorrow, so I couldn't figure out his patriotic excuse this time. Anyway, I had to work his section all night by myself. Got a few weird looks from fans who'd been following the murder stories, but nothing that caused me to lose a tip or miss the game action.

And what action! The Phils had been an amazing surprise contender so far, and with control specialist Robin Roberts going for them, I knew we'd have a tough contest. Made even tougher because winless and wretched Johnny Antonelli was starting for us. Maybe the unlucky day would reverse Johnny's non-luck.

Mays singled and got caught stealing to begin our 4th. I hate stealing, think more of the time it kills rallies than gets them going, but Cepeda made up for it with a line single on the next pitch. Then Willie Kirkland bombed a high arcing drive to right that got everyone in my section neck-craning and praying until Bob Bowman ran out of room out there and the ball dropped into the first row of bleachers for a 2-0 lead!

Naturally, Antonelli gave up a triple to Robin Roberts to start the next inning, the run scored on an Ashburn grounder and it was 2-1. Two innings later, Wretched Johnny gave Robert a one-out double, and he scored on a single by Ashburn to tie the game.

But this was our night; I could feel it. A run-scoring triple by Spencer and wild pitch put us up 4-2, and a costly error by Wally Post and double by Davenport made it 5-2 going to the 9th. Seals was charged. All Antonelli had to do was retire the dregs of the Philly lineup.

Except for a false alarm dispatch from Butch in the 7th inning, my Handy-Talkie was silent all game. I was afraid it needed a new battery. But around the time Chico Fernandez stepped up to the plate in the 9th, it suddenly crackled to life. I could barely make out a "You there?"

"You didn't hear me the first time, Butch? I told you, the guy we're after does not have a limp…" I heard no reply. "Butch? Come in, Butch."

There was another crackle. Then…

"You didn't recognize my voice, Milton. I'm insulted."

Fernandez whiffed and the stands roared, but I had stopped breathing. The entire stadium seemed to shrink around me.

"Who is this?"

"You know who it is… We didn't see each other that long ago."

"You sick, rat bastard. How did you get on this frequency?"

"Thomas was very nice to let me borrow his radio. After I put him to bed, of course."

"Tall Tom? What did you do to him!?? When I find you I'm going to turn you into hamburger, I swear to God!"

The fans around me normally would've turned their heads, but they were too busy worrying at the field, because Antonelli had just walked Solly Hemus.

"That's enough, tough guy. Now you better listen to me. I don't like these little trips you've been taking. You know, sharing intimate details with others about our special friendship—"

"We don't HAVE a friendship."

"Come on, Milton...When have we not?"

Antonelli then walked pinch-hitter Chuck Essegian on four pitches. Friday the 13th was pouring into the park like poisonous fog.

"Tell me your name."

"Hmm...Kind of like this 'Peanut Killer' they've come up with. Don't you?"

Richie Ashburn was up again. Richie Ashburn always seemed to be up. He smoked one down the line that dropped fair by inches, got past Kirkland and gave him a triple. It was 5-4. Everything had me in a panic now. I jabbed the red emergency button on the radio.

"Oh, you shouldn't have done that, Milton. Now I'll have to leave."

"You heard that? Where are you??"

"Close enough."

"You're a dead man!"

"Ha ha. Wrong. You are, and so are many others if you don't play along..."

Gordon Jones replaced Antonelli, who got booed all the way to the dugout.

"Play along doing what?"

"Just stick around and do your job like a nice little usher. Stop talking to strangers, especially the cops. Or that lady of yours is going away forever."

"WHAT? You have Liz??"

Granny Hamner singled in the tying run, of course, and the Peanut Killer killed his radio. Seconds later, Malarkey and his boys flooded the section.

"Where is he? You got him?"

I glanced around, wild-eyed. *Was he watching me this second? Was he seeing me talking to cops?*

"Uhh...It was nothing. Sorry. Some kid got ahold of Tom's radio..." On the field, Bowman singled and Paul Giel came in from the pen. "Tom must've dropped it somewhere. Look around, okay? See if you can find him."

They took off again. I dropped into an empty seat and sat there motionless for the last two dreadful innings. Turk Farrell infested the Giants' bats with termites, Hamner tripled in the winner in the 11th, and everyone went home miserable.

After learning Tall Tom had only been knocked out and left in a storage closet, I stopped at the Double Play for six beers. They didn't help.

How to Blow a Fuse

June 14th

I was back in my old section, and paired up with Dot again. After what happened to Tall Tom Tupper the previous night, Malarkey had so many extra cops in the stands the place looked like a giant coffee shop. With all the extra lawmen around, you'd think Dot would have felt safe enough to do her job. Nope. Two batters in and she was already clinging to me.

"We need some bonus money for this, don't you think? A guy like that wanted nothing to do with Tom, I'm convinced. He wants a girl he can terrorize. Like your friend Liz. He only hurt Tom because he didn't bump into ME."

"Dot? Can we just seat people for the game please?"

"I am, I am!'

"You're not. And section 16 is plenty big for you to work the top rows."

"I know that…I'd just rather work all the rows with you!"

"Obviously."

I had gone to see Tall Tom over at the hospital that morning. Unfortunately, he remembered nothing, having been knocked out in a dark stadium corridor. Didn't even remember smelling peanuts before he got hit.

I thought about calling Liz's parents or brother, but until I had more info there was really no point. The best thing I could do was keep my Handy-Talkie close, in case the maniac tried to talk to me again. If so, he'd be doing it from somewhere in or around the stadium, which explained all the extra flatfoots.

As if Dot and the Peanut Killer didn't have me enough on edge, the Giants were doing another collapse at the hands of the Phillies. This time Solly Hemus (!) and Harry Anderson both homered off Ruben Gomez in the 1st, a Hemus double and Bowman single got them another run in the 3rd, and it was 4-0 when Davenport finally clubbed a 2-run shot off Ray Semproch in the 4th. Another Bowman single added insurance in the 8th, Mays hit a solo shot, but that was all she wrote, and we were four games below .500 again.

"Can I work this section with you tomorrow?" asked Dot as fans filed out.

"I don't know. You should talk to Pence."

"Because Butch and Dominic stare at me too much and every time I work with Veronica she talks too much, and Lindee just doesn't get me—"

"Dot? Talk to Pence about it."

She revved up another question and I bolted for the nearest exit before she could floor the mouth gas. Wove my way through the crowds on Bryant Street, still in the usher uniform I didn't even feel like changing out of. All I wanted to do was hide in my place with a bottle and jazz record.

"Hey Snappy! Wait up!"

Oh no. It was Eugene Buzzbee again, from the *Tribune*.

"I thought I told you to keep away from me."

"You said your apartment. You didn't say anything about public places. I got it right here in my notebook if you wanna see."

"No thanks."

I kept walking. He closed the gap again.

"Heard the Peanut Killer talked to you personally last night. Care to tell me what he said?"

"Yeah. Shut up and none of your business."

"Was it about your girlfriend?"

I ignored him, kept walking.

"Not real sporting of you! Behaving this way when she could be tied up in some basement and needing your hel—"

He didn't finish the sentence because my right fist was smashing into his face. He dropped on the pavement like a skinny watermelon. The weeks of fear and frustration had boiled over on my stove, and I punched and kicked him until his face was the meat product I had promised two days earlier. Over a dozen fans stood and watched until one tried to yank me away. I shook free, wringing my hand, and continued the escape to my private chamber of torment.

Emergency Transportation

June 15th

Hours before I talked myself into reporting for work, I talked myself into getting out of bed.

What a mess my life had become. Cops and a killer were shadowing me, my rattled sexy girlfriend was missing, the Giants were heading for a mediocre finish, and now an annoying rookie reporter with a busted face was probably going to barbeque me in his paper.

The only piece of normalness I had left was my yearly summer job, despite all the recent shenanigans connected with that. It was the last game of the homestand, so after a shower, half gallon of coffee and some eggs I threw my uniform in a bag and trudged back to the ball park.

Pence Murphy appeared the second I put my hand on the changing room door handle.

"Got a sec, Drake?"

Pence never asked for a second. Most of the time he just blurted out whatever stupidity was on his mind. I nodded, and he pulled me around the corner, like he was afraid of anyone seeing us. Or me.

"We made a change."

"To the section assignments? Well that's good, because Dot was getting under every inch of my skin."

"No, no. YOU'RE the change."

"What's that?"

He sighed before he said the next thing. Pence Murphy actually sighed.

"You're fired, Drake. At least ten people saw you beat up that reporter, and the guy is pressing charges."

So this is what it had come to. Save the public image, and damn the investigation. I thought about bringing up the Peanut Killer calling me on the Handy-Talkie. But what good would that have done? And why waste intelligent words on this moron?

"So what? He was slime, Pence! A weasel with zits! I'll go talk to Stoneham—"

Tried to walk away and he grabbed my arm. "This came from Stoneham! I don't care how much of a jerk this kid was, we can't have ushers beating up reporters, get it?"

I stared at him, the back of my neck heating up while my soul began to evaporate.

"Sorry about this, Drake. You're a good usher. But we had no choice… Good luck to ya."

And he ducked into the changing room. I stood there in the hall a long moment. Then thought, *the hell with this place.* Dumped my uniform in a nearby trash can, wandered up the first tunnel I could find into the grandstand.

Found an empty seat in a mostly empty row in the far left field corner and sat there in a daze for the next three hours. If the world I lived in was a disaster, maybe I could transport myself into a baseball one for the day.

I even bought a souvenir scorebook to dive in deeper.

Mike McCormick was his usual awful self, gave the Phillies a triple, double, and single in the 1st and was behind 2-0 quick. At least he was able to plunk Ashburn on the noggin and put him out for the rest of the game. Kirkland homered to give us a run back, and then Jack Sanford fell off a cliff in the Giants' 4th. It started with a single, walk, single, single, walk and a double, and after a two-out Mays single we had a 7-2 lead.

My feelings of death and despair took a breather, but McCormick brought them back right away. Three Phillie singles in the 5th cut it to 7-3, and even after we scored the next seven runs off Sanford and reliever Hearn, Lopata homered to kick off a five-run Phillie 7th and bring in Gordon Jones, who was just as bad. By the time Bob Bowman hit a 2-run shot in the 8th off Grissom we were up 16-11 but I couldn't take it anymore. After what happened before the game, I couldn't watch our lousy bullpen cough up another one.

So I let Chumpo pour me a few at the Double Play instead, and heard us hang on for the win via radio.

"You don't look too good, Snappy."

"Can't imagine you would either, Chumpo, if you lost your job and found out you were being sued on the same day."

"You need trees, that's what."

"Trees."

"Yup. When my dog got hit by that milk truck, best thing I did was drive up the coast, lie on the ground and look up at them redheaded trees. Can't slap you with no lawsuit if they don't know which trees you're lyin' under."

He slid his rag down to the far end of the bar. For once, Chumpo was making a whole bunch of good sense.

The Bronx Bugle Sporting Life

| POST TOASTIES...MMMM GOOD! | Monday Late Edition, June 16, 1958 | SEE THREE HOLLYWOOD MOVIES A WEEK |

What's Wrong With the Braves?

by Archie Stripes
American League Beat

These are bad times out in "Bushville". The World Champion Milwaukeeians thought they'd have an easier road to a second straight pennant after topping our Bombers in the World Series last fall, but the potholes and oil slicks have been many and treacherous. Afer a promising early April, the Braves have been unable to reclaim any momentum, lurching from one disappointing series to another.

Their difference between runs scored and allowed is a healthy +57, best in the circuit, yet they are mostly winning drubbings. In one-run affairs they are a horrid 7-17. Worse, they have 19 blown leads, the most in either league. Most of the starters have done their part, but ace Warren Spahn is just 5-7 with a 5.51 ERA. Their on-base percentage and slugging marks are muscular, but "slugger" Joe Adcock has given them nothing, and home run leader Wes Covington butchers every baseball hit his way. Injuries haven't helped. In short, the parts just aren't meshing in a victorious way yet.

Lucky for the Tomahawkers, no other NL team has seemed juggernautical, and with over half a season left, good health and fortune may yet smile upon them.

**CARDINALS TOP REDLEGS,
GO TWO GAMES OVER .500**
Shocking details inside

"Notorious" Usher Missing After Reporter Assault

SAN FRANCISCO (UPI)— Melvin "Snappy" Drake, an ex-journeyman minor league pitcher turned Giants baseball usher, has been reported missing two days after he was seen beating and kicking a Bay Area news reporter in the street outside Seals Stadium.

Eugene Buzzbee, 25, of the *Oakland Tribune* has filed charges against the ball club and Mr. Drake, citing an "unprovoked, sadistic assault" that made it "impossible to do my best investigative job."

Mr. Drake has also been a person of interest in a recent spate of murders occurring in the city. When asked about Mr Drake's character, Giants owner Horace Stoneham replied, "No comment and get the hell out of my office."

≈ *The Cabin in the Redwoods* ≈

June 17th

I heard about the cabin from Allen Ginsberg, who knew about it from Gary Snyder, who knew about it from Gregory Corso, who was told of it by Kerouac before he skipped down to Mexico again. Around 240 miles north of San Francisco on an isolated stretch of the Klamath River, it was built some time ago by a hermit fisherman who lost his foot falling between slippery rocks and willed it to the public before drinking himself to death.

The perfect spot for me to hide from the world.

Not that I shouldn't have been out searching for Liz—maybe with her rockabilly brother—but where would I even start? Seemed to me the best way to find her was beat the location out of the Peanut Killer himself. This might not have been that hard, because wherever I went, the Peanut Killer had a knack for finding me.

So armed with Triples Trevor and an old fish-gutting knife I found in the cabin, I waited for him. Nestled in beside the gurgling river and grilled some hot dogs on a big enough campfire to attract a band of Wappo indians. I was never much of a fisherman, but maybe by tomorrow I'd catch myself a fat steelhead salmon.

It was invigorating to be out in the wild, especially under guardian redwoods. Gazing up at the planetarium-like sky was enough to make me feel humble, and the giant, swaying and creaking trees only added to it. It was rough not having a radio for music or ball scores, but that's what being a hermit's all about. I spent most of the time just listening to nature, and after shutting myself in the cabin for the night and flopping on the damp bare mattress, listening for the unnatural. The river ran directly behind the cabin, though, so it wasn't long before its comforting ripples blended with the cheap Cabernet I drank to put me out.

Until that damn cracking twig. Not sure what time it was, but it didn't matter. It was pitch black out. I grabbed Triples Trevor by the handle, crawled off the mattress to the window. Was hoping to see a deer, or even a salmon-hungry bear poking around, but saw nothing. I retreated to the mattress, made an attempt to fall back asleep.

This time heard someone whispering. And from a different direction than the snapping twig. I dropped the bat, grabbed the knife. Inched my way to the cabin door and slowly opened it.

Nothing out there but a dead campfire and moonlight on the river. I took a step into the damp air and an army of flashlight beams hit me in the face.

"Milton Drake?"

"Scare the tar out of me, why don't ya?"

"Are you Milton Drake?"

I squinted at the voice, then at his colleagues. The flashlights lowered slightly. The men were all dressed in official dark suits, white shirts and ties. Cops again.

"Maybe. What's this about?"

"It's about you going with us back to San Francisco."

"I can't believe it…One snot-nosed reporter presses charges and you track me down all the way up here? How the hell did you—"

"You stopped for gas, sir. The attendant remembered the make of your car, and the plates."

"Nice work. What's the matter, Malarkey had the night off?"

The guy doing the talking stepped forward. I could make out very short hair, a tight mouth and dead fish eyes chiseled into a big face. And when he flipped open his wallet, a monstrous badge.

"Special Agent Griffin Brewster, Federal Bureau of Investigation. Lt. Malarkey is officially off this case."

"You're kidding. The FBI? Since when did you get involved?"

"Since four hours ago. After the Giants game at Forbes Field tonight."

"Forbes Field?…in Pittsburgh."

"Afraid so, sir. A dead steel worker was found in the right field grandstand with Salty Dog peanut shells in his pockets and a sign taped to his back: SNAPPY WAS HERE."

Either the river or my blood was suddenly bubbling in my ears.

"Well, that wasn't me! Right? Because I've been out here—"

"We know it wasn't, sir. So does Mr. Stoneham, who now is prepared to meet with you and us."

"Get off your circus train…The guy just fired me! To meet about what??"

The guy didn't crack one drop of a smile.

"To discuss Operation Testa."

National League thru Tuesday, June 17

Chicago	34	28	.548	—
Philadelphia	31	27	.534	1
St. Louis	31	28	.525	1.5
Los Angeles	31	28	.525	1.5
San Francisco	29	31	.483	4
Milwaukee	28	30	.483	4
Cincinnati	27	32	.458	5.5
Pittsburgh	27	34	.443	6.5

American League thru Tuesday, June 17

New York	38	22	.633	—
Baltimore	38	24	.613	1
Boston	37	24	.607	1.5
Chicago	35	26	.574	3.5
Detroit	29	32	.475	9.5
Cleveland	28	35	.444	11.5
Kansas City	23	36	.390	14.5
Washington	16	45	.262	22.5

The Two Nicks

June 18th

It was seven in the morning. Horace Stoneham looked about as happy to see me again as he would a mysterious growth on his neck. Even though FBI Special Agent Brewster had done most of the talking.

"We know we're asking a lot of you, Mr. Drake. But with this new incident, the case has now crossed many state lines, and the Bureau thought we needed a radically different strategy."

"Operation Testa" was simple—at least on the surface. I was going to be secretly flown to Pittsburgh to join the Giants on the road, suit up and assume the identity of one Nicholas Testa, a career minor league backup catcher. Poor Nick played exactly one inning behind the plate for us on April 23 before getting sent back down without enjoying even one measly at bat.

"Great," I said, "And what's Nick Testa going to say about this plan?"

"Nothing," replied Brewster in typical emotionless fashion, "He's been successfully neutralized."

"Duly compensated, he means," added Stoneham with a sly wink.

"So what am I supposed to do? Hang out in the locker room for a week and a half and read girlie mags?"

"No," said Brewster, "You'll be in the bullpen in every park, taking warmup throws from pitchers whenever you can. We're fairly certain the killer has widened his net, and will follow the Giants for this entire trip. Keeping you undercover as something other than an usher will give you a chance to watch the stands, which naturally we'll be doing too. If he does spot you, it will only draw him closer and make him easier to catch."

"Yeah well, that was the idea at Seals Stadium, wasn't it?" I shot Stoneham a look but he turned to his window. "What about the Giant players?"

"They're on board," said Brewster. "We thought of passing you off as a reporter, trying to capture the mood of the team, except your picture's already been in the papers."

I sat there a moment, chewing it over. "And what about Liz Doomis?"

My question became flypaper for a swarm of blank stares.

"My girlfriend, remember? The one who's missing. The one who Peanut Head probably has."

Brewster fired a glare at Stoneham. "Why weren't we made aware of this?"

Stoneham threw up his hands. I suddenly had no choice. So I told them about my Handy-talkie conversation with the killer last Friday night, how he threatened some form of harm to "that lady" of mine if I went to the police, all after she had cleaned out of her place in L.A.

"Los Angeles is a big town, sir. She could be anywhere down there."

"I suppose…but you can count me out of your big costume party unless you put a few hound dogs on her scent. I got more important things to worry about than this team's attendance figures."

"Fortunately for you, Mr. Drake, Eugene Buzzbee of the *Oakland Tribune* won't be one of them."

"Oh really. Since when?"

"Since the Bureau discovered that Mr. Buzzbee has been dating a 13-year-old. Meaning he won't be pressing those assault charges after all."

"Come on Drake," said Stoneham, working up one of his famous hungover grins, "Haven't you always wanted to put on a big league uniform?"

He had me there. Temptation is one hell of a thing. And so was Forbes Field…

The Burgh Meister

June 19th

Our DC-8 landed in Pittsburgh late at night. Agent Brewster sat next to me the entire way, drinking coffee and reading three *Look* magazines cover to cover. I had two Camels, three gin and tonics, and fell asleep.

When we got to the team hotel, most of the Giants were across the street drinking at a place called Danny's, but we did bump into Bill Rigney in the lobby. Brewster introduced me to the skipper and we shook hands. Rigney had already had a few, muttered "Better not jinx us, Snippy…" and wobbled off.

◆ ◆ ◆

We were playing a matinee before grabbing a train to Philly for the weekend. I got to Forbes Field plenty early, headed straight to Rigney's office. Thankfully, he was more conscious. Fixed me up with the equipment guy and I was handed Nick Testa's baggy team uniform with the number 47 on the back. It felt strange putting it on.

I found a lonely corner of the visiting clubhouse to change in, two lockers away from utility outfielder

Bob Speake—who flat out wouldn't. Neither would Mays, Davenport, Spencer or anyone else. Cepeda and Gomez didn't seem to recognize me from that crazy night at the Mongo Room, and if they did, they weren't letting on.

Finally Valmy Thomas and Bob Schmidt walked over together. They were the first and second Giants catchers, played about equal time depending on the park they were in. They knew I would just be in the bullpen so didn't feel threatened at all. "You gonna be our four-leaf clover or black cat?" Valmy asked, and Schmidt pounded my back with one of his dog paws.

The visitors' bullpen was way down the left field line in foul territory, under a little sun canopy. The Pirates were playing sorrier than us, and maybe 9,000 people were on hand, the vast majority screeching kids just out of school. Suppose it might have been more packed if a body hadn't been found there two days ago. Poor Pete Szopa had been sitting alone in the last row of the deep dark right field grandstand when his throat was cut from behind, and Salty Dog peanut shells sprinkled on him like some twisted chef's holiday garnish.

"We didn't see a damn thing," said Valmy as he warmed up Ruben Gomez. "We were too busy trying not to lose, which we ended up doing anyway." Gomez kept sneaking glances at me. Maybe he wasn't as skunked at the Mongo Room as I thought he was.

His performance sure didn't inspire sobriety. Clemente nailed him for a run-scoring double in the 1st, a 2-run homer in the 3rd, and we were down 4-0 just like that. I took the last spot at the far end of the bullpen bench, listened to Paul Giel and Ray Crone discuss Philadelphia prostitutes and watched Marv Grissom fill up a paper cup with tobacco spit.

A Bressoud double and Wagner homer off Curt Raydon began the 6th and put us back in the game. Gomez had settled way down, but Rigney lifted him for a pinch hitter in the 6th. It was still 5-4 Bucs by the 9th, and I had a headache from sitting in the sun and the miniature screechers. Raydon hit Kirkland on the hand with one out, and Alou ran for him. Davenport worked a walk and my pal Valmy loaded them with a single. We were in this thing! I hopped off the bench and did a little clap-cheer.

"Sit the hell down, weirdo!" said Gordon Jones and I did, realizing I'd broken some kind of cool-acting bullpen protocol.

Roy Face took the hill. Spencer hit into a force to make it 4-3, but we were down to our last out. Reserve outfielder number two (we have about five of them) Jim King stepped in and roped a ball deep to right center. The outfield is bigger than Yosemite Park out there, and the thing dropped smack between Virdon and Clemente and rolled forever. Alou and Davenport both scored, King had a triple, and I cheered silently inside my grin.

Jones hustled in to save the 5-4 victory despite giving up a pinch triple to Stevens, and I was 1-0! I was so caught up in the game I had forgotten to even scope the stands for Brewster or the possible Peanut Killer. Brewster reminded me of this before I boarded the team bus for the train station.

"On a third-string catcher's salary?" I snapped back, "You'll take what you can get from me, pal."

The Man in the Corner

June 20th

I dozed off in my seat on the Keystone Limited, and in the early morning hours had that nightmare again. The one from when I had the stomach flu. This time the field was in a hospital courtyard. I had to pitch to a batter whose entire head was wrapped in bandages, and the mound was turning into quicksand under my cleats...

Then the train lurched, woke me up, and we were rolling into 30th Street Station. Philly was hot and muggy and my "private suite" at the hotel was the size of a mop room. I tried to track Brewster down to complain and find out if there was any news on the Liz search, but he was off at a local FBI meeting for most of the day.

Connie Mack Stadium was in a shabby part of the city. No surprise the Athletics split town five years ago. Unlike Forbes Field, the park was packed for tonight's opener. The Phillies were making fools out of the national writers who had picked them for last, starting the weekend just one game behind the Cubs after taking two of three from the Dodgers. They were doing it with smoke, mirrors, rabbit feet, leprechauns and voodoo, but also some real tough starting pitching.

"You watch," said Johnny Antonelli as I trudged down the right field line to the bullpen with Thomas, Schmidt, our starter Al Worthington and a few of the other pitchers before the game. "The pressure will get to them by mid-July and they'll start peeing in their jocks." Antonelli, still without a win, was looking for anyone and anything to criticize. He spent most of the game on the far corner of the bench, reading a local daily paper and whistling at ladies' undergarment ads.

Today's "lucky" choice for the Phils was Curt Simmons, who started pitching here when he was 18 and was now in his 12th season. Rigney stacked the lineup with his usual lefty-mashers, but it was fruitless. Inning after inning went by with Mays, Cepeda, Alou, Davenport and Hank Sauer flailing away at his drooping curveball, usually with men on base. The Phils were blowing chances too against Worthington, but they got the only run of the game when Dave Philley (perfect name) snuck a deep fly into the left center stands, just out of the reach of a leaping Willie. Maybe getting over .500 just wasn't in the cards for us.

A few of the Giants must have decided the shutout wasn't my fault, because I was invited along for drinks at a big smoky restaurant across the street from the Warwick Hotel. Cepeda, Gomez, Kirkland and Wagner felt uncomfortable walking in and took a cab to another joint in the colored part of town. As usual, there were a half dozen cute baseball tarts trying to chat it up at the bar—though none with me. The whole hour seemed pretty awkward, and not just because of the tight sport coat Brewster had given me to wear.

Right when I was about to order my third mug of Schmidt's, a waitress appeared and set a creamy, light brown cocktail in front of me. The thing looked more like a dessert.

"What's this?"

"Compliments of the man in the corner. Amaretto, shot of brandy, whipped cream—"

"What man in the corner?" I tried to look over her head. She turned and pointed, then twisted up her pert mouth.

"Oh. Well he was just there…Anyway, it's called a Peanut Pleasure. Enjoy!"

She walked away. I stared at the drink. Minced peanuts were sprinkled on the bed of whipped cream.

"Got a new girlfriend there, rookie?" It was Valmy Thomas, smirking beside me. I got off my stool, scanned the entire restaurant with my heart pounding. Saw no man in any corner.

"I sure as hell hope so…"

Hot Damned

June 21st

"Calm down, Drake!"

"I'll calm down when the Giants clinch the pennant on Labor Day, and when you start helping me out a little, Special FBI Agent Brewster. What were all your flunkies doing last night while I was being made with a Peanut Pleasure? Betting at the horse track? Shooting off rounds at the firing range?"

"I told you. We had a big mid-Atlantic division meeting. What I'd like to know is why you didn't initiate a suspect pursuit."

"Because he vanished, you robot! Like he always does! You expect me to chase a phantom down dark alleys in strange cities now? I'm a third-string catcher, remember? Not Marvel Boy."

"My apologies then…I'll increase our presence at the ballpark today."

"Yeah, well do the same to your brain pan, and bring along a tank and submarine while you're at it. And no more mystery meetings, please. The timing was so weird on this one it made me suspect YOU."

"That isn't even humorous, Mr. Drake."

"It wasn't meant to be."

◆ ◆ ◆

I was certainly in no mood to laugh at the afternoon game. I spent one third of it following the action and the rest anxiously looking for peanut phantoms in the shadowy Connie Mack grandstand. It was hot as blazes, and when the grounds crew watered down the infield I was of a mind to scamper out there and douse myself like a 6-year-old.

Wet towels around necks and over faces was the bullpen fashion the entire day, because Mike McCormick incredibly threw his first complete game since April. Our bats also woke up big time. With one gone in the 2nd, we strung together a Schmidt double, King single, McCormick single, Spencer single, Bressoud double, and two-run Willie Mays bleacher bomb, good for six quick runs off Sanford and basically the game.

As I said, the guys on the team were keen on what I was doing, and having a fun time with it. Davenport went to a costume shop later and bought me a Sherlock Holmes hat and toy pipe. Grissom and Schmidt took turns dropping their claws on my shoulder at quiet moments to make me jump. And when we were down in the hotel restaurant, Thomas tried to order me a Peanut Pleasure. Wiseacres.

At least the ribbing relaxed me a bit. When I got back upstairs it was also nice to see the maid had made up my mop closet. She even left a vase with a rose in it, next to a folded-up note. Which seemed odd. I picked up the piece of paper and opened it. The words were typewritten:

NICE DISGUISE, SNAPPY.
THANK YOU FOR NOT
INVOLVING THE LAW.

YOU CAN BET YOUR LADY
THANKS YOU TOO.

I dropped the note, grabbed the room phone. Dialed a number I had on an FBI card in my wallet. Dropped my voice to a whisper.

"Brewster? It's Drake. Listen good. For the next few days, you need to keep your men away from the ballpark, okay? And stay as far away from me as you can."

"What's going on?…Everything okay?"

"With me, yeah. Liz? God only knows."

Fatherisms

June 22nd

Flying to Milwaukee after sweeping our Father's Day twinbill in Philly, I actually dreamed about him.

Let's back up first. Ever since Dad was killed driving his Oakland bus years ago, I make it a point to call my mother on this day. Tried her from the hotel and got no answer because she was likely in church. (I can't seem to get this east-west time difference straight.) Anyway, Connie Mack was packed with dads and sons, and memories of playing catch with him and listening to episodes of *The Shadow* while perched on his lap bubbled up all day.

It was also another long, hot afternoon sitting in the pen, meaning plenty of bubbles. Antonelli took his scowl out to the mound in the opener and pitched it right off his face, giving the Phillies practically nothing but a Wally Post homer in the 2nd inning. That's right, after nine straight horrible losses, Johnny coasted on our five solo homers and got his first win of 1958! The locker room was so lively between games that Ramon Monzant went out for the nightcap and practically did the same thing, only needing a batter apiece of help from Giel and Jones to finish off the 9th.

Most of the players were phoning or telegramming their dads after, and I boarded our plane with mine still locked in my head. It was no surprise then, when my gin and tonic and the hum and light bumps of the flight put me under...

...and smack into the front seat of our dark blue Hudson sedan. Driving up into woods with my dad. Had my treasured glove in my lap, both of us wearing Oakland Oaks caps. Felt excitement glowing on the horizon, at the end of this two-lane road. The trees were dark green and leafy. Mosquitoes splatted the windshield. I thought I heard thunder. And my father just kept repeating the same words: "Hard and fast and middle up" like one of those Indian mantras.

It all seemed so real, like it might have really happened. I didn't dream about my dad much. Sure I missed him, but when he died it was like something in me switched off. Like a box of valuable china that gets glued shut and you don't dare try and break it open.

The plane bounced again, *and the Hudson turned sharply at a sign that said A.Y.B.L. and the road got narrower and twistier. The guard rails dissolved. Lightning crackled in the clumpy dark sky. "Hard and fast and middle up... hard and fast and middle up..." he kept saying, trying to calm me with it. A giant June bug got into the car and smacked against my arm. I tried to swat it away—*

And it was Valmy Thomas, nudging my arm on the plane. "Hey! You okay, rookie? Bressoud needs a new poker partner, so come on. Row 21."

I knocked the cobwebs out of my head and joined the game in back of the plane. It was Davenport and Grissom against me and Ed Bressoud, with others watching and stacks of dollar drink coasters and five dollar bills in view.

"Gee," I said, "I feel kind of honored here."

"Don't let it get to your head," said Bressoud, "I gotta win some money back."

I dropped a five-spot on the pile, looked at my opening hand. Nothing great.

"So how's the big psycho killer hunt going?" asked Jim King out of nowhere. I was afraid of that.

"Not really much action yet..." (Sure, if you count the guy buying me drinks and leaving notes next to my pillow not much action.) "If you notice, the FBI guys aren't even on the flight."

"Jerks..."

"Pansies..."

"No, I think they're probably just

checking other leads."

"Well don't worry rookie," piped up Thomas, "We got your back."

"Or at least Antonelli's cousins will," said Davenport. "Right Johnny?"

Antonelli waved a hand at us from two rows away. No doubt deep into a fresh girlie mag.

"Listen, if this situation becomes too much for everyone, I got no problems jumping the club when we get home—"

Spencer's face hardened. He pointed a finger in my face. "We just took three out of four from a team that's been pulling our pants down. Antonelli finally won a damn game and we're back at .500. You ain't going anywhere, chief."

I looked at my hand again. The plane dipped in a cloud and I was suddenly woozy. "I'll um…raise." Threw in a drink coaster. I'm not much of a poker player, but I did my best…*hard and fast and middle up.*

Welcome to Chillwaukee

June 23rd

Brewster had his hound dogs all over the airport and train station in Milwaukee, but as he reported by phone after I checked into my room at the Pfister Hotel, no one suspicious had turned up.

It wasn't exactly a relief. When someone is tailing and tormenting you, you're looking over your shoulder no matter what. For all we knew, Peanut Man could've flown to Chicago and driven up the Lake Michigan shore in no time—though the more I thought about it, it seemed unlikely he was dragging a bound and gagged Liz along with him.

Before I left for County Stadium I tried calling her brother Billy's car shop again and got another greasehead who told me he was "off somewhere on vacation." Great.

Except Billy Frack wasn't the only one who went AWOL. Our bats must've been left in Philadelphia, because against Lew Burdette tonight we could do just about nothing. The fans were packed in and loud, this being only eight months after they won a world title here. Their team was having a hard time getting over .500 but you'd never know it by how they painted the walls with us. Only the temperature was colder than our offense, which made sitting behind the outfield fence with icy gusts hitting our backs a brutal chore. Grissom and Crone were thrilled when they got to jog in with their mops, despite turning a 7-2 Braves lead into a rout by giving up five straight hits between them in the 8th.

Afterwards, most of the gang disappeared into the hotel bar again. I traded booze for blankets, went up the creaky stairs to my room to try and warm up. It was far too easy. The heater was turned up full blast, hissing and clanking, and I burned my hand trying to turn the knob. Unable to fall asleep I went for a walk through the hotel. Sat in the main lobby a few minutes to leaf through a magazine or two.

Someone was watching me. An older guy on the balcony, dressed in a musty, outdated suit. I looked back into my magazine, snuck another glance and he was gone. I suppose it could've been the Peanut Man, but he didn't seem nearly as big and tall as I figured he was. A laughing young couple swept in the front door, bringing a cold draft in with them. I shivered, ducked into the hotel bar after all.

The only player in there was Danny O'Connell, badly trying to sing "Stardust" to a girl at the bar who was drunker than he was. I started to order a drink, then stopped myself. We had another cold night game tomorrow, and I needed to go out in the morning and find some long underwear at a department store.

So it was back to my room. No scrawled note on the door or the pillow, no peanut aroma, no creepy phone calls. Just hot, stuffy air, creaks all around me and nightmares about some old guy staring at me. It's like that damn Pfister Hotel was haunted.

The Heckler

June 24th

Everywhere you go there's someone riding your behind. Starts with Mom and Dad, keeps going with your math and gym teachers, then your boss, then the guy sitting in section 3 behind home plate, maybe ten rows up from the field.

I told you about the heckler in Vancouver who had it in for me one night when I pitched for the Rainiers, right? This guy in Milwaukee tonight made him sound like Laurence Olivier. He was in the right field bleachers, just close enough for us to hear every word, and just far enough away to duck if one of our tobacco chaws happened to whizz at his head.

"Hey Crone! Your mother called! She wants her name back!" Ray Crone never got into games unless we were getting crushed, so insults made him feel special and just bounced off his cap.

"Don't start any crossword puzzles, guys! 'Cause every one of you's gettin' USED!"

That one wasn't exactly true. They only scored three runs and Gordon Jones was the only reliever to leave the pen, but as a team, everyone felt sort of used. We racked up a dozen hits on Rush and Robinson but left twelve on base, Cepeda got thrown out at the plate by Bruton to end the 8th, and we could only score one run all night. No wonder we'd dropped seven out of eight to them.

"Must be embarrassing to be called Giants when you guys hit like midgets!"

"Just let me brain him once..." I hissed to Bob Schmidt, "I'll find a back way up there and put him on the floor before he even—"

"No can do, Drake. One reason we make good money is to ignore this junk."

Down by two in the 9th, Rodgers and Bressoud singled with one out. The stadium got quiet and the heckler got louder.

"Nice ball park you got out there, Giants!! Down to only one murder a week, from what I hear!"

I turned, tried to get a view of him. The bleachers were too packed, the air too misty and smoke-filled to spot him. A few of the fans near him laughed, but most were fixated on the field. Mays hit one deep to right that Aaron flagged down, and then it was up to Cepeda.

"Oooh Giants, I'm scared! Big Orlando's up!"

"HEY SHUT UP, CREEP!!"

The words exploded from my mouth before I could stop them. The bleacher crowd grumbled, then booed us. Schmidt slammed an elbow in my ribs.

"Whaddya, stupid? What'd I just say?"

"Nice goin' down there, Testa!" yelled our friend in the bleachers. "Or how about I call you…MILTON?"

Oh no. I hadn't recognized his voice, but now I did. I hopped up on the bullpen bench. Looked frantically at the crowd.

"Don't worry about your lady, Milton! We're drinking wine and everything's fine!"

That did it. I never spotted him but I didn't care. Scaled the chain link fence like a mad Jimmy Piersall. Leaped into the bleachers. Grabbed the first big guy I saw with a peanut bag and knocked him over a seat. Cepeda whiffed to end the game. The stadium rocked and cheered and few noticed the scuffle in the bleachers, which lasted only ten seconds. Grissom and Giel jumped the fence too, pulled me off the baffled dad who was just sharing a peanut bag with his kids.

"I heard him!" I blurted to my teammates, "He was up there!"

"Bad enough we're stuck in the second division," snarled Giel, "now you're gonna get us suspended?"

Rigney had a different response later. For the last game I'd be banished to the dugout. I could think of worse fates. Like the one that evil, cunning rat bastard would suffer if I ever laid my hands on him.

Odd Man Out

June 25th

No one was happy to see me. Not the players at breakfast, or in the dugout, and especially not on the plane later to Cincinnati. The stewardess even watered down my gin.

To repeat the obvious, I should have known better. The Wisconsinites were nice and treated us with respect. One guy mouthing off like that was too strange, and should have raised an alarm that he was from somewhere else. Still, hopping into the County

Stadium bleachers to knock over an innocent fan was one thing. Suddenly being viewed as a bad luck charm was something else.

With me huddled at the far end of the dugout and avoided like a leper, we put on our third straight display of offensive offense. Scored just five runs during our stay, and left the home of the Braves three games below .500 with a season mark of 1-8 against them. The real sad thing was that Al Worthington threw like Bob Feller. Retired 16 in a row at one point, but the two hits he allowed, a key Covington single in the 1st and late Covington homer in the 7th were enough to beat us. We grounded into two double plays, left eight on base while Milwaukee left just one. What a stink bomb, and if that wasn't rotten enough, my new pal Valmy Thomas got plunked on the hand by Joey Jay in the 9th and would miss a whole week. Now HE wouldn't even talk to me.

So I sat in the last row of the plane, staring out at blackness and occasional signs of clouds. Agent Brewster had managed to find me leaving the park and ripped my head off because he obviously felt left out. He had no leads on Liz, of course, so I just walked away from him and boarded the team bus.

I had to figure our hitting would improve in shorter, steamier Crosley Field, but the question was whether our pitchers could keep Robinson and Lynch in the ball park. And every-one's favorite disappointment Johnny Antonelli would go in the first game. I tried to catch Rigney's eye when he passed me on his way down the aisle to the bathroom, thinking a little baseball chatter would lighten the mood. He just lit a cigarette and ignored me too.

No wonder I was shocked when we came down the plane's steps in Cincy at three in the morning and somebody whistled at me. He also yelled "Snappy Drake!" instead of "Testa!" or "Milton!" Standing outside the chain-link exit fence was none other than Billy Frack, soiled white T-shirt glowing inside his open, black leather jacket. I perked right up, broke off from the trudging team and ran over to shake the hell out of his hand.

"How'd you ever find me?"

"Queasy but easy, Pops. Headed up to 'Frisco, Seals cat said you were on the road with the team. Being my own boss-man, I can take a big vacater any time I like, right?"

"Sure, but why—"

"Gotta find Lizzie, don't we? May as well join forces, see some of the country!"

"Yeah, but I'm supposed to be with the team. Impersonating Nick Testa."

"Who the frack is that?"

"Forget it. Long story. Where you staying?"

"Where else? The El Rancho Rankin, out on Route 125! Place is a block long and there's an extra bed, so c'mon! You can fill me in on the way."

I was drifting away from the team

pack. Thomas spun around, eyeing me.

"No, listen. The FBI's involved now, and I have to be—"

"The feds? Big fat deal. Bunch of amateurs. Let's bounce, Pops."

He grabbed my sleeve, walked me ten feet. I began to shake him off but then stopped.

Got one look at his shiny, baby blue '58 Chevy Nomad station wagon, and damn near floated into the passenger seat.

Reds-Faced

June 26th

Ever try to catch a major league pitcher? Ever try when you've never used a catcher's mitt, you're more hungover than a midshipman in Bangkok, and the pitcher is a crabby Johnny Antonelli? Didn't think so...

I was elected because Thomas got injured our last inning in Milwaukee and Schmidt was taking a whirlpool when Antonelli was all dressed and oiled up. The reason I was hungover? Good old Billy Frack, who secured us a supply of locally-brewed Schoenling Lagers to drink ourselves to sleep with out at the El Rancho Rankin. Before that, of course, there was some half-baked sleuthing in his Chevy Nomad on the way.

"You're telling me this ape is following the team? That he's on to you? This is gonna be a cinch! You be the honey, draw him to the flower, and I'll

swat his yellowjacket ass when he isn't looking."

"May have to clear that with Agent Brewster. Assuming he's here now. You'll also have to be a lot quicker than I was. And smarter. This guy has barely made one mistake."

"They all make mistakes, Pops. Otherwise prisons would be out of business."

Anyway, Antonelli wanted to work on his curve in the bullpen before the game. At least curves—the baseball kind—were something I knew something about. Even though Johnny still tried to make me feel like an idiot.

"On a 3-2 count? are you nuts?"

"Surprise can work."

"You see the fences in this place, bud? My nine-year-old nephew could hit one out. Schmitty, Val and Westrum all say go with the heater in a pinch and that's what I do."

Fine, I thought. Get shellacked again.

It was much warmer in Cincy than Milwaukee, but not too humid. The pitchers told me the balls carried out like special delivery letters in Crosley, ever since they pushed home plate out for the second time. The park was only half full, but a lot of folks sat out in the Moon Deck, the steep right field bleachers also called the Sun Deck for day games. Our pen was on the field down the first base line, giving us a nice view of the Moon Deck, factories, and leafy green hills beyond the fences.

There were also Reds fans sitting

right behind us, and a guy named Billy who began pestering me in the top of the 1st.

"Psst! Hey Pops! How tall is he?"

"I don't know…Six feet at least."

"Psst! Hey Pops! Should I use my hands or a weapon?"

"Whatever seems right, Billy. Leave me alone and watch the game, why don't ya?"

I was still getting cold shoulders from my bullpen mates, and now Billy's endless questions were irritating them more. So it was a good thing Daryl Spencer started the game by belting Nuxhall's first pitch over the new five-story scoreboard in left field. Joe had 20 gopher balls on the season already (Antonelli had 18) when the game started, so we knew this could be a long night.

Antonelli made sure of that in no time. Served up a two-run shot in the 1st to Walt Dropo. We tied it in the 2nd, went back ahead on back-to-back clouts by Schmidt and Andre Rodgers in the 4th. Don Hoak made it 4-3 with a single, and then Lousy Johnny fired a 3-2 fastball to Haddix, who parked it in the Moon Deck to tie the game in the 5th.

"Psst! Hey Pops! Guess what?"

"WHAT??"

"Lila, Sue and Pinky are staying five doors away from us!"

"Who?"

"They just graduated Ohio State. You can meet 'em later. They have a record player!"

"Great…"

Antonelli fell apart an inning later, gave up three singles and walked Haddix with the bases loaded. Meanwhile our offense flat-out died. Felipe Alou, who Rigney stuck in the second spot to avoid double plays before Mays batted, rapped into two of them anyway. Grissom tried his luck on the mound and had nothing, giving up 8th inning triples to Temple and Ed Bailey, who went 4-for-4.

We were badly Reds-faced, and it was "my fault" again. I actually couldn't wait to hop back in Billy's Nomad and zoom back to the El Rancho Rankin, where he lured me down to a room of Ohio State co-eds for a night of cold beer, hot flirting and Bill Haley disks.

What I didn't know was that someone was sitting in the El Rancho parking lot the whole night, watching the windows.

Rank at the El Rancho

June 27th

He grabbed me by the back of my undershirt, hauled me into the El Rancho Rankin parking lot at six in the morning and threatened to pistol whip me.

"Really?" I said to Agent Brewster. "I think you could get reprimanded for that."

One of his FBI goons was busy dragging Billy—wearing nothing but his socks and underpants—out of the coeds' room to the other side of the lot. Billy was only beginning to wake up and get mad, but Brewster had a head start on me.

"We have an operation going here, Drake. remember that? You're supposed to be impersonating a ballplayer."

"Yeah, well…Don't ballplayers do this?"

"Don't get smart. Unless you want us to re-look at that breaking and entering charge out on Candlestick Point."

"Oh, heavens no. Not that. How's our old scam artist mayor doing these days, anyway?"

Brewster didn't answer. I shook him off, headed over to pull Billy away from his oafish captor.

"So who's your friend here from Los Angeles? Yeah Drake, we ran his plates."

"That would be Liz Dumas' brother. Who's going to help me find his sister while you guys are busy swimming in molasses."

"Watch it, Drake. I wouldn't exactly call all-night relations with teenage girls a quick way to find her, would you?"

"They're college-age, and I'm off duty."

"Then get on duty in a hurry. We know your cover's blown, but we need to keep you on the team to keep the suspect sniffing around. We're confident he'll be in custody soon."

Billy was back in his real room getting dressed. A half hour later he was across from me in the coffee shop, trying to enjoy breakfast with the feds peering at us through the window.

"This scene is just dead, Pops. Why don't I drop you at the park, cruise up to Chicago a few days early? Ain't that your next stop? If I set up near Wrigley somewhere, maybe I can scope him out before he scopes us."

I was in no mood to disagree. And Billy was right about Cincy being dead, because it sure was for the Giants. Scoreless into the last of the 4th that night, and then Frank Robinson went bananas. He'd doubled off Gomez in the 1st, after I spent half an hour warming Ruben up with my mouth shut. Then Robinson hit one over the scoreboard in left. Then after a Temple sac fly made it 2-0 in the 5th he tripled into the right corner to knock in two more. He waited to finish off his cycle until their five-run explosion in the 8th off Giel and Grissom, when his infield dunk single got tossed into the stands by Bressoud.

I was sorry Billy was leaving town. After going 3-1 in Philly we were now 0-5, and I was as welcome in the clubhouse as head lice. I needed a day on Ohio back roads in his baby blue Nomad wagon, bouncy rock blasting out the windows, our hair flying…

What I didn't need or want was the empty Salty Dog peanut bag I found taped to my room door at the Netherland Plaza after midnight. With a note scrawled on the back that said:

SAY GOODBYE TO YOUR
LITTLE CHUM.

Night Call

June 28th

Valmy Thomas didn't want to hear about it. Neither did Schmidt, Grissom, Giel or Crone. Rigney was so angry at our team you couldn't get within two feet of him, and I was still too afraid for Liz to get Agent Brewster involved.

Unless it was already too late. "*Say goodbye to your little chum*"? Who even says something like that? Was he talking about Billy or his sister? And how did this guy always know what room I was in? Our travel man Fred Coombs kept hotel assignments under brain lock and key till the last minute. Players couldn't even approach him, let alone stowaways. Nope. Peanut Man had to be stalking me big time.

But I had to try something. Before heading back over to Crosley for the night game, I snuck in a call to the Ohio State Police. Gave them the info on Billy's car. Of course all that did was distract the hell out of me while I was warming up Mike McCormick in the pen. It showed in the early part of the game, as Frank Robinson took him over the left field wall twice, once with a man aboard and the next time with two. Rigney marched out after the second blast and removed Mike from the mound before Robinson even crossed the plate, and I was the team leper once again.

Luckily, Joe Nuxhall was 3-9 for a reason. Hank Sauer got us close with a two-run homer in the 5th, before an Alou triple and Mays sac fly tied it up in the 8th. Giel, Jones and Grissom combined for four and two-thirds of 4-hit baseball after McCormick left, bench warmer Ray Jablonski hit for Jones in the 11th and crushed a Kellner fastball out of the park, and we broke our five-game losing streak with a clutch win.

For the first time in days, Giants players in the locker room looked me in the eye, and before heading back to the hotel I got a private phone call.

"Mr. Drake? Officer Reinhofer from the Ohio State Police. We've found your friend William Frack."

I was afraid to ask. But did anyway.

"Well, his Chevrolet Nomad wagon was in a ditch, two miles from the Ohio-Indiana border. There was evidence of tampering with the car's brake pads and tire treads. Appeared to be quite a crash."

"Thank god…"

"What was that, sir?"

"No—I mean, I'm glad it was just a crash. Which he survived, right?"

There was a long pause. "Stable condition at Dayton General. We'd like to see that note you told us about, Mr. Drake."

I said sure, arranged a rendezvous with an Officer Grundheinz for the morning and hung up. Valmy was inviting me out for beers again, and this time I went along, got loaded enough to sleep on the floor of his room. Enough with the notes. The rest of my plan was to hop a bus up to

Dayton for a quick Billy visit before Sunday's game.

But plans lately seemed to be made out of tissue. Or peanut brittle.

Punch-outs

June 29th

A note was slipped under the door of Valmy Thomas' room, where I woke on his bathroom floor with my face in a pile of wet towels. No doubt, it was scribbled by someone at the front desk:

Mr. Drake—
Officer Grundheinz called. Bring your note to Dayton General Hospital and he will meet you there.

How the front desk knew I was drinking myself into a stupor in another room was weird, but maybe word and screaming laughter till one in the morning gets around quick in a hotel.

Thankfully, it was a short bus ride to Dayton. I armed myself with the largest paper cup of coffee sold east of the Mississippi and was there in plenty of time to make it back to Crosley for the series finale. It took a bit of nurse questioning, but tracked down Billy's room in the recovery wing.

He wasn't pretty. Head bandaged, both eyes black and blue, his right arm and left leg in casts. He smiled when he saw me but it looked painful to do it.

"My wild and crazy blue baby…She never does that to me."

"Well, the cops said someone wrecked the brakes and took a switchblade to a few of the tires. I think you were meant to be our friend's next victim."

Rage filled Billy's eyes. His instinct was to smash his fist on the bed, but clenched his left one instead.

"You gotta get him, Pops…He's still got Liz alive somewhere, I know it. She's his trump card."

"I hope so. If I only knew what the lousy creep's beef with me was…"

I glanced out the third floor window. Spotted an Ohio State Police car parked in front of the entrance that wasn't there when I arrived.

"Call my folks for me, would ya Pops? Still got that phone number?"

"Yeah. Think so…"

"Hey…Feel like going out and snagging me a hamburger?"

"Uhhh…probably shouldn't. Have to get back in time to warm up Stu Miller."

"Aw c'mon, Pops. This hospital grub's gonna kill me faster than Peanut Jerk will." He motioned to a tray of uneaten grey toast and liquified eggs on his bedside table.

Next to it was a potted plant: a stalk of green leaves with yellowish flowers.

"That's nice. Who brought you that?"

"Dunno, actually…Was here when I woke up."

The plant looked familiar. Like something I'd seen out in the San Joaquin Valley once.

And then I remembered what it was. I walked over, picked up the plant and yanked the entire stalk out of its soil.

Peanuts were entangled in the roots.

"Damn...Listen Billy, I need to go talk to this cop outside. Back in a sec—" I took the plant with me, raced out the door.

The state cop saw me coming, swung open the car's back door. The morning sun was in my eyes, but I could make out his uniform, cap and burly frame behind the wheel. I reached the car and waved the plant at him.

"Officer Grundheinz, right? Listen, I think the guy who messed up my friend's car just left this! He's gotta still be around—"

"Did you bring his note?"

"Yeah! But look at this plant—"

"Get in and we'll look for him."

I hopped in back, shut the door. He screeched away from the curb, pinning me to the seat.

"Whoa! Where the hell are we—"

He turned sharply down the first alley he saw and threw on the brakes. His voice eerily dropped.

"Didn't I tell you not to call the police, Milton?"

I froze. In the split second before he turned and knocked me out cold with a fist, I saw the Peanut Killer's demonic, leering, misshapen face.

National League thru Monday, June 30

Chicago	40	34	.541	—
Milwaukee	38	33	.535	0.5
Los Angeles	39	34	.534	0.5
Philadelphia	36	34	.514	2
St. Louis	36	36	.500	3
San Francisco	35	38	.479	4.5
Cincinnati	33	40	.452	6.5
Pittsburgh	33	41	.446	7

American League thru Monday, June 30

New York	46	26	.639	—
Baltimore	45	30	.600	2.5
Chicago	42	33	.560	5.5
Boston	40	32	.556	6
Detroit	37	37	.494	10
Cleveland	38	39	.444	10.5
Kansas City	28	44	.389	18
Washington	20	55	.267	27.5

≈ *Sort of Fun at the Old Ball Park* ≈

July 1st

An usher wearing a bow tie and Wrigley Field cap shook me awake. Don't ask me how I got to Chicago. Don't ask me how I was dropped like a rolled-up rug between two rows of the left field bleacher planks. In fact, don't ask me anything, because the last two days were a big fat blur.

I remember getting my lights punched out by an Ohio state trooper who was really the Peanut Killer. I remember waking up gagged in a dark, stuffy motel room, obviously after he'd ditched the stolen police car and poor Officer Grundheinz's uniform. I remember being roped to a chair, the killer standing in a shadowy corner, wearing a baseball cap too small for his head with the letters AYBL on the front. Tossing a white ball of rolled-up wet socks at my face and chest over and over.

He had me drugged up on something, because I remember him talking but not much of what he said, other than "pray for your lady…pray for your lady" after nearly every sock-pitch. No use pussyfooting around here: the guy was some kind of freak.

After he had enough of me, a damp cloth hit my face and I blacked out again. Only to end up in the Wrigley bleachers an hour before the gates opened for our five-game, home-and-home series with the dangerous Cubs.

Anyway, the usher fetched his boss, who fetched Agent Brewster—who was stationing his men outside the park. As you'd probably guess, Agent Brewster was not a barrel of sunshine.

"They found the Ohio trooper dead in his trunk, a few miles over the Indiana state line. All just to get you into his clutches again. The gall of this suspect is beyond belief, and he's a step ahead of every one of us. Got any ideas on why he did this?"

"Gee, afraid I don't. When you're unconscious you tend not to think about things."

"How about when you're not? Any more details on the suspect?"

"Nope. Except his face was out of alignment."

"Really. Like how?"

"Like there's a dent in it at the top. From some car accident maybe." Brewster nodded to one of his flunkies, who jotted a note. "Can I go warm up Johnny Antonelli now?"

"Sure. And then you're sitting in the bleachers in street clothes, right next to Agent Culberson here. We're not letting you out of our sight until we leave Chicago."

The Giants players were glad to see me, gave me some healthy ribbing. I held back the grisly details, blamed my "wild" day and a half on my "out-of-control buddy" from L.A. Antonelli was in a good mood for a change and he pitched like it, whiffing eight Cubs, allowing just five hits and shutting them out in less than two hours, 3-0. A Mays walk and Cepeda double into the right corner in the 4th was all we needed.

One more game was left on this trip and then it was back to Seals. Brewster's guys were combing the streets and stands, and Liz Doomis was still a missing person of interest. I looked forward to going home, but even though I'd see Chumpo and Bob and my usher friends and be surrounded by friendlier fans, I knew I'd be feeling just as edgy and alone.

A Thrill on the Back End

July 2nd

Brewster backed down for our trip finale in Chicago and let me sit in the dugout again. The 100-degree heat played a part, because the bullpens at Wrigley were uncovered and we couldn't imagine the weather was fit for man, beast, or Peanut Killer. Only problem was that I had to listen to the same idiot fan heckle Mays every time he ran on or off the field.

"Hey Willie! You're good but you ain't no Ernie!"

Long as they kept race out of it, Mays was too nice and confident to let any barbs bug him. Each time the guy started in he just pounded his glove and tossed a fresh warmup ball out to Wagner as he loped out.

Of course, the fact that Ernie Banks walloped a two-run homer off Gomez in the 1st, then singled to start a rally in the 3rd only made the fan louder.

"Ya see what I mean, Willie? You're good but you ain't no Ernie!"

I snuck a peek out, just to make sure it wasn't our friendly suspect again, then retreated into the non-broiling shade. Moryn and Tony Taylor also knocked homers for the Cubs, and we were down 6-1 when Baby Bull Cepeda came charging and snorting into the dugout after the 4th.

"We can't take this, man!" he yelled, "Dick Drott is a lousy *payaso*, and I'm the only one hittin' him!" With a single and homer so far, Cepeda was right. He tossed cold, wet towels in many faces, and the dugout got a little electrified.

Except for me and Antonelli down at the far end. Johnny, off his second win and first shutout of the year, had his feet up on the dugout bench, scouring through movie starlet photos in the entertainment section of the *Chicago Tribune*.

"Can you believe it? Not one stinkin' Marilyn in here!" he growled.

"She does have to sleep once in a while, y'know."

"Says who?'

On the field, Bressoud and Wagner singled, but Mays popped out to Banks. Oh boy…

"YOU HEAR ME WILLIE? YOU'RE GOOD BUT YOU AIN'T NO ERNIE!!"

Cepeda barked something in Spanish to himself, marched to the plate and hit Drott's first fastball completely over the left field bleachers to put us back in the game. Antonelli got off the bench for a moment to shake Orlando's hand after he circled the bases, then went back to his newspaper.

Which was when I saw the item on the back page.

"FEMALE SCRIBBLERS CONVENE" the headline read over a photo. Ten or so ladies sitting in a large circle with notepads and pens, on what looked like the porch of a remote country lodge.

I peered closer. The woman seated closest to the camera was clearly the missing, nearly presumed dead Liz Doomis.

"Holy cow..." I muttered, and snatched the paper out of Antonelli's hands. The group was something called the McCullers Club, an "exclusive, two-week retreat for female writers" outside of Albia, Iowa.

"You find a Marilyn picture?" asked Johnny.

"Uh-uh. Much better."

A Davenport homer and two singles brought in ace Cubs reliever Bill Henry the next inning. Hank Sauer tied it up with a pinch single before Mays put us ahead to stay and shut up Mr. Loudmouth forever with a three-run smash homer.

Of course, by the time that hap-pened I had slipped out of the dugout, back into my street clothes and out of Wrigley without one FBI man spotting me. A half hour after that I had rented an old Ford sedan. That's right. To hell with Brewster, to hell with my Nick Testa costume and to hell with that sick, lying freak of a Peanut Killer. I was headed to Iowa.

The Iowa McCullers Confederacy

July 3rd

There wasn't a whole lot of anything going on in Albia, Iowa. Fifty years ago they used to mine coal around there, but now they were digging for suspicion. Seven men on seven separate porches watched me drive by like eyes in a spooky portrait painting. I stopped to fill up my Ford and buy a cold bottle of pop, and asked the guy manning the pump where the "McCullers Club" was.

"You got a dress?" was his first crack, before he finally gave me nutty, complicated directions involving hard rights, soft lefts, fence posts and particular trees.

It was late afternoon by the time I found the turnoff. The road leading in was unpaved and unfriendly. I bucked up and down in my seat like a rodeo rube. Finally entered a hilly section with some trees, and a smattering of cars with out-of-state plates parked in a clearing. Liz's T-bird was one of them.

There was a paved walkway between two big old rooming houses, both of them nicely painted and quiet. Said "hello?" in each lobby but no one was around. I stayed on the walk, repeatedly glancing behind me like I've been doing for months now. Then heard a faint round of applause in the distant trees and followed the sound.

I spotted a low, one-floor assembly hall down a narrower path. Located its back door, creaked it open and stepped inside.

I was at the back of the hall, a few yards behind at least four dozen women sitting in chairs. Standing in front of them, a notepad in her hand and looking refreshed and great in a white blouse and knee-length dungarees, was Liz. She didn't see me at all, because her eyes were glued to the paragraph she was reading from.

"Clara was clearly at the end of her rope. She'd done enough struggling with the heat, had enough of the pain in her feet, the pressure to produce, the lies, the half-jokes, the grueling labor of countless evenings, the transparent fabric of her being, the broken zipper that could not open into her soul. She would not, under any circumstances, bake this casserole."

She gave a little bow, and the audience erupted in cheers. Liz smiled and started for her seat. A spindly older woman wearing a pink head scarf took her place, was about to address the hall and then saw me standing there. Loudly cleared her throat.

"This is a private creative retreat, sir. How did you get in here?"

Everyone turned to look, including Liz, whose face went white.

"Well...I walked in. After driving in. Don't mean to intrude but Liz Doomis over there has kind of a family emergency."

"Who?"

"The lady who just read. Isn't that her right—"

"Do you mean Elizabeth *Dumàs*?"

"Yeah. Right. Whatever you say." I walked hurriedly up to the chair she had just collapsed into. "Miss Doomah?"

She stood up, her white face turning plum red with embarrassment. "Excuse me a minute, sisters..." she uttered, and yanked me to the door.

"How dare you follow me here!" she blurted the second we got outside, "Whatever is going on in your head?"

"What's in yours? I don't hear from you for weeks, your place in L.A. is cleaned out, meanwhile Mr. Murder tells me at least twice he's got you kidnapped so after a while I start to believe him. Thought you were cut to pieces in a shallow grave somewhere!"

She sighed. Walked me further away from the assembly hall. "I'm sorry, okay? Things weren't working out for me...in so many ways. I decided to just get out of town, and then I heard from this incredible writer's club I'd been trying over and over again to get into—"

"And you couldn't let me know that

you did?"

"No. That's the thing. The McCullers Club frowns on any outside contact. Especially with men."

"Gee, thanks. Carson McCullers told you this herself? Is she in there?"

"Oh no. She isn't able to leave her home back east, poor dear. She let us use her name for the club, and we use her work as inspiration. Have you ever read *The Heart is a Lonely Hunter*?"

"If it isn't a comic book or *Dime Detective* magazine, then no. And I wasn't kidding about the family emergency." I paused. "It's your brother Billy."

She averted her eyes, as if ashamed she hadn't told me about him. "What happened?"

"Stayed at his place one night in L.A. and he followed me to Cincinnati to help look for you. Now he's in a hospital in Dayton, thanks to our murdering friend."

"Oh no…We have to go see him! Get him out of there!"

"You got that right. Too bad you're trapped in Emily Dickinson's tea party."

"There's only one day left. I suppose I could leave early…"

"How about right now?"

She chewed on her lip. "Well, I guess. As long as you promise me you'll read all 900 pages of my novel when it's finished."

"Out loud and slow, baby."

She gave me a squeeze and a kiss. I'd forgotten how great those things felt. Then she ran back in to break the news to her sisters.

Really, though. Me read 900 pages of any book? It was a lie, of course. A big, necessary white one.

Bottle Rockets' Red Glare

July 4th

First order of business was to contact Brewster and put his mind at ease before he called out the military. Second order of business: simplify the road show. Liz reached her brother in Dayton, where he got healthy in a hurry, slipped out of the hospital and hopped a bus to St. Louis. Liz and I got there ahead of him in our two cars, and after I dumped the rental one we met him at the Greyhound station. Billy had his casts and a crutch, and I let them have their teary sibling reunion before we piled into the T-Bird and hit the road back to California.

It was July 4th, and it killed me to be missing our holiday doubleheader back home with the Cubs. Frankly, it killed me to be doing anything that didn't involve baseball, barbeque and a beer, so after heading down Route 66 a few hundred miles we started looking for the right eatery. Though Billy had other holiday ideas in mind.

"Gotta get us some Black Cats!" he said over and over, and right after we crossed into eastern Oklahoma he got his wish. One fireworks stand after another, and we stopped at one to load up on sparklers, spinners, bottle rockets, roman candles and a few packs of lady fingers.

"Maybe if Peanut Jerk gets on our tail, you can drop a few of those in his pants," offered Liz.

The restaurants we passed were either closed for the holiday or looked too decrepit in the first place. I would've been happy with a pack of baloney or beef jerky, but markets didn't look open either.

When we hit the outskirts of Claremore around dinner time, our noses perked up. Someone had a whole lot of meat cooking. A small town church came up, with lights hung in tree branches around the side, country fiddles playing and a hundred or so locals having a great old time. The First Presbyterian 4th of July Hootenanny would be our home for the evening.

Can't say we blended in, starting with Liz's car in a yard full of pickup trucks, but they all seemed friendly and ready to take our two dollars. The chicken and ribs were both spectacular, and the beer was like drinking heaven. Liz had a few and made a failed attempt at showing me how to two-step.

Then Billy limped over, barbeque sauce on his arm cast and mouth.

"Take a look back here, Pops. You won't believe it!"

I followed him around to an open back door on the church, where a handful of local cowboys were listening to a baseball radio broadcast. They tipped their hats when they saw me.

"Happy Fourth, friend," said the tallest one, "Got ourselves a right pickle here. 3-3, top of the 11th."

"Who's playing—"

"Hush a minute!"

Whoever was hitting hit a foul pop to third base for the third out. "DAMN!" said two of the cowboys, and one smacked his leg with his hat. Then I swore I heard the announcer say "Davenport", and squeezed closer to the radio.

"Is that a Giants game?"

"Huh?? Not on your life, podner. This here's the Cubbies! And if you ain't rootin' with us you better find yourselves another church."

"Oh no, we um…like the Cubs a lot!" Billy shrugged, hobbled away.

Seems that the tall guy, named Rex, had an uncle who played with Phil Cavaretta once and a grandmother who went on a date with Hippo Vaughn, so that was enough to make him a fan for life. And because Rex ran the ranch that employed his three cowboy friends, that made them Cub fans too.

"You from Chicago?" asked one.

"No…California. But not San Francisco."

"That's good. Too many commies, queerbates, and them darn cashew killers out there for my likin'."

Paul Giel was in his fourth inning of relief for us, and everything fell apart in the 12th. Cepeda, who had whiffed four times, threw a double play ball away before a Banks double kicked off an eight-run rally and had my new cowboy pals yahooing and grunting like it was the Fourth of July or something.

Liz was off at the fudge brownie competition, sampling entries, woozily trying to tell the local ladies about her writing exploits. Few understood, most just asked if she had a fella. Folks began lighting their fireworks just after dark, and Billy shot off every one of his in about five minutes.

And then the Giants exploded in Game 2. The Cubs took a short 3-2 lead before Cepeda put us ahead with a 3-run homer, Wagner and Cepeda homered in the next inning, I kept drinking and Wagner homered in the next inning, and then I was whooping it up like a San Francisco usher cowboy and suddenly there were four angry Oklahoma faces staring at me.

"You sure you ain't from San Franny town?"

"Well...maybe I am. It's a free country, and that's what we're here to celebrate, and no matter what team you believe in, it's your God-given right to root for it!"

They seemed to think about that for a moment, and maybe agree. But then Liz appeared, heard the score, yelled "Giants are killing 'em, yahoo!!!" and I was grabbing her arm and walking her in a T-Bird direction and pulling Billy away from a couple teenage Okie lasses, and like that we were back on Route 66 and sailing into the American dark.

Kicks

July 5th

The car was one of those one-eyed jacks. A ten-year-old Studebaker, maybe brown, possibly maroon. Its left head lamp out. It began following us somewhere outside of Amarillo and now we were over the New Mexico line and it was still there. Keeping a half mile back at all times, watching and waiting...

Excuse me if I was a little crazy from all-night coffee. Route 66 had been our home for the last thirty hours. We took turns making time in the T-Bird, Liz driving the day shift and me at night. Billy even took the wheel with his non-casted hand when one of us needed a break, or when Liz and I had things to discuss.

Which we did. The immediate goal was to get her brother back to L.A., but she was in no hurry to pull her stuff out of storage there or as I suggested, go back to the Bay Area. She was still on edge over the Peanut Killer, but who wasn't? He was haunting her dreams too, and her decision to ditch the west coast was related whether she copped to it or not.

Which is why I didn't bring up the one-eyed Studebaker right away. Even after we filled up in Tucumcari and the damn car tucked itself a half mile back behind a billboard. Waiting for us.

Liz knew I was jumpy. I said I needed food, so we stopped at a place called Joseph's Bar & Grill for hash browns, greasy links and yet more coffee. Five minutes into our meal, the Studebaker cruised by while we sat in the window booth. I tried to see the driver but caught only a hulking shadow.

Seeing the car pass by relaxed me. Liz took the wheel for the last stretch to California. Billy sat up front to fiddle with her radio and I curled up on the back seat.

I dreamed I was catching Christy Mathewson at the Polo Grounds. The grandstand was full of motionless, undead fans, and fog was wafting in off the Harlem River. A one-eyed Chicago Cub I didn't recognize stepped into the box, said "Howdy, Milton", knocked my behind with his bat and I snapped awake as the T-Bird swerved.

"Turn it off already!" cried Liz.

"So pass him!" said Billy.

"He won't let me!"

I sat up. The Studebaker was now a quarter mile in front of us, the only car in view on this barren stretch of desert between Gallup and Flagstaff. Its right directional signal was blinking.

"What's going on?"

"Can't you see? I've been staring at his damn signal now for fifty miles and it's making me blinking crazy!"

She gunned the gas to try and pass the Studebaker but it shot ahead and resumed the game.

"I've tried that over and over. What's his problem??"

"Try it again."

She did. Swerved into the left lane and pushed the pedal so hard I thought her engine would blow. We got about a hundred yards from the Studebaker's bumper before it jerked in front of us and zoomed ahead again.

"Okay Liz, pull off the road."

"What? Why??"

"Just do it please."

"Give me a reason!"

I didn't need one. Grabbed the wheel from behind and jerked us into the right-lane. A giant produce track honked and roared past out of nowhere, nearly sideswiping us. Liz shrieked and I swerved the car off the blacktop into a tire-slowing stretch of hot sand.

Liz and her brother were stunned, then furious. I let Liz yell at me and Billy whack me a few times with his arm cast. But the Studebaker had vanished, and the two of them slowly calmed down. After a toasty hour sitting there by the side of Route 66, we resumed driving.

By then, I had told them that the car had Ohio plates.

Home is Where the Good News Is

July 6th

The highway was open all the way to L.A., meaning no creepy Studebaker in sight. Billy wasn't convinced it was our taunting friend at the wheel, despite the car's Ohio plates, but I had my eye on the T-Bird's rear view mirror the whole stretch.

Anyway, Liz's brush with tragedy had changed her attitude about San Francisco. After we dropped her brother at his best friend's place in Van Nuys, she decided to give the Mission District apartment—meaning me— one more try. Another all-day drive got us into town in time to hear the last few innings of our second straight win against the comical Cards. They beat our pants off in the hit department, but Jim King of all people hit a giant 3-run homer, Gomez and Jones held the fort, and we were two games over .500 at the All-Star break.

More good news hit us when we got to the apartment: a FOR RENT sign on the unit downstairs.

"Poof!" I said, "Problem solved. You live downstairs with all the privacy you need for your novel, but you're still close by just in case."

"In case of what?"

"Aw, you know...danger...or dinner..."

Liz gave me a wink and a smile, more than I ever thought I'd get out of her.

I called the landlord to square things away for the apartment, and we made plans to go out for Italian food in North Beach. The old upstairs apartment was musty. Thankfully no one had broken in or left any strange notes. I took a long shower, listened to Russ Hodges interview Jim King on the after-game show.

There was a knock on my door around 5:30. I hopped up, checked my appearance and swung it open.

Agent Brewster stood there with a couple flunkies. He was in his shirtsleeves, tie loosened.

"Welcome home, Drake."

"Oh, for the love of..." I turned away. "Can't a guy have a day to get his life back in order?"

"Sure. Take the whole All-Star break. Take a month."

I turned back. Eyed him warily. "Why's that?"

He strolled through the door with his cronies. Knocked out a cigarette and fished for his lighter.

"Got ourselves a Peanut Killer, that's why. One Xavier Lawrence Chitwood turned himself in two hours ago."

The Bronx Bugle Sporting Life

| STAND FOR THE NATIONAL ANTHEM | All-Star Edition, July 9, 1958 | CLEAN YOUR EARS |

National League Puts it in the Banks

by Archie Stripes
American League Beat

BALTIMORE—In a gripping hit display rarely seen in these Maryland parts, the National League prevailed by a 9-7 score in the 25th All-Star classic.

Lumber was wielded aplenty, with seven balls hit out of the yard, five of them American solos. Staked to a 4-1 advantage, Mr. Ford of New York ran into 4th inning quicksand, giving up a walk and single, plunking Del Crandall, and giving up the first of two pinch-time triples to Cub slugger Ernie Banks.

A Ted Williams double put the A.L. ahead once more at 5-4, but leads in this snake pit slithered away in mere minutes. Stan the Man Musial popped a homer off Arnie Portocarrero to lead the 6th, and two outs later, Wes Covington of the first place Braves hit the longest ball ever witnessed in the mid-Atlantic, no doubt landing on a crab's back in some distant bay.

Undaunted, the Mick of the Bronx soon turned around a Don Elston offering and smashed it over the center fence. The American-leaning stands erupted, as the combatants went to the 8th in a 6-6 headlock.

But Baltimore's Jack Harshman would only be treated harshly. Singles by Aaron and Bailey and a walk to Mathews brought on Oriole-mate O'Dell, who wild pitched the go-behind run home. After whiffing Ashburn, Ernie B. did it again, jerking a ball into the right-center gap for his third and fourth RBIs on the day and a 9-6 lead.

The Americans' last hurrah was brave enough, with Bob Nieman homering off Craig, but Mantle's bounce-out to Banks proved to be a fitting finale.

Back to good old pennant race business now, as the Braves head to L.A. to take on the second place Dodgers.

Suspect Confesses to S.F. "Peanut" Killings

SAN FRANCISCO (UPI)— Ending a three-month-long manhunt for the notorious "Peanut Killer", Xavier Chitwood, a 41-year-old electric meter reader from nearby Fremont, turned himself over to authorities last Sunday. For the time being, Chitwood's confession has cleared the name of a local ballpark usher and eased the minds of nervous city dwellers.

≈ *The Other Killer* ≈

July 10th

Xavier Lawrence Chitwood—I decided to call him The X-Man—sat at a table in San Francisco's FBI headquarters, manacled and happy. He was sure big enough to be the Peanut Killer, that's for sure, with the same meaty hands that worked me over at Candlestick Point that night, and the same "dent" in his forehead I'd noticed in my recent half-conscious captivity.

"Good to see you again," he said, as Brewster showed me in.

"Good to see you too, Xavier. Especially in handcuffs."

"Care to tell Mr. Drake who you killed again?" piped in Brewster. He and the FBI guys looked like they'd been up all night.

"Sure. My first victim was John Blaziecsky on Opening Day. Had to use my blade on him, being it was kind of crowded. Then there was that Reggie guy in the park. Then the night watchman Vincent Grosso out on the Point. Stole the nylon cord from that same hardware store you bought the sign stuff to do that one. Pete Szopa in Pittsburgh, then Officer Grundheinz, that Ohio state trooper."

"So what do you have against me, Xavier?" He drew a big blank. "Why'd you kill one of my best friends?...You met him in the Double Play, right?"

"Oh yeah. Right. Had a few too many peanuts and beers with him, I guess. Followed him over to the park and was just gonna mug him but got a little carried away."

He blurted out a sick laugh and I lunged across the table at him. Brewster grabbed me from behind, hauled me into the nearby corridor.

"God almighty, Drake, get ahold of yourself—"

I ripped myself free. Took a deep breath and looked Brewster in the eye.

"It ain't him."

"What??"

"He's lying. About Reggie. And he didn't even smell like peanuts."

"Who cares? He confessed. He knows details. A guy matching his description was seen in a Pittsburgh tavern the day before Szopa died. You should see his flophouse room down near the wharf. Peanut Killer news clippings taped to every inch of the wall."

"So? Maybe he's just a fan."

"What makes you think he's lying about your friend?"

I hesitated. "Because he just is. Sometimes I get hunches just like you."

"Yeah, well how about you just congratulate us for getting a break in this case."

"Congratulate you? For what? Leaving your office door open so he could stroll right in?"

"Do me a favor, Drake, okay? Go back to Seals Stadium, put on your usher clothes and work the ball game. Mr. Stoneham said he'd take you back."

"Too late. Game started an hour ago."

"Then go home and romance your girlfriend. We have a statement to record in here."

♦ ♦ ♦

The romancing idea was a nice one, but pure gothic fiction. Liz had her phone off the hook, the door locked, and I could hear furious typing. She finally came upstairs after eleven for a highball and goodnight kiss, and certainly didn't want to believe that the X-Man might not be our man.

"I thought he confessed!"

Maybe she was right about him. Maybe they all were. But I still didn't feel good about blowing the whistle on Horace Stoneham, corpse mover, even though X-Man had told me he killed Reggie in the park across the street.

Before I went to bed I called Brewster one more time, knowing he'd be awake if anyone was.

"Where did this guy say he killed Reggie again?"

"In Franklin Square Park."

"Ah-hah…See, that's his mistake. I don't think that's true. I haven't been wanting to say this, but I found Reg-

gie sticking out of the Seals Stadium scoreboard."

"Oh. Well, that clears that up."

"Clears what up?"

"What Chitwood was talking about. He told us he stuck him in a 'strange place', then changed his mind and dragged him back to the park."

So that was that. I fell asleep, actually believing I could work tomorrow's game without looking over my shoulder.

Even though I still had a night full of weird dreams.

Snappy's Back!

July 11th

So my usher pals welcomed me with a devil's food cake and bottle of Napa red, like I'd just returned from Korea.

"You were kind of a crappy bullpen catcher anyway," said Cheesesteak Sid. There was also some funny talk about whether they wanted me back at all, seeing that being out of my usher duds seemed to put the team on a winning streak.

There was no way around it. Two weeks ago we were jockeying with the Pirates for last place, and now rookie Cepeda had taken charge on the field and in the clubhouse, Antonelli was on a roll, and we were suddenly nipping at the Dodgers' necks for second place.

Section 16 was a big party that afternoon, and Xavier Lawrence Chitwood being safely in the clink was a big reason. I got more back slaps and juicy tips than I'd had all year. It had to be a relief for the fans to not be seated by a suspected criminal.

Of course, there were the questions.

"Did you see the Peanut Killer in jail, Snappy?"

"What was he like?"

"Will they make a movie about him, ya think?"

"Will you get to act in the movie?"

These lasted right up till game time. Even usherette Dot stopped by to ask if the suspect was "as handsome and evil as his photo." Thankfully, the Giants rocked the scoreboard early and often, and my fan club was distracted in a hurry.

It was unbelievable, actually. Daryl Spencer popped one out off the 2-10 Nuxhall in our first at bat. Temple booted a grounder and Mays put one over the fence. Then Cepeda hit one out to center. Smoky Burgess clubbed one into the right field bleachers in the Cincy 2nd, but we scored six more times for Worthington in the next three innings, and handed the hapless Reds their 12th straight loss. Cincy eventually tried avoiding us altogether, walking ten batters, but it was a bad strategy.

With the Braves sweeping the Dodgers down in L.A., we were suddenly in front of our neighbors. Liz obviously wouldn't care to hear this, and because she was typing away on her novel into the evening, I stopped at the Double Play to see Chumpo

and Bob and tell them about my cross-country exploits as Nick Testa. The bar was packed and loud, talking about the Giants, the three big upcoming games with the Braves in town, and I should have been having as great a time as everyone else.

But with every drink, and especially with every peanut bowl that slid by my nose, I kept seeing Xavier Lawrence Chitwood's face. I then realized why I hadn't slept too well the night before, and it had nothing to do with my typically strange dreams.

Something about the X-Man was seriously bugging me, and I couldn't even name what it was.

That Nagging Thing

July 12

I sat with Liz down at Buzzie's Coffee Shoppe this morning. She was already hopped up from two straight days of novel-writing, and probably needed a morning martini more than coffee. When I brought up my nagging concern about the "X-Man", though, she was all ears and ears.

"Was it his voice?"

"No. He sounded a lot like what I heard, especially over the handy-talkie that night."

"His build?"

"Nope. Plenty big enough."

"His story?"

"Like I said, it checks out. Who the

hell else would know about sticking Reggie in the scoreboard? He even knew how to spell the Ohio trooper's name."

"So what is it?"

"Damned if I know."

"Well...neither do I."

"Yeah, I figured. Except sometimes you sort of...inspire me."

"Aww. I'm touched."

"You mean that?"

"Of course I mean that."

"See? I don't just like you for your ravishing figure."

"Mmm...And you haven't even seen my new bathing suit yet."

"Where do I buy a ticket?"

"You don't need one, mister."

"Nice...If there was only a good beach around here."

"Who says there isn't?"

"The climate."

"Well, I've heard good things about Stinson. A little ways north of the Golden Gate...Up for a drive?"

"Did you forget? There's a big game to work today. Braves in town."

"So when's the next Giants road trip?"

"Not for like ten days. What's your hurry?"

"Thought you were in one."

"Hurrying anything is a bad idea, doll."

"Sure is. Like believing the first Peanut Killer who walks in the door."

And with that, my coffee went cold. Talk about spoiling a party.

◆ ◆ ◆

No such party problems at Seals that afternoon, though. There were lines around the block for bleacher tickets as early as ten in the morning. Milwaukee was on fire but so were we, meaning something had to give.

It wasn't Antonelli. He did give us a scare when Mel Roach smacked his first pitch over the fence in left to start the game, and Leon Wagner scaled the wall to snatch it back. From that point on, Johnny was un-hittable.

Carl Willey was too good, the zero-zero score tightened the grandstand like a cheap Bulova about to snap a spring. Antonelli put one hitter on base in the first five innings, but kept escaping. The Giants had two aboard in the 6th, and second and third with one out in the 7th but got nowhere.

Then Johnny began our 8th with a walk. Up stepped reserve outfielder Jim King, who won a game against the Reds just days ago with a late 3-run blast. Rigney was batting him leadoff on a pure hunch. Willey tried a curve, King timed it and sent it on a mammoth arc into the right field bleachers! The Braves went meekly in the 9th and we were suddenly just two and a half games out.

The Double Play had fans spilling out the door all night. I couldn't imagine what Cepeda and Gomez were doing down at the Red Parrot. And if Liz was typing happily away on her opus, then I was more than happy for her. I just counted my lucky stars she wasn't a crazed Dodgers fan.

Prayers Answered

July 13th

I called Brewster, asked if I could go see the X-Man again. No dice. Chitwood was moved overnight to a more secure jail while he waited for his first arraignment on Monday.

"You ought to be in church anyway, Drake. Don't you know what day it is?"

Well, I did toil away at Our Lady of the Seals Cathedral all afternoon, where there was more prayer-inducing baseball to worship than I can ever remember. Liz at first threatened to join me, but when it came down to either taking in a heavenly ball game or clacking away on her typewriter, she was a devout atheist.

It was her loss. The weather was gorgeous. The crowd was even bigger than at Saturday's logjam. Plus, as was the case when I worked PCL games, the more the home team was winning, the bigger the tips got.

The madness all began with Ruben Gomez being wild. Mathews walked, Aaron singled, Covington got plunked and Bruton walked to put the Braves up 1-0. Then Cepeda doubled in two off Bob Rush. Mays scalded a triple into the gap for another run in the 3rd, before Davenport got him home with a single. In the 5th Rush ran for cover. Wagner homered, Mays and Cepeda singled, and a Davenport sac

fly and Daryl Spencer (!) homer made it 8-1. Trowbridge gave the mound a try for them in the 6th and with the help of a ball through Mathews' legs, three walks and a wild pitch, we were up 12-1 and heading for certain Sunday glory.

Celebratory beers dropped into hands all around me. In maybe one hour we'd be a game and a half out of first. I even saw a few fans leave early to get some local sunbathing in.

Being an ex-AAA pitcher, I know a few more things about baseball than most. But you don't have to be Van Lingle Mungo to know that no game is ever over. Especially against a club as good as Milwaukee.

The 7th inning was our sermon on the mount. Torre singled and with one out Aaron put one over the left field bleachers. Covington walked and Bruton singled and Marv Grissom came on. Crandall yawned and doubled down the line. Roach singled in another. After Logan whiffed Joe Adcock pinch-hit and launched one that was close to hitting Sputnik and it was suddenly 12-8.

Humberto Robinson set us down 1-2-3 and Seals got awful quiet. Then Mathews began their 8th with a line single off Giel and Aaron doubled. Mumbles erupted all around me, most of them prayers. A Bruton walk and another Roach single and it was 12-11. Logan and Pafko singled, loading the bases. The sun vanished behind dark clouds. Locusts were probably heading our way. Torre grounded out to end the inning and there was brief relief.

Cepeda and Davenport's back-to-back doubles gave the Giants a two-run lead back but Giel wasn't done torturing us, putting two more on with two gone in the 9th. Gordon Jones walked in to handle Crandall. I hadn't been to church since I was five and even I was praying. Del swung, popped it up to Spencer, and we had actually survived the ordeal.

Afterwards, sweaty but elated, I talked half the ushers and a few usherettes over to the Double Play. From there, a handful of us stuffed into my Coronet and Butch's Chevy and headed down to the Red Parrot, Cepeda and Gomez's Latin-Caribbean band haunt.

I'd done a bit of snooping down there with Liz a few months back, but it was a funeral home that night compared to the scene we encountered this time. I don't remember the S. F. Seals having any kind of Latino following, but the Giants—with Orlando, Ruben, Felipe Alou, Ramon Monzant, and Bahamian Andre Rodgers—were another story. Cepeda and Gomez recognized me from my recent guest stint as Nick Testa and had us smoking cigars and snaking through the tables in a conga line in no time, calypso beats pounding into our ears.

Much later and far from sober, I gyrated my way up the steps of my apartment. Liz's light was off, but it clicked on when she heard me and she poked her head out the door.

"So how was the Red Parrot?"

"Huh?"

"Or wherever the heck you were. Sounded like a good time."

"What are you talking about?"

"Don't mess with me, Snap. I heard calypso music."

"Heard it where?"

"You mean you didn't call me about two hours ago from the Parrot, whisper my name and hold the phone up in the air for almost thirty seconds?"

"Uhh, no."

"Well, somebody did." She shivered, tightened her robe. "And it sure couldn't have been your X-Man."

Just Here to Read the Meter, Ma'm

July 14th

I was done talking to Brewster. The guy couldn't find a bee if the stinger was in his behind. Here I was, letting down my guard day and night with Xavier Lawrence Chitwood "in custody," while someone was possibly tailing me around town and phoning my lady for terrorizing purposes.

Unless they were two different people with two different agendas. Maybe I could clarify one of them.

From a newspaper article I learned that X-Man read meters for the Pacific Electric Company over in El Cerrito. I got up early, crossed the Bay

Bridge, parked outside the P.E.C. office and waited for someone I could follow. A trio of meter readers in their little blue caps emerged from the building before long, coffees and/or cigarettes in hand. One overweight fellow seemed to be the friendliest, or certainly the one who knew the most co-workers. I waited till he drove away in his yellow truck and got on his tail.

The slow pursuit took me to a hilly neighborhood dotted with modest houses, thirsty flower beds and chainlink fences. If X-Man was truly diabolical, doing this job sure gave him plenty of easy access.

I parked and followed Chubby Boy down the sidewalk, keeping a safe distance. Let him duck down a half dozen alleys to read meters, then record the results in a big black binder. Waited for him to return to his truck and rounded the rear bumper to "bump" into him. The name GUS was stitched into his shirt.

"Excuse me!" I cried.

"No, no. My mistake, sir…" He tipped his cap and I pointed a finger at him.

"Say, you wouldn't happen to know Xavier Chitwood, would you?"

The question gave him pause. He suddenly wanted to flee. "Why?"

"Well, I'm an old buddy of his from grade school, see." I stuck out my hand. "Perry Dobbs." He gingerly shook it. "Drove up from San Diego when I read he confessed to these murders because I'll tell ya, it really

shook me up."

"Same here. None of us believe he was doing these things."

"Oh. So you're friends with him?"

"Not really. Just at work. Kept to himself most of the time but he was certainly friendly enough…Listen, I still got three more neighborhoods—"

"Yeah, I know. I'm just kind of searching for some answers. Been trying to call him off and on all year, but…Was he leaving town a lot?"

Gus shrugged. "Called in sick a few times if that means anything. Probably was hiding out at the library."

"Library?"

"Yeah the big one on Larkin." He was always doing some kind of 'research' there. At least that's what he said. Nice meeting you, Perry."

He hopped back in his truck and drove off.

◆ ◆ ◆

The library would have to wait, because I was due in section 16 for the Braves-Giants afternoon finale, with a chance for us to inch within half a game of first. No slugfest this time, just an endless death match. Rigney and Haney pulled out all the stops, and five straight innings of scoreless ball late in the day were as tense as you could imagine.

The game began with Mays dropping Roach's fly ball for a two-base error, and the 1-0 Braves lead lasted until Alou singled in Bressoud in the 3rd. McCormick pitched better than usual, but then gave up five straight hits and three runs to begin the 5th. It looked real bad. Then seldom-seen outfielder Don Taussig batted for McCormick with two outs in the 7th and popped one out of the yard off Spahn. It sparked the team. A walk and three singles in the 8th tied it up, and on we went into the extras abyss. We had chance after chance to win it off Spahn and Humberto Robinson but couldn't plate a crumb.

The 14th inning rolled around, Grissom pitching now, and I looked up from my rail perch to see Liz Doomis standing there in a big sun hat.

"I needed a break, Snap. Your friend Butch let me in the gate."

"Great. Any weird phone calls today?"

"I wouldn't know. Left it off the hook. So what's going on here any—"

WHOCK. At that very moment, Johnny Logan smacked one into the bleachers.

"That's what."

"Oh God! I jinxed them! I'm so, so sorry."

I put an arm around her for a reassuring squeeze, moved her aside so a handful of depressed fans could begin their exodus. After we went out 1-2-3, Liz ended up buying me dinner at the Cliff House, and all was soon forgotten.

Though I did urge her to just take a long walk in Golden Gate Park next time.

The Cable Gal

July 15th

I got followed again the next day, but not by who you think.

Started after I went to the city library after lunch and got nowhere with the snooty librarian. Don't ask me why librarians always seem to be snooty. They just are. Like they pump them out of snooty machines in library basements.

All I wanted was a list of books that Xavier Chitwood had recently checked out. "Absolutely out of the question," was her answer, as if I had asked the woman for her phone number and brassiere size. Aggravated, I hopped on a cable car to head down to the wharf and look for X-Man's hovel.

Which is when I noticed the strange lady. She climbed on back seconds after I grabbed a pole up front. She had a nice cream-colored dress, expensive white gloves and dark glasses on. Awkwardly changed her grip over and over, like she'd never been on a cable car in her life.

As people got on and off at the top of Hyde, I worked my way inside the car. So did the woman. Even with her dark glasses it was easy to tell she was eyeballing me—and trying to squeeze closer. When we stopped at Green I slipped into a vacant aisle seat. Waited for her to inch closer, then stood abruptly in front of her.

"Care for a seat?"

"Oh! Why thank you…" She slowly lowered herself into it, slipping me a brittle smile. Her voice sounded familiar, but I couldn't place it. I tapped her on the shoulder.

"We've met somewhere, right?"

She spun around. Lowered her shades and pretended to recognize me.

"Mr. Drake?"

"Mrs. North?

It was the wife of city grand juror Henry North, the Candlestick land swindle investigator. She had served us Waldorf salads and eclairs in Henry's parlor about two months ago.

"You never wrote that article, did you?" she said out of the clear blue.

"Article?" I had totally forgotten I had told North I was a reporter for the Sacramento Bee.

"Yes. Henry even drove out to the newspaper to look for you, and they said no one named Milton Drake even worked there. He could have used that support, you know."

"I'm sorry. I've actually been caught up in these murders revolving around the Giants, and I thought maybe the land deal had something to do with it."

"So you lied to him."

"Well, I guess you could call it that.

A white one."

The cable car gave a sudden lurch and Mrs. North nearly pitched into the aisle. I grabbed her in time and she suddenly began to cry.

"Mrs. North? You okay?"

She shook her head. "It's all gotten so ugly. My friends now…"

"Your friends?"

"They won't even talk to me… Won't even invite me to their parties. All because of this grand jury report the Mayor is trying to bury. I told Henry to back down but he just won't listen—"

She wept into the sleeve of my jacket. A few passengers stared. Most just got on and off the car at every street.

"Would it help if I saw Henry?"

"Definitely not…He's just so determined to pursue this."

"How about the Mayor?"

She violently shook her head. Yanked the cord to get off at the next street. "I'm sorry, Mr. Drake. I didn't mean to alarm you…All I can tell you is, if you're hunting for murderers, you may have been on the right track the first time we met."

And with that, she climbed off at Beach. The cable car was rotated around, and started climbing back up the hill.

I never even got off.

National League thru Tuesday, July 15

Milwaukee	48	37	.565	—
Philadelphia	44	40	.524	3.5
San Francisco	45	41	.523	3.5
Chicago	45	42	.517	4
Los Angeles	43	43	.500	5.5
Pittsburgh	41	44	.482	7
St. Louis	39	44	.470	8
Cincinnati	36	50	.419	12.5

American League thru Tuesday, July 15

New York	58	28	.674	—
Boston	49	36	.576	8.5
Baltimore	49	39	.557	10
Chicago	47	41	.574	12
Detroit	43	43	.500	14
Cleveland	44	44	.444	14
Kansas City	34	51	.400	23.5
Washington	23	65	.261	36

140 Words Per Minute

July 16th

It's hard enough just to talk to a dame. Try reasoning with one when she's been up half the night and into the next morning typing away on her first novel on a cigarette and coffee jag.

"She followed you for HOW long again?"

"I just told you. From the top of the Hyde line to the bottom of the hill."

CLACK-CLACK-CLACK-CLACK

"Liz, did you hear what I said? What does it matter if she followed me on foot twenty blocks before that?"

"If you feel like you need to go out on me, Snap, just say so."

"Who said going out? I said maybe tail her and see if it leads to some good Mayor creeps. That whole thing at Candlestick Point could be a cover-up and this Peanut Man guy, whoever he really is, could have been hired by them. Wasn't that the first place I 'met' him?"

"Hmm…Sounds like a big old conclusion-jump. If you ask me, a lady in distress curdles your milk every time, and that's what this is really about."

CLACK-CLACK-CLACK-CLACK

"What, you don't think the Candlestick Point business is a big sleazy pit? That all kinds of crimes can be linked to it? Both Henry North and now his wife have hinted that."

CLACK-CLACK-CLACK-CLACK

"Liz, you're really being no help at all here."

CLOCK-CLOCK!!

She practically used her fists on the last two keys. Pulled out yet another cigarette and lit up. The ashtray beside her already looked like Mt. McKinley.

"Snap. What do you want me to say? You want to follow Mrs. Drake all over town, then go ahead. If I were you I'd just go see the Mayor and smack an answer out of him."

"I tried that."

"Then try harder."

New clacking erupted. I stormed out of her place.

◆ ◆ ◆

Down at City Hall, Mayor Christopher still had the same unbearable secretary he had last time, Mrs. Bluebottom. Like Liz, she was also busy pounding a keyboard into submission. At least she stopped when I entered.

"Remember me?"

"No sir, I don't." She went a bit pale, reached for something under her desk. Came out with a piece of tissue to remove a stray muffin crumb from her chin.

"Milton Drake. I was here about two months ago, left you a note to give to the Mayor. Which you did, right?"

"Yes. I suppose I must have."

"Well, suppose you pick up that phone and let him know I'm here. And don't give me any moose dung about him being out to lunch or in a meeting or at the doctor or playing golf or in a steam bath, okay?"

"I don't have to, Mr. Drake. The Mayor will see you now. Just walk down the hall to the first door on the right. I believe he's alone in our conference room."

"Oh…okay. Thanks."

Wary, I left her office, made a left and headed down the hall. Walked into the open conference room and two large brutes grabbed me from both sides, hauled me into a back stairwell and began punching. I could have gotten my arms free and knocked out both of them, but my head got in the way of their fists.

Apparently, seeing the Mayor was going to be a recurring problem.

Taking the Cake

July 17th

As I figured, Liz wanted me to press charges against the Mayor.

"Are you kidding? He'll rope in his cops, lawyers, and judges and before you know it they'll have me up on breaking and entering. Forget it, Liz. I've been barking up the wrong fire hydrant with this one. The Mayor's gang is too openly stupid to do anything cunning and calculated like plan a string of murders. Another ice pack, please."

My mother had a different remedy for my beat-up head in mind: her annual birthday dinner. She had this joint in Jack London Square she liked me to take her called the Seafood Grotto. Surf 'n turf, baked potato with cheese and chives and a big glass of wine for $4.99.

"We'll have a good time," she said. "It'll do you some good to get your mind off all this nonsense."

Mom wasn't wrong, and after the game (we won again!), I even talked Liz into driving and having dinner with us. With the usual third degree attached.

"Why do I need to meet your mother again?"

"Because some day you may have to."

"And why would that be?"

"Another ice pack, please."

◆ ◆ ◆

The Grotto was packed for a Thursday evening, and Dorothy Gladys Drake actually got along fine with Liz—especially after her second Chablis.

"So what do you think of Mr. Baseball Usher here?"

"Oh…I guess he's okay by me," said Liz. She tickled my leg beneath the table.

"Yeah, he's a good son. Make a good darn good father, too."

"Mom, stop…"

"I'm only saying. I know the qualities. Woodrow sure had them, bless his soul. Would do anything for his boy…"

Her voice tailed off, and she polished off her wine to fill the gap. Caught the waiter's eye to signal for a fresh glass.

"Spent every dime we had on that silly camp…"

"Camp?" asked Liz.

My mother paused. Shook her head violently, like a giant twitch. "Shut up, Dorothy…"

"You were saying—"

"Oh you know. Sleepaway camp. How's your chicken marsala, dear?"

"Just fine…How's your dinner, Snap?"

"Good enough."

"Still got that headache?"

"The beer helps."

"Oh, you'll be right as a rainstorm tomorrow," said my mother without thinking. Her trademark.

"What makes you think so?"

"I'm your mother, remember? Known you for a while. Heck, every time you blacked out you were always good as new the next day."

It was too late. Mom was cursing herself again and Liz was staring at me.

"You used to black out?"

"Yeah. Fainting spells of some kind when I was a teenager. Not too often."

"We had a GREAT doctor. Jerry Donaldson. A real cutie pie. Married three times but he knew his stuff so you couldn't hold it against him. Remember Dr. Donaldson, Milton?"

My mind sharpened for a second. But it wasn't on the name you'd think.

"Milton! Did you hear me?"

"He never said that…"

"Huh?? Who never said what?"

I looked at Liz, suddenly tongue-tied. She was as baffled as my mother. The traditional slice of chocolate bundt birthday cake arrived on the table, complete with lit candle. Liz and I managed to sing a soft rendition of "Happy Birthday", and as Dorothy Drake wobbly rose to blow out the candle, I gazed at the flame as if it were a miniature light bulb that just switched on in my brain. The nagging thing that was bothering me was nagging no more.

At the FBI office the other day, the X-Man never called me Milton. Not even once.

Night Games

July 18, 1958

I called Brewster first thing the next morning and told him that the X-Man never called me by my given name, something the Peanut Man always seemed to do. Naturally, he wasn't impressed and didn't want me going back to see him, but did manage to slip out the name of the facility out in Livermore where Chitwood was being held.

So I gave myself a little daytime road trip before tonight's weekend opener with the Pirates. Lucky for me, it was visiting hours when I got there, and I talked a looming red-haired guard into passing the suspect a note that "Uncle Snappy" was waiting to visit him. They set us up in a private room with a glass wall between us and an extra guard on hand to announce we had three minutes.

"Nice to see you again…Uncle" the X-Man began, trying not to laugh.

"Same here. But did you forget something?"

He paused a moment, then pointed to my bruised face. "Somebody hit you?"

"No, no. When you said hi to me just now. You didn't use my real name."

"Sure I did. Uncle Snappy."

"Not that one, Xavier…My REAL name…"

He squinted at me through the glass. I saw a trickle of perspiration over one of his eyebrows.

"Why are you messing with me?"

"I can ask you the same question, bud."

His eyes went vacant, like he was searching through some kind of weird memory bank in his head. Then he grinned.

"I have no reason to mess with anyone. Except for those poor saps I killed…Milton."

I slumped in my chair. Nothing I was coming up with was working.

"It's been nice playing this game with you, Milton, but I'm a little tired now. Do you know someone who can write a book about me?"

I didn't, and I never would. Turned and asked the guard to let me out. I was frustrated, and when I hit the hallway had to shove a janitor out of the way who was mopping the floor.

By the time I got back to town it

was nearly ushering time, and drove over to Seals. The X-Man was still bugging me, and I decided I'd duck out early and head down to the Wharf to get into his flophouse.

But I had a new twist waiting for me at the ballpark: Agent Brewster on his night off, holding tickets with his wife Bonnie Brewster in MY damn section.

"You don't mind if I give you a big tip tonight, do ya Drake? I'm feeling a little accomplished these days."

Good for you, I thought, not wanting to drop one word about my trip out to Livermore. And I would have to fake a little sickness to cut out early.

When we fell behind 5-0 on two rare Bill Virdon home runs, it seemed like my plan would be easy as pie. Except I wasn't counting on upside-down cake. Mays and Wagner popped 2-run homers off Ron Kline, and it was 6-4 Bucs going to the 8th.

Bonnie Brewster was slim and kind of mute, and her husband spent most of the game explaining the rules to her. Lassoed me to fill in some of the blanks and I was starting to get annoyed with the both of them. We loaded the bases with one out and El-roy Face came on to face the usually disappointing Willie Kirkland.

"Why do they call the bases sacks, Drake? Bonnie wants to know."

"Why you think? They look like them."

"No they don't. They're flat."

"So they're flat sacks. Do you mind if I—"

WHOCK!! Kirkland hit one on a rising line over the right field bleachers for a grand slam, an exploding crowd, a certain win, and my perfect cue to duck out the nearest exit.

◆ ◆ ◆

Finding Chitwood's hovel was a cinch. I knew the general seedy neighborhood down on Fisherman's Wharf, and then it was just a few questions to local merchants and locating the police tape over the door. I climbed up a fire escape, forced open a window on his room. Clicked on my flashlight.

Brewster was right. Chitwood's walls were plastered with newspaper clippings on the "Peanut Man" killings. I even found my name in a few of the early stories where I was a person of interest. My name "Milton" circled in pen. Hmm…

I looked around some more. Eventually lifted up his stained, moth-eaten bare mattress. Saw a black scrapbook secured below it with a strap. I pulled it out.

Inside were pages and pages of other clippings, some from newspapers, some ripped out of library books. All about murderers. Leopold and Loeb made an appearance. So did a lot of clippings about Ed Gein, the demented killer up in Wisconsin last year.

Xavier Lawrence Chitwood was into murder, alright. But there was a slight chance he was just a diehard fan.

Haven't the Foggiest

July 19th

Liz was less than thrilled about me breaking into crime scenes late at night. We were having morning coffee on her porch, and I knew after ten seconds there was no way I'd be telling *her* about my trip out to Livermore either.

"You're getting cuckoo over this, Snap. You're a ballpark usher, not Phillip Marlowe. The case is closed when the guy confesses."

"Not if he's lying."

"Okay, well…a bunch of newspaper clippings and library visits doesn't make anyone a liar. Even if he didn't call you Milton that time you saw him."

"Actually—" I stopped myself, but a second too late.

"Actually what?"

"Nothing…forget it."

She gave me an odd look, then convinced me I was driving myself too hard and needed a day off from both ushering and sleuthing.

"To do what?"

She shrugged. "I don't know. You can always…get lazy with me." She followed this up with a hand on my knee and one of her famous juicy smiles.

* * *

Two hours later, we had showered and dressed and were packing lunch for another picnic in Golden Gate Park. Liz had hit page 300 of her novel and was in a rare giddy mood. As we lay under the trees with her head on my chest, I tried to get the book's plot out of her but she kept saying it was "in progress and off limits."

A guy on a nearby blanket had the Giants game on his transistor radio. Russ Hodges' voice was just faint enough to miss the action, but I could tell the Pirates were winning by his muted tone. On the other hand, it was just loud enough to distract me from Liz's dreamy ramblings on our fantasy future.

"I bet if we ever had kids they'd be talented wiseacres."

"I suppose…"

"Ever think about what you'd name your kids?"

"Not really…"

This dragged on for a bit. Then some mid-afternoon fog rolled across the treetops, and it got a little clammy out.

It also felt like someone was watching us. I sat up, peered around. The guy with the radio had packed up and left. I wished I had caught the damn Giants score.

"You okay?" asked Liz.

"Think so. It's probably nothing."

We finished off our small bottle of wine and started out of the park. Took a path through a thick grove of tall pines and the clammy feeling returned with a vengeance. I grabbed Liz by the arm, quickened our pace. Twigs snapped on all sides and Agent

Brewster suddenly appeared in front of us. Flanked by his mini-FBI army. The relieved look he had on his face at Friday night's game was completely gone.

"Uncle Snappy, I presume?"

Uh-oh. This wasn't good.

"What happened?"

"You tell me, Drake. How did your visit to Livermore go yesterday?"

Liz just about popped her cork. "Your what??"

"Yeah, I couldn't help myself. Had to see if he'd call me Milton. Which he did."

"And what about last night?" continued Brewster. "Knew your way around that place pretty good, I imagine. Like which guard was on duty at what time."

"What the hell are you talking about, Brewster?"

He glanced around at his flunkies, who moved a step closer to me like it was in their genes.

"Xavier Lawrence Chitwood was found in his cell this morning. Drowned."

"Drowned?? How is that possible?"

"Head forcibly held under water in his own toilet. The guard on duty was found strangled, his uniform and key ring gone."

"Jesus…"

"Where'd you go after the game last night, Drake? Or should I say…before it was over?"

"Had some errands to run, that's all. We had the game in the bag."

"Errands, huh?"

"Yeah. As in, cleaning my laundry."

"And was one of them going back to that hardware store to buy yourself a stapler?"

Now I was baffled. Brewster took a small plastic bag out of his pocket, held it up in the shadowy light so I could read the scrawled note that had been tucked inside:

WHO ARE YOU KIDDING?

"It was stapled into Chitwood's lower back. Same kind of marker you used out at Candlestick Point. And if you ask me, Drake, I'd say it appears to be your handwriting."

I looked closer. Supposed it did. But that wasn't the only thing.

It was written on San Francisco Giants stationery.

And Now… This

July 20th

Whoever the Peanut Killer really was, he knew how to ruin my life. I spent all last night being grilled by the FBI and most of this morning attacked by reporters. Even my old pal Lt. Malarkey stopped by to breathe more scallions and snide remarks in my face. Luckily, a handful of Fisherman's Wharf witnesses gave me an alibi for the time X-Man was getting his head stuffed in a toilet. Unluckily, I had to 'fess up about breaking into Chitwood's taped-off apartment.

The killer's note was certainly explainable. The bastard left a victim's wallet in my place back in April and probably nabbed a piece of my hand-writing then. And S.F. Giants stationery? There was a supply room filled with the stuff over at Seals—if he knew how to get in and where to look. And so far, this guy knew how to do everything.

Horace Stoneham, meanwhile, was floored. Like most everyone, he thought the murder stories were over. That the fans could go back to thinking about the pennant race and buying Giants concessions.

"Watch the game from my suite today, Drake," he told me over the phone before I was allowed to leave FBI headquarters with an extra-long leash around my neck, "I'll have two guards outside the door and if you're interested, a new bottle of Glenlivet in my office."

I took him up on the scotch between the third and sixth innings, and it did make the game and the day more bearable. Antonelli was masterful again, throwing a two-hitter at the Bucs, and with the Braves losing at Wrigley, we were suddenly just two games out again.

Liz didn't know what to say to me yesterday after Brewster cornered us in the park, and nothing changed today. She was too disgusted with my hijinks and too wrapped up in her novel to even retrieve the day-old mail from her box. I pulled out the postal clump and rapped on her door. She swung it open, her hair down and makeup nowhere to be seen.

"Gee. You're not in prison."

"Thanks. Nice to see you again, too."

"I'm in the middle of a tough scene, Snap. I'll stop by in a little while, okay?" She started to close the door, then opened it again to grab her mail. "And thanks."

I trudged upstairs, tossed a few lamb chops into a pan and began frying. If Liz never showed up I would have been happy to eat both of them.

And then I heard her shriek.

I killed the burner, ran down the porch steps. Burst into her place.

She had her back against the far wall. Hand over her mouth. Shaking.

"What happened??"

She said nothing, just pointed to an open letter on her desk. Beside it was a plain envelope with no stamp or postmark, addressed to THE FUTURE MRS. MILTON. I picked up the letter and read:

Pestering Milton has gotten stale, so now it is your turn.
Thank you a head of time for a greeing to be my published voice. Your news paper the Los Angeles Herald will print the letters I send you while you travel with the Dodgers team on their next trip. For every letter that is not printed, there will be a fresh killing.
This I can promise.

"What the hell does he want?"

"I don't know, Liz. Other than to create terror."

"But why me??"

"Because you're with me, I would think."

"Oh God...he's been following us!"

"And probably because of your newspaper connection."

"What connection?? They booted me off the staff, remember?"

"It doesn't matter now. Trust me. Call your editor back, read him this letter, and they'll put you in the Dodgers press box in thirty seconds."

The Bronx Bugle Sporting Life

| SALUTE THE FLAG | Monday, July 21, 1958 | DRINK MOXIE NIGHTLY |

Bombers Fly West on Pennant Mission

by Archie Stripes
American League Beat

Our Yankees are off to Detroit, riding the clouds on a fat nine-game cushion, and the junior circuit will be hard pressed to provide meaningful ball news for the last two months of the campaign.

"They're all good clubs out there," said Casey Stengel before he climbed the steps of the team's chartered plane. "Ain't no dog in the pound. Get Cerv or Colavito or that Kaline kid on a hot streak and who knows what and then some. I could tell you Boston'll stop hitting one of these days except I can't do that because they probably won't. All you can do is freeze as many steaks as you can in case September's a hot month and your whole supply melts, and then it's you that's cooked instead and Ted Williams is standing over your carcass with a big bottle of A-1 Sauce."

With his deep pitching staff and crack bench, Casey's gang can never be counted out of a game. For that reason, baseball

GRAND OLD BRIGGS STADIUM, DETROIT

wags are stumbling over their Smith-Coronas lately to predict another Braves-Yankees World Series, but in the far more interesting and meaningful National League, the race isn't close to being decided.

Milwaukee is finally playing like the defending champs they are, but the Giants, Cubs and even the Phillies are all capable of a late run. The upcoming County Stadium series between the Giants and Braves beginning August 1st should be a rip-snorter, and I will do my best to provide you with a firsthand account.

Girl Reporter to be Peanut Killer "Ghost Writer"

SAN FRANCISCO (UPI)—Following the shocking murder of "Peanut Killer" suspect Xavier Chitwood late Friday night, a fledgling *Los Angeles Herald* girl columnist named Liz Dumas has been apparently chosen by the still-at-large real killer to receive and publish his letters while she travels with the L.A. Dodgers on their just-launched road trip.

"Naturally we're concerned for Miss Dumas' safety and the FBI will take every precaution," said Herald publisher George Hearst, "But no newspaper on earth can resist a story this entertaining." Miss Dumas' beau and recent person of interest in the case Milton "Snappy" Drake, would not comment.

≈ *Traveling Circus Begins* ≈

July 22, 1958

So with the blessings of the FBI, Walter O'Malley, and the Hearst family, Liz was suddenly the new "personality columnist" in the *Herald*'s baseball section. What a circus. Fans knew about it, and the players were fighting over who would get to flirt with her, all while Brewster and the feds were trying to keep her on 24-hour guard.

And yet they couldn't. The Peanut Killer wanted his letters printed, so somehow they had to get to her. Brewster, of course, was livid that the *Herald* had leaked the whole setup to the public, though if they hadn't, our murderous, attention-loving friend probably would have done it himself.

Liz flew to Pittsburgh this morning, and was pretty torn up about it. Back when I first met her, she was getting her *Herald* feet wet as a celebrity grandstand sighter for the "Gaddy's Gadabouts" column, but this was much bigger. This was a career break that could put her on the national map. It was also creepy and dangerous, and would take gobs of time away from her novel—which she decided to bring along for "good luck and idle moments."

Plus there was this other problem.

"Explain to me why you can't come along."

"Brewster's orders, baby. And I get it. With the killer threatening to rub out more victims, he doesn't want us doing anything that might upset the psycho even more."

"But wouldn't the psycho want this? I thought you were his personal obsession or something."

"I was. Until the letter to you arrived."

"I'm scared, Snap. I'm not sure I can go through this alone."

"You're hardly going to be alone. And didn't you drive to that woman's writer camp in everlovin' Iowa by yourself? To me that place looked a lot more scary." She started to jab my arm, turned it into a desperate hug. "You'll be fine, Liz. I'll call you as often as I can."

In the meantime, like most people I planned to be all over the *Herald*'s morning editions like flies on a cow.

For the first game of their trip I followed the score by listening to the Giants' battle in Philly. Man alive, those Phillies were tough. Errors by Jones and Ashburn helped us to an early 4-1 lead, but Gomez was in boiling oil every inning till the 8th, when Jones and Giel ladled him out of a two-out, second and third jam. Cepeda doubled and singled and drove in three, to add to his team-high 63 RBIs. It was also nice to rough up Curt Simmons, a crafty lefty who shut us down on our last trip there.

Russ Hodges didn't bring up the Peanut Killer once on the broadcast, but was certainly aware of audience interest because he gave a Dodgers update practically every inning. They scored five times for Drysdale early, but as usual, their bullpen and defense plain evaporated. Forbes Field, site of the last fan murder, was apparently packed to the gills and sprinkled with over 100 cops.

About a half hour after the game ended, Liz called. She didn't sound too good. The first letter had somehow arrived in the Forbes Field press box, sent special delivery from Topeka, Kansas. It took some doing for me to calm her down enough to read it over the phone.

There once was a writer named Liz
Who everyone said was a whiz
She did favors for a killer
Provided good filler
Till some poor fan's life went kafizz

"Great," I said, "So the jerk is going to kill somebody anyway? Then what's the point of doing this?"

"He isn't well, Snap. I think it's hard for him not to kill. Brewster told me all we can do is follow along until he slips up on the other end. Unfortunately, no one in Topeka remembered seeing him. He dropped it in a mailbox there days ago."

One thing was clear to me, though. When this thing got published in the

morning, Forbes Field attendance would be dropping for the next game.

Mission Statement

July 23th

I was wrong. Instead of Pirates fans being scared off in droves by the Peanut Killer's published limerick, even more showed up at Forbes Field the next night. Maybe with the hope of being the one to actually catch the lowlife.

Me? Just another boisterous evening at the Double Play, watching the Giants barely outlast the Phillies again at Connie Mack Stadium. With Warren Spahn putting the Cards away in Milwaukee, we stayed a tight game and a half out of first and the saloon's giddy tension mirrored this. Like Liz, Bob and Chumpo thought I should've gone back east.

"I kind of liked you playing Nick Testa," said Bob, "Except you should've pestered Rigney to let you bat."

"Couldn't have done worse than them two lummoxes we got behind the plate now," offered Chumpo, wiping his nose with the bar rag I was praying he'd retire.

"I'm a pitcher, remember?"

"You was a pitcher. And that don't mean you gotta hit like one. Didn't Spahn go deep tonight?"

Indeed he did. But even just being

a bullpen catcher on their last trip was grueling. Despite Liz's ordeal, I'd been looking forward to a nice few weeks following the pennant race from afar—with nothing but some cold ones.

After the game ended (along with my fifth cold one), I meandered back through the Mission District to my apartment. Just in time to hear the phone ringing. Oh boy, I thought, maybe Liz could lull me to sleep with tomorrow's creepy limerick.

I entered and grabbed the receiver. Didn't hear anything right away.

"Liz?"

"Surprise surprise, Milton."

Blood rushed up my neck, filled my head. I was sober in an instant.

"You again."

"What's wrong, Milton? Thought I would let Mrs. Drake have all the fun?"

"Stop calling her that."

"Oh, I'll call her anything I feel like. Seeing she's working for ME now."

"How the hell did you get to Chitwood at Livermore?"

"Hmm…How did *you*? It appears we use our heads in a similar creative fashion, Milton. See, there's always custodial work available in most institutions."

And then I remembered: the "janitor" who was mopping up that I briefly collided with outside Chitwood's visiting room.

"How's Kansas, you bastard?"

"Old news. These days it makes more sense for me to keep moving, right?"

"So where you headed now?"

"You expect me to tell you that?"

"Sure. So I can meet you and grind your nose into your skull."

He sighed. "Still a malicious brute after all these years…This letter-publishing business is great fun, Milton, but I'm not sure it'll achieve the outcome I'm looking for."

"Which is what?"

There was a long pause. I swear I heard a seagull cry, from outside whatever open phone booth he was standing in.

"Heroes depart…and hearts are forever crushed."

"Excuse me?"

Another long pause. "The Giants and Dodgers leaving New York was a horrible crime, punishable by many deaths. There is no doubt about that. But right now I am less concerned about the Los Angeles team. It seems obvious they are lacking enough hitting, pitching and fielding to make a serious run at the flag. The Giants are another story. They are red-hot this month, challenging Milwaukee. I cannot sleep at nights thinking about this. You are their employee, Milton, so you need to help prevent more of our hearts from being crushed."

"What in god's name are you—"

"Do whatever you must do to stop this from happening, Milton. And tell no one. If the Giants win the National League pennant I can't begin to count the number of bodies that will be found in their wake. Beginning with your favorite lady."

CLICK. I held the receiver in the air a few moments, gently set it back in its cradle. In a rush, the very first note found in the pocket of John Blaziecsky in section 16 on Opening Day became crystal clear to me.

a band on

The Peanut Killer tended to not glue some of his words together. And I bet if we ever found the second half of that torn note, the whole thing would read "abandon and die."

Snap Decision

July 24th

I was knocking on Stoneham's door before he even had his first scotch of the day. I asked him to get Brewster on the phone from Pittsburgh, and then laid out my latest scheme.

"He may be messin' around with Liz now, but I'll bet you nickels to nicotine he's doing this to drive me nuts."

"We're aware of this possibility," said Bewster in his usual velvety know-it-all-tone.

"Well, while we're waiting around for you to do something about that, how about I take the lead? Both the Dodgers and Giants are visiting the same cities on this trip, right? Philly, Pittsburgh, Cincy, Milwaukee, Chicago and St. Louis. Usually playing pretty close to each other. If I do my Nick Testa bullpen catcher act again,

there's a good shot it'll drive Peanut Man a little batty."

"Distracted, at least. Between two places at once."

"Right. Which will make him more likely to slip up."

Stoneham puffed his lips. "The boys on the team better not be distracted. Look how lousy the Dodgers are playing. We got a pennant to win here!"

"Er, the boys on your team didn't want me to leave last time, remember? When do you think they started playing better?"

The owner muttered something foul. He knew damn well I was right. Brewster less so.

"I am a bit concerned about splitting my men between the two of you."

"So don't. Stick a few in the stands near the bullpen and one in every hotel the Giants stay in. I can handle myself."

"You didn't do too well last time, from what I heard," said Stoneham.

"I'm a fast learner. And Billy Frack is back in his car shop."

They agreed to let me join the club on Saturday in Pittsburgh, but Rigney must've gotten wind of it because he called me later at home. I could just about smell the cigarette smoke in his voice.

"Grab the first plane tomorrow morning, son. The Phillies just waxed our behinds and used them to ski home."

I wasn't completely upset about this fact—but wasn't about to tell him why.

Two-Timing

July 25th

At least Antonelli was glad to see me. Shook my hand with his non-pitching one and insisted I warm him up in the Forbes Field bullpen. I'd become his accidental good luck charm, you see. Ever since I got him limber in Philly last month, he'd been pitching like a champ and the Giants had hopped back into the pennant race.

Johnny threw another gem tonight, but by the time we boarded the team bus to the hotel, it was the hitters who didn't want to look at me. Against a journeyman named Bob Porterfield—with the help of Roy Face's 16th save—we couldn't score a run to save each other's lives. We hit into three DPs, left ten on the bases and sent all 22,000 fans of the suddenly scorching Pirates home with a happy, hot glow.

The good news was that I barely watched any of it. Brewster had set up a special phone line to the Dodger press row across the state at Connie Mack Stadium so I could talk to Liz every other inning. What we talked about wasn't important; the idea was for the Peanut Killer to *see* one of us talking and get flustered about it. Assuming he was around, of course.

"I hate being the only female up here," said Liz. "Sportswriters are perverted drunken louts. I'm like a walking gas station pinup calendar."

"How are the Dodgers doing?"

"You have to ask? Look at the scoreboard."

I turned and did. It was 2-0 Phillies after seven.

"Sure you can't come visit me after the game?"

"Pittsburgh's 250 miles away, Liz. Not exactly around the corner." The line got quiet. I could practically hear her pout. "So no strange letters yet?" I asked.

"Not tonight. Haven't been any for a few days, actually. Makes me think he's planning something new. Do you see him in the stands over there?"

"I still haven't gotten a good look at his ugly puss, remember? And it's awful crowded. If he was here I probably wouldn't know. "

"This is nerve-wracking."

"Just hang in there, baby. It's only a matter of time before he slips up on this trip."

"I was talking about the jerky writers."

"Oh. Well, just tell them your boyfriend will rearrange their jawlines if they don't cut it out."

"Thanks…Except my boyfriend needs to be here to do that."

Bob Schmidt chucked a couple ice cubes at me. "Hey Testa! Go warm Grissom up!"

"Dang it. Gotta go."

"Thinking about ya, Snap…"

"Yeah. Ditto."

Grissom never even got in the game and we lost 2-0. When I got back to my room I ordered a couple of room service beers. I took the tray from the teenage waiter and stared at it.

Someone had stuck a folded-up note to the bottom of the empty glass when the waiter wasn't looking. After I grilled the kid I dropped two quarters in his hand, waited for him to leave and opened the note:

The Braves lost today too. Which is not good. And the Giants put way more runners on base than they had a right to. Get a little more serious about helping them lose, Milton. Or you know what.

Ripped Asunder

July 26th

Ray Crone walked over to me after the first inning. The Pirates had just scored three times off Gomez on a leadoff Clemente triple, two singles, two walks and a passed ball.

"We took a vote, Dresta. You need to go sit in the dugout."

Dresta was my new nickname, artfully combining Drake and Testa. At the moment, though, I didn't care one dew drop about cleverness.

"And you guys need to relax. Don't you see Bob Friend out there? The man's given up like 450 hits this year." (Actually it was 164, but in only 133 innings.)

Baseball players are way too superstitious. I was certainly one of them in my minor league days, but now that I was just moonlighting with the Giants for suspect pursuit reasons, that

kind of mania was bugging me.

We got one run back in the 3rd, but they got it right back on a Bob Skinner triple and wild pitch. The game in Milwaukee against the Cubs didn't start for another half hour, and I was already nervous. Who knew what would happen to Liz or some poor slob if we crept to within half a game of first?

And then Friend did what he's famous for, dishing out hits like Christmas stocking stuffers. A ringing Cepeda double and four singles gave us two runs in the 4th, and after Cepeda wiped Mays off the bases with a DP in the 5th, King, Davenport and Kirkland all singled to tie the game and send Friend to his friendly shower.

"Never mind, Dresta!" yelled Crone from the other end of the bullpen bench. I shook my head and leaned back to chew a fresh stick of Doublemint. Would've checked in with Liz at the Dodgers-Phillies game again, but they were playing at night and to be honest, we didn't have much to say to each other that didn't frustrate the two of us.

On the scoreboard, the Braves had a 1-0 lead on the Cubs through three, which calmed me a bit. Gomez then lost it altogether, giving the Bucs four runs in the 5th on four singles, three walks, and a sac fly. I didn't know where these Pirates had been the last two months, but they were sure back now.

"Dresta! Skedaddle! Scoot!!"

"Live with it, Ray!"

The six-foot-two Tennessean got to his feet and ambled over. Spit a jet of tobacco juice a few inches from my cleats.

"I don't get to pitch a lot around here. But one thing I got plenty of time for is keeping my bullpen brothers happy. Now I won a World Series last season with Milwaukee, so I know a thing or two or three about team happiness."

"I ain't moving."

"No need to. 'Cause if you don't get your fanny into the dugout after this inning, I'll just pick you up by your ears and put you there myself."

I peered around him. Grissom was being warmed up by Schmidt, but every other pitcher in the pen was giving me the aggravated eye. I grabbed my mitt and trudged down to the dugout. Told Rigney I had a bit of a cold and it was too drafty out there. The game was in serious jeopardy so he had other things to worry about. On the scoreboard, the Cubs tied it up and the Braves went back ahead 2-1 with Rush on the hill. All seemed safe for the time being.

Grissom threw two perfect relief innings and even Ray Crone had one. Ron Blackburn, who had bailed out Friend earlier, took the ball again to begin the 9th. Bressoud led with a sharp single. Mays walked. Cepeda singled and Gross came on to face the lefty King. Rigney put righty Hank Sauer in and he doubled down the line to make it 8-6. Davenport singled and it was 8-7.

The crowd was howling for blood. I was sweating more than them. Kirkland finally made the first out, but Thomas singled and so did pinch-hitter Alou and we had the lead!

"I knew it, Dresta! I knew we could do it!" It was Crone, pounding my back after he joined us in the dugout. When Bressoud singled again and Mays launched a grand slam into orbit, trash flew out of the upper decks. I did my best to look thrilled when Mays returned to the celebrating dugout, but I was ripped in all directions. We scored nine times in the 9th, racked up 23 hits, but at least the Braves would win. Right?

"Cubs got three in the 8th and won! Yahoo!" Crone yelled later, running through the shower with his uniform still on.

Good god. We were only a half game out of first. I tried dialing Liz in Philly but she wasn't in the press box yet.

I'd be calling every hour until she was.

Cruel Twist

July 27th

After our nine-run, 9th inning sap to the side of the Pirates' head yesterday, I was offered practically every non-playing job on the team other than Bill Rigney's. I invented something called Bat Rack Custodian, which was to make sure the batboy in each park put everyone's lumber in the right slots. The last thing I wanted to do was take Johnny Heep's job. Our clubhouse assistant worked his tail off for us and was a great kid.

There was nothing murder-related in the Philly or Pittsburgh papers this morning. No word from Brewster on a killer-written poem in the *Herald*. More troubling, no peep whatsoever from Liz. And she still wasn't answering her phones.

"Do your job, Brewster. Look for her!"

"Way ahead of you, Drake. She just left her hotel and is on her way to Connie Mack."

Which only confused me more...

We had to wrap up our Forbes business with a double-header in swampy heat before heading to Cincy. Lousy Mike McCormick started Game 1, and after he gave up a Frank Thomas homer in the 3rd to put us behind 3-0, the team figured it was because I hadn't been out in the pen to warm him up. Mays in particular was chatting up the dugout, rubbing his bat handle on the side of my face before he started the 4th.

With a single, naturally. And Cepeda doubled, and Thomas booted one, and a walk, and a sac fly and a double by McCormick and a three-run homer by Daryl Spencer later off Kline and shazam! We had six runs. Spahn would be taking the hill in Milwaukee soon. If he had a bad day we might even be in first place, and then what?

Praise the heavens for Mike Mc-Cormick. A Maz single and Hank Foiles bomb right after our big rally knocked him out. But Giel and Jones threw 5-hit shutout ball the rest of the game, and we took the opener by one run. Thankfully, the Braves got three runs against Moe Drabowsky in the 1st inning.

I reached the Connie Mack press box between games, was told Liz was there but "too busy" to come to the phone. Then Ramon Monzant took the hill for our nightcap and shut the pesky Bucs down like a butcher locking flies in his freezer. They whiffed eight times, made three errors, Mays homered after rubbing his bat handle up my backside, and we rolled them.

The club was practically petting me like a furry mascot, but all I wanted to do the whole game was keep calling Liz. I swear, somebody needed to invent a little telephone you could just walk around with in your pocket.

Spahn barely eked out his win at County Stadium, so we tied the Braves for first, just points behind them. I did my best to seem happy about this during the steak dinner and beers that were bought for me afterwards, but it was a struggle. A drunk Jim Davenport kept whispering in my ear he was going to start a coup and get me Rigney's job "if the old man messes up even once".

In a beer-induced stupor around 1 a.m., I woke to a creaking floor. Sat up, eyes focused on the darkness. Was it in my room? In the hall?

It creaked again. Then there was a knock.

"Hello?" I said.

I climbed out of bed. I had no weapon, but grabbed a heavy aluminum ice bucket to cold-cock the possible intruder with. Crept my way to the door. Silently undid the latch. Curled my sweaty hand around the door handle and yanked it open.

A shaking, half-crazy Liz fell into my arms.

"You've GOT to go to Milwaukee with me! PLEASE!!!"

I pulled her into the room, shut the door. Shook her some more until she spoke.

"He got me alone...in the elevator..."

"At the ballpark?"

"In my hotel...Said he just killed someone..."

"What?? WHO?"

"Said there'd be more...lots more..."

She was clutching something in her coat pocket. I pulled out her hand. It was wrapped tightly around four sealed envelopes, marked with different days of the week.

"The next things we have to print..." She dropped them on the floor and collapsed on my bed.

I didn't dare open or even touch them. That was for the FBI fingerprint men. By morning I would hear about the one Liz didn't have with her. The one that was already printed in the *Herald*:

How cruel is life?
With its salty twists and turns?

When loyalty is dumped
Like morning trash
As if it were last night's ash

And then I saw the morning paper in our lobby. Rudy Creech, 45-year-old vendor on the streets outside Connie Mack, had been found dead. His battered head roasting inside the flame on his hot pretzel wagon.

Knaves of the Keyboard

July 29th

So it was me and Liz, rooming together at the creepy Hotel Pfister in Milwaukee. Telling her about my last shaky visit and the place's haunted rumors would have been a big mistake, though. There's a whole binder full of women in the world that can do without added nervousness.

The Giants weren't too keen on me departing the club again, but Brewster approved. Provided us a private escort of federal lawmen all the way into County Stadium.

And then we reached the press box.

"Whoa! Look who the cat dragged in!"

"Should we go load our guns?"

"Keep him away from our dope sheets, he's a Giants man!"

It was the Dodger writers doing the mouthing. I didn't know any of the Milwaukee scribes, and the only Dodger one whose name I recognized was Frank Finch, the hard-working, often hilarious beat man for the *Times*. After their warm welcome, though, I had no desire to shake any of their hands.

Liz had filed a few stories about how she received the killer's cryptic letters (and how she felt about this as a woman), but when the first one didn't create boffo ad sales for the paper, the next few were buried in the "Dodgerisms" column. The Philly pretzel vendor killing changed that again, but Liz and I

The Bronx Bugle Sporting Life

| PLEDGE ALLEGIANCE TO THE FLAG | Monday, July 28, 1958 | DRINK RHEINGOLD BEER |

N.L. Update: Of Giants And Lesser Men

by Archie Stripes
American League Beat

With the American League flag race providing as much excitement as a church pie sale these days, it was time for this scribe to take leave of said league and focus on some bona fide suspense. Namely, the recently christened San Francisco Giants.

I reached manager Bill Rigney by phone after his club had drubbed the hard-fighting Buccos twice on a Pittsburgh Sunday. The 40-year-old Californian and ex-infielder has done a yeoman's job of skippering, especially taking into account the ghastly murder case shadowing the team wherever they travel (See accompanying telewire story).

"Mr Stoneham has been vocal about this all year, and I tend to agree with him," said Rigney, "We have a pennant to win. The players are too busy trying to hit curveballs to worry about what some disturbed fool might do next."

Their recent play has been anything but distracted, a fierce 19–6 in July. Rookie Orlando

Cepeda leads the club with 67 runs batted in and after a slow spring has upped his average to .311. Willie Mays has been his usual excellent self, with his batting mark climbing to .354.

"You don't think I leave the park every night looking over my shoulder? Of course I do. So

do the players. But you can also walk down a sidewalk and have a tree trunk fall on your head."

The murder case certainly hasn't dampened the local fans' spirits. Seals Stadium only seats around 23,000, but owner Stoneham reports that the park has been 80% filled most days. With the FBI announcing a substantial reward for information leading to the killer's arrest, it's been said that many Giants rooters are clamoring to "cash in."

"Leon Wagner told me he'd take his bat to the guy's head if he catches him," said Rigney, The boy's got gumption, but I told him to just worry about Bob Purkey's fastball for now."

No Clues Yet in Pretzel Vendor Slaying

PHILADELPHIA (UPI)— Police in this city are baffled over the Sunday evening murder of 45-year-old Rudy Creech, a likeable Lehigh Avenue pretzel vendor outside of Connie Mack Stadium.

Early speculation was that the killing may be the work of San Francisco's notorious "Peanut Killer," even though only salt and mustard drops were found on the victim's body.

Liz Dumas, gossip and crime columnist for the *Los Angeles Herald*, has been in town with the Dodgers team, and a poem printed in her newspaper the next morning contained the line "salty twists and turns."

Milton Drake, the San Francisco usher once thought to be linked to the crimes, seemed to be out of town and could not be reached for comment both agreed the advance letters she'd gotten should be opened one a day as instructed. We'd had enough victims for the time being.

County Stadium was rocking and rolling. Even more so after four hits off Stan Williams gave the home folks a quick 2-0 lead. But Walt Alston had tinkered with the Dodgers lineup big time, and it paid off. A homer by new cleanup man Snider and run-scoring double by new second hitter Norm Larker tied it up by the 3rd.

On the scoreboard, the Giants were also coming back from an early 2-0 deficit at Crosley Field. Other than following the away action, I didn't have much to do but sit beside Liz and give reporters who tried to flirt with her dirty looks. A lady reporter up there was like a doe in a den of mountain lions. Even a 14-year old press box ruffian dropped his pencil a few times when he passed behind her chair. She spent most of the night scoring the game so she wouldn't have to look at anyone. After a while, I feared for her sanity.

Then the Dodgers exploded against Lew Burdette in the 8th. A single, walk and Snider triple broke the tie, and Roseboro greeted Bob Trowbridge with a shot into the right field bleachers. This got the Milwaukee writers aggravated, and one barked out that it was "time for that girl to go cook us a late dinner." I stood, tried to see who said this but there was so much cigar and cigarette smoke in the air it was hard to see five yards away.

Stan Williams, who had issued 79 walks in 115 innings coming in, didn't walk one Brave and retired 23 in a row at one point. With the Giants crushing the Reds in Cincy by a similar score, my team was suddenly back in first place! It was a relief they'd found a way to win without me, but dread over how the Peanut Killer would react ruined the rest of my night. To complicate things even more, a note was waiting for me at the front desk when we got back to the hotel.

But this one was on L.A. Dodgers stationery:

> *Stick around, kid.*
> *—Duke Snider*

Swooning to the Crooning

July 30th

"I don't care if he's the Duke of Flatbush or Windsor, you're staying with me in the press box."

Liz's response was what I predicted, and I didn't blame her, even though the Peanut Killer's latest published passage was more bizarre and harmless than the others:

> *Summer's moon on the wane*
> *And no threat of rain*
> *A rocky field of grain*
> *Is a neighbor to pain*

"He can rhyme from now till doomsday," I said over toast and eggs at the Pfister in the morning, "Long as he keeps his peanuts in his pants."

The Dodgers had another night game in Milwaukee, so Liz and me had a nice day strolling the big lake, Kosciusko Park, and the incredible Basilica of St Josaphat in Lincoln Village. The church was cavernous and half-empty, every footstep behind us echoed, and there were plenty of nooks inside crannies for someone to watch us from. Liz was handling this press box deal pretty well, but I was still nervous about leaving her alone for more than an inning.

My presence seemed to give the Dodgers crazy luck again. Joey Jay walked Larker, Snider and Roseboro in the top of the 1st and Dick Gray cleaned off the bases with a line drive grand slam. The Braves chipped back against Podres, but the most dependable fireman other than Roy Face—Roger Craig—came on with the bases stuffed in the 6th to shut them down on one hit the rest of the way.

More Jay wildness in the 7th and a horrible two-base error from Logan later, the Dodgers won the game on only four hits. Another note from Duke Snider was slipped to me, this time inviting me to after-game beers at an old saloon called Kneisler's White House. I was going to invite Liz along but she had a headache and was no doubt tired of being in rooms full of men.

It took a while for me to escort her back to the hotel and into her room. Then I had to think of an excuse to leave again ("need to track down some cigarettes"). By the time I finally got to Kneisler's, all of the Dodger players had come and gone except Don Zimmer, their chunky little shortstop. And I had no idea what to say to that guy.

I found a seat at the far end of the bar and ordered a draft. It was cold and delicious and went straight to my head. So did the next one. I heard the bartender mention to someone that Antonelli and the Giants had lost badly. It shouldn't have helped my mood, but it did.

And then I heard a song in the air. The bar had an old juke box in the corner, and Bing Crosby's rendition of "June in January" was suddenly playing. The music swirled with the lager in my brain. I felt woozy. Buried images, snapshot memories. Clawing their way to the surface. *A white room. A distant water tower. Crosby's crooning voice drifting up a long hallway with a polished floor...*

There may have been a lot more, but I don't remember. By then I was losing my balance, falling off the bar stool and hitting my head on the tavern's floor.

Das Blatzkrieg

July 31st

"What does Bing Crosby have to do with anything?"

I couldn't even answer her. Liz had to come fetch me from a local emergency room after midnight, and despite a big ugly bandage where I gashed my head on Kniesler's saloon floor, she wasn't the kindest of morning nurses.

"I don't know about you, Snap. If I left you in a church you'd fall out of the choir balcony."

The Peanut Killer's morning dispatch had been another incomprehensible limerick, and Liz had to get to County Stadium early for the matinee finale. I chose to stay at the hotel, tend to my scalp with ice and watch the game on television.

It was a good idea. They had Blatz Beer on the room service menu. The TV reception wasn't great, but I smacked the rabbit ears around until Don Drysdale didn't look like the creature from the black lagoon.

Unfortunately, he was pitching like him. Torre doubled and Mathews homered in the 4th, and the Braves put six straight people on base off him and Ed Roebuck in the 6th to put the easy win away. Meanwhile, after whacking away on Burdette and Jay for two nights, Carl Willey had the Dodgers' number. Fairly and Snider homered late, but L.A. ran out of outs. At least I wouldn't be getting any after-dinner invite this time from the Duke.

Liz would be heading to Cincy later and after the Giants finished their last game there (they were getting hammered again, 8-1 the last time I checked), they'd be on their way to Wisconsin for the weekend. So I definitely had some time to kill at the old Pfister. I had three Blatzes in me, and

didn't even feel my gash anymore.

Coming back from the bathroom I happened to walk past the room's writing desk, where I noticed a nondescript cardboard box sitting there. I had an idea what was inside, and pried off the top.

It was the manuscript for Liz's novel, the one she was working on at that women's writing camp in Iowa that I rescued her from. It was called *Wool Over Their Eyes*, "a novel of suspense by Liz Dumás", and there were at least 400 typewritten pages so far.

I read the first line:

Clara was angry enough to skin a dog alive.

And was instantly hooked. I was also pretty Blatzed, so sat on the bed and got into the rhythm of the thing pretty quick.

It also began to disturb me. The lead character was a female killer whose father abandoned her. Let's just say she had many axes to grind against many men, and used an axe on most of them. She toured the country collecting bodies, getting away with every murder through her looks and charm and the fact that no one would suspect someone like her.

There was even a stooge of a steady boyfriend named Melvin, who happened to be an usher at a movie theater.

I ordered one more beer from room service and began to think. What was I doing sharing a room with this woman? What if SHE was the Peanut Killer, racking up victims like the girl in her book? Maybe the guy I encountered a few times on the phone and in shadows was her accomplice!

All I know is that I read all 400 pages in one sitting. Got so wrapped up in it that the ballgame ended and a polka show called *Dairyland Jubilee* was on the next time I looked at the TV.

And then Liz rushed in, out-of-breath, and started packing.

"Got your stuff ready? Press bus leaves for the airport in twenty minutes."

She looked over and saw her manuscript pages, turned over and strewn on the bed.

"Oh…You read it."

"Damn right I did."

"Why are you looking at me like that?"

"Like what? A little paranoid? Maybe, yeah."

She walked over, started collecting the pages.

"You should have told me you were going to do this."

"And maybe you should have told me you were going to write your murderous life story."

She walked the pages over to the desk. Turned and just glared at me.

"Ever hear of the word 'fiction', Snap?"

"Sure. And do you know any ushers named Melvin?"

"No, but I know one named Milton who's being a first class jerk."

I wobbled to my feet. She stuffed her manuscript back in the box. Dropped it into her open suitcase. Picking up speed as she went.

"Maybe this was a bad idea. Counting on you to watch over me…"

"How do you think I feel? Sleeping in the same bed with someone who fantasizes about collecting man-corpses!"

"ARE YOU CRAZY? It's a book! A novel! How do I know the killer isn't YOU? You're the one who's always stumbling over the dumb bodies, right? 'Blacking out' every chance you can get—"

"Take that back, Liz."

"No way. And guess what? I'm taking my life back."

"Which is what? Traveling around with a bunch of press box creeps?"

"It's a gig, whether I like it or not. And creeps come in all sizes and shapes, Snappy."

She clamped her suitcase shut and carted it to the door. I tried to go after her but tripped on the carpet and fell like a fool. All I could think about while I lay there and she slammed the door after herself was how good it would feel just to be warming up Johnny Antonelli again. Which said a lot.

National League thru Thursday, July 31

Milwaukee	54	45	.545	—
San Francisco	55	46	.545	—
Chicago	53	49	.520	2.5
Philadelphia	50	48	.510	3.5
St. Louis	47	50	.485	6
Los Angeles	48	52	.480	6.5
Pittsburgh	48	52	.480	6.5
Cincinnati	44	57	.436	11

American League thru Thursday, July 31

New York	68	35	.660	—
Boston	56	44	.560	10.5
Baltimore	56	46	.549	11.5
Chicago	55	48	.534	13
Detroit	51	50	.505	15
Cleveland	52	51	.505	15
Kansas City	39	62	.386	28
Washington	31	72	.301	37

Wake Up and Smell the Curve Balls

August 1st

Four games in three days with the Braves, the Milwaukee mashers just percentage particles in front of us. Meaning for two or three hours Friday, Saturday, and six on Sunday, I had less space in my life for diabolical killers, angry girlfriends or booze-induced headaches. It was serious baseball time.

Spent the first half hour warming up Al Worthington before we faced Spahn in the big opener. The County Stadium parking lot was stuffed with people cooking kielbasas, and the smell was wafting over the outfield walls and making our bullpen brigade batty. Worthington is a good ol' Alabama boy turning 30 next year who came up with the Giants when they were in New York and earned a spot in the rotation with his decent work. Thought he was going to break for the lot and stab a sausage between every warmup he threw.

The team was jazzed up to see me again and gave me a choice spot to watch the game in the middle of the dugout. When Davenport doubled and Mays waited on a Spahn curve and drove it high and deep and into

Kielbasaville in the 1st, I was even allowed to shake Willie's hand in the subsequent mob scene.

Worthington allowed a double to Torre and two singles to make it 2-1, and after Alou creamed another slow gopher out of the yard in the 5th we were up 3-1 and first place looked very possible again.

Except they don't call these players Braves for nothing. Spahn smashed his own homer soon after, and after a walk and Covington double, Paul Giel relieved to face lefty Bruton—who singled to tie the game.

It was a warm night when we started but as the barbeques died, cold Canadian air shot across the field and into our faces. The mood changed with it. Mathews hit one over the fence in right with two gone in the 7th that Alou managed to leap and bring back. We cheered the play but had only ten seconds to enjoy it before Aaron lined one way over the bleachers in left. 4-3 Braves.

Spahn was dealing now, smelling his eight straight victory, and Rigney strolled through the dugout to reinvigorate the troops. It may have worked. Cepeda led off the 9th with a double but Valmy Thomas whiffed for the third time. Spahn had a knack for giving up untimely hits, though, and Daryl Spencer took him up the middle to tie the game! Win or lose, cold extra innings, were not on anyone's wish list.

No need to worry. Marv Grissom took our hill and Eddie Mathews ended things minutes later the way he did against the Pirates on Opening Day: with a leadoff game-winning homer.

The team trudged into the locker room, and as usual, I had to play along with the outrage and depression. As much as I wanted to, how could I tell any of them that because they lost, at least no one would be murdered that night?

The Post-Game Spill

August 2nd

So the Giants banished me to the bullpen again after last night's loss. Mike McCormick didn't even want me to warm him up, but the guy's been so unreliable he didn't have a cleat to stand on.

Agent Brewster had tried calling me at the hotel, but I wasn't answering the phone. If there was a break in the case or another murder, I'm sure I would've seen it in the *Milwaukee Sentinel*. Hadn't heard from Liz, either, since our blow-up on Thursday, but wasn't too surprised. Me suspecting her followed by her suspecting me was a sign of how silly and desperate we were all getting for a solution. Here I was thinking having both of us on the road would mess up the killer's head, when it was suddenly the other way around.

Meanwhile, my half hour squat in

front of McCormick gave him a full afternoon of Irish luck. All he allowed the first three innings were three scattered singles, while we were busy knocking Lew Burdette around. With two gone in the 1st, Wagner, Mays, and Cepeda all singled and Davenport lined a double down the line for a 2-0 lead. A run-scoring Spencer triple and boot by the usually spotless Frank Torre at first made it 4-0.

McCormick began putting more guys on but four double plays bailed him out, and by the time we racked up three more digits on Juan Pizarro in the 9th, a third of the once-chirpy Braves fans had headed home to their wigwams and we were tied for first with them once more. Everyone in the league had a doubleheader to play tomorrow, and if Antonelli was on his game, we could have a two-game lead before heading to Chicago.

Naturally this concerned me, and I had to fake my elation again in the locker room. Beers and roast goose at Karl Ratzsch's were on the evening agenda. "I don't drink," said Willie Mays to me as we were about to head out, "so you can drink all four of mine."

Suddenly...

"HEY! WHAT THE HELL??" yelled someone in the far corner of the locker room. It was our backup backup rookie outfielder Don Taussig. Don never played, so liked to keep his uniform on as long as possible and was always the last to dress. He was

standing there in front of his just-opened locker, mouth agape.

Someone had filled the thing top to bottom with peanuts, and they had spilled onto the clubhouse floor and covered his baseball shoes like blood out of a slaughtered pig.

Dinner at Karl Ratzsch's would be delayed.

Toil and Trouble

August 3rd

Some days are so bad you wish they were phonograph records, so you could just pick up the needle and drop it back at the beginning.

Don Taussig's locker was one big peanut party, and the thing became a crime scene for half the night. Every County Stadium worker, from senior ushers down to teenage kids selling Braves Booster badges, was either questioned or grilled by the FBI. The back door to our clubhouse had been mistakenly left open by an after-game caterer, but no one had seen anyone enter with a carton of peanut bags.

Salty Dog peanuts, I should add.

"No foul play reported here or in Cincinnati," said Brewster this morning over weak coffee at the hotel, "It had to be a warning of some kind, right?"

I shrugged, lit a Camel. "You got me. His daily jabberings are being published on schedule, right? What was today's?"

Brewster flipped open his little spiral notebook and attempted a dramatic reading:

Whippoorwills and fireflies
That's where it begins
Skeets and moths and fastballs
The worst of many sins

Brewster snorted when he finished. "Sounds like some kind of nature deviant."

"Forget handwriting analysis. You need to hire a bad poetry professor."

"We could do without your sarcasm, Drake."

"And I can do without the Bureau turning every ballpark into a Spanish inquisition. We got a pennant to win."

It felt good saying that, Horace Stoneham's favorite line, but the irony was lost on my square-jawed friend. He cleared off the coffee cups and my half-finished plate of eggs, flipped over my paper placemat and sketched out a quick map of the United States on the other side. Made six large black circles in specific places and turned the map around.

"What do you see?"

"I don't know. Big dots?"

"Right. Every one where an alleged peanut killing took place. What else do you see?"

"Not much. Except a big coffee stain in Nebraska."

"No, genius. Look where the killings are. All over the place, from San Francisco to Pittsburgh, across to Ohio, back to Philly and who knows where else next. This person gets around, but I'm not buying the trav-eling salesman angle. They don't have this kind of money. The Peanut Killer is loaded."

At that moment, I wished I was loaded, and not with cash. Better yet, I was eager to get to the ball park, because as I said, we had a doubleheader to play.

"Look, Brewster. If you're fishing around for connections you may have to try the Rockefellers. You're wasting your time. Only rich guy I know is named Willie Howard Mays."

He shot me a sly eye. "When did I say you you were connected?"

"You didn't. But why else would you be here? Why buy me breakfast?"

"Believe me, if we still suspected you we'd have you in a windowless room by now with a light in your face."

"You see too many movies." I slid my plate back on top of his map and finished off my eggs.

"I guess I see you more as some kind of lightning rod, Drake. I don't believe this guy has one ounce of interest in your girlfriend. He's been trying to get to you from Day One."

"Guess he'll have to try a little harder then. Thanks for the grub, chief."

♦ ♦ ♦

I scooted onto the team bus, rode over to County Stadium for seven hours of double hell. Antonelli badgered me again during his warmup throws, then fell apart after retiring the first nine Braves in a row. Aaron had a double and homer and our feeble hope for a split rested with Ramon Monzant.

Monzant was better, but the result

was about the same. The problem this time was our unholy, hole-filled defense, which after making two errors in the opener flubbed five balls leading here to four unearned runs. After we cut Milwaukee's lead to 3-2 in the 6th, Spencer and Kirkland made errors to start their 7th and one out later Bressoud kicked one. No wonder we were 4-13 against this team.

The only good news was that we had a short bus ride down to Chicago later instead of a long plane trip. Liz and the Dodgers, who also dropped a pair of stink bombs today, were heading to St. Louis for two games before we swapped cities. As we cruised past the big lake, the temptation to call her bubbled up to the surface again. Try as I might to stop it, my heart was making trouble for my head again.

Let's Play One!

August 4th

Chicago revisited. And the Cubs hadn't gone away like they usually do. Just a game and a half behind us at 55-51, not the team we were in the mood for after getting spanked three times in Milwaukee.

On top of that, my room at the Del Prado Hotel was smaller than Superman's phone booth, and the lighting was so bad I didn't even notice that the clothes in my bag needed cleaning until the morning. The shirt I was wearing when I fell off my bar stool and gashed my head the other night

was in there, still stained with blood. I rang the front desk for laundry service, dumped the rest of my clothes out while I waited. There was even a blood-stained Milwaukee Braves cap in there I didn't even remember having on my head. What did that damn Bing Crosby song do to me? And why?

I warmed up Ruben Gomez without incident, but the game had the same depressing theme from yesterday. A hittable sidekick named Taylor Phillips hurled for the Cubs and we collected a total of three singles off him the whole afternoon, two by Mays. Chicago's defense was sloppy and gave us every chance to score more but it was hopeless. Old pal Bobby Thomson doubled and homered and the Cubs won without breathing hard. By the 7th inning I asked Rigney if I could get dressed and sit in the half-empty stands, with the idea it might change our luck, me being the unofficial team mascot and all.

Gotta tell you that sitting right next to the Cubs dugout, being able to study Ernie Banks in the on-deck circle in the late afternoon shade, stroll to the plate and coil up before every pitch may have been the most relaxing five minutes I've had all year.

I was so calm when I got back to my room tonight—where I soon learned the Braves shut out the Bucs—that I picked up the phone and tracked down Liz. Her opening sigh lasted a good fifteen seconds, and it wasn't just because her Dodgers had just gotten their pants pulled over their heads. I could hear loneliness in her voice.

"How's your room?" she asked.

"About as big as a bowling alley. One lane's worth."

"So ask for a bigger one."

"It's okay. Without a television it'll force me to go to sleep earlier."

"Why don't you read a book?"

"Didn't bring any. Maybe you can read one to me."

"Ha ha. Don't think you'll care for a gothic romance."

"Try me. I hear there's always a couple of saucy pages in there."

She laughed under her breath. "Flirt."

"It's what I do best."

"Yeah. That and falling off bar stools. Why are you in such a good mood? Aren't you three games out again?"

I wasn't about to tell her that the worse the Giants played, the safer she was. So I said nothing.

"Anyway, be thankful you guys got out of Milwaukee before they found that drunk."

"What drunk?"

"Oh. You didn't see the papers? Some drunk Braves fan was found dead and stuffed in a trash can about half a mile from Kniesler's. Wasn't that the place you passed out in?"

I suddenly felt warm. In my head, my neck. On my sweating hands.

"Um, yeah…Why don't I talk to you tomorrow, okay?"

"Is something wrong, Snap?"

"No…Nothing. Just tired."

I said goodnight and hung up the receiver. Turned and gazed over at my open bag.

And at the bloodstained Braves cap sitting inside it.

Stu Miller Can Wait

August 5th

Willie Kirkland was knocking on my hotel room door.

"Bus about to leave, Cap'n!"

"Thanks, Willie…"

"You okay in there?"

"Yeah, I'm fine. Thanks. I'll get myself a cab."

The hallway floor creaked. "Suit yourself!"

After finding that bloody Braves cap in my bag I was more tempted to just ditch the team altogether, hitch-hike west and relocate in some desert cave until I pieced all this junk together. Other than get drunk, hear a Bing Crosby song and fall off my bar stool, what the hell did I do the other night in Milwaukee? According to the *Chicago Tribune*, Tim Kruger had been found with his face in a puddle, signs of a struggle in the alley, and his hat gone.

Was that how I gashed my head? I blacked out a lot when I was younger, so was this problem back to stay? Were John Blaziecsky, Reggie, Vincent Grosso, Pete Szopa, Ohio Officer Grundheinz, Rudy Creech and now this Kruger guy done in by me in some unconscious state? Maybe Brewster and the S.F.P.D. were right to suspect me in the first place!

No, said my saner half, that was plain crazy. Szopa was killed in the Forbes Field grandstand when I was hiding out in a Pacific cabin on the other side of the country. And wasn't there an actual creep calling my place, appearing over my handy-talkie, scaring Liz and knocking me out with chloroform?

Or was he triggering a darker side of me?... Just in case, before I left the hotel I located an incinerator in the basement and threw the bloody cap in it.

"Drake!" yelled Bob Schmidt an hour later as I continued to sit and ponder in a clubhouse stall, "Miller's ready for ya!"

Stu Miller could wait. I smoked two more Camels in there, then trudged down the tunnel and out onto Wrigley's Field to warm him up.

"You all right?" asked little Stu when he saw me, "Looks like you seen a ghost get hit by a truck." It was something like that, but I shrugged off his question and asked for a fastball.

Leon Wagner gave us a kick out of the gate with a long homer onto Sheffield off Glen Hobbie. But Miller was shaky. Bobby Thomson doubled and Dale Long parked one and we were behind in no time. Our bats turned back to lead and produced nothing. With two gone in the Cubs 5th, Miller plunked Dark, Thomson

singled, Long doubled, and we were well on our way to dropping our fourth straight and six out of seven on the trip. The dugout was a sweaty morgue.

And I sat there like the perfect cadaver. Thinking about Liz now. It was nice to have a silky talk with her again last night. Obviously this was going to be one of those on-and-off switch relationships, but was she safe with me? What might I do to her if I had another blackout?

CRACK!

Baby Bull Cepeda brought me and us back to life like he usually did with a leadoff triple in the 6th. A Kirkland single cut it to 3-2. Hobbie recovered with a spotless 7th, but the 8th was a different and better story. Daddy Wags walked, Mays singled, Cepeda walked, and reliever Don Elston took over for Hobbie. Davenport lined out but Kirkland singled hard past a drawn-in infield to put us ahead, Banks booted a Valmy Thomas grounder, Miller beat out a bunt single, Spencer hit a run-scoring grounder and poof! We had a 6-3 win in the bank.

Next up was a happy team train ride to St. Louis. The Pirates had just beaten Warren Spahn, and the beers were flowing in the bar car. I sat in the back by myself, half-smiling, not drinking a drop. Thankfully, Jerry Lee Lewis was playing on someone's radio. Maybe I wouldn't have blacked out at all, but I was taking no more chances.

Speake Experience

August 6th

The St. Louis air we played in made our uniforms feel like wet carpets. The team stuck me in a room at the Chase Hotel with Bob Speake, our 27-year-old sixth outfielder from Springfield, Missouri, and I guess the heat made him feel right at home. Me? I was dumping cubes from our ice bucket under my sheets and laying on top of them.

"Spook" was in the minors for a while before making it to the bigs with the Cubs in '55. He showed a bit of power his first two seasons, belting 28 combined homers, but with Mays, Wagner, Kirkland and Alou starring for us out there he's been lucky to get some late pinch-hitting spots.

"Hell of an occupation we got, huh?" he said before our first game at Busch Stadium. I'd told him about my short career pitching in the Pacific Coast League, and we had similar journeys to talk about. Like everyone else on the Giants he also knew I was posing as Nick Testa to try and help catch the killer.

"If you ask me the murderin' bastard got bored and went back to 'Frisco. With all that fog it's easier for him to do his handiwork there."

It sounded possible, but I wasn't buying anything until these last two games and the three coming up in L.A. were over—without news of a fresh murder.

Ripe to be killed were the Cards, who were playing better lately but still 2-9 against us for the year. Naturally, Blasingame gave them an early lead with a cheap homer off the right field foul pole. Wagner tied it with a 4th inning single but was gunned down at the plate to end the inning by Bobby Gene Smith, trying to score on Cepeda's double. It would be important.

Back-to-back homers by Kirkland and Thomas gave us a 4-1 lead which Al Worthington cruised into the St. Louis 8th with. Bressoud booted one, and a wild pitch and two singles made it 4-2. Paul Giel came to the rescue and fell off his ladder, as Ken Boyer whacked a three-run shot into the bleachers for the shocking 5-4 Cards lead. Even more shocking was something called Nelson Chittum getting us 1-2-3 in the 9th, and Speake and I were back at the Chase in no time so he could find the bar and I could collapse on some new ice cubes.

Then the door opened at two in the morning. I opened my eyes, saw Speake just standing there, silhouetted. Staring at me.

"What's wrong?" I sleepily asked.

"I don't know. You tell me."

God, now what? I put on a light and he walked over to hand me a note, written in pen on a Hotel Chase bar napkin:

Watch out for your roomie. He'd KILL for some attention.

"What's this about, Drake?"

I didn't even answer him. Threw on my clothes and ran down to the bar in my bare feet. The only people left in there were a bartender, an old couple, a passed-out woman and a chain-smoking piano player. I showed the napkin to the barkeep.

"See anybody write this?"

"You can't be in here without shoes on, sir."

I grabbed him by his tie and yanked him close. "I don't care if my pants and jockstrap are missing. Answer the question."

He was scared. Glanced at the note. "I don't know, okay? There were lots of people. Salesmen. Ballplayers and the like."

"What kind of salesmen? The traveling kind?"

"Of course. What other kind would stay here?"

Two cops were walking their beat outside the bar's window. I let go of him. He edged away, grabbed a couple of empty bowls left on the bar. Peanut shells had been in them. I turned and studied the piano player, the old people. The drunk woman.

The person who wrote on the napkin may have been watching me that very second, from a corner. A phone booth. A shadow. But at least one thing was clear: I wasn't following myself.

Bazooka Jerk

August 7th

It was 5:30 p.m. in the Busch Stadium locker room. I sat there pulling on Nick Testa's uniform, watched the Giants players gradually fill the room and slowly lost my mind.

Sure, I'd been on the road with these guys for weeks, but I still barely knew any of them. Until last night, I hadn't spoken two simple syllables to Bob Speake.

Suspecting any of our regular players of monkey business was certifiably cracked, but what about frustrated benchwarmers like Speake, Jim King, Ray Jablonski or Don Taussig, who "found" his locker full of Salty Dog peanuts in Milwaukee? Maybe one of them had an axe to grind or use.

Then I warmed up Antonelli, who couldn't possibly be involved but had an atomic scowl on his puss that left me wondering after every bullpen session. Tonight he was going against Sad Sam Jones, the league's premiere hard-luck case, so Johnny should have been relaxed.

He was after we gave him a 3-0 lead after four, but then he got sloppy. Plunked Ken Boyer on the arm to knock him out of action a few games, got his mind all scattered and served up a Stan Musial bomb into the pavilion to cut it to 3-2.

Mays was on fire, though. Singled to start a rally in the 5th and homered to begin the 7th. 5-3 Giants to the last of the 8th, with the Braves struggling 1-1 vs. the Pirates again up north. The first two Cards singled to begin their 8th, Gordon Jones entered, and I had to run out to the pen again to warm up Paul Giel. Paul had to use the toilet when he was set to go and left his glove sitting beside me.

I stared at the glove. I was chewing a big wad of Bazooka, and whether I did it subconsciously or not, I put some sticky-sweet gum saliva on my fingers and rubbed it in Giel's webbing. It was a goof some of us did to each other up in the Pacific Coast League in idle moments. This moment was hardly idle, but I really thought Jones would put out the Cards' fire.

Jones was terrible. Surrendered singles to Irv Noren and Gene Green, and Giel jogged in to face pinch-hitter Wally Moon. Who he walked. So did light-hitting Eddie Kasko on four pitches. So did pinch-hitter Don Blasingame. Four St. Louis runs were across, we were behind 7-5 and it was likely my fault. Giel stood out there staring at his glove a minute. Discovered the sticky substance, smelled it, and shot a glare in my direction. He asked for a towel from the dugout, wiped the glove clean, and proceeded to get Smith, Cunningham and Ruben Amaro on harmless grounders.

When he got back to the dugout, I apologized for "dribbling some gum juice" on his mitt. He wasn't pleased, walked away without a word and

started talking me up to his mates. Phil Paine, off two painful relief outings in a row for the Cards, suddenly became a Giants punching bag. Bressoud singled, Wagner and Mays (4-for-5 on the night) doubled, Blasingame threw one into the Mississippi, and we had an 8-7 lead just like that. Giel got three more ground outs without batting an eye, and Rigney had me in his office ten minutes later.

"I didn't like this Nick Testa ruse from the first day," he said, wiping off his glasses with a tissue, "Sabotaging my pitchers' equipment like that has no place on our ball club. The team wants you gone and so do I. Sorry, Drake."

I packed up and left the clubhouse without even raising my eyes. Called Liz where she was wrapping things up in Chicago, said I'd meet her at the L.A. Coliseum tomorrow. Brewster would be taking me on a separate, government plane.

"Why would you do something like that to his glove?" she asked.

"If I told you, you wouldn't believe it."

"Try me."

I would have to be careful here. "Peanut Man said if the Giants win the pennant many people are going to die."

"Are you kidding?...Hmm...What the devil does he have against the Giants?"

Come to think of it, it was a damn good question.

Nighthawks at the Deli

August 8th

Liz was happy to be "home" in L.A. again, which turned out to be the Hotel Figueroa. A family of Greek people were now living in her vacated house in the hills, and she had no clue what she'd be doing when the weekend was over.

We met at the counter at Canter's Deli on Fairfax for some late coffee and dessert after the Dodgers game. Which I skipped. The Giants had smacked Drysdale silly again but the Braves had also won back in Philly and to be honest, I wasn't in a baseball mood. Getting booted off a team you have no business being on is like getting double-fired.

Considering the way the road trip went, Liz was pretty friendly. We had a fine time talking about the different towns, the murder victims, and the insanity of our lives. We were like an old married couple—without the married and old parts.

"John Blaziecsky!" she began over her warm cup. "The Opening Day guy with the knife in him. He was the only one that wasn't an ordinary joe!"

"Cops checked him out right away, Liz. Vacuum salesman from San Jose, remember? If that ain't ordinary I don't know what is."

"Yeah, but think a second about the others. Grosso the night watchman,

your friend Reggie in construction, Pete Szopa the steelworker, a cop, and a Philly pretzel vendor. Maybe that first guy sold a defective vacuum to the wrong character."

"Uh-uh. As they say, I think we're meowing up the wrong scratching post. The question you threw at me last night is our ticket."

"Which was…"

"What would someone have against the Giants?"

She shrugged, snatched the last bite of cheesecake off our shared plate. "Insane Dodger fan? They've gotten awful rotten. Maybe it's Ralph Branca's brother."

"Or Ralph Branca. Seen him pitching anywhere lately?"

We chuckled over that one. It was almost midnight, and I still had to ride with Liz back to the Figueroa. She offered me part of her bed but I was wary. That business needed a bit more time, a stronger heart and stomach. And as the coffee suggested, a long walk under an L.A. moon felt more like it.

She paused outside the hotel doors. "Oh! Before I forget, Billy invited us over for a barbeque after Sunday's game."

"Great. Guess he's healed up enough to flip a few burgers."

"Try top sirloin."

"Then I will. Thanks."

We kissed. It was still sweet, still electric. I watched her through the lobby doors, waited until she vanished into the elevator, then headed up the sidewalk. Got about half a block and then…

"Mr. Snappy, is it?"

The voice was tough, vaguely ethnic. From no one I'd ever heard before. I turned.

It belonged to a six-foot-tall man mountain, with slicked-back hair and a broken Roman nose. He wore an expensive black suit with a black shirt and black tie. Two henchmen, less fancily dressed but no less creepy, had just gotten out of a bright red Eldorado with him.

"Maybe."

"I say most definitely. Allow me to say good evening. Braggo Farfadecchio."

He put out a hand the size of Sicily, and I shook it. Half his knuckles felt out of place.

"What's this about?"

"It's about you taking a little spin with us."

"No, I better not. Spinning makes me dizzy."

"Too bad. 'Cause my boss might get a trifle upset."

"Who's your boss?"

"Just get in the car, asshole."

"I'd like to know who I'm about to sue."

"You ain't suing nobody but your doctor. After he messes up the spleen surgery you're about to need."

I threw up my hands. "Sorry!" Began to walk and his two goons stuck matching .38s in my ribs.

"Let's just say that Mickey would've sent Johnny Stompanato instead of me, except for the fact someone stabbed the hell out of him four months ago."

I froze. Because I suddenly realized which Mickey he was talking about. And it wasn't the mouse.

I Scream, You Scream…

August 9th

Turned out that I didn't need to worry where I was sleeping last night, because Braggo Farfadecchio kept me up till dawn and most of today waiting until Mickey Cohen could make time for us. When you're a full-time crime boss it tends to clog your schedule a little.

It was 7 p.m. by the time he finally met us in the Carousel Ice Cream Parlor he owned with his sister on San Vicente Boulevard. The guy was all of five-foot-two, with an old boxer's face and a mouth on him that could drive a sailor into the priesthood. Thankfully, he was more interested in putting ice cream inside it and making eyes at his dish of a girlfriend, who also happened to be named Liz.

"Seeing I got vending machines to collect on tonight, I'll make this quick for ya, Drake. Word on the street is that this sick murderin' bastard followin' the Giants around might cost them a shot at the World Series, am I right?"

"Well, if they lose I'm not sure the

murders would have anything to do with it. More likely their lousy bullpen ERA—"

"Hey! Did I just ask you for details? If I want a fancy math lesson I'll call Albert Einstein. Braggo! Put the game on!"

Braggo snapped a finger at an 18-year-old kid behind the counter, who nervously fumbled with a radio until Vin Scully's voice came in from the Coliseum. It was already 5-1 Giants in the 2nd.

"Looks like they're winning tonight," I said. "Didn't know you were a baseball fan."

"Whaddya, nuts? I'd rather watch blood dry on somebody's face. Problem is that this sunavabitch bookie out in the desert talked me into laying 50 large on the Giants back in March, and now I'm a little worried I might gotta pay him."

"So don't."

"You tellin' me what to do, shit-for-brains?"

"No. I'm telling you what NOT to do."

He glared at me. I was already regretting what I'd said. Thankfully his girlfriend was waving her little spoon at him.

"Mickey? Can I have your cherry?"

He cracked up laughing. "Hell, I'm supposed to ask YOU that!" A few seconds later, Braggo and his goons laughed too, and I forced a smile after getting a smack from one of them.

"Thing is," continued Mickey, "I gotta feel good about this investment

I did. The boys up north seen your name in the papers, news gets down to me here, I figure hey—maybe this Snappy character knows a thing or two of the inside tip variety."

"A little, maybe. Not sure I know more than the average fan—"

"Tell ya what, Brainiac. Why don't we sit here a while and see how this game turns out? If the Giants look like they got it in the bag, let's say a little while after halftime, maybe I'll feel a lot better and you can just go."

With our 5-1 lead I agreed to that plan. Mickey Cohen obviously knew less about baseball than I did about girls' lacrosse.

"And get yourself a sundae, why don't ya? They're damn good here."

"That's okay. Trying to watch my waist."

"You makin' fun of me now? Have a Hot Fudge Banana Dreamboat and shut the hell up."

So I did. And it was good. But then the Giants stopped hitting, I mean really stopped. After smashing Johnny Klippstein around early he threw five hitless innings at us, while the Dodgers begin chipping back. Our suddenly swiss cheesian defense helped out. Daryl Spencer made two errors, Cepeda one, and after Mays dropped a Gil Hodges fly in the 6th, the Dodgers scored twice and it was 5-4. When Reese tied the score with a pinch sac fly in the 7th, Mickey sent his Liz home in a cab, sat across from me again and folded his arms.

"Sounds to me we got a problem

here."

"Uhh…not yet. And the Giants have a good record in one-run games and extra innings."

"You gettin' mathy with me again?"

The bananas and fudge were curdling in my gut. It was nearly ten and the last customers were emptying out.

"Doesn't this place close soon?"

"Aw no, we're open all night. Keep your panties on."

Vin Scully's voice floated across the room like whipped cream on pudding. *So Klippstein, Koufax and now Babe Birrer have no-hit the Big Bad Giants for the last nine and two-third innings! Can you believe it?*

It was the last of the 11th. Gilliam walked and Furillo singled him to third. Ramon Monzant replaced Giel and walked Gray to load the bases. I was a dead man. Roseboro lined out but Snider lofted a fly deep to Kirkland and Gilliam ran home with the Dodger winner.

Bullet in the head? Wire around my neck? Hopefully he'd give me a choice. Instead…

"You're a pretty sharp guy."

"Oh…really?"

"Yeah. Knowing about their lousy reliever pitching and all. So now I'm thinkin'…I got an easier way to make back this investment of mine and you're gonna help me pull it off."

"I am?"

"Giants and Dodgers are playing a super-long series in both places this coming Labor Day weekend."

"Right. Think it's like eight straight games using both parks. Kind of nuts."

"Yeah well, this bookie I spoked about should be going to the games down here. So I'll need you to follow him afterwards, get my 50 large back and waste him for me."

"What?? I've never done anything like that in my life!"

"Gotta start sometime."

"No. I don't. I can go to a phone booth right now, call FBI Agent Brewster and have your ass back in the slammer."

Braggo chuckled once. Mickey just smiled. The ugly kind.

"Brewster the Rooster's the reason I picked you up, Brainiac. He's been on me like flypaper for years. See, he got tired of taking my contributions to the Police Activities League when he was on the force out here. Decided to get all high and mighty in a federal kind of way and make me his personal project."

He leaned in, a smidgen of whipped cream melting on his menacing puss.

"And now I got me his little play toy."

To Sirlon, With Love

August 10th

As Mickey Cohen might have said, *oy gevalt.*

Here I was, a month and a half left in the season, saddled with a serial killer who wanted me to help the Giants lose, and an L.A. mob boss wanting me to help them win. Or at least kill some bookie stooge to get his 50 grand back.

One thing I knew I *wasn't* doing was telling my Liz about Mickey Cohen. She had enough drama on her dining table. We met today for a late breakfast at the Pantry, and had an intriguing time going over the most recent batch of published Peanut Killer notes. They had become even more cryptic and strange, the poetry was even worse, and readers were having a field day trying to make sense of them.

"There's definitely a pattern," she said, "Lots of stuff about loyalty and abandonment. But every time I think I've nailed it down, he throws one out about moonlight or crickets and I lose track again. He is one scatter-brained fellah."

From the Pantry it was on to a relaxing afternoon at the Coliseum, watching the Giants pummel the now-last place Dodgers. The L.A. boys have used the second half of the season to unravel like a cheap watch, despite still being second in the league with 130 homers.

Later on, though: Beer and melt-in-my-mouth barbeque steaks at Billy Frack's place in North Hollywood. Liz's brother was healed, rested, and ready to ride us.

"See, here's what you love-cats are doing wrong. You forgot to hire Billy Frack to be your all-purpose assistant, bodyguard and Peanut Killer groin-smasher."

"You left out gourmet barbequer. This steak is the tops."

"And I'd cool it with the 'love-cat' stuff," added Liz.

"Oh? Trouble in Shang-ri-la?"

"It's never been Shang-ri-la, Billy. More like a fire escape in *West Side Story*."

"You ain't kiddin', Maria" I said, pinching her behind.

He asked what we were doing next and it was still pretty much up in the air. Liz had a chance to get her place in the Los Feliz hills back, but wasn't sure she wanted to live there alone and was starting to like the Hotel Figueroa. I was a pariah on the Giants now, but Brewster didn't want me straying too far with the suspect constantly hovering around the team. So that pretty much made up my mind. After dinner and my fourth beer, I called Pence Murphy at his home in Daly City.

"Section 16, Murph. Can I have it back?"

"You mean it? Every young usher we got is about to head back to school. You are music to my ears, Snappy. Just do me a big favor."

"What's that?"

"Keep your murder sleuthing shenanigans away from my ballpark."

I promised I would—like a good liar. Because even if I wanted to, it wasn't up to me.

The Bronx Bugle Sporting Life

Bombers Frightened of No One
Not even S.F. "Peanut Killer"

by Archie Stripes
American League Beat

It was a relaxed clubhouse late Sunday after the Yanks edged the Bosox in their second straight afternoon thriller. So relaxed I had a chance to ask our beloved Bombers about one of their favorite off-field topics: San Francisco's notorious "Peanut Killer."

For those in a cave, "P.K." has been touring the country, leaving corpses in scattered, unpredictable locales while terrorizing a Giants usher, his reporter girlfriend, and leaving federal lawmen flatfooted and flamboozled.

"We get a lot of time together, between the planes and trains between cities, "Hank Bauer told me, "so it's fun to try and guess about him sometimes."

"I got fifty bucks on [Johnny] Antonelli myself, "said the Mick, "Woulda gone with Sal Maglie, of course, but the Barber's on a different team now."

"It was a little scary on our last western trip," admitted Bob Turley, "especially when we were way out in Kansas City. Who the heck knows where this guy is lurking?"

"His killings are unpredictable, too," added Gil McDougald, "but they always seem to be in and around ballparks. I'm just waiting for someone to be found stuffed head first in a ball bag, or hanging from an outfield foul pole."

"It's obvious to me he's a weak, frightened individual with a bone to pick about something in his past," said brainy Ryne Duren through his thick specs.

Naturally, Casey Stengel had the last word.

"Got no time for thinkin' on that character. Not with Boston comin' in now and us goin' to Boston next, and a big cushion for us that could pop like a balloon whenever, so no peanut butter killer in my book, no sir. Don't care what he did to his momma or what his pappy did to him or what teacher smacked him with a yardstick or what bad food he used to eat, 'cause that's what's always made killin' characters and always will and if I see him here or Detroit or in my backyard murderin' squirrels I'll make him wish his being born was just the Lord makin' a big accident in his pants," said Casey.

≈ *This Is My Life* ≈

August 12th

A crystal clear, fog-free Tuesday evening at 16th and Bryant. A packed Seals Stadium. A rollicking, pennant-hungry crowd with St. Louis in town.

And section 16 was an endless freak show.

"Snappy! Take a picture with me!"

"Who izzit, Snappy? You gotta know by now, right??"

"If they make a Hollywood movie about the killings, make sure they hire me to play you, okay?"

I had this same neo-celebrity problem back in June, but with everything going on since and my name in a few national papers now, it had cranked up to a new decibel. And that was just the fans. Dot and the usherettes were swooning by every other inning. Gus and Russ Nicholson both wanted autographs for their wives. Tall Tom Tupper invited me over for dinner—and he didn't even cook.

Too bad, because the mayhem caused me to miss most of a great game. Joe Cunningham, the Cards' outfielder who's been redbird-hot ever since they parked him at the top of their lineup, hit a two-run homer in the 1st, triples in the 2nd and 5th, a single in the 19th, and a double leading off their 13th to help him hit the cycle for the night.

It was a battle of loser-heads, Sad Sam Jones and Mr. Antonelli, and after Wagner tied the game with a homer in the 7th, it seemed like it might go on forever. Not so. Cunny's double in the 13th off Gordon Jones was followed by a Musial single and Boyer triple off Giel, and we bombed a chance to gain half a game on the idle Braves. I didn't care which killer was happy nor angry about the outcome; I was just glad to get out of there, back to my place, platter up Sinatra and hit my favorite bottle.

Then Liz called, to cap it all off.

"Got the new Peanut Killer note going in tomorrow's edition. Want to hear it?"

"No. But sure."

She cleared her throat first:

High and tight
With all your might
Snap off a curve
To do what's right

I let the words sink in, paddle around in the gin.

"Ring any bells?"

"About what?"

"Well, he used your name in it."

"Yeah…Sort of."

Actually, the *high and tight* is what bothered me, for some reason.

"Maybe this is connected to your

minor league pitching days."

"I thought I'd looked into that."

"Looking deeper probably wouldn't hurt."

She had a point. And after 13 innings of the Snappy Drake Seals Show a little road trip to visit Phil Todd wasn't the worst idea.

Kicked in the Head by a Mule

August 13th

I was itchy, the Coronet needed to stretch her tires, and a visit to my Pacific Coast League scout buddy Phil Todd was in order. Lucky me, his Spokane Indians happened to be 75 miles north in Sacramento, playing a series with the Solons. Bingo.

After calling Pence to inform him of my food poisioning, I hit the old highway. The drive took about an hour and a half through hot, dusty fields. Spent the time listening to Russ Hodges' call of our matinee with the Cards. It ended even more badly than last night's game, so no sense detailing that tragedy. I killed the radio when I hit Sacramento, cruised around a bit till I found Edmonds Field.

It was an ancient yard on the corner of Broadway and Riverside. With the sudden demotion of the PCL to Triple-A status, it would possibly be demolished soon. The Solons were in sixth place, just in front of Spokane but well back of first-place Phoenix.

The rickety stands were two-thirds full of farmers, families, scattered migrant workers in the cheaper seats. I wandered down to a box rail during batting practice, caught the eye of Glen Gorbous, one of the brief friends I made during my couple of days with the Indians back in late April. Naturally, he dragged Norm and Larry Sherry over from the cage.

"What the hell YOU doin' here, Drake?" Gorbous asked "Bored bein' a celebrity?"

"Actually I'm looking for Phil Todd. Tried his office and they said he was on the road with the team."

"You kiddin'?" said Norm Sherry, "We're lucky if we see him once in a purple moon. Guy's off watchin' high school and little league games half the time. You fly up here to see him?"

"No, my trusty Coronet. If he shows up tonight, tell him I'm here, okay?"

Their game with the Solons was pretty grim. I remembered how feeble they looked up in Spokane, and they hadn't exactly risen in the standings since. After the 12-2 drubbing, I walked out to my car and saw a typed, folded note under the wipers:

SNAPPY—
    MEET ME AT THE OLD IRONSIDES BAR FOR A MOSCOW MULE.
                                    —PHIL

So my old pals had come through. And I was dying to find out what a Moscow Mule was.

♦ ♦ ♦

Ginger beer and vodka, that's what. Papa Bill Bordisso's house special since his place on 10th Street opened in 1934. The Ironsides was packed with summer night revelers. Billiard balls cracked from a back room and a local combo played some old jazz and swing favorites that thankfully didn't include Bing Crosby. By the time I finished my first Mule, Phil Todd hadn't shown up, and by the time I finished my second, I'd forgotten he was even coming. Instead of taking over our schools and government, the Commies could've just poured us a few million of these.

"Tell ya...what" I burped to the out-of-focus bartender, "Iffa guy name Phillip...Todd shows up...have him...call me." And stumbled outside.

First thing I did was lose my car. Second thing I did was turn down the wrong sidewalk while looking for my car. It was a pretty residential area with some nice front porches. I was tempted to curl up on one for a nap, or if they didn't have a porch, knock on a front door and use the closest living room couch.

It was also a quiet area, and I could tell because my shoes were making echo sounds on the sidewalk. At least I thought they were echoes. When I paused to light a Camel, though, and the echo kept going a few extra seconds, I wasn't so sure.

I picked up my pace. Reached a modest rectangle of greenery called Roosevelt Park and ducked into some trees. Peered out. Thought I saw a quick shadow move off the walk.

Turned and another shadow stood in front of me. A shadow with a dark hand holding a revolver.

"Gimme that wallet now."

His cohort appeared behind me. "Best listen to the man."

"How about I do neither?"

"Then you be dead."

The rear mugger brought up a knee, caught me in the liver. I collapsed like an upside down cake, got a kick to the back of my head. I felt rough hands going through my pockets. One came out with my wallet.

Suddenly, the warm night air shifted. The wallet fell to the ground, a few inches from my aching head. Moments later its thief dropped on the grass, clutching a bleeding stab wound in his gut. A horrible gurgling followed. I looked up in time to see the first mugger drop his gun, pathetically try to keep the blood gushing from his neck while he fell and bled to death.

I then heard a third voice. Gruff. Out-of-breath. One I could recognize on a foggy night through tin cans.

"You owe me one, Milton. Actually...make that two."

It was hard for me to sit up, but when I did, two negro muggers lay dead on either side of me. And the Peanut Killer was gone again.

Right Field Brain Thinking

August 14th

The speedometer on my Dodge was busted, but I knew I was driving back from Sacramento last night at close to sixty-five miles an hour because the windows were rattling. Sure, a highway cop might've stopped me. But try telling that to the adrenalin in my foot and the eggs I was trying to unscramble in my brain.

Peanut Man had left that fake Phil Todd note on my car at Edmonds Field to get me to The Old Ironsides. Meaning he followed me all the way up there and overheard the conversation with my Spokane pals. His aim was to get me plowed and do something else dastardly, but what? Kidnap me again and throw more sock balls in my face? The muggers he killed had messed up whatever plan he had, and with the law about to arrive, there probably wasn't enough time to pull it off.

So for those of you scoring this insane game at home, I now had a serial murderer, a mobster, and Sacramento cops to worry about, not to mention City Hall goons in 'Frisco if I got any deeper into that Candlestick Point scam. What better way to forget about it all but to take in another ball game, right?

Called in "sick" for one more day and parked myself in the right field bleachers for a change. One bonus of sitting out there is that if I felt frazzled I could just turn around between innings and gaze at the trees in Franklin Square Park. At least until they reminded me of poor Reggie again.

Al Worthington did his best to ease my mind-pain. The Cards swung feebly at his offerings all afternoon, and even though he struck out nobody, thanks to an early Davenport solo shot he took a 1-0 lead and no-hitter into the 7th. The Seals stands were starting to electrify again, like they did for Jim Brosnan's no-hit gem here back in April against us. First up was Musial, though, and he worked a walk. Worthington bore down against Bobby Gene Smith but he walked too. Up stepped Irv Noren, who killed us with a late three-run homer yesterday.

Well, he whacked the first pitch deep in my direction. I stood and watched the ball sail on a bay breeze over the bleachers, bounce between a pair of passing Oldsmobiles on 16th Street and roll into the grassy park. 3-1 St. Louis and here we went again. Worthington departed after giving up just one hit, Grissom redeemed himself with two shutout innings before Monzant gave up three singles in the 9th. But it didn't matter. Jackson and Paine put the termites back in our bats and the Cards, 3-10 against us going in, pulled off the dreadful three-game sweep. All we have now are the blue-hot Cubbies, red-hot Reds and ever-dangerous Braves coming to town, so if you ask me, this is our biggest two weeks of the year here.

Afterwards, I checked an evening Sacramento paper for any dead muggers news, and didn't see any. Which was strange. Maybe Peanut Man had gone back and disposed of the bodies himself after I left. Or maybe negro victims didn't warrant space in the local paper. It wasn't that uncommon.

I stopped at Pete's Liquor for a new bottle of gin, and headed home.

Only to hear a loud sneeze as I rounded the corner to my steps. Parked at the top with one of his goons was Braggo Farfadecchio, blowing his schnozz into a monogrammed hankie.

"Damn weather up here ain't fit for an Eskimo, Mr. Snappy. How d'ya do it?"

"Can I help you, Braggo? It's not exactly Labor Day yet."

"No it ain't. But Mickey's Giants seem to be laborizin' a little too much this week."

He stepped up to my face. Even his nose hairs looked scary.

"I don't care if you're puttin' opium in their chewin' tobacco or crabs in their jock straps. But if you enjoy wakin' up every day you better knock it the hell off."

Business as Unusual

August 15th

Typical Giants. Get swept by the Cards, then pull one out against the much-better Cubs. Typical Snap-py. Showing up for work with ten things on his mind and none of them good. A morning phone call with Liz helped a smidgen, at least until we got onto the murder subject. Seems that Peanut Man's daily missives for publication have gotten less frequent. I told her maybe it was because he was busy chasing me up to Sacramento and stabbing muggers to death, but all that did was launch a zillion questions from her about what the hell I was talking about.

"Did you check yourself later, Snap? Was there blood on your clothes? Scratch marks on your face and hands?"

"What's that supposed to mean?"

"That maybe you were...imagining Peanut Man being there. I'm not saying you did anything on purpose, but you do have this weird history of blacking out, right?"

"Liz, I saw and heard the bastard. He was talking to me while I lay on the ground."

"Okay, okay! Don't take this the wrong way, geez..."

"How else am I supposed to take it? Don't you have a last place team to get meaningless quotes from today?"

I hung up on her for a change and headed for the park. It was Johnny Heep's 16th birthday, and it cheered me up to rub the top of our ball boy and clubhouse helper's head while he fetched batting practice balls before the game. Sometimes I think I would have been better off applying for Johnny's job instead of the usher one, even though it probably would've required stepping into a time machine.

"Hey mac! I can't see the field because some lady down there is wearing a big sun hat with feathers!"

So I went down to the third row to ask the lady to remove her hat.

"Not on your life!" she shrieked, "This was my Aunt Dolores' hat, she was a big Seals fan, and I won't take it off for Dwight David Eisenhower!"

I suppose I could have forced her. If Braggo and his goons were somewhere in the park to lend me a hand, that would be one thing, but I just didn't have the energy. I ignored her and did my best to focus on the ball game, which was a rare Mike McCormick pitching gem for eight innings, when he crumbled in seconds and dished up a three-run shot to Bobby "Who Else" Thomson. Monzant and

Giel finished off the win, and I went home to throw on normal clothes and head back up to the Double Play for some cold ones.

It was good to see Bob and Chumpo again, and offered to buy Bob a Hamm's right away. I fished in the pocket of my coat I dragged myself back from Sacramento in, looking for change.

Felt something cold and metallic instead. Reached in deeper and slid out a long silver knife. Complete with dark red, two-day old bloodstains on the razor-sharp blade. Bob and Chumpo saw the thing and just stared at me.

"Um…guys? I can explain this."

"You damn well better," said Bob, sliding a few inches away.

Truth was, I couldn't explain crap.

National League thru Friday, August 15

Milwaukee	64	50	.561	—
Chicago	64	54	.542	2
San Francisco	61	55	.526	4
St. Louis	56	58	.491	8
Philadelphia	54	58	.482	8.5
Cincinnati	56	61	.479	9.5
Pittsburgh	54	61	.470	10.5
Los Angeles	52	64	.448	13

American League thru Friday, August 15

New York	73	43	.629	—
Boston	64	51	.557	8.5
Baltimore	62	52	.544	10
Chicago	63	53	.543	10
Detroit	58	56	.509	14
Cleveland	60	58	.509	14
Kansas City	46	69	.400	26.5
Washington	36	80	.310	37

≈ Cheers and Beer on a ≈ Late Summer Breeze

August 16th

"Stay up here till we figure this out, Snappy. It's for your own good." Chumpo's "apartment" was a two-room hovel atop the Double Play. Furnished with a lumpy bed, girlie calendar and hot plate. He and Bob were committed to keeping me "safe" until it was clear that Peanut Man had planted the knife on me. But how could I prove it if I was stinking drunk at the time?

"One thing you ain't doin' is turnin' that knife over to the Sacramento cops," said Chumpo this morning, "They give jaywalkers five years up there."

"Yeah," asked Bob, "but what if the sicko's prints are all over the thing?"

I shook my head. "Doubtful. This guy's nuts but he isn't sloppy. If he was we would've caught him by now. If you ask me, best thing I can do is usher today's game like nothing ever happened. Like I didn't even find the knife. Wait for him to try something else."

"No way, San Jose," said Chumpo, "You found that blade when you were in my joint, and I ain't losin' my license over it. One day to keep cool, that's all I'm askin' here."

So I went along with it. He brought me up a burger and fries and bottle of Royal Crown, then switched on Russ Hodges' broadcast for me.

Not like I needed it. The half-open dirty window brought crowd noise and Hamm's brewery odor wafting into the room all afternoon. And just my luck, I missed the Giants belting five solo homers as they handled the Cubs again and picked up a game on the Braves.

Later, I used Chumpo's phone to call Liz and tell her about the knife. There was a good ten-second pause on the line when I'm sure she was deciding whether or not to hang up and call the FBI on me.

"You're my best friend right now, Liz. I need you to believe me."

"Really? What happened to your saloon buddies?"

"Okay, change that. You're my smartest best friend."

"I'm not saying I don't believe you, Snap. But every weird thing that happens to you tests me a little more. Maybe you should come back down to L.A. so I can keep an eye on you."

"Don't think so. I'll see you plenty end of the month during that eight-game series." (I left out telling her about my "assignment" for Mickey Cohen.)

"Geez. Don't remind me about that.

One day some hack's going to write an article about the most idiotic baseball scheduling in history."

"Yeah, but for now, I don't want you any more involved."

"I already am, remember? I'm Peanut Killer's ghost publisher. Just take some aspirin, calm down, and I'll talk to you soon."

I hung up. Wandered into Chumpo's World War I trench of a bathroom and rummaged through his medicine cabinet. Found a bottle of three-year old morphine pills his doctor must've filled after Chumpo got back from Korea. Popped a few of those and laid down on the lumpy bed for a while to think about what I could do on Sunday. Until I gradually stopped thinking at all…

On the Backstop of Madness

August 17th

I dreamed about murder and fast balls, all to the sound of crickets. Woke in my morphine haze and slipped out of the Double Play without Chumpo seeing me and found myself in the Giants clubhouse at Seals Stadium. Knew I was supposed to be ushering and had already put my uniform on but then remembered I had to warm Ruben Gomez in the bullpen. The only person in the room was Johnny Heep who was hanging the clean uniforms in every locker.

"What are you doin' here, Snappy?" I think he asked, followed by "You okay?"

"Yeah yeah, gimme some baseballs. Gomez is waiting…"

"What?? There's no one here yet, and I thought you were off the team."

"Don't get smart with me kid," I think I remember saying and stumbled back out.

Then I was in section 16, watching a game that was like a morphine haze all by itself. Home runs and back and forth and fans yelling at me from behind for some reason, we tied it in the 9th on a Mays homer and single and three-base error by Bobby Thomson of all people but all for nothing when the Cubs scored three times in the 11th on a Don Elston leadoff triple and bunch of garbage.

By then I was wandering in section 17 down the right field line for some reason and Stan Lowsack and Tall Tom Tupper were shaking me.

"Better 'fess up Snappy!" said Tom, "Like right now before the cops get here."

"Huh? Why are you…"

"They just found Johnny Heep, that's why," said Stan, "Stuffed head first into a ball bag with your usher cap hanging off his foot."

A twig snapped in my brain. Whether it was the booze or morphine or something deep and dark inside didn't matter. I felt over 20,000 grandstand eyes on me. Tore myself away, smashed through the crowd toward the home plate area. Reached the backstop screen and began climbing it like a madman. Screaming at the field, the scoreboard, the fog-licked San Francisco sky—

"YOU WIN, YOU BASTARD! I DID IT! I DID IT! YOU HAPPY NOW?? I DID IT!!!"

Felt hands on my legs, around my waist. Wrenching me back down into a human stew. The last thing I heard was a siren, which I now realize was not a police car's.

The Bronx Bugle Sporting Life

| BELIEVE IN THE BOMB | August 19, 1958 | BROCCOLI BUILDS CHARACTER |

BALLBOY IN A BALL BAG!
Will Latest "Peanut" Murder Affect Frisco's Play?

by Archie Stripes
American League Beat

The major league circuits were abuzz on Monday following the grisly discovery of a teenage employee's body in the Seals Stadium clubhouse.

Judson "Johnny" Heep, the 16-year-old ballboy and locker room attendant for the San Francisco Giants was found toward the end of Sunday's contest versus the Cubs with his body stuffed head first in one of the team's ball bags.

Cause of death appeared to be strangulation, though authorities are awaiting details of an autopsy report. Milton "Snappy" Drake, the Seals Stadium usher unofficially connected to some of the other "Peanut Killer" murders, suffered a mental breakdown in the grandstand when he was informed of the killing, and despite being admitted to Atascadero State Hospital for observation, has yet to be ruled out as a suspect.

"It's distrubing for sure," said Giants skipper Bill Rigney, "but

S.F.P.D. crime sleuths make careful notes outside suspect Milton "Snappy" Drake's Mission District apartment yesterday.

thank God we have Cincinnati in town to think about instead."

Special agent Griffin Brewster of the FBI has vowed to put extra men on duty in the Giants clubhouse, although that plan has failed to nab the killer in several ball parks thus far.

"Right now we are questioning as many employees as we can. Mr. Drake will be one of those as soon as he's coherent again."

Giants owner Horace Stone-

ham also expressed some optimism. "Our new facility out on Candlestick Point will be a wonderful place to bring your family, but Seals Stadium is still one of the safest ball yards in America," he said by telephone, "The Braves and Dodgers will be here soon for five games apiece, and we're looking for enormous crowds to help us hoist our first west coast flag, so come on out!"

In the White Room

August 20th

Those damn crickets were back. Chirpy little demons. Bent on hopping into my head and driving me more crazy than I already was. Wished I had a barn cat handy to pounce and chew them up.

The bugs just didn't go well with the spongy white walls and harsh lighting in my private room. Wherever the hell it was. Five different docs had come and gone, each one more bearded and four-eyed than the last. Armed with stethoscopes and note pads. One even wore a big sweater and smoked a pipe.

My arms and legs were strapped to the bed to "protect" me, and it wasn't too comfortable. The morphine had worn off but not my paranoia, and I was still punching my brain trying to figure out how I might've killed poor Johnny Heep.

Liz and my mother were right: I had a history of blackouts. That still didn't explain why I kept hearing Peanut Man's voice, seeing and feeling his looming presence. And I wasn't the only one who did that. Maybe I climbed the Seals backstop screen to just put an end to this season of craziness. Here I was after years of waiting for big league crowds to work, and the city a big part of the first National League pennant race they've even sampled, and I've had to spend eighty percent of my time worrying who was going to kill or arrest me next.

Then I met Darwin. A colored hospital orderly who moved down here from Seattle, he gave me a few sticks of Juicyfruit, promised me cigarettes when I was "better," fetched me the ball scores and helped me keep my head on straight.

"You got more folks out there wantin' to see you than a piano's got keys, Drappy." (He insisted on calling me Drappy.) "But don't you worry. I'll tell 'em you're all drugged up and loonaphrenic until you're ready to see 'em."

"Why are you being so nice to me, Darwin?"

"No sense bein' any other way for nobody, right?"

The doctor with the bushiest beard and thickest glasses—Muffinstein was his name—stopped by to let me know he'd be "deep-analyzing" me in his office sometime soon. Of course, I told him I wasn't crazy at all, just a little pressured at work lately. My sentence seemed to take an express line through both of his ears. He sniffed, faked a smile, and promised they'd unstrap me soon if I "cooperated and improved," whatever that meant.

Dr. Muffinstein also asked what I'd been dreaming about. I told him the truth: that it was too hot and humid in the room, and the crickets and thunderstorms were too loud to allow me to dream about anything.

He made a special note of that.

Visiting Day

August 21st

Darwin woke me at the crack of dawn to make me happy again. As in, my morning pills. Can't remember what their names were, but there were two, and it even felt wonderful to get my gown changed after I took them.

Actually, I felt so great and was being so polite that the docs said I could lose my straps and see a few of these visitors Darwin said were "queuelined up" outside.

Unfortunately, the first one was Brewster. He sat in a chair next to the bed and shook his head at me a good thirty seconds before saying one word.

"How'd we ever get to this, Drake?"

"Thought you were the detective here."

"I'm a Special FBI Agent. We have a broader scope than that. And I can tell you Mr. Stoneham is about to have heart failure. He's got the Reds, Braves and Dodgers in town on this massive home stand and the papers are calling his park Sealed Tomb Stadium."

"That's his problem. Maybe he needs to offer fans a big reward for capturing the killer."

"Over 22,000 amateur cops in the place? I don't think so." He leaned in and squinted. "But tell me something Drake. For my own peace of mind. What really happened when you were on morphine the other day?"

"Think I know? That stuff doesn't even help you remember your name."

"Right. But two employees we questioned saw you go in the club-house with your usher hat on, and one saw you leave without it."

"And that means I killed the kid? Maybe I dropped it in the stupor I was in, and the killer used it for a decoration later."

"It would certainly help if you could re—"

"It would help if you could figure out who the hell has been shadowing me and ruining my life!"

"I'm afraid that's going to have to be *your* job, Drake. You're the one with the sketchy past. Just waiting for the pictures to be filled in."

I said I needed a nap. It got him out of there. Darwin brought me a soggy tuna sandwich for lunch and then I had a surprise visit from my other personal investigator.

"They couldn't even give you a window? This is what you get for not listening to me," said my mother.

"And hello to you, too."

"What did I tell you, Milton? About your blackouts?"

"Mom, it doesn't matter what you told me. It wouldn't matter if two hundred doctors and their priests told me. How was I supposed to prevent another one from happening?"

"By eating vegetables and staying out of the ocean air, that's how."

"Science fiction, mom."

"A mother's advice is not fiction. It's gold in your pocket. Just remember that."

"Well, what I really need to remember is when my very first blackout happened and why."

She clammed up. Scratched at a cuticle on one of her fingers.

"Please don't make me bring up your father…"

"What's he got to do with it?"

She sighed. Stood and paced around the tiny room. Like she was hoping a window might magically appear.

"I told him it was too much money. But he wouldn't listen and he took you there…"

"Took me where?"

"Then that coach called. Soupy or whatever his name was. Said you fainted and hit your head and when you came out of it…You came out of it and you weren't talking—"

She choked back some tears, then looked up in a sudden, scary rage.

"Why are you making me do this Milton??"

Grabbed her purse and stormed out of the room. I was tempted to ring for Darwin, tell him that a new mental patient had just escaped, but I couldn't. After all, she was my mother.

20 Questions

August 22nd

The following was transcribed from an analytical session between Dr. Seymour Muffinstein (Ph.D. in Abnormal Psychology, Germantown University, Columbus, OH) and Atascadero

State Hospital patient #6736, Milton "Snappy" Drake, on 8.22.58, 8:16 a.m.

DSM: Would you describe your childhood as being a happy one?

MSD: Yeah. The part of it I can remember.

DSM: And which part can you not?

MSD: I don't know. A lot of things after I was twelve are fuzzy. Like I had a stocking over my face or something.

DSM: What does the term "Hard and fast and middle up" mean to you? An orderly reported you saying that repeatedly in your sleep.

MSD: Well, it's a good way to start pitching a tough hitter. To knock Henry Aaron back off the plate, for instance.

DSM: And the reason you would repeat that in your sleep?

MSD: My father may have said it to me once…I need to think about it…

DSM: Are you now, or have you ever been a member of the Communist Party?

MSD: Hell no.

DSM: When did you first have problems containing your rage?

MSD: That's a pretty loaded question, Doc. Unless someone gets me mad and I have to smack a bunch of sense into him, I'd say I'm a pretty calm guy.

DSM: Do the fans at Seals Stadium ever "get you mad"?

MSD: Only the stupid and annoying ones.

DSM: What about the San Francisco Giants?

MSD: Antonelli is a jerk, Stan Spence

could be a homo, and I won't drink with Cepeda and Gomez ever again, but otherwise no.

DSM: And how about the way they play?

MSD: They're doing the best they can. At least they're in the stinkin' race.

DSM: If Rigney plugged Giel into the rotation and sat McCormick, would you say they have a better chance to catch Milwaukee?

MSD: (unintelligible response)

DSM: Do you need me to rephrase the question?

MSD: I'm not a bookie, Doc. Let's stick to discussing me. And anyway, (in loud whisper) I'd be just as worried about the Cubs if I were you.

DSM: Would you consider your lady friend Liz Doomis a substitute for your mother?

MSD: Why, because they're both loony birds? I would say no to that. None of my 48 lady friends have ever pinch-hit for my mother.

DSM: What is your saddest childhood memory?

MSD: The movie projector breaking down when I was in a theatre watching some Little Rascals movies.

DSM: And how did that make you feel?

MSD: Sad.

DSM: Pretend I'm a man who comes to your front door. I've just told you that I've stolen the wheels off your car, gotten you fired, proposed to your girlfriend and written a damaging letter about you to President Eisen-

hower. What would your response be?

MSD: I know you want me to say I would rip out your entire spine and strangle you with it, but I won't give you that satisfaction. It's more likely I would kill you on the spot.

DSM: Do you like the length of my beard?

MSD: What??

DSM: Should I trim the bottom? Or maybe mutton chops would suit you—

DR. CHISHOLM (bursts into the room with nurse): Seymour! Leave this nice patient alone! I'm sorry, Mr. Drake, was he bothering you?

MSD: Is that the next question?

DR. CHISHOLM (motions for a nurse to inject Dr. Muffinstein with a sedative): Seymour frequently dons a lab coat and pretends he's a doctor. We've been trying to keep tabs on him but sometimes he pays patients "house calls". Come along now, Seymour…I'll take back Mr. Drake's file now. That's right…

(The door slams shut.)

A Lady Vanishes

August 23rd

Atascadero Hospital's big egg-in-their-face helped spring me from the place faster than a jack-in-the-box. But not before one last visitor stopped by in the morning.

"Phil Todd!" I grumbled as he walked

in, "Better never than late." My scout friend from the Spokane Indians was the whole reason I went to Sacramento a few weeks ago, and him not being there the whole reason I found myself lying next to two dead muggers. Not that he needed to know about that.

"Yeah, sorry I missed you," he said, "There was a kid shortstop at Modesto High I had to go see."

"How'd you find me here?"

"How d'ya think? Looked you up at Seals, boss said you got carted away. I'm a scout, remember?"

"Speaking of which...Need a washed-up arm for three months of mop-up duty? Anything to bail me out of my hell up there."

"Yeah, and straight into mine. We're chasing the Rainiers for last place." He gave my side a little nudge. "Holdin' up okay?"

"Like a circus tent. Actually I'm out of here in two hours if you're up for giving me a ride."

"No can do. Gotta see a Mexican lefty in Salinas. Think there's a bus line nearby, though...Why'd you come looking for me in Sacramento?"

I had to think a moment. It felt like it was six months ago.

"This creep who's killing people has a thing for me. I mean, a personal vendetta of some kind. Was wondering if you remembered anyone from the old PCL days who had it in for Younger Snappy."

"Well...there was that crazy heckler in Vancouver."

"Thought of him."

"That baseball tomato in San Diego with the red bobbie sox who you proposed to."

"That was a girl. And shut up."

"Could be anyone, Snappy. For any reason. Maybe someone who had ten grand on you throwing a shutout once."

"That would've been one stupid bet."

"Maybe, but you get my point, right?"

I'd already been down that dead end gambling road with Paulie Suggs back in May. Then I remembered something.

"Hey—Did we ever have a coach named Soupy?"

Phil scratched his crewcut, then his chin. "Kind of a goofy name. Be a tough one to forget...I knew a Soapy once. And a Droopy. Droopy Drummond, with the hairlip. But I think he was a utility player."

No dice. I thanked him for stopping by, wished him luck in Salinas, said a special goodbye to my new pal Darwin, and prepared for my exit.

I was fully expecting to see Agent Brewster waiting for me outside, but there was a game about to start at Seals and he was probably on hand to man another fruitless grandstand watch. Sure enough, Brewster wasn't there, and I started down the two-lane road, past a half mile of fields and migrant workers toward the bus stop.

Suddenly a shiny black Cadillac town car rolled up beside me. The driver was very fat and wore a goatee and dark glasses. He rolled down his window.

"Mr. Stoneham paid me to come pick you up."

"He did?" I laughed. "One mental breakdown in his ballpark wasn't enough?"

He had no clue what I was talking about. "Do you want a ride or not?"

I shrugged, got in the back seat. The car was so plush I could barely feel it moving. I tried some more conversation with the driver but he was basically mute. He kept looking at his watch every few minutes, finally switched on the Giants game at 1:30 p.m. The last of a 5-game set with Cincinnati and a thriller. We got stuck in a lot of traffic heading back to the city through San Jose and were able to hear the whole thing. As we drove past Seals Stadium the cheering inside matched the madness on the radio. The Giants had come from behind with two in the 9th to win 7-6.

I thanked the driver as I climbed out at my place, and then he said "wait a minute." Opened a folder on the seat next to him. Inside were two white envelopes, one marked IF THEY WIN. He handed it to me and drove away.

What the hell? I tore the thing open, unfolded a one-page note in a familiar scrawl:

SORRY I TOOK YOUR LADY, MILTON.

BUT I WARNED YOU ABOUT THE GIANTS WINNING, DIDN'T I?

I suddenly couldn't breathe. Tore up the steps into my apartment and grabbed the phone. Dialed long distance, got the L.A. Coliseum operator to put me through to the press box.

"Liz Doomis, please! I mean *Dumás!*"

I heard nothing but phone-fumbling for a moment. Then somehow, Liz's sweet voice.

"Hello?"

"Liz. Thank god you're okay. Find a cop, quick!"

"What's going on, Snap? Are you still in the—"

"No! I got out, but Peanut Man impersonated Stoneham on the phone, sent this guy to drive me back to town."

"Why would he do that?"

"Why does he do anything? Anyway, he left me a note, saying he either killed or kidnapped you!"

"Well…that's sure news to me. He used my name?"

"No. He just said—"

I stared at the note again. In mounting horror.

"Snap? You there?'"

"I'll call you later."

Hung up, ran out to my Coronet and weaved through the crazy postgame traffic. Roared all the way across town and over the Bay Bridge. Got to a residential street in Oakland, hopped out and ran to the front door.

It was unlocked, with a window around the side smashed open. I swung open the door, stepped into an ungodly mess of a house.

"Mom?"

There was no answer.

The Box on the Shelf

August 24th

I was out at my mom's house with the Oakland cops most of the night. A neighbor had seen an Impala speed away—Peanut Creep had obviously changed cars—but didn't catch the license plate. Somehow she had been kidnapped in broad afternoon daylight, though the fact she was on her first Saturday bottle of Cabernet must have helped. Window glass was on the dining room floor. Clothes were strewn around her room, like she'd been forced to pack in a hurry.

The Oakland cops were more business and less nonsense than the S.F.P.D. Dusted for fingerprints, asked the right questions ("Can you think of any reason she might have had to skip town?") and then Brewster showed up around midnight to take over and dump all their work in the toilet.

"No, Brewster. I don't think I'd have a reason to kidnap my own mother."

"It's not what I'm saying—"

"It's what your fricking implying!"

He took me to an all-night diner to let me calm my nerves with some eggs. Promised the FBI would cover the Bay Area like a "wool blanket" and follow up every lead, but somehow I wasn't convinced.

When he dropped me back at my mother's house, now taped off, quiet and spooky-dark, I got inside and switched on a few lights. Wandered into her bedroom again. Her jewelry box was still on her dresser, half open and filled with broaches and necklaces. Stuff her kidnapper had no interest in. I knew she kept a few valuable fur coats in her closet, and those were there, too. A cardboard box on a high shelf tipped over when I was rummaging around, and I caught it a second before it fell. It was small and rectangular, like something you'd store office documents in. On one side it said "MILTON PAPERS," written in my father's handwriting. I opened it and leafed through the contents.

My birth certificate was in there, pediatrician bills clipped together from age one to ten. Receipts of two train tickets from San Francisco to New York, dated June 23, 1935, and a rental agreement for a Hudson sedan from Arrow Autos in Yonkers, NY dated four days later. A New York State road map. None of this rang an immediate bell. I would have been around 12 years old at the time.

Then I found two old letters. The first was from a Randall Nathan, director of the Adirondack Youth Baseball League up in Loon Lake, N.Y. It was dated July 14, 1935 and addressed to my father:

Dear Mr. Drake:

All of us at the A.Y.B.L. have been thinking about the well-being of your

*boy Milton. How is his recovery going?
We realize an incident such as that can
have a lasting detrimental effect on a
young lad, and when you informed us
he has been subjected to recent "brain
faints," it had us all the more concerned.*

*If there is anything I or my staff can
do to help Milton through this difficult
period, please don't hesitate to write us.*

I stared at the letter. Suddenly
those weird nightmares I'd been having about crickets and mosquitoes
and June bugs and my father driving
me through woods past an A.Y.B.L.
sign began to fuse together. But an
"incident?" What the hell happened?
Did I accidentally kill some kid at this
place? Did I fall and bust my head on
a rock? Both of the above?

What I really needed to do was ask
my mother.

Curious and Curiouser

August 25th

Liz showed up at my door in the
morning, fresh off an airplane.
I was on the telephone, trying to
reach the Adirondack Youth Baseball
League, but there were thunderstorms
back there and the lines were down.

"Any word on your mom?" she
asked, pulling off a shoe to rub the
bottom of her foot.

"Not yet. Supposed to meet Brewster before tonight's game for a report."

"You're actually going to work?"

"Know a better distraction?"

"Oh, I can think of one…"

"Please. What are you doing here,
anyway? Don't you have a killer letter
to publish?"

"You haven't been following? They
stopped four days ago. No surprise,
seeing what he's been up to lately."

I nodded. Handed her the letter I
found from the summer camp. She
skimmed it, arched an eyebrow.

"You went here?"

"Apparently. All those weird dreams
I've been having? With the crickets
and the driving with my dad and the
ball field in the middle of the woods?
Bingo."

"So what's this 'incident' he's refer-
ring to?" A drowning? An archery accident? A midnight panty raid?"

"Ha ha. It's a baseball camp, honey.
Boys only."

"Sorry. Didn't mean to…"

She munched on a new thought.
"Hey—why not ask that doctor?"

"What doctor?"

"The one your mom mentioned at
that seafood place last month? Don
something or other…Dr. Donaldson!"

"Oh…Right…"

"Got a phone book around here?"

◆ ◆ ◆

Berkeley "Psychoanalyzing Specialist" Dr. Jerry Donaldson was incon-
veniently on vacation in Hawaii, but
it was no problem. After I produced
one of Brewester's FBI cards, the
timid receptionist let us peruse his file
cabinet.

The folder on DRAKE, MILTON was so old it had cobwebs. My mom had taken me to see him six times in 1937. Reading the doc's session notes was like trying to read inscriptions on Tut's tomb, but we could at least make these out:

- *post-trauma effs.*
- *sig. memory loss*
- *no contact acc. victim*

Liz pointed to the last line. "Accident victim?"

"None that I remember."

"Yeah, well…We've established that."

"We better get over to Seals and meet Brewster," I said, checking a clock on the wall, "If he finds my mother we can just put a brake on this Holmes and Watson crap."

"Elementary, my dear Snap."

I kissed her, just for saying that.

◆ ◆ ◆

Antonelli was a pitching master, and the game was even better. A 2-0 win on a Daddy Wags Wagner home run off Lew Burdette in the 10th inning. The Braves had suddenly dropped two and a half games behind the Cubs, and we were just half a fly's wing behind *them*.

We sat in the grandstand because when we arrived I didn't feel quite ready to face my fellow ushers again—and also because Brewster never even showed up. Was he being a no-good slouch again, or was he chasing a lead on my mother?

I took it as a sign of hope.

Ruben's Sandwich

August 26th

I was half right about Brewster. He *was* off chasing a lead on my mother. A gas station attendant in Utah had filled the tank of a blue Chevy Impala matching the description of the one leaving her street in a hurry on Saturday. The attendant also said he heard "thumping" in the car's trunk when it pulled away. Turned out the pump jerk was color blind, and the driver had kidnapped his own bowling ball and forgot to zip its bag shut.

Liz was back working on her novel and knew I needed baseball to distract me, so was happy to have me go to the matinee game. After starting the big series with a 4-13 mark against the Braves, we had nabbed the first two, and the line for bleacher tickets nearly stretched to Potrero Avenue. I was really intending to reunite with my usher pals—assuming they'd have me—but Ruben Gomez cornered me when I got to the employee gate.

"You see Johnny A. pitch last night? He get all good after you warmin' him, so now you go back to warmin' ME."

Bill Rigney had kicked me off the team on our last road trip, but Ruben had already cleared this with the old buzzard. As long as I was off the field before the game began.

So I suited up in my fake Nick Testa duds, and let Gomez work me in the pen for a good half hour. His curveball was dropping, his fastball popping. A few of the guys, Valmy Thomas and of course, Gomez's night club buddy Orlando Cepeda, stopped by to either rib or console me on my missing mother. The alleged kidnapping had made the Oakland papers and already been linked to the Peanut Killer.

"Can't believe you're here at all and not out there huntin' this animal down," said Valmy. "You get along with your mom, right?"

"Zip it."

There wasn't a seat to be had for the game, and one of the *Examiner's* photo bugs let me join him in his box. The Braves had Crandall out with an injury and had been suffering at the plate, but a Covington double and Logan triple over Mays' head gave Joey Jay a 1-0 lead in the 2nd. Jay then hit Davenport to start our 3rd, which really pickled our herring. Gomez laid down a perfect bunt, Bressoud singled in the run with two gone and we were tied.

Then Ruben just dangled his cheese and ate them for lunch. Milwaukee got a leadoff single by Covington in the 4th a leadoff double by Schoendienst in the 6th, a leadoff single by Rice in the 7th, a leadoff walk and single by Aaron in the 8th, and a leadoff single by Logan in the 9th—and couldn't score one more run. In our 8th, Gomez singled, went to third

on a Spencer single, scored on a wild pitch and that was the game.

In 28 innings on this latest visit to our fair stadium, the Braves had scored just two dinky runs. And we had hopped over them into second place.

I got home to see an envelope pinned to my door. Liz was inside, frying up steaks for us.

"Exciting game, sounded like."

"Yeah. You didn't hear anyone knock?"

"No. I was too busy on my second act problem to hear it anyway. Why?"

I held up the envelope. She frowned, and at that moment the telephone rang. I walked over and grabbed it.

"Yeah."

"You're not big on listening to warnings, are you Milton?"

"Shut your yap and let me talk to my mother."

"Oh, sorry. She can't come to the phone right now. A little tied up. Gagged, too."

My hand tightened on the receiver. Imagining it as his neck.

"Another win for the traitors today, Milton? I'm so disappointed. You and Mommy better hope the Cubs or Braves win this thing."

CLICK. I dropped the phone, opened the envelope.

Good job, kid. Keep Mickey happy and keep them Giant wins coming. See you next week in L.A. —Braggo F.

A Mother of a Phone Call

August 27th

For cryin' out loud, today they had me warming up Al Worthington. Don't know what kind of mojo magic my hand has been putting on the ball, but if the Giants keep winning there's a good chance they'll make up a bed for me in the clubhouse.

The poor Braves were spooked, suffering and anemic again. Carl Willey pitched his arm off, but a one-out Bressoud single in the 1st and Wagner double past Bruton was somehow enough to beat him, because Milwaukee:

- Couldn't score with the bases loaded and one out in the 1st
- Couldn't score with first and third and nobody out in the 4th
- Couldn't score with first and second and nobody out in the 6th
- Couldn't score with first and second and one out in the 8th
- Didn't score in the 9th after pinch-hitter Warren Spahn belted a one-out, pinch-hit double that missed leaving the park when a sudden wind gust from Alcatraz forced the ball to graze the top of the fence for a double. Torre walked, but naturally Giel came on to get Mathews and Aaron with ease and end the game.

Hammerless Hank has totally stopped hitting, and the team has followed suit. They've now scored a grand total of two runs in four games here, with the finale against McCormick tomorrow.

I watched this surreal epic with the photo bugs again, but somewhere around the top of the 8th, Pence yelled from the Giants dugout that I had a phone call. I ducked into the clubhouse tunnel to answer it.

It was a terrible connection, choked with static, but I thought I heard a seagull cry.

Or was it my mother's voice?

"…wanted to let you know I'm all right…"

"Mom? Is that you??"

Static. Then…

"…a lot nicer that I thought he'd be…"

"Where are you, Mom? I'll come right away, and I'll kill the bastard—"

"You eating okay?"

"What?? Forget about me! How are YOU? He said you were tied up."

"…Sometimes I'm cold, but I can manage…"

"WHERE ARE YOU??"

Someone took the phone from her. A static-filled man's voice said "she's gotta go" and hung up.

"Hello??"

I smacked the receiver against the tunnel wall, left it dangling. Tracked down Brewster outside Stoneham's box the second the game ended.

"My mother just called. A pay phone, near a beach."

"How did you know that?"

"Because I heard a seagull."

"Any idea how many phone booths

are near beaches?"

"Yeah. Which is why I'm telling you now. You have an entire division, right? Get on it."

"Certainly, Mr. Drake. Oh—and would you like us to check the entire Atlantic coast, too? Or just the Pacific."

I said that was up to him. You gotta start somewhere.

In Search of a Wild Goose

August 28th

Brewster knocked on my door at 9 a.m.

"We're hitting the road today, Drake!"

"You serious?" I was half asleep. "McCormick needs me to warm him up. The Giants can sweep all five from the Braves if—"

"Someone found a body down near Santa Cruz. Thought you should tag along."

I wasn't asleep anymore. "What kind of body?"

"Older female. Caucasian. That's all I know so far. Think you can handle this?"

Liz had already gone to read her manuscript pages at some coffee joint in North Beach. I left her a note, called in a second one for McCormick—that I had a bad stomach ache and couldn't squat—and headed out with Brewster.

Sharpson, his chain-smoking, right-hand flunkie, rode beside him down the coast. Gabbed about this new Natalie Wood movie he had just seen most of the way, interrupted by the occasional squawk of their police radio. I was getting nervous, and would have settled for hearing Nat King Cole or Frank, but was stuck in the back and had no vote.

Our route took us through Pedro Point and Half Moon Bay. They didn't seem to be in any hurry, stopping for coffee twice along the way. Sharpson gave me shady glances once in a while, like he thought I was hiding something. The thing is, I was. But until I figured out what connection Peanut Man had with my past, if he did at all, I didn't see any point in blabbing about it. And believe it or else, the telephone lines in Loon Lake, New York were still down from the storm.

♦ ♦ ♦

Thankfully, the body in Santa Cruz belonged to a vagrant, and was a far more experienced wino than my mother. Strangled with her own shoelaces and dumped in a trash can behind a Shell Station on Route 1. Local cops were on the scene when we arrived, and were kissing up to Brewster and Sharpson like they were popes.

Ambulance guys hauled out the stiff, laid her on the muddy ground. Which was when we noticed the small, empty bag sticking out of her shirt pocket.

"Don't tell me," I said. "Salty Dog Nuts."

Bingo. Except this bag had a small note tucked inside:

Getting warmer, Milton. Sorry for her ragged appearance, but get the point?

"What the hell's that supposed to mean?" asked Sharpson.

"It's a goose chase," said Brewster, "A scavenger hunt. He's leading us to Mrs. Drake."

"It's a place," I said.

"A place? What do you mean a place?"

"Ever been down Big Sur Highway? A spot at the southern end is called Ragged Point."

And so we kept driving. Sharpson finally gave in to my pleas and tuned in to the Giants broadcast. Thanks to me not being there to warm up McCormick, he was his old batting practice self and the Braves woke up for a day and shellacked him. As we hit the curvy, spectacular Big Sur road just past Carmel, and Russ Hodges' voice vanished into static and pounding waves, at least I was sure the killer would be satisfied for another night.

The Point of It All

August 29th

I forgot that cops tend not to get hotel rooms. Brewster and Sharpson were perfectly fine dozing in their Ford, halfway down the Big Sur coastline in the muddy parking lot of Hank's Fine Eats—and Sharpson stinking up the car with his Tareyton filters.

"I'd rather fight than switch, mac. You don't like it, find yourself a room."

"Best idea I've heard all night."

"Yeah. Come to think of it, maybe your murdering boyfriend will come knocking on your door."

The trek down to Ragged Point had gotten us nowhere. Not much there except a mailbox, hamburger stand, and dumpy motel. Brewster questioned every living person he saw, and there weren't many. He was mad at me, mad at the Peanut Killer, mad at the wasted work he'd been doing the last three months.

"If you ask me," I said, "We missed something back there."

"Nobody's asking you, " said the ever-charming Sharpson.

"I'm serious. He wouldn't have left that note about Ragged Point unless there was something for us to find."

"Maybe it wasn't a place. Maybe Ragged Point is the shape of something. Like your head."

I glared at him. "Ever wonder what it's like to swallow an entire lit cigarette?"

"Oh, I'm all impressed now. Being told what to do by a menial ballpark employee—"

I tried to vault over the back seat at him, but Brewster caught me in mid-lunge.

"Watch yourself, Drake. You're one

guilt by association away from getting a pair of cold metal bracelets."

"Really, Griffin? I didn't think you cared."

He scowled, and I backed off with a new thought.

"How about this? Drive back to Ragged Point and let me snoop around for fifteen minutes. If I don't find anything we ditch the idea and head back to the city."

"You're a real card, aren't you?"

"Yep. And you gotta play me if you want that royal flush."

◆ ◆ ◆

It was nearly morning by the time we got back to Ragged Point. They parked in the nearly empty motel lot, watched me while I circled my way around the building. The place sat atop a cliff over the ocean, but as dawn light painted the air, the fog that was everywhere hours ago had begun to lift, and I could make out the rocky beach below.

And a weird, pink-colored shape.

I found a path that zig-zagged down the cliff. Kept my eye on the shape at every turn. It was starting to look fleshy.

Scampered back up and whistled at Brewster and Sharpson. They got out, followed me down the path to the beach.

The man's legs sticking out of the sand were, cold, bloated. His black trouser pants bunched down over his fat knees. Brewster and Sharpson eyeballed each other, put on plastic gloves and hauled the rest of the body out of the sand.

It was the limo driver the killer had hired to pick me up at the mental hospital. Another empty Salty Dog Nuts bag was stuffed in his mouth. Brewster carefully plucked it out and we looked at the brand new note inside:

You came in high
So your name is a lie
And for that you will die

I felt dizzy. Something new and clear was taking shape in my brain.

"I think this is it…" I uttered.

"It?" asked Brewster, "It what??"

I stared at them. Smiled for the first time in a week. "The clue I've been needing to solve this."

Fog Lifting

August 30th

"Okay. It's coming back to me now."

"I'm all ears, Snap."

Liz sat on my couch, both of us armed with gin and tonics. I had managed to stall Brewster and Sharpson, who were off investigating the death of a fat limo driver. After spending most of today's second straight Giants win trying to pester Liz up in the Seals press box, she was finally ready to listen.

"The dream. About driving with my dad, the crackers, the clearing in the woods with a ball game going on—"

"The A.Y.B.L."

"Right. The Adirondack Youth Baseball league. When I was reading the note our nasty friend left with the limo guy, it started to put itself together. My dad spent half our life savings to send me to that place. Which is why he had to get a second job…as a bus driver."

"Which caused him to die in an accident. I'm still so sorry."

"Yeah…"

"So what happened at the camp?"

I took a long sip of gin. Knocked out a Camel.

"'Hard and fast and middle up'. Dad drilled it in my head the entire way there. And then…in maybe my first game pitching…I think I hit someone."

"You think?"

"It was getting dark. The field didn't have any lights. I remember gripping the ball, whipping it in…and wishing right away that I hadn't. Too late though. That sickening sound—"

"Who did you hit?"

I took a long pause. Painfully trying to conjure the crickets back into my head, the sticky midsummer heat.

"I don't remember."

"That's too bad. Guess we'll have to talk to that camp director after all."

"You don't think I've been trying? Damn phones have been down for days."

"Then we better take another road trip. Or tell your FBI buddies to send someone on a new goose chase."

"Forget that. I don't trust those clowns to wind their watches."

"Maybe, but all we need is the name of the person you hit!"

"I need more than that. It's pretty obvious that my blackouts started around that time. If I go to that camp again—and that field—it might bring every detail back and cure me forever."

"Okay, so what are we waiting for?"

I finished my Camel. Dug out the pack to keep the chain going. "For these eight straight games with the Dodgers to end."

"Why's that?"

"Let's just say…I got a new commitment."

"To who?"

"To a certain powerful L.A. hoodlum I'd rather not talk to you about."

"Hey. I don't care if it's Mickey Cohen. Right now you need to be honest with me."

I gazed at her. The words I wanted to say were stuck in my throat like a bunch of chicken bones. She got the message from reading my face.

"Oh god, you know what? You're right. I don't want to know."

"If we can just wait till next week, Liz."

"Wait? We've waited long enough. There might be two more people dead by then!"

"Yeah, well…One's going to be me if I don't take care of this thing."

"Fine then. I'll go myself."

"What?"

"Why not? I'm not getting those creepy notes anymore. Meaning the *Herald* doesn't care if I write a column or fall off a cliff."

"I'd worry about you up there. And this is my past we're dealing with, not yours."

"I'm a big girl, Snap. Just lend me that old bat of yours and if he tracks me down I'll bash his peanut of a head in."

I didn't like lending Triples Trevor to anyone, let alone a dame. But this was one time I knew I'd be giving in.

Glassy-eyed

August 31st

So Liz was off again for the East Coast, presumably to track down camp director Randall Nathan in Loon Lake, New York. The fact she left with her novel and fresh notepads made me think a side trip to Manhattan publishing houses was not out of the question.

Me? Business as unusual. With my mother still missing, I needed a day escorting Giants ticket-holders to their seats to keep myself calm. Naturally, Brewster showed up five minutes before the first pitch to make that impossible.

According to his "report," the dead limo driver was apparently bound and gagged before he was strangled, maybe in the killer's trunk. He hadn't been seen since he dropped me at my place eight days ago, and his limo was found abandoned outside a sandwich shop in Daly City.

"The marks on his neck were awful fresh," he said, "Meaning our friend was keeping him alive for a while. He's got to be operating out of some local lair."

"Where he might also be keeping my mom."

"You would think."

Norm Larker was stepping into the box against Stu Miller, and there were a dozen fans waiting for my help.

"Guess I'll talk to you later," he said, "Oh—one other thing. Fingerprint people came with up nothing visible at your mother's house. Not even on the broken window."

He left. I helped two families and two priests find their seats, and the game got going. Miller was effective as always, but the shock was that this skinny guy with big ears named Johnny Klippstein, who came over from the Reds in June, was even better. After Ron Fairly singled and Dick Gray tripled to put L.A. on top 1-0 in the 6th, Klippstein struck out our side right after. It seemed to spark the last-place Dodgers, as Gilliam doubled, Furillo put one into the parking lot in deep left, and with a Mays homer the only pimple, the Klipper Kid beat us 3-1 to keep us a game and a half out. The Cubs could very well spend their Labor Day tomorrow bombing the suddenly pathetic Braves twice, so we needed to keep pace by doing the same to these Black and Blue Boys.

I wasn't in the mood for the Double Play, or being at home without Liz. Brewster's comments were still swimming in my head, and were enough to drive me over the Bay Bridge for another look in my mother's house. Before going in, I knocked on the door of Ben Mudge, her 80-year-old retired postmaster neighbor who could still be nosy on a good day.

"Already told the police I didn't hear no screams, Milt. Can't you all just leave me alone?"

"And you didn't see that blue Impala tear out of here?"

"Nope. That was Flo across the street, but she's half blind so I wouldn't listen to her. Did see a strange old jalopy pull away a bit later, though. One of its headlights out."

"No kidding. A Studebaker?"

He shrugged. "Might've been."

I thanked him, mulling it over. Went in the house, put on some lights. Wandered over to the broken window.

This time noticed something odd. A few pieces of glass that were still intact in the frame were bent outward, not inward. I looked down. Some of the window glass was on her carpet, but not all that much.

I hurried back outside, circled around. There was a little broken glass under the windowsill, but a bunch of it was gleaming at me from a bush a few feet away.

I crouched. Carefully spread its leaves open with my hand. A brown glass container was wedged in there, and I pulled it out. It was a bottle of Hamm's. Its stale beer smell still wafting out the neck.

Unless I was crazy, it was possible the kidnapper hadn't broken in this window at all. He had flung his empty beer bottle through it—from the inside. Did the Peanut Killer drink Hamm's?...

National League thru Sunday, August 31

Chicago	74	58	.562	—
San Francisco	72	59	.550	1.5
Milwaukee	69	61	.531	4
St. Louis	65	64	.504	7.5
Cincinnati	67	66	.504	7.5
Philadelphia	61	67	.477	11
Pittsburgh	58	73	.443	15.5
Los Angeles	56	74	.431	17

American League thru Sunday, August 31

New York	81	49	.623	—
Chicago	76	54	.585	5
Boston	70	59	.543	10.5
Baltimore	68	60	.531	12
Cleveland	70	62	.530	12
Detroit	62	66	.484	19
Kansas City	50	79	.388	30.5
Washington	41	89	.315	40

≈ *The Blue Car* ≈

September 1st

Funny, but today sure didn't start insane. There was my steaming coffee cup. There were my eggs and morning paper. Liz called from somewhere outside New York, saying she'd rented an auto and was en route to Loon Lake to find the camp director. Hopefully she would find him, because I was flat out of recollections.

The Giants had two Labor Day contests with the Dodgers before heading south and then east for their final trip of the year. I walked into the usher's room to suit up and was stunned to see a surprise gathering and birthday cake waiting. My head had been so scattered lately that September 1st had snuck up on me.

"Even though Butch and Dominic tried to talk me out of it," said Pence, "we thought we'd all thank you for being born." I blushed, thanked them back. Tall Tom gave me a snazzy new cigarette lighter, Stan Lowsack assured me in his baritone that my mother would turn up safe, and everyone else vowed to buy me a draft at the Double Play later.

Naturally, Valmy Thomas tried to get me to warm up Al Worthington before Game 1, but I declined. Turned out he didn't need my help, because Johnny Podres was so god-awful again for the Dodgers that Red Skelton could have pitched for us. Podres took a 2-0 Dodger lead into the 4th, then promptly gave us nine runs in the next four innings for the 10-5 wipeout. And with the Cubs busy getting spanked twice in Milwaukee, everyone in Seals suddenly realized we could slip back into first by winning the nightcap.

"Drake!" yelled Valmy from the field as soon as the first game ended, "Ramon Monzant just promised you a box of cigars!"

Oh boy. Tough to resist that. I had about twenty free minutes, so got into my Nick Testa duds, found a mitt and warmed up a grinning Monzant in the Giants pen.

Next thing I knew, Pence Murphy was yelling at me from the stands.

"Snappy! Just took a call from your mom!"

"YOU WHAT??" A Monzant fastball nearly sawed my head off.

"Yeah! Said you have to come get her! She's in a place called Guerneville, up past Santa Rosa I think. Wrote down the name of the park—"

"Is she all right??"

"Dunno. Sounded a little shaken up. She was sneezing too."

"You positive it was my mother?"

"Whaddya, given' me the third degree here? Yeah, it was your mother. You want I should call that FBI guy—"

"NO!" Monzant's next heater nailed my shin. "I'll go myself. Valmy, take over!"

"We got to win this!" yelled Monzant.

"Get some faith, Ramon." I told him.

◆ ◆ ◆

The Coronet hadn't been pushed hard since my drive to Sacramento, but I did 50 with ease heading over the Golden Gate. On my radio, we took an early 2-0 lead on Koufax thanks to Cepeda's second of three doubles on the day. A Fairly sacrifice fly cut it to 2-1, but then Koufax started walking the park like he's done all year, and we scored four times off him and Craig in the 5th. I picked up speed, in case the killer decided to let the inevitable sweep set him off again. Pence always had one foot in a beer keg. What if the killer was impersonating my mother on the phone?

Guerneville was a tiny old resort town from Victorian times that was part of Sonoma County. I found the park Pence had written down, a shady public facility on a bank of the Russian River.

And I couldn't believe it. Mom was sitting alone at a picnic table, wearing a rain slicker that wasn't hers, carrying a bedroll, and blowing her red nose into a wad of tissue.

"There you are!" she exclaimed, as I parked and climbed out, as flustered and confused as I ever was. "Happy birthday, doll face!" I let her hug me.

"Where the hell have you been? It's been a week! I was worried to death! There's been an all-points bulletin!"

"Really? For me? That's just silly. Might've been rough for the first few days but I was never in danger for one—"

"Where is he?" I uttered, with a sharp dagger of a voice. She looked at me as if I were nuts.

"You mean Jack? He's right over there!"

I turned. Twenty yards away, a half dozen young men and women were hanging out of the back of a little camping truck. Parked at the edge of the lot beside a shiny blue Impala. I walked over. Recognized the stocky, handsome, T-shirted ringleader right away.

"Kerouac?"

Jack spun, saw me and burst into a huge smile. "If it ain't Brother-Man, son of Good Lady Drake! Thought you might arrive event-u-ally."

"You're the one who kidnapped my mother?"

"Kidnapped? What are you, blotto? Actually got back in town after a floating raft of glorious days and nights down deep Mexico way and came looking for YOU to outdoor celebrate said days and nights but forgot where you lived and your mama was helpful, so so helpful, and had a bit too much of my wine bottle and asked to go camping with us, that's right!"

"Camping!" my mother squeaked, "Never did it until now!"

"You broke her damn window!" I barked at Kerouac.

"Oh no. Oh no no no, Brother-man, that would have been Dwight. He had a bit of a beer problem and liked throwing things around including bottles that night and there you have that. We lost Dwight somewhere on the way up to Eureka, and where was that, Bonnie-ola?"

Bonnie, a young blonde girl with very red eyes, peered out from the back of the camping truck. "Redding?"

"Redding, righhhht…"

I glanced around the lot. Even looked into the shadows on the nearby road. "You guys didn't have an old Studebaker with you? With a headlight missing?"

"Uhh…nope. Say, you ever feel that dark soul I told you to feel?"

"You better start making some sense, pal—"

"Your baseball-killer! He ever turn up?"

"Oh. Well…We're getting close. I can smell him."

"Uh-uh. Uh uh uh uh uh. You can't smell or taste him, you gotta BE him. Thanks for makin' that soup, Mama Drake!" He nudged me with a wink. "Be good to the ones that put you here. Because years mean wisdom, mister. Years means wisdom…"

And with that he was back with his vagabond friends, and I was driving back to the city with my beaming, apple-cheeked mother. She actually looked healthier.

"Jack is a well-known writer, you know."

"I'm aware of this, mom."

"And he's much nicer than I thought he would be."

I dropped her off, ideas tumbling in my head. Peanut Killer *was* at her house that night, but only *saw* my mother's "abduction" go down. More than enough to inspire his "kidnapping" scheme.

I got back to my place, and another note was pinned to my door to cap off a most laborious Labor Day:

Bookie's name is Sal Flores. L.A. Coliseum upp grand sec 9, row LL seat 12
*   —Braggo F.*

My sinister gig for Mickey Cohen was on, whether I liked it or not. And I knew just the person to help me…

Drysdaled

September 2nd

"Yes Milton, you beanballed someone."

"What was his name?"

"I don't even remember. Some rich kid. Now can you fix my toaster please?"

After helping my mother straighten up her house this morning and attempt to do the same with her life, I hit Route 101 for my last trip of the year to L.A. The Giants pitchers naturally hoped I'd be warming them up, but I had darker plans for the evening.

Like he told me over ice cream last month, Mickey Cohen had a target he wanted me to knock off: a bookie named Sal Flores he'd placed fifty grand on the Giants with. Of course, with the Giants now back in first, I wanted to be sure Braggo's note last night was still relevant.

Unfortunately, it was. Mickey still didn't trust the Giants' bullpen to get them across the pennant finish line. He didn't like being nervous, didn't especially like Sal Flores, so why not rub him out and retrieve his money ahead of time?

I met Braggo at a hot dog stand on La Cienega called Tail of the Pup, where he slipped me a snub nose .38 and reminded me how useless my body and face would be if I didn't do the job. I hid the gun in my glove compartment and drove across town to the monolithic stadium, pulling into a lot thirty minutes before the game.

Not having the tragically injured Roy Campanella on their team this season had finally caught up with the Dodgers. His longtime batterymate and buddy Don Newcombe had a terrible start and was sent packing to Cincinnati, and their record since the all-star break was an abysmal 14-40. We had taken four out of five at Seals, and with their ace loser Don Drysdale on the hill, the place looked emptier than the Roman Colosseum for Black Plague Day.

I bought myself a cold one, easily found an empty seat behind the row Sal the bookie was booked for. A few families filed in around me, but the crowd was mostly groups of guys or first-year diehards wearing Dodger hats studded with goofy buttons.

Halfway through the 1st inning, a thin character excused himself into the row in front of me. Tropical shirt, porkpie hat, and shades. Puffing on a thick, smelly cigar and carrying a folded up sports section and racing form, he dropped into seat 12. If this guy wasn't Sal the bookie, I was Grace Kelly.

Meanwhile, Antonelli must have been cursing me between pitches, because even without the injured Snider, the Dodgers lit him up for four home runs. Sal stood and cheered, left his hat on his seat at least four times to go make phonecalls, then came back and kept on puffing. I didn't really want to kill this guy, but his cigar smoke wafting into my eyes was making me think otherwise.

After Ray Crone took over for mop-up duty and Furillo bashed his third round-tripper of the night—the second time he'd done that this season—Sal clapped again and dumped some hot cigar ash on my pants leg.

"Hey, watch it!!" I barked.

He turned, lowered his shades to reveal a jagged scar under one eye, and fixed me with a wordless death stare. I forced a friendly grin, then quickly ducked up to the restroom to relieve myself.

When I returned two minutes later, he was gone. His hat and newspapers with him. What kind of baseball fan leaves a game in the 7th inning? And with Drysdale taking a rare shutout into the 8th! Rats. I would have to follow him home the next night.

◆ ◆ ◆

I drove up to Liz's old bungalow in the Los Feliz hills, still unrented and vacant. I got inside via the same open window crack, laid out a blanket I'd tossed in my trunk and tried to get some sleep.

Tough to do. Aside from the hellish crickets, someone was having a cocktail party a few houses away or across the canyon and playing far too much Louis Prima. Except for the crickets, the racket all died out around midnight.

Which was when I heard the car motor. Idling close by. I sat up, crawled over to the window and peered out. A ghostly glow came through the trees, and I couldn't tell if it was from one headlight or two. Maybe a hundred yards from the house. I stood up in the window and the car drove by, rounded the corner and vanished.

I laid back down. Let the crickets conjure up my high and middle-in fastball, rushing toward a faceless boy's head…

And the car motor woke me again. I sat up. Someone definitely was watching the house through the trees. Was it Sal? Braggo? I would have been happy with either one, but when I stepped out the front door this time, the car sped away again.

Further sleep would be out of the question.

To Live and Drive in L.A.

September 3rd

Nobody was watching me or Liz's house this morning. I rolled out to my car, groggier than hell, drove downtown to have breakfast and a pot of coffee at the Pantry. Afterwards, I found a pay phone and tracked Liz down at the only hotel in Loon Lake, New York. Randall the camp director had been taken seriously ill and wasn't seeing visitors yet. That figured. I suggested she go all Snappy at the A.Y.B.L. office and get into their records. We had to get the name of this kid I hit.

In the meantime, there was another night game at the Coliseum to follow Sal Flores home from. But I needed a partner this time. Headed over Cahuenga Pass to Ventura Boulevard and straight into the narrow driveway for Frack Automotive. It was busier than ever, but Billy was pretty hopped up to see me.

"Didja ask my sister to tie the knot yet, Pops?"

"Nothing personal, but sometimes it feels more like a noose."

"Ha! Well, yeah…She's a piece of job, that's for sure."

I told him about my predicament, disguising it as a simple errand to "try and get my money back from a hustler" and conveniently leaving Mickey Cohen's name and possible murder out of the stew. When I promised him a nice little cut—something I prayed I could arrange later—he took the bait.

"Just make sure I don't break no more bones. Business is through the roof and I gotta be able to turn a wrench."

◆ ◆ ◆

A much bigger crowd showed up, what with the Dodgers' 10-3 demolition of the Giants the night before. The other reason for the mob was the return of Duke Snider after a two-week absence. It was Billy's first Dodger game, and he armed himself with a beer and weenie in no time. The congestion made it tougher to find empty seats behind Sal's row, but we managed.

Sal showed up halfway through the 1st again, sporting a different colored tropical shirt and smoking a fresh cigar. He arrived just in time to see the Duke line a single into right off Gomez to score Fairly with the game's first run, then rob Bob Schmidt of a three-run homer in the 3rd. With Billy on hand, we were able to take turns going to food stands or the restroom without losing sight of him.

It was still a tight contest, 3-3 into the 4th, when Mays' third straight single off Erskine gave the Giants a 4-3 lead. After that, things got ghastly in a hurry. Dodger pitchers had nothing, and the Giants repeatedly reminded them of this, shellacking Erskine, Roebuck, Birrer and Kipp for 19 total runs and 27 hits. The game was an abomination by the 6th, and this time I didn't squawk about Sal leaving early, because three-quarters of the Coliseum was following his lead.

But Sal was a quick walker. "Good thing he's wearing that awful shirt," I said as we struggled to follow him out the exit tunnel. Billy stayed on his heels while I circled around to pick Billy up with the Coronet. Sal drove a shiny white T-Bird convertible, gave a parking lot kid a ten-dollar bill to lift a barrier for him. It took a little lurching and weaving, but we closed in behind him as he headed east.

He drove straight through teeming downtown. At each light we could hear a different male crooner on his radio. Billy blew gum bubbles, beat out a rhythm on my dashboard. I was starting to wonder what I was getting this poor kid into.

Sal drove into Boyle Heights, pulled up in front of a rundown Victorian. A beefy Latino guy wearing a yellow satin jacket came out, got into the passenger seat.

"Who's the doorman?" asked Billy.

"Hell if I know."

We kept following them. They were heading further east. By the time we went through Chino, cold, dry wind gusts swept out of the desert and started buffeting the car.

"Santa Anas, Pops. Beware of crackling hair."

"I thought Santa Anas were hot!"

"Give 'em twelve hours."

The T-Bird stopped at a petrol station. We hung back, waited for them to leave and quickly zoomed in to fill my tank. The further east we drove, the more house lights began to vanish, and a few tumbleweeds bounced across the road. I splattered a jackrabbit. Billy crossed himself, said it was bad luck.

It was midnight when we entered the Pomona Hills. Sal's T-Bird led us down a twisting two-lane road flanked by swaying oaks. Went through the gate under a sign reading HARRAH RANCH.

We killed the headlights, parked on the side of the road. Hopped a fence and made our way toward the sprawling, lit ranch house. We saw Sal and his buddy climb out of the T-bird, shake hands with a tall, cowboy-hatted gent, who could only be Mr. Harrah. Sal's friend went into the house while Sal and Harrah headed toward a large barn.

We went around the back of the house, approached the open barn. We could hear Sal and Harrah laughing, and then Harrah said in a pronounced drawl, "This one here's a demon. He'll mop the floor with Del Mar." So Sal was also in the horse trade. Billy was getting anxious, and I had to keep him quiet and restrained.

When Harrah went back toward the house promising " a bottle of my best," I saw my chance. Told Billy to stay put, felt for the .38 in my back pocket and walked around the corner and into the barn.

Sal, cigar still in mouth, was petting the nose of a gorgeous brown stallion. And he was all alone. I took a few steps forward and took out my gun. He turned and saw me, yanked off his sunglasses. I raised the gun.

"Don't make this any tougher, Sal."

"Who the hell are you?"

"Mickey Cohen sent me. He changed his mind about that bet."

"Then ya better tell him he's got a screw loose. They won 19-4 tonight! They're in first place—"

"I know, but I'm sorry. I need his fifty grand back."

"Why you little punk. This is how he does business now? Following guys from ballgames? Don't think I didn't see ya."

"Please. I don't wanna have to use this."

"Aw, don't worry. pea-brain. You won't."

Another gun clicked behind me. I glanced around. Sal's yellow-jacketed henchman had one arm under Billy's neck, and a much bigger gun to his head. I slowly dropped mine.

"I'm sorry, Snappy. He came out of nowhere—"

"Shut up!" yelled Sal, "the both of you!"

He found himself a riding whip and walked up to my face. At this distance, his ugly scar looked like the Panama Canal.

"Braggo Farfadecchio is the only guy I know who does jobs for Mickey Cohen. What makes you so special? Huh?"

"Guess I'm in training."

He nodded, then whacked my face with the whip. I dropped to my knees in pain.

At that moment Harrah returned with a champagne bottle and two glasses. Whistled when he saw us.

"HOO-boy…Sure didn't expect no bake sale."

"I'll be with you in a few, Rusty."

Harrah winked, retreated and shut the barn doors after him.

"I didn't really want to do this, Sal. I've been giving the Giants good luck most of the year, and when it turned all of a sudden, Mickey blamed me. Said I owed him one."

"How heartwarming. Except now you owe ME one. He looked at his buddy who threw Billy on the ground, then calmly smashed his shoe down on Billy's right hand and broke it.

"You son-of-a—"

I leapt to my feet, ignoring the ferocious, stinging blows of Sal's whip. But I couldn't ignore the butt of his friend's gun. It hit the back of my head like a polo mallet. Knocked me nose first into some hay, my consciousness along with it.

The Unusual Suspect

September 4th

Little things were digging into my back. Pinching my neck. I opened my eyes in near-darkness. I had been thrown into some kind of wooden, coffin-shaped box. Pressed up on the top and all it did was rattle a padlock that kept me inside. I reached under my sweat-caked shirt, picked off a handful of chicken feed.

I heard low voices. One was Sal, the other Harrah. The faint wimpering was clearly Billy Frack's. I balled a fist and pounded the top of the feed box.

"HE'S ALIVE!!" I heard Sal yell in mock-Frankenstein sarcasm. Footsteps drew closer, then the entire box shook like an earthquake fault.

"Better do something with him quick", added Harrah, "I got that trainer and his wife comin' by in two hours."

"Pardon my spanish, amigo, but could you hold your horses?"

Their wave of idiotic chuckling was suddenly cut off by the creaking sound of the barn door.

"Who the hell are YOU now?" asked Sal.

The voice that answered was loud, raspy. And instantly recognizable.

"Don't you know that he's mine?"

There was an odd, whizzing sound. An awful gasp. A horrible gurgling. Something heavy landed on top of my box, rolled off. A single gunshot rang out. A man screamed. More gurgling.

Then, total silence. I lay there, afraid to breathe. A new set of heavier footsteps approached my box, and a key carefully slid into the padlock. Turned. I heard the footsteps leave the barn again.

I laid there another thirty seconds, then braced myself. Slowly raised the box's lid. Sat up, hay still in my hair, my nose sore and red. Gazed around.

Blood was absolutely everywhere. Sal, Harrah and Sal's satin-jacketed friend lay on the floor, either stabbed to death, their throats cut, or both. Billy was propped awkwardly in a corner. Both of his hands mangled, a bullet hole in his forehead, his eyes lifeless.

My entire body deflated. I had no clue how I was going to break news of this nightmare to Liz, but there was no time to think about that. I said an atheist's prayer for the poor kid, picked up Braggo's .38 that had been dropped beside him.

Morning light filtered into the barn through the door's slats. I stumbled outside. Saw one dead ranch hand draped over a barbed wire fence, another head first in a pig trough. I walked over to the house, quietly walked inside.

Mrs. Harrah and what looked like her sister were both lying dead in the kitchen. Strangled with their own apron strings. A coffee cake was burning in the oven and I turned it off.

I spotted a few dollar bills on the counter and grabbed them. Opened a cookie jar and found a few more. Located Sal's study, went through his desk and nabbed a few wads of bills from the drawers. Checked the pockets of every corpse for extra cash and hurried back down the ranch driveway.

Braggo's Cadillac was parked just outside the gate, a few yards from my car. Braggo was slumped over the steering wheel, wheezing out blood, almost dead from multiple stab wounds. He was trying to whisper something.

"Miser…"

"What's that?…Listen Braggo, I have to find Mickey. Where's he live?"

"MISER…"

"Shut up! Where's Mickey live?"

His eyes fluttered for a moment. "Brentwood…Moreno…513…" And he died right on the wheel.

On the Dodge steering wheel, a note from my infamous friend was waiting for me:

Nice work, Milton. But don't stop now. You're getting oh so close.

◆ ◆ ◆

I high-tailed it back to L.A. Made it to Brentwood around noon. 513 Moreno was a sweet property, but no one seemed to be home. I'd heard Mickey Cohen had a complete security system installed, but for some reason it wasn't on, because I walked right through an unlocked gate around the side.

The pool area was empty. Its perfect water shimmering in the hot midday sun. I was about to leave again and heard a glass shatter in the open pool house. I crept over to the door.

"Mickey?"

Heard nothing. Stepped inside. Its blinds were lowered. The plush furniture looked pretty unfestive.

I heard someone breathing. Stepped around the bar and saw something I never thought possible: Mickey Cohen cowering on the floor. Still in his bathrobe. Armed with a corkscrew, and even that was shaking. He stared at me, his eyes bugging out.

"It's you...You're him!"

"I'm him? Him who?"

"MISER SOLSTEIN!"

"Who the hell is Miser Solstein?"

He lowered the corkscrew. "He's supposed to be Jewish. Some say his father was Italian. Which is sort of the same thing...Anyway, nobody believed he was real. Nobody ever saw him or knew anybody that ever worked directly for him, but to hear Bugsy Siegel tell it, anybody could have worked for Solstein. You never knew. That was his power. The greatest trick the Devil ever pulled was convincing the world he didn't exist."

"Yeah, well...Nice fairy tale, Mickey. Meanwhile, another buddy of mine is dead and it's all your fault."

"He killed them all, I tell ya! He's a heartless butcher! And now he'll get me! I believe in God, and the only thing that scares me is Miser Solstein!!"

"Oh, cut the crap. It was the damn Peanut Killer, and you're the least of his worries. Here—" I tossed the cash I'd collected from the ranch at him. "Comes to about two grand and change. Sal's dead, and your Giants might win anyway, so you can leave me alone now."

I left him cowering, grabbed an ugly alligator shirt off a chair to change into, and headed back to the Coliseum.

◆ ◆ ◆

It was the best of the three matches there, and the season series finale. Dick Gray popped a two-run homer off McCormick to put the Dodgers up 4-3 in the 6th, but three innings of good pitching is too much to ask of L.A.'s inflammable bullpen. Craig gave up a Mays single and Cepeda homer in the 7th, a Hodges error was followed by a Bob Schmidt homer in the 9th, and that was that, the Giants easily taking the series for the year, 14-8.

Seconds after Cimoli flied out to end the thing, someone smelling of Asian cologne dropped into the sunny seat beside me. It was Valmy Thomas, dressed in his street clothes already.

"Nice whack from Schmitty, eh?"

"Sure was. What are you doing up here?"

"Oh, Rigney and the boys thought you might need a personal escort and a bit of coaxin' to the plane."

"Plane?"

"Three games at Wrigley with the Cubs start tomorrow. Did you forget?"

"Um, no. But I have to—"

"Come with us, right? Great idea, Mr. Goodluck!" He helped me to my feet, looked straight at me. "Listen, Drake. I don't care if Adolf, Benito, Jack the Ripper, and Leopold and Loeb are after you. We're only one game ahead of those jokers, the Braves are alive again and we gotta widen that lead."

I sighed. Hated to leave my wheels, but come to think of it, getting out of L.A. at that moment wasn't the worst idea.

≈ *Take the "W" Train* ≈

September 5th

I tried calling Liz first thing in the morning from our Chicago hotel to tell her about Billy, but she didn't answer. Left a message with her nun-like innkeeper that I'd try her again later, then hopped on the el train to the north side.

It was packed to the hand straps with Cub fans, everyone blabbing excitedly about the big weekend series, a few betting on how many homers Ernie Banks would sock. The teams had an ancient rivalry that predated the Giants' move west by half a century, when Fred Merkle's famous boner helped the Cubs steal the 1908 pennant at the Polo Grounds. Most of the faithfuls around me didn't know Merkle from Spackle, but it didn't dampen their spirits.

I wove my way through the street mob and into the park. Suited up, warmed Stu Miller in the pen—his stuff was crackling—and took a seat in the cramped Giants' dugout for the game. I was right about Miller; the Cubbies couldn't touch him. Taylor Phillips didn't look bad either, but the game quickly got away from the Georgia lefty in a nightmarish 4th. Alou doubled, Mays tripled, and Cepeda homered right in front of me for a 4-0 Giants lead, but for me it was a different kind of nightmare: All I could see was poor Billy's dead face.

The crowd that had been so vocal before the game sat there mute. Soon after, our dugout phone rang. Cubs broadcaster Jack Brickhouse wanted me as an in-game guest up in the booth. I'd get $30 dollars and a free dinner at the Blackhawk. Not the best timing.

"Does he think I'm Nick Testa or Snappy Drake?" I asked Rigney.

"Didn't say" he said, "Keep your uniform on just in case."

I climbed up some rickety stairs to the television booth, and Brickhouse was there to greet me in a criminally ugly sport jacket.

"Hey-hey! Nick Testa!"

So that settled that. At least I wouldn't have to answer any murder case questions. He set me up beside him before they came back from a commercial break. Slid a big WGN microphone in front of my face.

"Joining us in the booth for the last of the 6th is Nick Testa, bullpen backstop extraordinaire. According to the Giants players, you've become quite the good luck charm for them."

"Um, that's right, Jack."

"There's a called strike on Tony Taylor…Nick, maybe you can share some of your secrets with our viewers."

"Er—secrets about what?"

"How you bring them good luck! Admit it, you hide pixie dust in that mitt of yours, right?"

"Well no, it's probably all a coincidence. Started when I first warmed up Johnny Antonelli before a game in Philadelphia—"

"Taylor bounces one to third and Davenport throws him out! One away…Would you say Antonelli is the toughest customer on the team you have to deal with?"

"Yeah, I'd say so. Johnny has a temper, likes to do things his own way. He's a lefty, you know."

"Oh, don't I know that…Cal Neeman up there now, grounded out his first time…Say, you seem like a nice young fella. You think the pressure of the race and that murder business surrounding the team is getting to you, too?"

I was tongue-tied. "Well…it sure isn't affecting the team's—"

WHOCK. "High fly ball by Neeman! Sauer back to the track and this one is WAY OUT OF HERE!! HEY-HEY!!! WHOOOOOO!!!"

Brickhouse stood and cheered and made a fool of himself and the park went crazy. He wiped his face with a hankie, slapped me on the back when he sat back down.

"Looks like you brought us some luck too, Nickie! Maybe I oughta tie you to that chair!"

"Mr. Rigney probably won't like that, Jack."

The inning and game would end

quickly, but not as fast as me getting out of that booth with my cash and Blackhawk voucher.

Miller was brilliant, giving up just three hits but getting three double play balls. Chicago left just one runner on base the entire game. Our lead was up to two games, and with the Braves getting skunked by the Pirates again, the champs were three back.

Our usual post-win celebration carried over to an Italian joint downtown, but I ducked into a phone booth after one beer and a hunk of calamari to call Liz again. This time she answered, but sounded congested and confused. She had caught a bad cold and was trying to sleep it off.

"Is something wrong?" she slurred. Obviously, being in upstate New York she hadn't heard the awful news from L.A. yet. I filled the phone line with a long moment of dark hesitation. "If not, try me tomorrow when I'm more conscious, okay?"

I hesitated agin, then promised I would and hung up. Hell. It would've been tough enough for her to hear about her brother *without* a stuffy head.

Bombardment

September 6th

Oh, the best laid plans of Snappy and men…

With our 1:20 start time, I was hoping to make the big call to Liz around noon, but it got postponed. So did my life.

The second I neared the players' gate, two Chicago television crews and three local reporters swarmed all over me like flies on a steer. Apparently my guest spot in Jack Brickhouse's booth got the old press wheels rolling, and it took a lot for me to not go all Eugene Buzzbee on someone. The Giants players ribbed me up until game time. Davenport was calling me "Marilyn" and Antonelli was chuckling so hard he could barely warm up.

But nobody on the Cubs or in the stands was laughing. After his last bad outing at the L.A. Coliseum, Johnny was smoking again. Occasional Cubs would get on the bases, but none of them went anywhere. Meanwhile, Chicago's defense betrayed them in the 2nd. A hit batter, single and unforgivable walk to Antonelli loaded 'em with two gone, and after Glen Hobbie uncorked a wild pitch for the first run, Bobby Adams booted an easy grounder at second to bring in another, and Bressoud's cheap single made it 3-0. The booing in the grandstand over our heads was practically making the dugout shake.

Hobbie was beside himself, which may have been why he lost his mind two innings later. First he walked Daryl Spencer, then gave up five straight hits to Bressoud, Mays, Cepeda, Alou, and Davenport. That was about the time the first draft beer came spilling into our dugout.

"Hey Testa!" yelled the beer's former owner, "Get your ugly leprechaun ass outta there!"

Right. Like this was somehow MY fault. And I certainly wasn't Irish. The Giants tried to console me, but with a 9-0 lead now, the verbal abuse was only going to increase. Rigney eventually said I could go get dressed and wait in the clubhouse, so I did.

Heard the last few innings on the radio, and missed a near-donnybrook when Banks reached third to start the Cub 9th and Rigney brought the infield in to try and keep the shutout. After the next two guys whiffed, Cal Neeman put one on Waveland Avenue, then cussed Antonelli all around the bases, causing the next pitch to nearly dent Bobby Adams' forehead.

Before the victorious gaggle invaded the locker room, I ducked into the hall to try Liz again on the pay phone. While I was fishing out some coins, three sets of arms grabbed me from behind. Someone dropped a burlap bag over my head. I could smell stale beer.

"Party's over, O'Testa."

"What the hell—Who are you??"

"The Bear Cub Brigade, that's who."

One of them punched me in the gut. I felt myself being dragged out a service gate, tossed into the back of a cargo van. The only thing I heard after that were screeching wheels.

Not Exactly My Kind of Town

September 7th

Mel was stocky, wore a muscle shirt over his beer paunch and rolled-up jeans, and drank Old Styles for breakfast. Andrew was thin and creepy and had a face like the surface of the moon. Heckie was hopped up on something, or maybe it was just because they were using his third floor apartment to bind and gag me in.

This Bear Cub Brigade may have been nothing but certified goofballs, but they were deadly serious about their ball team. In their odd world, the risk of a kidnapping charge was small potatoes compared to letting me warm up Ruben Gomez and causing a three-game sweep of good Giants luck.

At least they fed me Saltine crackers and water.

"Most of the time, we're real nice guys," said Mel while he roped me to Heckie's Barcalounger. "But it's gotten a little desperate around here, and we can't take chances. Do you know the Cubs haven't won a World Series in fifty years?"

"Haven't even been to one in thirteen!" piped in Heckie, "It's gotten out of hand."

"Yw gza gnn bsor!"

Mel took out a portion of the gag. "What's that?"

"I said, you guys are gonna be sorry."

"Uhh...nope. That would be you for showing up with the team, going in Brick's booth and putting the whammy on us."

"Hey, it's been your crummy pitching and defense that lost you the first two games. Nobody in your outfield has any range—"

"GAG HIM!" barked Heckie, and Mel did.

Today was a warm Indian summer day, and the temp was rising. I was pretty delirious by the time the game began. They dragged over kitchen chairs, sat around me while we watched Heckie's Philco.

Gomez and Dave Hillman were both throwing fantastic, and it was scoreless after three. Mel finished off the last of Heckie's beers and took turns snarling at the TV or glaring at me. Andrew stared at the screen in a silent, scary stupor, puffing on Winstons. Heckie paced the floor, mumbling something.

"Root and Cavaretta...Root and Cavaretta..."

"Don't mind Heckie," said Mel, 'In close games he likes to repeat the names of his dad's favorite players. Keeps him normal.'"

Scoreless into the 6th, the tension in the room made it feel like 100 degrees. When Walt Moryn made a nice grab on a deep drive, I heard a faint explosion of cheering. We were pretty close to Wrigley.

And then Heckie's telephone rang. He ran over to answer it.

"Yeah!...Uh-huh...Uh-huh...

You're kiddin' me...Jesus, Mary, and...Okay, thanks Boppo."

He hung up, turned to his pals with an even more crazed look than he had before.

"Boppo found him. He's living outside New York. The Giants paid him to go along with it."

Whatever this was about, I was intrigued. Mel stood, grabbed an empty beer bottle and smashed it open on the kitchen table. Walked over to me, armed with its long, jagged neck.

"See, our buddy Boppo has an uncle who happens to know Nick Testa. As in, the actual one you're pretending to be. The one who never even got a big league at bat and got paid off to stay out of the picture."

Now I was really sweating. And not because Hillman had just retired Bressoud, Wagner, and Mays 1-2-3 in the 6th.

"What d'ya say, Brigands? Should we carve up his face, or just sic the press hounds on him? Anything to mess up the Giants, right?"

Andrew and Heckie hooted and hollered so much I couldn't even tell which choice they made. Mel leaned over and tickled my cheek with a sharp point of broken bottle.

"Fifty years is way too long, whoever you are...don't you think?"

"AHL TL YW WHW YAM!"

He pried loose the gag again."What's that?"

"I'll tell you who I am. And you better listen good."

"We're all ears. Talk while you still got two of yours."

"I'm Snappy Drake. The usher from Seals Stadium?"

They frowned. Obviously, their knowledge of the world didn't extend past the north end of Chicago.

"There's a mass killer who's been stalking me and the team the entire season. A half dozen more people just got massacred in L.A. and for all I know you guys are next. He could be outside your door right now."

Heckie turned a little white. Ran over to the door. Opened it and looked into an empty hall. Shut it again.

"No one there. He's gotta be kidding us, right?"

Mel didn't looked convinced. Suddenly Andrew let out an excited yelp.

"Dark and Thomson singled! Two on, nobody out for Long!"

They shifted their attention back to the TV. Dale Long walked to load the bases and bring up Banks. I thought Heckie was going to wet himself. Banks drew another walk for the first run of the game. Thomson was tagged out at the plate on a Jim Marshall grounder, but then Moryn hit a sac fly to make it 2-0. They were crazed.

"It's working, Mel!!" It was the first English Andrew spoke all day.

Lee Walls was up next, clubbed a Gomez curve into the left field bleachers and I thought the roof of the apartment building would blow off. 5-0 Cubbies, my life was suddenly less in jeopardy, and if the Peanut Man was in the neighborhood, he had to be happier. After Hillman kept his two-hit shutout through the 7th, the Brigade got all giddy and soft and worried about their futures. Mel broke down and cut me loose. I've found most Midwestern folks to be

pretty friendly, and even these nut-cases proved it.

"Just stay the hell away from the park the last two innings or we'll track you down again."

Naturally I headed straight back to Wrigley, cutting through alleys.

The Bronx Bugle Sporting Life

VISIT ALL OF OUR NATIONAL PARKS	September 8, 1958	BEWARE OF SLAVIC NAMES

Will Yanks Throw This Away?
Schedule Favors Chisox; 3 Weeks to Play Means No Room for Blasé

by Archie Stripes
American League Beat

Only five minutes had passed since the Bombers' shocking flop in both acts of yesterday's double-header with the pitiful Washington Senators. Casey Stengel, looking 88 years old rather than his spry 68, shuffled silently past his players to the clubhouse food spread and violently knocked over the entire table. While the team stared mutely, he bent over, snatched up a baked chicken drumstick and gnawed off a bite. Dropped the rest on the floor and smashed it into fowl pulp with one of his cleats.

"Chicken's for winners only, boys," he said, before shuffling into his office and barricading the door.

The Yanks have been a .500 team since the third week in July, while the Pale Hosiery Gang from Chicago has gone 27-7 since August 1st and sparked dreams of an El Train World Series with the Cubs.

This reporter would find that scenario most entertaining, but I can't speak for the masses of Yankee fans expecting the American League pennant flag to show up at their lordly arena like the annual holiday catalog from Gimbel's. With their first-place lead down to just three digits in the loss column, the Bombers' two matches this weekend at Comiskey Park have become the hottest tickets in the midwest.

Though the Giants recently pilfered the National League lead back, despite distractions from a certain notorious mass murderer, it is the Yankees who seem to have come down

with a case of the willies.

One would think the Dodgers' recent eight-game war with the San Franscisco squatters would have put a dent in the front-runners' pennant hopes, but the Angelenos have been playing as bad as the Senators since the halfway mark, and dropped six of the contests in a vulgar, half-hearted fashion. Brooklynites who also saw their club ripped away from them surely have little remorse, but the ones I spoke to last week were still rooting for a Gigantic collapse. The rivalry, it would seem, will be in their baseball blood forevermore.

Regardless, the remainder of the pennant pigpiles sort out this way:

BRAVES: 11 home, 5 away
CUBS: 3 home, 12 away
GIANTS: 5 home, 10 away
Giants at Braves, Sept. 16
Cubs at Giants, Sept. 23-24

YANKEES: 3 home, 13 away
CHISOX: 14 home, 3 away

When I caught the Giants scoring two runs in the 8th from a cabbie, I picked up my pace. Banks singled one in to make it 6-2, but Mays homered in the 9th off Don Elston. By the time I reached the players' gate again, the 6-3 Cubbie win was in the books, and the Giants were packing up for Pittsburgh, where'd they start a two-game set on Tuesday.

"What the hell happened to you, Drake?" asked Valmy.

"You're better off not knowing."

There were also three phone messages for me from upstate New York. Damn. I went into Rigney's office before we left and made the call. Like I feared, Liz was crying and hysterical.

"You knew about Billy and didn't even tell me???"

"I was going to, okay?" You were sick—"

"He was my brother!!"

"I know! I'm sorry. I was shaken up about it, too...And I know it was the Peanut Man who did it."

"What?? How would you even—"

"Because I was there!!"

The line went dead for a moment.

"I can't...I just can't..."

"He said we were getting real close. Did you get that kid's name yet?... Hello?"

"No...Tomorrow....The director's feeling better...We're supposed to meet at noon."

"Liz? Hang in there, okay? I'll be there by eleven."

Into the Wilds

September 9th

I wasn't even sure which pickle was worse: escaping Chicago without Brewster and You-Know-Who on my tail, or picking the correct road to get me out of Pittsburgh. Eventually, I found myself crossing Pennsylvania in a cheap rented Fairlane, en route to the northern regions of the Empire State—and Liz.

On the plane, I had told Bill Rigney about Liz's brother, and why I had to be with her for both emotional support and Peanut Killer investigation reasons. "Don't sweat it," Rigney said. "This good luck charm business is all a bunch of hooey, anyway. A pitcher will blame a bad outing on sunspots if he can."

◆ ◆ ◆

The middle of Pennsylvania looked like the Deep South minus cotton and tobacco fields. I veered north around Scranton and crossed into New York State. Blue-black clouds gathered over the looming Adirondacks, and a hellish thunderstorm hit as I neared Loon Lake.

My mind began to drift. I was suddenly my dad, buzzing from too many coffees and cigarettes, young Milton sitting beside me in the Hudson and pounding his ever-ready mitt. "High and fast and middle-up," I blurted robotically, the words burning into his little brain.

The dark green turnoff sign for the

Adirondack Youth Baseball League appeared through the driving rain. I slowed the car. The swish-thump of the windshield wipers, the peeling sign were lulling me, but not into sleep. Into a dark, rot-filled cavity of my mind…

CRACK! A thunderclap exploded overhead, woke me the hell up. Shaken, I spun the Fairlane's tires in the mud, turned up the baseball camp road.

The place was already closed for the season, the kids being back in school. I was early, and pulled into the small, empty lot. Waited for the rain to subside a bit and climbed out.

The air smelled fresh and earthy. I spotted a few ball fields in the distance, seemingly in prime condition. Didn't remember ever playing on those. A small office was about fifty yards away, and beyond, a series of bunkhouses flanked both sides of a wooded path.

"Hey…"

I spun around. Liz stood there, her blonde hair dripping wet. Wearing a deeply forlorn expression.

"I parked on the other side—"

And took her in my arms. Hugged her like I've never hugged any gal.

"I'm the one to be sorry," I said, "Billy never should've been there. He was only trying to help me out—"

"I know, I know. It's alright. I loved him…and I'll miss him…But he was just too much of a wild one."

A shiny green Studebaker rolled into the lot at that moment, and Randall Nathan the camp director climbed out in a yellow rain slicker. He was in his 60s, and blowing his nose into a hankie. Wouldn't let us shake his hand but managed a creaky smile.

"Second day out of my pneumonia bed and look at the weather I get!"

"We really appreciate you meeting us," said Liz.

"You better. Let's do this in my office."

His office was small. Cluttered. With a big activities chalkboard for the entire summer behind his desk that looked like Patton's plans to invade Germany.

"So you were the kid that hit this other kid?"

"Right. I kind of had no memory of the beaning after it happened. My father's passed away since and my mother wasn't much help. Wondered if you could tell us who I actually hit."

He blew his nose again. Poured himself a glass of seltzer from a stash in his bottom drawer.

"Kids get hit all the time here, y'know. And you're talking what, twenty years ago?"

"Twenty-three, actually," added Liz.

"Said your name's Drake, right? Hmm…I kind of remember a bad one around then. It was a late afternoon or early evening game. Technically we don't start games after 5, but technicians aren't usually around by then, if you know what I mean…Let's see. The ambulance showed up late, that I remember…And the father was a day or two late getting here to take you home…"

"That sounds possible."

He swallowed some seltzer, let a belch out. "Actually it's coming back now…The kid's dad was some rich pain-in-the-ass from Westhampton."

"Great. What was his name?"

"C'mon, you have any idea how many rich pain-in-the-asses from New York enroll their kids here? You'd have better luck tracking down Soapy. Your coach!"

The name lit a fuse in my head. "Soapy…Phil Todd mentioned a Soapy last month when he saw me in the hospital…And I think my mother called him 'Soupy'…

"Phil Todd? He still scouting?"

"Wasn't Phil the guy you saw in Sacramento?" asked Liz.

"Yeah, and up in Spokane. He still scouts for the PCL Indians." I looked at Nathan. "You know him?"

"Know him? We both went to Rutgers! Different classes, of course. Who the hell you think got you back in the PCL this year?"

"Phil Todd did."

"Congratulations. Except he wouldn't have signed your jockstrap if it wasn't for you gettin' recommended by Pete 'Soapy' Szopa."

Liz's eyes bugged out. "Pete Szopa? From…Pittsburgh."

"You bet, beautiful. One of the best coaches I ever had. The guy was a Pied Piper. Kids followed him everywhere. Damn shame he gave it up and went back to his steel plant. You like working with him, Drake?"

"Guess I did…" I uttered, trying to form a picture of him, "Szopa" swimming around in my brain. Liz poked my leg.

"Think hard, Snap. Really hard."

"His name definitely rings a bell."

"It sure as hell should."

She leaned in, excitement flooding her eyes. "Pete Szopa! The retired steelworker they found dead in the Forbes Field grandstand back in June."

Smoke Gets Out of Our Eyes

September 10th

We spent a sleepless night on a lumpy bed at the musty and creaky Loon Lake Inn, then ditched Liz's rental car and took mine back into Pennsylvania. The Giants were finishing up their season series with the Bucs that night, and with any luck, we'd be able to talk to Pete Szopa's widow before game time.

No such luck. The address Randall Nathan gave us in Swissvale was old. Fran Szopa had sold the house right after Pete died and moved in with her sister Lotte down in Donora. Meaning it took a lot more time to track them down in the factory-filled birth town of Stan Musial.

Lotte Pieknik's house was perched on a hill overlooking the murky Monongahela River. She had survived the horrific Donora smog disaster ten years ago, but her husband hadn't, so having Fran move in seemed to be the right choice.

After explaining to Lotte why we were at her front door, she let us in. Fran Szopa sat on a flowered living room couch watching a daytime television drama. It took her a while to focus on us.

"You better talk to them, Fran," said her sister, "Any help we can give the Giants to beat out those Cubs will put us in good with the Lord." A Cardinal and Stan Musial fan, as I expected. Fran finally sighed and looked up at us with blue, gloomy eyes.

"Who killed my Peter? That's all I wanna know."

"That's what we're trying to find out too, Mrs. Szopa. But we need to ask you about the time he coached kids up in—"

"He lived for baseball. And the Pirates. Knew they were having a bad year but it didn't bother him. After his shift at the factory he'd clean up, take the bus to Forbes Field and sit in the grandstand most every game…"

"Did he tell you he was being followed before that night?" blurted Liz, hijacking my approach. I shot her an annoyed look.

"Followed? Maybe by that charlatan of a lawyer. Not by a killer."

Liz was intrigued. "A lawyer?"

"Please, Mrs. Szopa." I said, laying a comforting hand on her arm, "You need to concentrate on this. Do you ever remember one of his kids at the Adirondacks baseball camp hitting another kid on the head?"

Her expression sharpened. Her voice rose a full octave.

"That's the lawyer I'm telling you about! From New York! Pestered us forever until the judge threw the case out!"

"W-what case are you—"

"The lawsuit! From that millionaire devil D. L. Tressip! Said it was intentional. That the Drake kid hated his precious little Ricky, hit him on purpose and it was Pete's job to put a stop to it!"

I sank into a chair across from her. Decades of smoke cleared from my mind and I saw *Ricky Tressip's goony little face, peering out from under his A.Y.B.L. cap. My hard and fast and middle-up pitch accidentally nailing him square in the forehead…blood spilling down his creamy A.Y.B.L. tee shirt… his little legs kicking on the ground, his mouth screaming…everything going fuzzy and then dark around me in the sticky, early evening heat.*

Then Lotte was handing me a glass of mint lemonade. "You okay, Mr. Drake?" Fran was gazing at me, dumbfounded.

"YOU were the Drake boy??"

"Yeah…Unfortunately." Across the room, Liz was staring mutely out the window. "Something wrong?" I asked her.

"D. L. Tressip. You have any idea who he is?"

"The Devil, that's who!" barked Fran Szopa.

"Maybe. He's also one of the richest

people in New York. Made his fortune in the food distribution business." She turned to me, her face slightly pale.

"Snackful Enterprises. And I'm pretty damn sure they sell peanuts."

◆ ◆ ◆

I floored the Fairlane all the way back to Pittsburgh, discussing the case with Liz the entire way. She was ready to rope in Brewster, but I wanted to wait until we had something completely solid. First thing we needed to do was find D. L. Tressip.

"Who do you know in New York?" I asked her. "Any publishing company pals who might know him?"

"Whoa, there. I'm not exactly a published author yet."

"What about newspaper guys?"

"Suppose that's possible. One of my *Herald* cronies might know."

I racked my brain. And then it hit me. That guy from *The Bronx Bugle* I was reading earlier in the year. We stopped at a pay phone on the outskirts of Pittsburgh. The long distance operator couldn't find a number for the paper quick enough, so I had her put me in touch with the New York Yankees press office. Got a night watchman instead.

"Better you try back in the morning, mister. They open at 9."

"Can I leave a message?"

"You can try. And I can try to remember it long enough to write it down."

"You're a big help, mac. Anyway, if you're feeling inspired, tell them Snappy Drake needs to contact the guy who covers the Yanks for *The Bronx Bugle* right away, or talk to someone who might know how to reach D. L. Tressip."

"You mean Snackful Tressip? The billionaire?"

"Yeah! Heard of him?"

"Surely did. My uncle Roy drove a car for him couple of years back. Still would be, too, if he was alive."

"You mean your uncle?"

"I mean Tressip. You didn't hear? The man died almost a year ago. Hung himself in his coat closet."

The City That Always Creeps

September 12th

"Up and atom, Snap!"

Coffee and nagging early morning thoughts will get me up every time, Not so much bouncy enthusiasm from a dame. And I certainly had things on my mind this morning.

My plan was to call the Comiskey Park press box later to get the goods on D.L. Tressip from that *Bronx Bugle* writer. If he wasn't there for the big Yankee-White Sox series I might not find him anywhere, but if that was the case, either Casey Stengel or one of the other Yankee players or writers could likely give me what I needed.

"That's crazy," said Liz, "You need to be at Connie Mack Stadium to warm up those Giants pitchers. How about if *I* actually GO to Chicago?"

"That sounds even more crazy."

"Not at all. I want to see my folks in St. Louis, anyway. You know, about Billy. I can stop at Comiskey tonight and talk to your writers on the way. I bet some of my cronies from the *Herald* will even be there."

"How do you know that?"

"Come on. Would YOU want to write about the Dodgers right now?"

She had a point. But I wasn't wild about her going off by herself again.

"Hey, a press box is the safest place I could be. Besides, if Peanut Face is going to be anywhere, it's in Philly."

"That's sure nice to hear."

I said I would try and reach her at Comiskey right after the game started. This Tressip business was bugging the hell out of me, though. Lollygagging in Philly seemed like the wrong move. The second Liz took off for Chicago, I hopped an express train to New York.

◆ ◆ ◆

It was only the second time I'd been in Manhattan, and my first brief one as a kid didn't count. After years of getting around in serene west coast cities, walking in Times Square was like being sucked into a pedestrian meat grinder. I had a late lunch at an automat, where I heard a lot of businessmen and shoppers discussing the big Yankee game in Chicago later. That gave me an idea, but my first stop was the archive room at the *New York Times*, where I found plenty of info on D.L. Tressip.

His death in a closet of his upper west side townhouse was indeed ruled a suicide, in November of '57. He was a widower, his wife having died twenty years earlier. He never remarried. He was survived by his only child, 38-year-old Richard. I even had the address of their townhouse, but was "Richie" still living there?

I made my way by dirty, crowded subway to the upper west side, where I checked in at an upper crust tavern off Central Park West—a half dozen blocks from Tressip's 84th Street address. The Yankee talk at the bar was more muted here. A few more references to summer homes and sailboats thrown in. I caught the bartender's eye.

"Say, did you ever see D.L. Tressip in here?"

He frowned. "You mean the deceased millionaire D.L. Tressip? No, sir."

"How about his kid?"

He shrugged. "Didn't know he had one. I stay out of rich people's business."

"But you knew he was dead."

"Doesn't everyone?"

I didn't tell him that my girlfriend and I never had a clue, but what good would that have done? New Yorkers have a way of assuming that everything that happens in their city is world news.

I walked a few more very long blocks. The Museum of Natural History passed on my left, but it had closed an hour ago. Too bad. After a few cold ones I was in the mood to take on a wooly mammoth.

The next tavern was called Shorty's. Decidedly less snobby, and luckily they had a TV over the bar tuned to the Yankee game. Don Larsen and Early Wynn were warming up when I got the ear of the gum-chewing bar-keep.

"Who do you like tonight?" I asked.

"Yanks big time. Larsen's something like 13-4 and Wynn's a fat old man. Still got a few minutes to lay down a wager if you like."

"No, that's okay. I'm actually look-ing for a guy. Thought maybe drank here sometimes."

"I know 'em all, mac. Try me."

"Richard Tressip? He's the son of D.L.—"

"You mean Richie? Damn yeah! Stops by pretty often, but never drinks."

"Oh. He places bets?"

"No, no. Just drops off a few of his newspapers."

I stared at him. "Newspapers?"

He reached under the bar, handed me a copy of the *Bronx Bugle*. It was yesterday's edition, the first I'd ever seen with a bright color photo.

"No kidding…So what, he works for them?"

"If he doesn't I don't know where the hell he gets 'em. Drops off a little stack whenever they come out."

Weird. I flipped through the little 8-pager. The front was well done, but the rest of it–stories from the Bronx community and cheap little ads—

looked like it had been slapped to-gether by a sixth grader. The bartend-er looked curious.

"See the name Richie Tressip in there? I thought maybe he wrote for 'em and was too modest to tell me or something. To tell you the truth, the guy's a little strange."

I looked at the front page again. This time the lead story's byline stuck in my eyes:

Archie Stripes…Richie Tressip

"Holy Jesus."

"Huh??"

I snapped the paper shut. "He lives right up the street from here?"

"Yeah. In the Park West Arms. Good chance Richie won't be there, though."

Slapped down a dollar for my beer. "Why's that?"

"Ants in his pants. He always seems to be going out of town."

◆ ◆ ◆

I thought about calling Brewster, getting him there right away with a search warrant, but I was much too impatient. Instead I called Liz in Chicago. Sherm Lollar had just hit a homer off Larsen to put the White Sox up 5-0, and there was much groaning in Shorty's, but the phone booth gave me a little peace.

"Well, you won't believe this, Snap. Those interviews Archie Stripes was doing with Stengel and the Yankees? Complete baloney. No one ever talk-ed to him. Yankee press secretary told me they'd sue the creep if they could find him."

"Makes sense, Liz. Because he's not only a liar. I think he's our killer!"

"What??"

"Look at his last name! It's 'Tressip' all scrambled. And I just read this new front page story. He's lost his marbles! The whole thing is a lunatic's rant against the Giants!!"

"That makes him a killer? He could just be a Dodger fan."

I could hear Comiskey explode behind her. The White Sox were having

The Bronx Bugle Sporting Life

BRUSH TEETH FOUR TIMES A DAY	September 11, 1958	HORACE STONEHAM IS A COMMUNIST

BRAVES, CUBS BEST BETS TO BE GIANT-KILLERS
"Carpetsquatters" Threaten to Pilfer Pennant!

by Archie Stripes
American League Beat

As the Chicago Cubs roll into Cincinnati and Milwaukee Braves welcome the Cardinals this Friday, it has dawned on the baseball populace that in less than three weeks, the illegally transplanted San Francisco "Carpetsquatting" Giants may very well abscond with the National League flag. I don't mind saying it will be the worst discgrace to the game since the 1919 Black Sox went belly up for gamblers.

While America slept last fall, owner Horace Stoneham cowardly chose to uproot his team from metropolitan New York, destroying a loyal fan following in the process that had endured for nearly three-quarters of a century. The tales of heartbreak and woe from Giants supporters could fill the abandoned palace at the foot of Coogan's Bluff ten times over.

True, the Blue-garbed

Brooklynites also departed for western environs, but every ball aficianado knows that the recently successful history of the Dodgers cannot compare to the lordly heritage of John McGraw, Christy Mathewson, Bill Terry, Carl Hubbell and Mel Ott. Their recent 1951 playoff win and championship sweep of the Clevelanders just four years ago galvanized the city like no sports crown ever has. Anyone who has ever paid a Polo Grounds ticket and poured their believing soul into their team has been insulted. Violated. Kicked to the curb. Discarded like yesterday's laundry lint. Left to wait 24 hours for a newspaper game result from that faraway urban sewer of free-thinking Marxism and bohemian decay.

We cannot stand for it! Write Comissioner Frick at once! Telephone your congressman! Demand our New York Giants BE RETURNED!!!!

YANKS ARRIVE IN WINDY CITY

The Bombers' final two games with the second-place White Sox (barring a one-game playoff) begin tomorrow night, with Don Larsen facing Early Wynn. Saturday afternoon Art Ditmar will take the ball against Jim Wilson. Comiskey Park is sold out both days.

—A.S.

their way and the A.L. race was still very alive.

"Well, I'm going to try and go ask him. Talk to you later."

"Be caref—"

I hung up. Left the bar in the dark and huffed and puffed up the final endless blocks to 84th Street.

The Arms was on a brownstoned corner overlooking Central Park. It also had a doorman. I lingered by a mailbox until the guy went to the curb to help an elderly resident out of her chauffeured Cadillac, then ducked past him and into the building. Quickly found the mailbox for TRESSIP in Apartment 1203 and passed up the elevator for the stairs.

My Camel-smoking didn't help the climb. I was beyond winded when I reached the 12th floor. Found the door to 1203 and knocked. Stood back, ready for anything.

No one answered. A few yards up the hall, I saw faint neon light filtering in from outside. I walked around a corner. A closet, fire extinguisher and window were there, a ledge visible just outside the glass. I went over, lifted the window as high as I could and climbed out onto the ledge.

Tried not to look down. Tried not to let the gusting wind and flapping pigeon wings bother me either. Facing the building, I inched my way along the dark ledge. Curtains were drawn on the many windows of 1203. The last window was open just a crack. I slowly crouched, wedged my fingers underneath and lifted it

up. Slipped inside.

It was a vast, high-ceilinged townhouse, but it looked like it hadn't been cleaned in two months. Piles of newspapers, nearly all of them *Bronx Bugles*. Dirty clothes, empty food containers drawing flies, and a dirty dish here or there. The place stank of old perspiration and something else.

Ink. I found a lamp and switched it on. Sure enough, a giant metal contraption took up half the far wall.

It was a home printing press.

Bureau of Best-Laid Plans

September 13th

The manager of the Park West Arms set up a cot for me in his office while we waited for Brewster to show up. It was a long night.

First I had to exit Richie Tressip's 12th floor apartment via the same scary window ledge. Tressip was "away on business," according to the doorman, and I decided to act like I'd just shown up at the building on a "serious hunch." No sense putting Brewster's knickers in another twist.

He arrived with his flunkies at eight this morning, armed with a search warrant. The super let us into the apartment more legally, and I played stupid as long as I could. Brewster didn't even have to play.

"So you're telling us D.L. Tressip's kid became a mass killer because you beaned him when you were 12 years old?"

"No, Brewster. I think it's more complicated than that. And if you'd only let—"

"Why didn't you share this background information with us?"

"Share WHAT with you? What do you think I've been trying to do since Opening Day, for cripes sake? Figure this all out!"

"Calm down, Drake. Proper procedure is important in any investigation."

"Yeah, well the reason we're here at all is because I flushed your procedure down the crapper."

That shut him up, briefly.

"Still, If Tressip is as smart as we think, he won't try and come back here. His publishing days are over."

"Too bad. I'd sure love to send him a letter to the editor."

Brewster eyed me. "Maybe you can. How about sending one to the *Cincinnati Enquirer*?"

"Why them?"

"Because that's where the Giants play a doubleheader tomorrow. We can wire them the letter tonight. Tell the killer we know who he is now. Plead with him to stay away from Crosley Field. Better yet, taunt him. Challenge him. And we'll have that place blanketed like a toddler in a blizzard."

"Okay, but he's gotten away from every trap we've thrown at him."

"Not Operation Shakespeare."

◆ ◆ ◆

The FBI was already looking into Richie's past. Not so much why he was still living in a haunted Polo Grounds in his mind, but other things. Like the beaning giving him severe head trauma. By the time we had driven halfway back to Philly, they'd unearthed records of appointments with surgeons, specialists, and eventual psychiatrists straight through the 1940s.

None of us were sure Tressip would take the new bait, but it wasn't the worst idea. Sitting in the back seat, I scribbled out a letter to the *Enquirer* per Brewster's instructions, handed it off to him.

Meanwhile, I missed the entire Giants finale at Connie Mack, with Robin Roberts suffocating our bats to the tune of 6-1. The players looked very relieved when I boarded the team plane to Cincy, especially Valmy Thomas.

"Thanks for not forcing me to hunt you down again," he said over Eastern Air gin and tonics, "We need all the help we can get against those pain-in-our-ass Reds."

After we landed, we learned the Braves had pulled out another miracle win against the Cards, and we were suddenly two back in the loss column. This may have made Richie Tressip happy for one night, but I wasn't relaxed for a second. I tried calling Liz at Comiskey again but the game there was over, the Yanks having survived a battle royale with the White Sox 8-6, and she hadn't even been in the press box. Most likely, she was safely on her way to

St. Louis to be with her folks.

Or so I prayed.

Dying in Wait

September 14th

My letter to the *Cincinnati Enquirer* was short, and not too sweet:

Dear Richard Tressip,
(AKA the "Peanut Killer"):
Now that the authorities know who you are, it's only a matter of time before you are captured. Why make this difficult and sacrifice more innocent lives? Whatever personal beef you have with me can be discussed face-to-face, like real men do. I look forward to it. But please, stop your cowardly crimes and stay away from Crosley Field today for the Reds' doubleheader with the Giants. When you're ready to talk, you know where you can find me.

                   —M.S. Drake

The letter was a local sensation. Nervous jitters about the killer maybe being at the ballpark scared away some ticket-holders, but the ones that happily took their place had an armed, hair-trigger charge to them, no doubt eager to nab any potential reward money. Add to that a gorgeous day and the state of the Reds—still alive in the race and ready to further ruin Giants hopes—and the place had lines wrapped around the gates.

My phony Nick Testa act had apparently been leaked, and a small mob of fans clamored for my autograph while I was trying to warm up Al Worthington. Three Cincinnati TV stations wanted to interview me before the first game. I declined them all. With Liz safely bunked at her parents' house in St. Louis, I should've been more relaxed. To hell with that. Telling Tressip we'd discovered his identity could very well disrupt things in his sick mind, and Brewster and I had no idea how.

Operation Shakespeare also was an unqualified mess. Brewster and Crosley Field management had replaced a big handful of ushers, grounds crew, and food and beer vendors with FBI men in disguise. They tried this with my crew at Seals a few months back, but today's operation made that one look like the invention of the Model T.

Ushers were putting people in the wrong seats, hot dogs were being dropped and beers were spilling, and if there's one thing you can't do in Cincinnati it's spill a patron's beer. Some guy down the first base line was practically tackled by the FBI peanut vendor he tried to buy ten bags from. Some of the reward-hungry fans patrolled the grandstand and bleachers like amateur bounty hunters, and I counted at least four miniature brawls by the fourth inning.

Which was when the tense atmosphere started rattling Al Worthington. Up 3-0 with the help of a two-run Daddy Wags homer in the 1st off Purkey, a single and two doubles suddenly cut our lead to 3-2. Then, after Temple singled and Pinson doubled in the 5th, that likely MVP Frank Robinson hammered one over the left field scoreboard and we were down for good, 5-3. These Redlegs were more dangerous than pythons on a chipmunk farm. If they'd gotten any pitching at all the first half of the year, they would've been clinching the pennant around then.

Between games, a note was handed to me by a Crosley clubhouse attendant. It was a fourth request for a TV interview, and I almost crumpled the thing before I finished reading. I'm glad I didn't:

Dear Milton Testa,

Ten minutes of your precious time at Buckabee Television Studios would be greatly appreciated. No compensation is available, but another dramatic piece of your mystery puzzle awaits you.

161 North Main Street, Walton, KY

I found Brewster behind the home plate seats. He wore a striped apron, straw boater, and was struggling to sell fans popcorn. I showed him the note.

"Think it's him?"

"Nobody else calls me Milton except my mother."

"Where'd you get it?"

"Clubhouse guy. Someone must've given it to him."

He nodded. Dropped his entire popcorn tray and yanked a portable radio out of his apron.

"Brewster here. Heckler 1 may be in reach. Repeat. Heckler 1 may be in reach."

Commotion rippled through the stands as Brewster's Comedy Players ditched their disguises, began darting around. I stayed on Brewster's heels. Found the clubhouse guy who never saw the killer. Said he heard a loud knock on the clubhouse door and found the note taped to it.

"Where the hell's Walton, Kentucky?" I asked him.

"Over the state line. Not too far."

Brewster shot me a look. "Come on. You're riding with me."

"But I have to warm up Ramon Monzant in ten minutes!"

"He'll survive."

Ramon didn't. Lasted all of one-and two thirds innings, giving up nine hits and eight runs, and Cincy shellacked us 11-0 in the nightcap. We'd have a day off in Milwaukee before playing our final game there Tuesday, and with the Braves edging the Dodgers again today it was basically going to mean win in Suds Town or die.

And on that note, it only took us about half an hour to get to the eerily sleepy town of Walton. 161 Main St. was not a TV studio at all, but a small white house set back from the road with T. BUCKABEE painted on a mailbox at the end of the driveway. There was a pickup parked there, but knocking on the screen door produced zero response. Brewster took out his gun. Tried the door handle. It was open.

The living room was a complete shambles. Furniture knocked over, peanut shells covering practically everything. Tim Buckabee wore dirty overalls over a T-shirt, and the bottle of beer he'd been drinking was smashed on the floor beside his armchair. He seemed to be in his 50s. The reason I wasn't so sure was because it's hard to pinpoint a man's age when his head and shoulders have been shoved straight through the glass of a TV screen.

For good measure, Tressip had stapled another note to Buckabee's overalled behind:

I STAYED FAR AWAY FROM CROSLEY FIELD, JUST LIKE YOU TOLD ME TO.

DOES THAT MAKE ME A GOOD BOY?

The Bronx Bugle Sporting Life

THERE IS NO PLACE TO HIDE, MILTON	September 15, 1958	YOU WILL BE THE LAST TO DIE

D.L. TRESSIP:
HIS LIFE FOR HIS TEAM

by "Archie" Tressip
Roving Bugle Reporter
and Victim

Next month marks the one-year anniversary of the death of Donald Lincoln Tressip—Founder and President of Snackful Enterprises, grieving husband, loving father, and New York Giants fan extraordinaire.

Donald saw his first game at the Polo Grounds at the tender age of eight, in 1904. That squad won the pennant easy that year, by 13 strides over the Cubs, but John McGraw decided—rightfully so—that the champion Red Sox of the upstart American League were not worthy of being on the same field with his mighty men, and refused to play in this new, money-grubbing charade called the World Series.

Young Donald was heartbroken, but being deprived of the spectacle only made the 1905 campaign even sweeter, when the Giants took the NL flag by nine games over the Pirates and took the Athletics in five games, shutting them out in every win. From then on, Donald was hooked like a trout with an eagle claw through its mouth. He smelled the actual flames of the 1911 fire. Attended their 1933 Series win. Rode the El train to West 155th and 8th Avenue routinely. Kept every scorecard in a trunk in his closet. A trunk he stood upon in 1957 when, still in mourning ten years after the death of his wife to polio and shattered by the beaning injury suffered by his only child Richard earlier, heard the news the Giants were being ripped from his heart and took his very life. A tragedy like this can NOT and will NOT go unavenged.

PENNANT CONTENDERS' REMAINING GAMES

NATIONAL LEAGUE
Braves-10: S.F. (1), @ STL (2), @CIN (3), PHL (1), CIN (3)
Lying Traitors-9: @MIL (1), @STL (3), CHC (2), STL (3)
Cubs-10: @PHL (2), L.A. (3), @S.F. (2), @L.A. (3)

AMERICAN LEAGUE
Yankees-10: @DET (2), @BAL (3), @BOS (2), BAL (3)
White Sox-11: BAL (2), @K.C. (3), DET (3), K.C. (3)

National League thru Monday, September 15

Milwaukee	81	63	.563	—
San Francisco	79	66	.545	2.5
Chicago	77	67	.535	4
Cincinnati	75	72	.510	7.5
St. Louis	69	74	.483	11.5
Pittsburgh	69	77	.473	13
Philadelphia	68	76	.472	13
Los Angeles	61	84	.421	20.5

American League thru Monday, September 15

New York	88	56	.611	—
Chicago	85	58	.594	2.5
Boston	77	67	.535	11
Cleveland	76	69	.524	12.5
Baltimore	74	69	.517	13.5
Detroit	72	71	.503	16.5
Kansas City	55	89	.382	33
Washington	48	96	.333	40

The Wigwam Willies

September 16th

After the Tim Buckabee murder outside Cincy, the feds turned Milwaukee into an impending battle zone. Tressip's photo, a fuzzy, ten-year-old number showing him sitting at a Paris café with his lordly father, was printed in all the local papers and copies handed to nearly every employee at County Stadium. The train station and airport looked like dark suit conventions. But what could they do? As the killer proved in Ohio, you can't guard every baseball fan within fifty square miles.

And none of the Milwaukee Wig-wammers were going to miss this game tonight. A line for standing room tickets snaked around the park by 3 p.m. The aroma of beer and sizzling brats rose from the huge parking lot like alluring smoke signals that had gulls off the lake spinning in circles. We were three games behind the Braves in the loss column, and would only meet again in a playoff series, so you might say this contest was critical.

To ensure their good fortune after Sunday's double disaster—not counting the murder—the Giants players first rose to the occasion by cloistering me inside the ballpark like some kind of religious talisman. Reporters, fans, everyone but those in San Francisco uniforms were kept far away from me.

They even tried to bribe Brewster to keep him away, before remembering he could be a protective asset. And occasionally smart.

"That 'latest edition' of the *Bronx Bugle* yesterday? A phony. Or at least one he printed way ahead of time. Tressip may be insane, but he's sure clever." Brewster gave me a Handie-Talkie to use, which Bob Schmidt soon lifted from my back pocket and "stored away somewhere" for safekeeping.

I happily lost myself in the game, perched on the bullpen bench beyond the outfield fence, wedged between Ray Crone and Marv Grissom. Their body warmth helped alleviate the early fall chill blowing through, and I was careful to ignore any and all catcalls from the nearby bleachers. Especially after what happened there back in June.

Mike McCormick was pitching against Warren Spahn. It really wasn't the mismatch people thought, because Mike had been throwing better after many shaky outings, and Spahnie could be either brilliant or wretched. As it turned out, this was a nerve-wracking game neither team deserved to win.

A walk to Cepeda and singles by Davenport and Thomas broke us in front 1-0 in the 2nd, but McCormick coughed that up immediately by hitting Andy Pakfo, giving up an infield single to Schoendienst that Spencer threw in the seats, and a sac fly to Logan. In the 4th, a second Pakfo plunking and Logan sac fly put the Braves briefly ahead, but that would wrap up all home fan cheering for the night.

The killer at the game was not Richard Tressip at all, but one Melvin Earl Roach of Richmond, Virginia, a 25-year-old, spectacled utility player for the Braves. Roach had a nice bat, had mostly been filling in at second base but against the lefty was stationed out in left field tonight. "Stationed" being a figure of speech.

First he let us tie the game in the 5th when a two-out Spencer single bounced in front of him and he kicked it away. Then with a man on and one out in the 6th, Davenport lined a single to left that Roach let bounce happily through his legs, scoring Cepeda with the go-ahead run. The big crowd went mute, along with the Brave bats, which had been doing a lot of that lately. Thirteen out of the last fourteen Milwaukee hitters couldn't get the ball out of the infield. We were suddenly two games out in the loss column, the Cubs had also won in Philly, and the horse race was back on.

The feds didn't want us out celebrating, even though we didn't have another game until Friday in St. Louis. We were expected to board the team bus and head straight for the airport. That was good news for me, because I knew Liz was there, and we already had dinner reservations for tomorrow. It was a weird but fun scheduling quirk; many of the players were going to sit in the stands and take in the Braves' two games there on Wednesday and Thursday.

But then the bus wouldn't start.

"Are you kidding me??" yelled Davenport. "To hell with this!" piped in Mays, and he bolted off the bus with Wagner and Kirkland to hail a cab. Within seconds, so had everyone else.

I followed them out, but lost most of the players in the mad rush of exiting fans. Luckily, a cab pulled up behind me.

"Airport, buddy?" asked the driver.

"You read my mind," I said, hopping in. "Step on it."

He knew what he was doing, quickly got us out the exit, nearly hitting a few fans still wearing their feathered headresses. As soon as we were away from the stadium, I thought I heard something thump in the cab's trunk.

"Did you hear that?"

He glanced back, then pulled down a dark side street and climbed out. Went around and popped open the trunk. The thumping suddenly stopped. I turned my head and he opened the back door on my blind side. Lunged in and put a familiar wet cloth over my face. Before I passed out I heard him say,

"Once a sucker, always a sucker, Milton…"

Darkness on the Outskirts of Town

September 17-18th

Sore wrists, clammy air, and peanut dust: the first sensations I had when I came to.

I was strapped to some kind of conveyor belt, feet on a slight incline, in a dark, cavernous room maybe the size of an airplane hangar. A bare, sputtering light bulb hung over my head from the rafters. I had no clue where Tressip was, but I couldn't undo the nylon cords binding my wrists and ankles if I tried. And believe me, I tried.

The place seemed to be some abandoned factory or warehouse on the outskirts of some town. I mean, what mastermind villain doesn't use something on the outskirts of town? Getting into that cab after the game in Milwaukee was stupid; I should have known better. But it was also dark, and hectic, and I was trying to keep up with the Giants players, and it never occurred to me or anyone that the team bus failed to start because Tressip had screwed with the engine.

Finally I heard a metal door slide open at the far end of the room, and my abductor strolled toward me out of the shadows. He was taller, beefier than I remembered from the last time he nabbed me in Dayton, though I was a lot more delirious on that occasion. He wore crisp slacks, a black polo shirt with some kind of aviation emblem under a weathered New York Giants ball cap. Had a ruggedly handsome, clean-shaven face but slightly off-kilter eyes.

He carried a large paper bag. Stopped a few feet away from me and worked up a wet, frosty smile.

"Hello again. Isn't this exciting? We

get to follow a ball game together."

"No kidding. So what the hell's in the bag? My foot-long wiener?"

"Hardly."

He set the bag down on a small table I hadn't noticed. Lifted out a brand new Zenith Universal portable radio, still in its packaging box.

"There's a good appliance store a mile away. The merchant wanted 70 dollars for this but I Hebrewed him down to 60."

"Really? With the type of cash you've been throwing around you're worried about saving ten dollars?"

"It isn't the savings, Milton. It's the joy of negotiation. The power of victory. Oh, but I forgot. You haven't experience many of those."

He ripped open the radio's packaging, took the device to a nearby wall outlet and plugged it in. Hunted through crackly static until he found Jack Buck's voice on KMOX in St. Louis—reasonably clear.

"Where are we, Tressip? Indiana? Kentucky?"

"Why would we be there?"

"Because I think you're more clever than Agent Brewster gives you credit for. You can't risk taking me to St. Louis so you stopped as close as possible in a bordering state that could also pull in Cardinal games on the radio."

He strolled back over.

"See? This is why I haven't killed you yet. Though you did something unforgivable that ruined my life and ultimately led to the death of my fa-ther, you possess a level of intelligence that is rare in these times and is well worth studying."

"Gee. Thanks, Professor. Except I have no holy clue how me accidentally hitting you with a summer camp baseball caused your father to hang himself."

He took off his cap, bowed slightly so I could see the faint purple scar and lopsided depression that was still visible atop his forehead.

"A germ entering the bloodstream finds its way around the body, Milton. And my severe injury and even more severe trauma was too much for my polio-stricken mother, who died of a stroke when I turned 16. An event my father never emotionally recovered from. The Giants abandoning him was merely the lever that dropped the noose."

Something happened in St. Louis which caused Jack Buck to exult into his microphone. Larry Jackson bailing himself out of an early jam.

"Mmm. Unfortunate. If the Braves don't win this game and your traitorous Giants inch closer to first..." He shrugged, "I may just have to kill you tonight."

"You'll never get away with this, Richie. Come to think of it, driving all the way here in a Milwaukee cab wasn't too brainy."

"Please call me Richard now. And the taxi car never made it out of Wisconsin. Found a nice, nondescript Plymouth on a street near the Illinois border. Do you like this factory,

Milton? One of the few that Snack-ful closed after my father died, but I kept a few peanut-related contraptions around, for nostalgic reasons of course. That one you're attached to water-blanches the peanuts to separate the red skin from the kernel. Helps remove unwanted things. For your sake, the Braves will emerge victorious tonight and we won't have to switch it on."

The Braves did, though I must have sweated out five pounds in the pro-cess. Burdette was as shaky as ever, giving up eight hits in the first three innings but just one run, while the Cardinal defense stayed home in bed. When Musial homered in the last of the 9th to cut it to 5-3, I got pretty nervous.

"So now what? You're letting me go?"

"I'd love to, Milton. I'd likely get more pleasure from hunting you down again. Except the Braves have one more game in St. Louis tomor-row night, so…"

"You're not serious."

"Oh, I'm dead serious. Don't wor-ry, though. It's an afternoon game. Starts in only 14 hours. Get a little sleep, why don't you?" He slid over a chair, opened a thermos of coffee and poured himself a cup.

◆ ◆ ◆

I was hungry, thirsty, and delirious by the time Thursday's matinee be-gan. Tressip had refused to feed me or share any of his coffee. I tried cursing him for a while, but that got me no-where. Taunting was next.

"Sure must be nice being as rich as you. Richie. Go anywhere you want. Kill people on a moment's notice. Show up in my local saloon to leave a *Bronx Bugle* and peanut shells in one of the booths—just so I can see it, right?"

"Yes, I did enjoy that. Stalking can be so rewarding."

"As much as killing? What the hell do you do when you're done with me and the Giants lose the pennant? Re-tire in the Caribbean and spend your inheritance? They might win in '59 and you'd be miserable and vengeful all over again."

"I live for the moment, Milton. The future is a black pit not even worth contemplating. And these are my mo-ments."

Jack Buck yelled a Joe Cunningham home run call at that moment, the first run of the second game going to the Cards. Tressip's face visibly tight-ened. Moments later, Bobby Gene Smith hit a 2-run shot, the Braves were down 3-0 and Tressip was pac-ing frantically, talking to himself.

"Not do at all…This will not do at all…" He walked over to the blanch-ing machine I was strapped to and flicked a switch. The entire thing vi-brated beneath me. "Didn't think I'd need to use this tonight…"

"Are you crazy??"

"That's what they've all been saying. Kind of an insult, if you ask me."

There was a weird bubbling sound. I turned my neck around, saw a glimpse of a giant tub of boiling oil. Baseball was literally going to be the death of me.

"Most unfortunate, Milton. I've enjoyed your company. Of course, the San Francisco Traitors would be eliminated by now if Eddie Mathews was hitting over .220 and Wes Covington had hit at all in the last month and a half. See, this really isn't my fault at all."

"You bastard…"

"Now now, Milton. I happen to be very legitimate. You can relax a short while, though. It's still early in the game."

It was, and the mediocre Cards stopped hitting Carl Willey altogether after the 1st. And guess who homered to tie the game up in the 6th? Wes Covington. Then Mathews sprained an ankle and was replaced by Felix Mantilla, and Tressip was pacing again. But Torre singled in the go-ahead run in the 7th, doubled in another in the 9th, and I wasn't a dead man yet.

"Even if the Braves win this, a two-game lead in the loss column doesn't exactly comfort me." he drolly said.

And then St. Louis started rallying in the 9th. Juan Pizarro walked Flood, hit Cunningham, and walked Blasingame. Only one out. Tressip poised his finger over a second button.

"Don't do this, Tressip. I can talk to Mays. And Cepeda. And Antonelli. I can get them to lose, I promise."

"You mean CHEATING?? I never cheat, Milton. Maybe I remove people from the earth on occasion, but I never…ever…cheat."

Humberto Robinson took over to face Stan Musial. The count went to three and two, before he grounded into a force to score a run and cut it to 5-4. Next up was Ken Boyer. Tressip started the conveyor belt. All he had to do was cut loose my straps and I'd slide into the hot, bubbling oil.

"Boyer hits one out to right!" yelled Buck, and I clenched my teeth. "but Aaron nabs it and the Redbirds lose!"

"Nevertheless," said Tressip, and took out a long straight razor.

I struggled. He moved toward me.

Suddenly the far door exploded open. The force knocked over the peanut blancher, loosened my straps.

"SURRENDER,   TRESSIP!" shouted a man with a megaphone that sounded a lot like Brewster. Tressip bolted for cover and shots rang out. He popped back up with a revolver, fired back. The air in the factory lit up with gunfire. A bullet tore through shirt fabric, just missing one of my arms. I got free, crawled on hands and knees off to the side. Tressip tried to come after me but I eluded him, slipped out an open window and fell into some high grass. Stumbled my way along a dank, smelly river. As far away from the dark, hellish factory as I could get—with nothing but St. Louis on my mind…

≈ *Home Improvement* ≈

September 19th

Two miles away from the gunshot-riddled Snackful Peanut Processing Plant #5 outside Terre Haute that night, I thought about going back. Saw distant flames licking the place and knew it had caught on fire, probably from the spilled hot oil. I knew the lawmen could have taken me in. But in the moment, my body said flee at all costs, and it did.

A late-night trucker picked me up along the first westbound highway I stumbled upon. Offered to drop me at a hospital but I asked for downtown St. Louis instead. Got there by dawn, found the address for Liz's parents in a phone booth and soon dropped myself on their front porch like a tossed morning newspaper.

Mr. and Mrs. Doomis were a straight-arrow midwestern couple, right out of an Andy Hardy movie. Dad was a retired science teacher, now garbed in dungarees with a screwdriver in his hand. Mom, an apple-cheeked, never-retired homemaker, stood there in an apron. I heard bacon crackling from the kitchen. They had a framed photo of their dearly departed Billy on a small table by the door, draped with a black ribbon.

I told them I'd had an accident. They were startled by my appearance, but didn't seem to recognize my voice from the rushed long distance call to them months earlier.

"Well, I'll be!" said Liz's mom, "Guess that explains it. Lizzie was expecting you two days ago, Mr. Snappy!"

"It's Drake. And she's here, right?"

"I'm afraid not. When she heard you disappeared after that game in Milwaukee, she just went off searching for you yesterday with a girlfriend. I suspect she'll be calling in this morning. You look like you could use a nice hot shower!"

If I had my belongings I would have moved right in at that moment. The shower was heavenly, the four-course breakfast even more so. Mr. Doomis sat with me, re-pouring my coffee, and I divulged some of my Terre Haute torture tale.

"Baffling, that's all I can say. When a young man comes from such a fine genetic line as that, and turns a dark corner. Baffling."

Two wonderful things happened in the next two hours to improve *my* genetics: Liz called from her friend's house in Bloomington, exchanged phone joy with me for a few minutes and said she'd be there in the morning. And there was a news bulletin on the radio that Richard Tressip was believed to have perished in a factory fire in Terre Haute. I couldn't believe it. Naturally, it also announced I was missing again.

"You need a few days for recuperation," said Mrs. Doomis. "Stay until Billy's memorial service on Sunday, at least, and then you can talk to those policemen all you want. I'm sure Lizzie would appreciate it too."

"Certainly. It's the least I could do, ma'am."

I spent most of the day napping, the rest helping Mr. Doomis build a work shed in their huge, leafy backyard. After everything I'd been through that year, it was like spending a day in an alternate American universe. Mrs. Doomis cooked some fresh tarts later, we ate roast chicken and golden potatoes and I drank a bottle of Griesedieck lager that tasted like something from the Lord's private brewery.

My hosts were avid Cards fans, and I sat with Dad Doomis after dinner and watched the Giants battle them at Busch Stadium while Mom knitted a sweater in an adjoining chair. Antonelli sure didn't seem to be missing my warmup tosses. He took a 6-2 lead into the 5th thanks to a horrendous 2nd inning from Mizell that featured a Daryl Spencer grand slam homer.

"Darn that Vinegar!" barked Dad. "If anyone can get us out of this eight-game losing streak you'd think it was him." I was going to remind him that the Cards were already eliminated, but I'm sure he knew and didn't care. The most loyal baseball fans live through their team day after day, regardless of where they are in the standings.

Mrs. Doomis went to the kitchen to bring back the pitcher of her mint lemonade for refills, and I thanked her for the ninth time that day.

"Oh, never you mind. It's nice having a young man here. Especially this weekend—"

She choked back a few tears, was about to say something else when Harry Caray shouted on the TV and her husband yelped with joy. Ken Boyer, who'd homered earlier, had just tied the game in the 6th with another grand slam. Uh-oh. It was the third homer Antonelli had given up in the game. If Brewster wasn't out looking for me, Johnny would be soon.

He'd give up a fourth, a solo shot by Gene Freese that broke the tie in the 7th. Chuck Stobbs pitched four great innings of relief, the Cards snapped their losing streak, the Giants were three back in the loss column with the Braves having creamed the Reds, and were Richard Tressip alive he would have been a happy man.

Over tea and a giant slice of devil's food cake, Mrs. Doomis joined me for my final hour before bed.

"I'm so glad Lizzie met you. You seem very nice and she really needs to plant her feet with someone. Seems like she's been willy and nilly for half her life."

"You mean with jobs? Or um, romances."

"Oh, both. There was the editor of

that Chicago paper. The doctor in Des Moines. That crazy rich boy in New York."

My eyebrow arched. "Crazy rich boy?"

"Yes, she had an internship with a book publisher there, right out of college. Met some wealthy boy at a company party and dated him for a while. His father made himself a fortune in the food business, I think."

The teacup suddenly quivered in my hand.

"You wouldn't...remember his name, would you?"

She chewed on her wedge of cake for what seemed an eternity.

"Archibald, I believe. Archibald Priests. Rather an odd name...Anyway, he pestered her for a long while after they broke up." She dropped her voice to a whisper, even though no one was around to hear us. "I think he even proposed to her."

Extra Inexplicable Innings

September 20th

I was either angry, annoyed, flustered or flabbergasted. Until I heard the absolute truth from Liz it was tough to pick the right selection from that emotional juke box.

It was even tougher to hang around her parents' house waiting for her to show up. After nursing three cups of coffee for three hours I left her a message with Mommy and Daddy Doomis: *Meet me behind the Giants' dugout at Busch Stadium this afternoon.* My Giants had pennant race ground to make up, and I was pretty sure they needed me.

Antonelli, who got bombed for four homers the night before (and led all major league pitchers in that nefarious department with 40), nearly kissed me when I showed up an hour before the game. Ruben Gomez was so thrilled when I donned my catching gear I thought the first thing he was going to toss me during his warmup was a bouquet of red roses.

"We figured for sure you was in that factory fire," said Vamly Thomas, "the place becoming a big ash pit and all. How else could you explain us getting ambushed by these Cardinal clowns last night?"

I wanted to tell him that Stan Musial and Ken Boyer were hardly clowns, but kept my mouth shut and asked them to please do the same. Brewster didn't know I was still alive yet, and I wanted to keep it that way as long as possible. With Tressip presumed dead, the FBI presence at the park was minimal, anyway. So were the Redbird fans. I was able to dress after the game started and slip into a box seat just behind Bill Rigney's perch in our dugout.

Soon after Wagner and Mays doubled and Cepeda gave us a quick 2-0 lead, I felt a thin, smooth hand touch the back of my neck.

"Oh, Snap!"

It was Liz alright. Radiant as ever, blonde mane glowing in the autumn Missouri sunshine. She sank into the empty seat beside me. Kissed my cheek with her warm mouth.

"I thought you were dead…"

"You ain't the only one. Where were you?

"Oh, Indianapolis. Then Chicago. By the time I heard about the factory fire in Terre Haute I was almost in Wisconsin.

"So you were just looking around for me aimlessly? With a girlfriend? At least that's what I heard."

"What's that supposed to mean?"

"Never mind…"

The Giants were lighting into Bob Mabe again in the second inning. Four runs were across and fans practically booed him off the mound. While Lindy McDaniel came in, Rigney and coach Salty Parker eyed us from the lip of the Giants dugout, a hint of snicker on their faces.

"Is something wrong?" Liz asked.

"Why don't we take this to the shadier and more private upper grandstand, okay?" Grabbed her hand and led her up the aisle.

"You're being very strange, Snap. What's—"

"*I'm* being strange? The almost Mrs. Richard Tressip is telling me I'M being strange??" I dropped us into a row about twenty steps up. "Or wait… Maybe his name was Archibald Priests."

Her entire face sagged. Lipsticked mouth quivered.

"He was nothing to me. Okay? You have to believe that. Just a rich, jerky kid I dated a bunch of times. How did I know he'd grow up to be a killer?"

"You sure knew who he was that day in Donora, Pennsylvania. Soon as Fran Szopa mentioned D.L. Tressip. When were you going to tell me?"

"I wasn't positive it was Richard yet. I had to find out for sure. But I was scared to."

"Which is why you went to Chicago instead of New York."

"He was so creepy after I broke things off with him. Left dead flower petals on my apartment doorstep. I was afraid of actually seeing him again."

"But he was killing people, Liz! How could you only think about yourself??"

"I know, I know! I'm sorry. I just…I just couldn't bear to tell you, Snap—"

"Why not??"

On the field, Boyer singled in two Cardinal runs following a dropped fly by Wagner. Liz paused, grateful for the distracting cheers.

"Because I love you."

Musial grounded out to end the inning. The crowd groaned. I didn't know what to feel.

"Still?"

"I always did. After all we've been through, no matter how many times we've knocked heads, I can never stop thinking of you. Don't you…feel the same way?"

I believed I did, but it took three scoreless middle innings of quiet reflection to let everything churn in my mind. The grandstand around us was thinning out. Loyal, tipsy fans stayed to yell at the umps and players. I walked Liz out a side gate, went around and got us into the right field pavilion where most of the negro fans were, recalling Sportsman Park's segregated days when they sat behind chicken wire.

The Giants erupted for four more runs in the 7th and started to run away. I guess I enjoyed that, but the weightier subject was keeping me mute. Liz was patient. Cradled her sweet head in my collarbone, lightly brushed her fingers up my arm. I sat there in delicious, dizzying agony.

Suddenly the pavilion fans all around us were talking excitedly, gesturing at the scoreboard in left. The Braves had just miraculously lost in 11 innings at Crosley and the Cubs had inexplicably done the same to the Dodgers in 12 innings at Wrigley.

I took this as a sign. Finally turned to Liz and kissed her full on the lips.

"I want to marry you."

She smiled, nodded, and cried. The second Daryl Spencer homer in two days brought in the Giants' 12th run. We were about to be a full game closer to first. And I had just raced around third for home.

See You on the Flip Side

September 21st

We clued in Liz's folks last night on our marriage plans. Mom was over the moon, but Dad just looked under the weather.

"You'll support my daughter by seating people at ball games six months a year?" I assured him I'd be finding a winter job, and also that Liz couldn't go a week without working somewhere herself.

The saving grace was that they were a bit preoccupied with today's memorial service for son Billy at their local church in Webster Grove. It was an event Liz helped put together the last few days, and our engagement bit would fit right in. After the solemn service she planned a celebration of Billy, and had booked the adjoining church hall and yard for a summer-style barbeque. Knowing her brother's love for rockabilly, she even talked Eddie Cochran, his famous musician buddy he'd met out in California, to perform at the party.

This morning we got a congratulatory call from Brewster, who'd finally discovered I was still alive when a local cop alerted him to a last-minute notice on the *Globe-Democrat*'s society page. His present to us would be a few FBI men stationed at the church because they needed something to do.

Of course, I also needed to calm

down some of the Giants players. They were facing Jim Brosnan, who'd already no-hit them back in April, and this was a game they had to win. Thankfully, Stu Miller—our best pitcher—had a cool head, didn't believe in superstition and said he'd "stick one in Musial's ear" for me and Liz.

The church was stuffed to its upper pews. The Doomises had many friends, a lot of family, and a gaggle of Billy's car-crazy pals from L.A. even made the trip. Father Grundy gave a heartwarming eulogy, praising Billy for his "big soul and wayward spirit," even though he "never fulfilled his academic studies."

The party afterward was a relieving hoot. I had never tasted more delicious ribs. Mr. Doomis walked around taking handshakes and embraces, never removing the earplug wired to the transistor radio in his suit pocket. (Giants were up 3-2 in the 5th). Liz was bravely spirited. She'd been very emotional all day, about me and the resolution of the Peanut Killer case, and really, the only mystery left was whether I'd be dusting off Seals Stadium chairs at the World Series.

Mrs. Doomis announced our engagement to the cheering hall, Eddie Cochran took the stage for a few numbers, and Liz even got me out on the dance floor. One of Billy's buddies smuggled a case of Griesdiecks in, and I joined them for beers, cigarettes and auto talk around the side of the church. It almost felt like my bachelor party.

Mr. Doomis tracked me down after a while and asked where Liz was, because a friend of his wanted to snap a few pictures. Somebody had seen her playing catch with her five-year-old cousin Maxie behind the church, but a quick scout of the yard didn't turn them up.

"Maybe they just took a walk together," said Mrs. Doomis.

"Past two FBI men? Doubt that."

And then a side exit door of the hall banged open. Little Maxie ran in, dirt on his face and both of his bare knees. Tears streamed down his cheeks.

"The bad church man took Cousin Lizzy!" he cried. I crouched, grabbed him by his little shoulders.

"What church man?? Father Grundy is right over there!

"No, no!! The one in the parking lot! The one with the burned-up face!"

This Means War

September 22-23rd

Crazy me. Thinking Richard Tressip was dead. He knew damn well where I went, read the St. Louis society page and found himself a priest outfit before the church barbeque coals were even lit. With plenty of time to take out the two bored FBI agents, abduct Liz, scare the bejeezus out of Little Maxie and ruin what was a damn good party.

So last night, having pocketed the nice little portable-printed gem below that he left for me in the Doomis' mailbox, I was soon on the California Zephyr back to San Fran. Screw Brewster and his incompetent G-men, screw my backup catcher act, screw being patient and to hell with the consequences. This thing was down to two games with the Cubs, and me against Him.

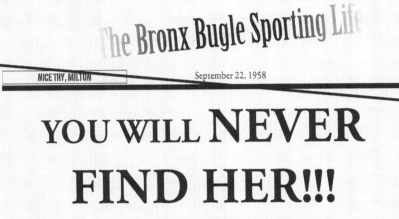

The Bronx Bugle Sporting Life

NICE TRY, MILTON　　　September 22, 1958

YOU WILL NEVER FIND HER!!!

by The Haunter of
Your Dreams

*There once was an usher
named Milton
Who would give anything to
stay at a Hilton
But he suddenly got
famished
Because his Liz-lady vanished
And this thing will ryhme if I
say it does*

Like that one, Miltie? I wrote it extra special for you, which believe me wasn't easy with Liz-lady squealing in the background through the tape over her mouth.

My face really hurts. The tube of Johnson & Johnson first aid cream I used today just isn't cutting it, and I hope I don't get an infection from all these burns because I hear those can make you a little crazy.

Really now? You thought you could abandon me and go off to live a happy life with the girl who broke my heart? The girl I was destined to marry?

I suppose if you cared enough about her, if you really tried to do something useful with your life and find her, I might even have a chance to do away with both of you together. I would certainly enjoy that, after everything you've put me through.

Well, if you must know

where I've taken her, the answer is in front of your insipid face. If you're at Endangered Seals Stadium tomorrow, think of the battery you can see out there, and Spencer, and that old lefty who served, and showed me the way. Think about Liz who will never be Dumas to me, screaming a bit more each night, and though Giant wins will make her scream even more, I have a new revenge in mind.

Your unsnappy, lethal pitch kept me from ever having a normal life, Milton. Or even a wife. Now I'm afraid you'll have to lose yours. Good luck with your bad luck. —R.T.

≈ *Mays the Force Be With Us* ≈

September 24th

It was a gorgeous afternoon in the Mission District. A perfect contrast to the dark, raging clouds in my head. Bleacher seats at Seals were gone by 8:30 a.m., and every local politician needing favors called in had flooded the switchboards. Like a modern Coogan's Bluff, there were fans sitting in trees across the street in Franklin Square Park. I even had to bribe Pence Murphy with an after-game beer to get me in the usher gate.

After 150 games we were dead even with the Cubs at 82-68, three behind Milwaukee in the loss column with just four to play. If Chicago beat us again that day we'd be history, and all 25,000 hearts in and around the ballpark rested on the Say Hey Kid for salvation.

His double and two homers yesterday raised his imminent batting title average to .354, his homers to 34, RBIs to 115 and whatever the hell OPS is to 1.005. His heroics also brought us back from an early 10-2 deficit to tie the game and lose it in extras. Did he have another miracle left in his bat?

I didn't need a miracle to find where Tressip had stashed Liz, just my good old noggin. The rat bastard liked to play games, and the Christmas stocking of hidden clues in his final, demented *Bronx Bugle* had topped them all. Let's start with the "battery," which was Thomas and Antonelli for us, Neeman and Hillman for them. Didn't see anything revealing there,

but I was afraid to run any of this by Antonelli. He would've forced me to warm him up again, and I was trying to stay incognito.

That plan worked for as long as the scoreless first inning, which was when usher pals Tall Tom, Butch and Dominic, and usherette Dot arrived in my high corner of the left field grandstand. Thanks a lot, Pence.

"Don't you guys have people to seat?"

"They already are, Snappy," said Tall Tom. "No seats left!" said Dominic.

"And your poor, poor fiancee!" piped in Dot.

So that had made the local paper. One question led to another answer and soon they were playing Sam Spade with me whether I liked it or not.

Banks led off the 2nd with a bloop double and one pitch later, Walt Moryn bashed a two-run homer into the right field bleachers. Gopher balls were Antonelli's bugaboo, up to 41 of them now, and Seals fell as silent as an abandoned Polo Grounds.

"*Spencer* has to be our Daryl at shortstop, right?" asked Butch, "What's he done so far?"

"Nothing for two."

"But he did turn the first two outs of the game," said Dominic.

"So what?"

"Maybe he's wearing something," offered Dot. "Like tell-tale undershorts."

"What the hell are tell-tale undershorts?" asked Tom.

"Can you people shut up??"

Then Willie shut their yaps for me. He had led off the 2nd with a walk and got stranded, and now singled with one gone in the 4th. Cepeda singled him to second, and Kirkland walked. Davenport, wobbly after being out a few days with a bruise, whiffed to elicit more groans.

Up stepped Valmy Thomas, my best buddy on the team. I glanced around nervously, he being part of the battery and all. Was Tressip perched somewhere with a sniper rifle?

CRACK! The sound came from Valmy's bat. The ball whistled into the left field gap, scoring all three runners to give us the lead! Once again, the thrill of a big Giants hit collided with my fear for Liz.

"Valmy and Johnny? Vajlohn? Thomanelli?"

"Shut up, Butch."

The game stayed 3-2 us until the 7th, when Wagner misplayed a Dale Long single into a two-base error and a scrub named Jim Bolger tied it back up with a pinch-hit sacrifice fly.

Andy Anderson took the hill for the Cubs because three of the next four Giant hitters were righties. Antonelli was the lone lefty, and he tripled down the right field line. Here was Spencer, and he doubled down the LEFT field line!

"Wait! What's Spencer backwards? RECNEPS?"

"Shut up, Butch."

Bressoud made out and Bill Henry, Chicago's perfect relief man (10-0, 1.60 ERA) came in to face lefty Wagner. Felipe Alou batted instead, doubled again, and we were up 5-3!

But I hadn't warmed up Antonelli earlier, and after a Banks single to start the 8th, Johnny hung another meatball, Dale Long splattered it into 16th Street., and we were tied 5-5!

"'A lefty who served,'" mulled Tom. "Gotta be Antonelli, right? Serving them up!"

The game had gotten too intense to focus on anything else. Kirkland doubled to start our 8th and was left there. So was Spencer after a leadoff walk in the 9th. Gordon Jones was in for his second relief inning in the top of the 10th. Walt Moryn stepped up and launched a V-1 rocket, his 31st of the year, high and way out to right, and we were down again, 6-5.

Henry retired Cepeda and Schmidt easily in the last of the 10th. Davenport sort of redeemed himself with a single to keep our meager flames lit, but with everyone standing and praying, Valmy popped out to Banks to drive the stake into our 1958 season.

None of us could speak to each other. I trudged toward the exit. Like everyone else in the place I was happy to see the Giants stay in the race that long, but my quest to decipher Tressip's weird clues had gotten me nowhere.

"Meet you at the Double Play?" asked one dour fan to his counterpart walking in front of me.

"Naw. Already promised Harry I'd get plowed with him at O'Doul's if they lost."

And I stopped in my tracks in the exit tunnel, a half dozen fans slamming into me from behind.

Of course. The "lefty who served." The legendary manager of the San Francisco Seals. The part-time hitting coach for the Giants who owned the most famous tavern/eatery in town. The guy I hadn't had a conversation with all season: Lefty O'Doul.

I got down to his joint as quickly as I could. The place was stuffed with Giants fans drowning their sorrows. Lefty wasn't even there, "home sick" according to the barkeep. I said it was an emergency, and after a call to his house, I was told he'd meet me for breakfast tomorrow.

I spent a sleepless, torturous night waiting for morning. An occasional siren or howling cat, but no phone calls, knocks on my door or messages under it. The Giants were eliminated, no doubt making Tressip happy, but if his last "newspaper" indicated any-

thing, I wasn't sure it was enough to keep Liz alive. And what did Lefty know?

Luck of the O'Doul's

September 25-26th

Lefty never showed up for breakfast. Or lunch or dinner, for that matter. Not much else I could do but down cold ones in his restaurant bar and follow results of the only game of the day at Comiskey Park. The White Sox—even with ace Billy Pierce on the hill—dropped dead for the third straight day against Detroit and handed the American league pennant to the Yankees. It was downright ironic, what with all the decoy Bronx reportage compiled by our trusty mass murderer. If he had only become an American league fan when the Giants left town…

O'Doul's was a spiffy joint, the walls covered with framed photos of Lefty from his playing, managing and Japan touring days. I even saw a glimpse of myself, ushering a Seals game in the second row from a few years back, O'Doul posing with Ken Aspromonte by the on-deck circle.

O'Doul finally called me at home later after I was pretty much soused for the night. He apologized forever. Said he had been meeting with Japanese dignitaries all day about another possible goodwill baseball trip to

Japan. Promised me a giant plate of apple flapjacks and sausage at 10 a.m. sharp on Friday, which sounded good to me.

◆ ◆ ◆

Lefty was 61 years old, and in tip-top shape. He'd been working with Mays and some of the younger Giant hitters on a part-time basis, but I rarely saw him at the park. He kind of recognized me from the last six years I spent working Seals games, but he wasn't sure. Still, he was a good-natured, helpful guy, and saw the desperation in my face right away.

"Looks like you need something in that coffee."

"All depends on what you tell me."

"Yeah, that. Your message was a little foggy, for starters. Something about the Peanut Maniac? Gotta tell you, I've been too busy all year to pay much attention to that idiot."

"He left me a bunch of clues the other day. And I think you might have been one of them."

"Hey John-Boy!"

Hotshot rookie John Brodie of the 49ers walked in at that moment with a small pack of admirers. O'Doul motioned for a waiter to get them a prime booth, then turned back to me.

"What was that?"

"The clue said 'a lefty who served'."

"Yeah. Well, maybe he meant Lefty Grove who served up his mean 'sailor' pitch to mix with that fastball. Or Lefty Gomez. Didn't he serve during the War?" He chewed on a thought. "Actually, Gomez didn't serve during the War, he took a job at General Electric...But anyway, why me?"

"Because you happen to be here in town. Ever remember serving food or drink to somebody weird who asked a lot of weird questions?"

"This place hasn't even been open a year, kid. I see a ton of new faces and sports stars every day. This is kind of a wild turkey shoot, don't you think?"

"What about Daryl Spencer? You've worked with him this season, right? Nothing strange about him? Or any of the Giants' pitchers and catchers?"

"Listen. You're a good kid. And I'd like to help you out but I got stuff to do—"

"I'm sorry to bug you like this, Lefty. But if you haven't heard, he's taken my fiancee, and I'm sort of at the end of my rope."

He hung his head with a dash of guilt. I kept at him. "You just seemed like a good hunch. I mean, you do have my photo behind your bar."

"I do?"

I nodded. Quickly got up and walked him over to look at it.

"Well I'll be..." He glanced at me, then back at the wall with growing clarity. "Come to think of it...Turns out you're the second fella to bring up that photo since we opened."

I stared at him. "No kidding. Who was the first?"

"Oh, I never got his name. Some good looking rich boy from back east. In here on the second day, asking about my time in Japan, my work with the Giants, about Seals Stadium, who all the people in that photo were. I didn't know your name at the time so couldn't tell him—"

"What else?"

He shrugged. Waved at a couple City Hall types coming in for morning beers. "Nothing special. Best places to stay, where all the local landmarks were. More like he was writing a school paper than wanting to visit any of 'em."

"Coit Tower? Fisherman's Wharf? The Presidio?"

"Yeah, the usuals. Even military stuff like Treasure Island and Battery Spencer."

Every drop of color left my face.

"Battery what?"

"Battery Spencer! Other side of the Golden Gate! Where they used to have those big cannons."

"You mean that creepy old abandoned fort?"

"Hey, it's really something. Do yourself a favor sometime and give it a visit—"

"I've been there. Years ago. Walked through it to take pictures of the bridge with an old girlfriend. I just… never knew its real name."

"How were those flapjacks, kid? Still hungry?"

"Umm, no. But now I think I'll have whatever you offered to put in my coffee."

Bottom of the Ninth

September 27th

Tressip woke me this morning from a pay phone. He was definitely on the Marin side of the bay. I could hear the unmistakable dull whooshing of cars crossing the Golden Gate. But I played dumb.

"Sorry your beloved Traitors couldn't take the pennant, Milton," he said. "Any luck with my riddles?"

"Working on 'em, Tressip. And that was your team more than mine."

"How DARE you say that to me!"

"I haven't even started saying things. How's my fiancee holding up, and it better be swell."

"If you insist that's who she is…just fine. For now."

"How about giving me the number of that phone booth you're in and I'll buzz you back when I find out where it is."

"Not on your life. But I'll give you 24 hours to find us and then…season's over."

He hung up. I smirked. This was one day I wouldn't need coffee.

◆ ◆ ◆

I had paid a pal of Billy Frack's to drive my Dodge back up from L.A., and by late afternoon I was tossing things in the trunk: a flashlight, rope, my .38, and all forty hard, wooden ounces of Triples Trevor. Stopped at a hardware and sporting goods store near the Presidio and bought some ammo for the gun. The guy had just folded over the top of the bag when none other than Agent Brewster entered the store with another new goon. Strolled over to me. He didn't look too good. Or pleased.

"Well, well. Doing a little home hardware-ing, Drake?"

"Yeah. The usual loose screws. What did you do, follow me here?"

"Damn right I did. You sure bolted out of St. Louis like Snappy's Comet. Got a lead you'd like to share?"

"Why would I have one of those? Isn't that your job?"

"Come on, Drake. I wasn't born yesterday."

"Could've fooled me."

"We did find Tressip's private plane, y'know," said his stooge, "At an airstrip outside of Berkeley. Was wondering how he was gettin' everywhere. "

"Congratulations. Stop by later and I'll give you both little gold stars. Meanwhile, call me if you think of anything useful to say."

I walked out. Knew they were going to follow me again and gave the Coronet a little gas to lose them in the park with some extra weaving. As it turned out, the weather cinched it for me. A fog bank higher and thicker than a plague of Egypt rolled in from the Pacific and cut visibility to three car lengths. I crawled across the Golden Gate, barely able to tell I was on a bridge, took the first exit on the other side and looped up to the cliffs. Turned into the dirt lot for the old gun battery and parked.

One of the spookiest things about fog is how quiet it makes things. I knew the bridge was just below the embankment, but it could've been on a distant planet for all I could see or hear of it.

What I did see, after stuffing the .38 behind my shirt and arming myself with Triples Trevor, were the looming, gothic shapes of Battery Spencer. The fort was built in 1897 to guard the Bay with three giant M1888s against foreign invaders that never materialized, then was finally scrapped in the middle of World War II. And it had a haunted, menacing feel to it. Perfect.

It also seemed abandoned, and now way past sunset, was smothered in darkening fog. There were two rows of abandoned former barracks, rusted out and filled with military spirits. I inched through every one. The air smelled like old urine and was beyond clammy. If Tressip was camping out up there with Liz, they both might've caught pneumonia already.

I was ready to give up staking out the place when I suddenly heard a ghostly sound in the fog. It was a faint woman's cry—more a sob than a scream—but did I imagine it? Did the wife of a fallen soldier throw herself off the cliff once?

Another wave of frigid fog fingers groped through the encampment. I wrapped my coat tighter. Listened hard.

And heard it again. It was coming from a barrack across the path I had just been inside. I retraced my steps. Took out the flashlight.

In the far corner of the structure, beside a small heap of discarded newspaper, pop bottles, and animal dung, was a door I hadn't noticed. Fitted with a shiny new padlock. The female sobbing was clearly somewhere behind it.

It took me a few minutes, but I found an old hair clip and managed to jimmie the lock open. Quietly opened the door. Saw a flight of steps leading to an underground bunker or storage chamber. Tightened my grip on the bat and crept down them.

Liz was nylon-corded to a girder, stripped to her soiled slip and bra, tears streaming from her eyes. Looked like she hadn't eaten in days. Unable to see me with the flashlight beam in her face, she immediately began shrieking through the black tape over her mouth.

"No baby, it's me!!" I put the beam on my own face to show her, then set the flashlight on the floor. Reached up to undo her mouth tape and her eyes practically popped out of her skull. I turned a fraction of a second too late: Tressip was behind me and yanked the .38 out of my shirt.

"Well done, sir. Extremely well done. Now get those hands up, please."

He hadn't seen the bat yet. I leaned it against the front of my leg, raised both of my hands.

"So the Giants ending up in third place just wasn't enough for you, was it?"

"Curiously…no. This damage you did to me runs deeper than I ever imagined. But we're a lot alike, you and I. Both of us lost our fathers. Both of us could have been big league stars, if not for one sloppy pitch—"

"Oh shut the hell up, you sick scum. I am nothing like you."

"Apologize for that, Milton."

"Never."

I heard the .38's chamber click. Felt its cold barrel on the back of my neck.

"How about now?"

"Gee, I don't know…How about THIS—"

Whipped the bat around and nailed the side of his half-burned head. The gun went off, narrowly missing my ear and putting a hole in the ceiling. I hit him again and the weapon went flying. He crumbled in a bloody heap on the floor. I ripped the tape off Liz's mouth, madly undid her cords.

"KILL HIM!"

"I knocked him out! Let's just go—"

"Where's the gun?? I'LL do it!!"

"No, Liz—"

I grabbed her arm and Triples Trevor and raced us back up the stairs.

It was so dark and foggy we kept slamming into barrack walls. Finally got back outside and headed toward the parking lot. I pulled off my coat, wrapped it around her.

"Nice swing in there, Snap," she said, "Never knew you could hit."

"Two for eighty-two lifetime. But they were both triples."

We reached the wet dirt of the parking lot and stopped. A familiar shiny black Mercury was parked about ten yards away. Brewster's car.

"What the hell? I ditched them over an hour ago. How'd they find me?"

"The FBI? That's a good thing, right? Come on."

She broke away, ran up to the passenger side of the Mercury and shrieked. Backed away from the car.

Brewster's stooge was sitting there with a large bullet hole in his forehead.

"Tressip got him!" she yelled.

"Wrong, Miss Doomis," said Brewster's voice behind us. He stepped out of the fog, brandishing a bigger revolver mine could only dream of being. "My partner of the day was getting a little too curious on the way over here."

"I don't believe this…" said Liz.

"But not too shocking," I added. "I thought his investigative work was a little slow and shoddy. And nice little phony factory siege you staged in Terre Haute, Brewster."

"Do either of you losers have any idea how much money Tressip has? How much he was willing to pay for some simple cooperation?"

"So he bought you off."

"No, I'd call it more of an under-the-table contract. He knew some federal men through his father's friends. Heard I was unhappy at the Bureau. That I wanted to retire early and sail around the globe on my yacht. Thought correctly that I could be persuaded to be his 'inside man' for a very pleasing sum."

"You lousy—"

I charged him. In a flash, his weapon was in my nostrils.

"Now now, Drake. One more day till the season ends—before I help Tressip leave the country and get the rest of my payoff. I don't want you blowing this deal. Where's our friend now?"

"I killed him."

"Baloney."

"Go take a look. He's downstairs."

"Not anymore, Milton…"

It was Tressip, also stepping out of the fog. Blood oozing from the scalp wound I gave him. He was wobbly but still looked ferocious.

"Hello, Richard," said his buddy Brewster.

"Good evening, Griffin," said Tressip. "And thank you. But I think I can manage from here." He raised my .38 and blew Brewster's brains out from four feet away.

Everything happened fast. Tressip grabbing my arm, knocking the bat away. Liz slipping in the mud trying to run. Me lunging after her and Tressip getting a burly arm around my neck, slamming my head on the Mercury's door. I dropped in a daze. heard Liz's screams muffle as he pulled the stooge's body out of the passenger seat, shoved her in and peeled out of the lot.

I staggered to my feet, somehow got to the Dodge and roared after them. Nearly went off the winding road three times trying to catch up. The Merc tore through a red light at the bottom, got back on the bridge to 'Frisco. I broke the same law, pumped my speedometer up to 55. Saturday night traffic was as thick as the fog going into the city, and we bobbed and weaved through it like lunatics.

But then we could go no further. Ran into a murky sea of red tail lights. Tressip jammed on his brakes right in front of me. I hit the Merc's bumper head on, slammed my mouth on the Dodge's steering wheel. Groggily climbed out half a minute later, spitting a couple front teeth on the road. A few motorists ran over to help, but I was already stumbling past them. Followed Tressip as he pulled Liz between oncoming cars to the sidewalk on the eastern side, the .38 lodged in her spine.

"Stop, Tressip!" I yelled, "It's over!"

"For you, maybe! She told me she loved me once, I believed her, and now we're going away!"

"Going where?? Every cop in the city you weren't paying off is about to be after you!"

He paused at the rail, spun around with a beaming, insane expression.

"Going where it's wet…and quiet…and we can be together. Come darling."

He hoisted himself on the rail, yanked her up beside him.

"DON'T!!"

She struggled with him. I hobbled up and he shot the sidewalk two inches from my foot.

"Uh-uh, Milton. You threw an evil fastball. You lose. You don't get the girl in the end. I do. Forever."

He stood on the rail, gripped a cable with his free hand. Hauled Liz up by her hair.

"Ready to say your vows, my sweet?"

He was really going to do this. Any motorists who tried to intervene were fired at. The fog whipping across the bridge made it even more nightmarish. I begged my brain for an answer. And then…

"Okay, Tressip! You're right! I KNOW she loved you, because she told me a few days ago! She even… she even told me about your son!"

Tressip paused, stared at me in wonder. So did Liz.

"My son?"

"Right. The little boy she had nine months after she had…relations with you. She was afraid to tell you, and when I proposed to her I agreed to help raise him."

A half-confused, half beatific expression enveloped his ruined face. I kept going.

"Don't you remember him? Little Maxie! You scared him away at that memorial service for Liz's brother!"

"That was my son…"

"I was going to name him after you, Richard," said Liz, playing along, "I just wasn't sure I'd see you again."

He stroked her hair with the gun still in his hand. "In your heart you knew you would…"

"Kiss me, handsome."

He smiled, leaned in. She put her mouth on his, then kneed him full force in the groin. He howled, slipped off the damp rail. Pulled her off with him. She clamped an arm on the top rail as she dropped. I raced up.

Tressip dangled from her ankle, high over the fog bank of death, volcanic rage and hurt in his doomed eyes. And they were staring right at me.

"You shouldn't have hit me, Milton…"

"For God's sake, Tressip! It was an accident!"

"There are no accidents…" Liz tried to kick him off but his grip was otherworldly. Her hands were slipping. "Worse than that…You didn't pick me for your team that day, Milton! YOU DIDN'T PICK ME AND LOOK WHAT HAPPENED!"

Police sirens approached. Tressip heard them, sighed deeply… and let go. "LOOK WHAT HAPPENED…" he cried as he fell into oblivion, cold fog and seawater silently entombing him.

The helpful mob swarmed in. Helped me pull Liz back over the rail to safety. I kissed and hugged her until a police officer made us stop.

For the Love of the Dame

September 28th

"Snappy Appreciation Day? You're kiddin' me, right?"

"Not at all," said Horace Stoneham over the phone at eight in the morning, "You're the biggest story in town, kid. Probably in the whole country. Forget about taking down the Peanut Killer, you exposed a crooked FBI man."

"He sort of exposed himself, pardon the expression."

"Yeah well, be at the ballpark by 12 noon. And bring your sweetheart."

It was awful tough to leave the bedroom, let alone my apartment. Reporters clogged the sidewalk outside for a change instead of snoopy lawmen. But after taking our sweet time about rejoining the world, I skirted Liz out my famous back exit and hiked us up the hill on the next street to Seals Stadium.

All my usher and usherette pals were there to greet us with gifts of flowers and alcohol. Then Stoneham lured me out to a microphone at home plate. Slimy Mayor Christopher was there to shake my hand, Cards and Giants lined up on either side. Flashbulbs popped in my face. Liz watched from a few yards away, beaming through misty eyes, and I decided to say something after all.

"Today…I consider myself…the luckiest son-of-a-bitch in San Francisco. I've been ushering games in this park for over a half dozen years, and have never gotten anything but kindness, and encouragement, and good tips from you fans. My fiancee and I have been through quite a lot this year, survived many tough breaks, but thank God we still have an awful lot to live for. "

"I'm sorry the Giants couldn't finish first, even with helping out their pitchers as much as I could. But it's only their first year in town, and I'm sure Willie and Orlando and Valmy Thomas—and I better not forget Antonelli—will give you folks plenty of pennants and world titles the next ten years in their beautiful new ballpark at Candlestick Point. So thanks again for coming out to support us, even with a dangerous criminal stalking me and the club all season, and GO GIANTS!"

The crowd roared, and for a retired ballplayer and amateur sleuth I felt pretty good. I watched the ballgame with Liz in a front row box, signing a raft of baseballs and programs throughout, and enjoyed an absolutely thrilling season finale. The Cards took a 1-0 lead, before Mays tied it with his 36th homer, a shot off the left field pole. Cunningham put the Cards up 2-1 with a homer and Sad Sam Jones pitched a classic Sad Sam 6th: walk-walk-double-Bob Schmidt homer, four runs across the dish and there would've been more if Mays hadn't been gunned down at the plate by Bobby Gene Smith.

Then your inevitable Leon Wagner butchery in left ignited a three-run Cards rally and Phil Paine and Paul Giel pitched us into extra innings tied 5-5. It was a gorgeous day, and nobody rooting for either club wanted the game to end. But

National League Final Standings

Milwaukee	89	65	.578	—
Chicago	86	68	.558	3
San Francisco	84	70	.545	5
Cincinnati	76	78	.494	13
Philadelphia	75	79	.487	14
St. Louis	72	82	.468	17
Pittsburgh	70	84	.455	19
Los Angeles	64	90	.416	25

American League Final Standings

New York	92	62	.597	—
Chicago	90	64	.584	2
Cleveland	84	70	.545	8
Boston	83	71	.539	9
Baltimore	81	73	.526	11
Detroit	77	77	.500	15
Kansas City	58	96	.377	34
Washington	51	103	.331	41

it had to. Leading off our 12th, Ed Bressoud rifled a double down the right field line, Irv Noren kicked it off his shoe a few times like a buttery soccer ball and Eddie raced all the way around to score the unearned game-winner.

After meeting the press some more and shaking too many hands, Liz and I made our escape. More fog was rolling in, and we cuddled as we walked downtown in search of a quiet, celebratory dinner.

"Been meaning to ask," she said, "How did you ever come up with that bit about Tressip and me having a son?"

"It was the last of the 9th on that bridge, doll. I had to think of something. Plus the man was insane, desperate, and delirious. He was likely to believe anything. And you went along with it like a pro."

"Well, at least I really didn't have to kiss him again. Did that enough on our small number of dates. Oh—and guess what? The editor of the *New York Herald Tribune* wants to add me to their World Series coverage team! Maybe I can talk them into letting you write a column from the stands. You got nothing special to do this week, right?"

"Naw. Just recuperating. But I got a lifetime for that."

I kissed her. We had already made our wedding plans lying in bed that morning, which would be a quickie job in Reno without friends, flowers or little Cousin Maxie. After that, who knew if I would still be an usher? It was a fun summer job, but not exactly a full-time living.

I certainly wasn't too shy about calling Phil Todd back, trying my luck with the Spokane Indians again. I was still a few years shy of forty, plenty of time to get that old Snappy Curve snapping again. And maybe, just maybe, I'd be ready to resurrect the old fastball I had as a kid. After all, it's kind of become the way I've gone through life: high, fast, and middle-up.

The End

≈ Appendix: The World Series ≈

Spahn and Pain and Unfortunately No Gain

October 1st

You'd think the Yankee brass would've given me a choicer seat after my killer-catching heroics out west. I guess sticking me out in the right field bleachers was how they felt about anyone from the National League.

I was surrounded by wall-to-wall hooligans out there. Most of them had camped out the night before to buy tickets, and many with hidden flasks to lubricate the experience. The good thing was that none of them recognized me or even knew who I was. The bad thing was that I still had to listen to them.

"Spahn? He's a bum! Whitey'll mop his clock."

"You told me three Ballantines, a Coke and a red hot."

"No, meathead. I said two Ballantines, two red hots and a Crackerjack!"

"Mathews? He's a bum! What'd he hit this year, .195?"

Actually, it was .215, but what difference did it make? With a half hour still to go before the first pitch, I dreamed about being up in the press box beside Liz.

Five minutes after the first pitch, Warren Spahn was wishing he was dead. Carey laced a double down the line with one gone in the Yankee 1st. Slaughter singled him in. Mantle singled Slaughter to third. Berra dumped another single into center to make it 2-0. Skowron walked. I had a full house of cheering nuts shaking the bleachers and dozens of rollicking armpits in my face.

Fred Haney came out to calm Spahnie down, and it worked, because Warren got McDougald on strikes and Richardson on a dinky fly to end the inning. Logan got them a run back against Ford with a two-out single in the 2nd, but then Spahn was back on his slippery slope. He started by whiffing Whitey, but Siebern blasted a ball that landed two deafening rows behind me, Carey ripped the next pitch into the left field stands, it was 4-1, and Spahnie was gone for the day.

Warren did have trouble against lefties all season, but no one saw this disaster coming, not even the bleacher creatures around me.

"It's ovah!!" one of them yelled to Aaron out in center, "Ya hear me Henry?? O-VAH!!!"

What was really over was the Yankee offense for the rest of the game. Spot starter Juan Pizarro took over and pitched one-hit ball for four and two-third innings before Bob Rush escaped jams in the 7th and 8th.

Crandall socked a solo homer in the 6th, and after Roach singled and Mathews walked in the 7th, Aaron strode up there as the go-ahead run. All mouthy shenanigans ceased in the bleachers. You had the certain Cy Young winner (23-8, 2.56) facing the possible NL MVP (.336, 40 homers, 120 RBIs, 17-game winning hits) with the game on the line. Breathing was suddenly a luxury.

Aaron worked Ford to 3-2, then rapped a ball up the middle that McDougald grabbed and flipped to Richardson to start a killing double play. Ford snuffed out the last six Braves with ease, and New York had first blood in the Series.

I had to wait around forever for Liz to finish her game story, and we were both too drained to do anything but return to the Piccadilly and order room service. Tomorrow it would be Burdette against Ditmar, with Wes Covington back in action, and I told Liz if she couldn't get me into the press box or a grandstand section containing actual adults, the marriage was off.

Game One:
MLW 010 001 000 – 1 5 0
NYY 220 000 00x – 4 11 0

W-Ford L-Spahn

U.S. Steel Shows Record Profits

Bombers Drop 19-Run Atomic Device on Braves, Lead Series 2-0

By Liz Dumás
Herald Tribune
Female Columnist

October 2nd

Fred Haney sat in his Yankee Stadium office with the remains of his head in his hands. His Braves had just been shot, stabbed, hung, set on fire, drawn, quartered and tossed to a pack of ravenous back alley dogs, and it would be a good half hour before his scratchy voice could utter an intelligible syllable.

Because how does one react to such carnage? After Spahn came out of the pen armed with nothing for Game One, Lew Burdette began Game Two by serving up a Siebern line shot homer into the stands in right, Norm's second of this young Series. In literary parlance, it was gothic foreshadowing. Walks to Carey and the Mick soon followed. Yogi

Berra, slower than Nikita Khrushchev on a basketball court, then legged out a triple past Covington to left center, and it was 3-0 home fellas before the first punches were even thrown in the bleachers.

On the Yankee hill, Art Ditmar was not himself either, but the Braves helped him out all afternoon by grounding into double plays and stranding runners. And unlike Burdette or the four doomed souls who followed him out to the rubber chopping block, Ditmar at least showed he belonged on a professional baseball diamond.

Are you sitting down, dear readers? Good. Berra was on base all six times to the plate, with two homers and two singles to go with that triple. Mantle was on base all six times to the plate, with four walks, a single and an upper deck homer. Norm Siebern, MVP of the first two affairs, was on base six of seven times to the plate, with two walks, two singles, and two homers, his second clout a grand slam in the 5th on the first relief pitch Bob Rush threw.

Later, Casey Stengel was typically gracious in victory. "I won't say nothin' bad about no Braves. You win 89 you deserve all the deserving you get, and that's a bunch of sweet, talented grapes hangin' over there, so don't tell me we got this thing licked headin'

over to that frozen tundra they play in, with all the good pitching no one saw today that I wish we had sometimes when we're stuck in one them barnburners with no hoses in sight," he explained.

The one silver lining for Milwaukee was the reappearance of slugger Wes Covington, who singled and homered in four tries. But Frank Torre, one of their best pressure hitters, made out all five times to McDougald at second and Aaron rapped into another death-dealing double dip in the 3rd. Then there was poor Eddie Mathews, who missed a sure homer and surer bloop single thanks to mysterious, swirling Bronxian wind gusts.

The Yanks hadn't crafted a stomping like this in a long time, and the Braves had rarely been a stompee all season. Baseball can be funny, though. Teams often come out cold after getting every break and blessing in the Bible, and a frosty Wisconsin climate, loud, bundled-up wigwammers and Joey Jay will be primed to make that happen to the stately Gothamites.

Game Two:
MLW 010 100 000 – 2 9 2
NYY 302 052 16x – 19 22 0

W-Ditmar L-Burdette

Brave New Brat Tub

October 4th

It was great to be on another planet for Game Three. Open fields, open sky, Wisconsin-nice people, and a ballgame for the ages that reminded me why the sport is one of the two best things on Earth.

First I had to manuever my way through the vast, sweet-smelling parking lot. I'd become a minor celebrity in these parts, and ten different "tail-gating" groups tried to rope me into parties behind their open station wagons. I picked the one that offered me an extra grandstand seat and served me an early lunch from a "brat tub". This was just what it sounds like: an army of Usinger's bratwurst simmered in Blatz beer and onions.

Braves fans were ecstatic to be back in the Series, nonplussed about having their headresses handed to them two days ago. "I sold Joe Adcock new whitewalls at my shop last week," said Freddy Skiba, "The man had a rough year with the stick but he still gave me a five dollar tip. How can you not root for a fella like that?"

Two brats, too many onions and a few bottles of Schlitz later, I waddled with my new friends into County Stadium a few minutes late. It was a godsend. I missed Siebern opening the game with a slice double to left which Covington—naturally—kicked into the corner. An Elston Howard single one out later put Joey Jay behind 1-0 and made the crisp October air a little icy. The crowd never got down though, tooting horns, waving plastic tomahawks, urging on their heroes as pleasantly loud as they could muster.

The Braves responded to this in the 2nd. Crandall walked, Roach singled him to third. Crandall was nailed at the plate on a Logan grounder, but a ball got past Berra to advance the runners and Jay hit a sac fly to tie it up.

Big fat deal, said Mickey Mantle, who turned around some Canadian air with a solo missle last seen heading for Lake Michigan. My rowmates squirmed, got a bit quieter. The Braves had put runners aboard each of the first six frames off Larsen, but managed only one run. After freshly-whitewalled Adcock pinch-hit for Jay and grounded out to end the 6th, Larsen then smacked a homer to left to begin the 7th. Winter was truly coming.

The seventh-inning stretch featured a fun group sing-along to a small polka band atop the Milwaukee dugout. It seemed to lift everyone's spirits. Bruton singled with one out. Covington lined a single to get him to third, but Wes pulled his fourth bonehead play of the Series, rounding first too wide and getting tagged out by Skowron. Groans and maybe a boo or two filled the air, but Aaron singled in Bruton and it was 3-2. Stengel replaced Larsen with his favorite set-up reliever, Virgil Trucks.

Here was Eddie Mathews now, saddled with a low batting mark but always capable of a big hit, like his Opening Day homer to beat Roy Face and the Pirates. Eddie looked at a few pitches, then swung.

The ball was clean out of the yard before we even reached our feet. 4-3 Braves! A half dozen of my new pals rubbed my head. One stuck a headress on it. I warned them that my good luck charm deal with the Giants never paid off, and sure enough, Yogi clubbed a homer to tie it again in the 8th.

Humberto Robinson was pitching now, and put us through the ringer. After Aaron and Mathews stranded two more runners to end the 8th, Enos Slaughter pinch-hit a triple to begin the 9th that dropped two inches fair. Haney brought the infield in. Robinson bore down, got Siebern on a grounder, whiffed Carey and Howard grounded out to end the threat. Ryne Duren mowed the Braves down in the last of the 9th, so extra innings happened.

Mantle, Berra, and Skowron went out 1-2-3, and Milwaukee was forced to hit for Robinson. Adcock had already been used, Pafko was in left field for Butterfingers Covington, so up stepped Harry Hanebrink. Yes fans, Harry Hanebrink. Maybe ten at bats all season. He bounced the first pitch he saw out to McDougald at second, but the frigid air put a spell on Gil's grip, and his throw sailed into the first base boxes for a two-base error!

Torre, 0-for-5 on the day and 1-for-13 in the Series, singled him over to third. The place became a nice, pleasant asylum. Billy Bruton dug in. He had singled his last three times up. Everyone was standing. Duren looked in…stretched…threw…

And Bruton ripped a liner into center for the ballgame! Schlitz showers for over thirty thousand! I glanced up at the press box while I got wet, imagining that Liz was having a lot less fun. But I'm sure she was cheering inside.

Game Three:
NYY 100 100 110 0 – 4 9 1
MLW 010 000 300 1 – 5 15 3

W-Robinson L-Duren

Whiteywashed

Ford Rolls Over Braves with 4-Hit Shutout, Parks 3-1 Yanks in Series Driver's Seat

By Liz Dumás
Herald Tribune
Featured Columnist

October 5th

He showed up for his last outing of the year against Baltimore, this port-siding blonde demon, with a boozy head and nothing on his pitches. New Yorkers were actually worried. Then Whitey Ford handled the Braves rather easily in the opener, a mere warmup act for his 7-0 command performance in Game Four today. Milwaukee never had a chance, and this World Series is one Yankee win from a too-early closing curtain.

Actually, the Chairman of the Board and Carl Willey both looked wonderful for the first three innings, but Willey was the resident mortal. He walked Carey, gave up a Slaughter single and run-scoring grounder to Mantle in the 4th. A Siebern single, Carey walk and Berra RBI single in the 6th made it 2-0. One run would have been enough, because Whitey's stuff was demonically good.

The Yankees even tried to make it a rough day for him, and he wouldn't have it. Skowron booted a grounder hit by Mathews in the 1st, but after a Roach single, Aaron grounded into his third twin killing of the Series. In the 4th, Hank started the inning by reaching first on catcher's interference, and guess what? Adcock grounded into a double play. Felix Mantilla hit a pinch single to start the 8th, but oh yeah—Roach grounded into an inning-ending double play.

Meanwhile, the Bombers were lobbing soft grenades all over the field and exploding them. A Mantle walk and Berra bloop double began their 8th. Willey gave up a sac fly to McDougald to make it 3-0, and when Trowbridge came in to face lefty Kubek, said lefty Kubek lined a home run to right that just made it over Pakfo's leaping glove. For the sheer fun of it, they scored twice more in the 9th with a Carey double and obligatory Johnny Logan error in the mix, and County Stadium was so quiet you could hear obnoxious tavern cheering all the way from the Bronx.

Unless you were a Yankee fan, there was nothing good about this game. It will now be up to Warren Spahn to save the day in Game Five, a man who couldn't get out of his own ghastly way in New York. He'll face Bob Turley, prone to be wild, with the hope that another midwest miracle is in the cards. And the dice.

Game Four:
NYY 000 101 032 – 7 13 2
MIL 000 000 000 – 0 4 1

W-Ford L-Willey

Out with a Wisconsin Whimper

October 6th

There was nothing we could do. Nothing.

I sat with my tail-gating pals from Game Three in the same grandstand seats. It was even colder out than on Friday, but we were prepared with our Braves garb, Indian blankets, and nuclear flasks. I even let them put warpaint on my face.

The irony was that even after he surrendered a home run to Norm Siebern on the first pitch of the game, it wasn't Warren Spahn who needed our good luck smoke signals. It was the Milwaukee offense.

Against Bob Turley, walker of 134 men in 257 innings and sporting a perfectly average 15-13 record and 3.56 ERA, the Braves' bats were spooked from first inning to last. Witness:

1st inning—Leadoff double, Mathews, Aaron and Covington do nothing.

2nd inning—Two leadoff walks, Roach, Logan and Spahn do nothing.

4th inning—Crandall single with one out, Roach and Logan do nothing.

5th inning—Torre single and Mathews walk with one out, Aaron and Covington do nothing.

6th inning—Bruton walk and Crandall double with nobody out, Roach, Logan, and Spahn do nothing.

7th inning—Torre and Mathews walk with nobody out, Aaron and Covington ground out, Wes's into a double play.

8th inning—Bruton leads with single, Crandall hits into a double play.

9th inning—Mathews and Aaron single with two outs, Covington flies out to end the Series.

Game Five:
NYY 100 000 001 – 2 9 0
MIL 000 000 000 – 0 9 0

W-Turley L-Spahn

Without a doubt, considering what was at stake, it was the worst display of clutch hitting I'd ever witnessed. The Braves left 13 aboard, eight of them by Covington. Except for the leadoff Siebern dinger and a stupid leadoff triple to Turley in the 9th that led to New York's other bookend run on a two-out Carey double, virtually none of this was Warren's fault.

When Siebern caught the last out and it was finally over, I trudged through the exit tunnel with the massive funeral procession. Waited around in the slowly-emptying parking lot drinking Schlitz until Liz found me. Yankee champagne spray still twinkled in her blonde hair.

"Well, that was sure awful," I said. "Bet the Giants could've done better."

"Not with their bullpen. That Siebern played like he was in a higher league. 13-for-24 with four homers."

"He won Series MVP?"

"Him and Ford. Clean split by the writers."

"Nice. Who'd you vote for?"

She smiled mischeviously. "Harry Hanebrink, of course."

"That's my Liz…"

I kissed her and we started walking, into the end of summer.

About the Author

Jeff Polman is a journalist, produced screenwriter, and baseball blogger. In addition to being Arts Editor of the *Vermont Vanguard Press* its first five years, he has written for the *Advocate* newspapers, *Boston Phoenix, Huffington Post, Baseball Prospectus, Hardball Times, Seamheads, Chicagoside Sports,* ESPN's *SweetSpot Network*, and other Web sites. *Mystery Ball '58* was adapted from the third of his five fictional replay blogs, which also include *1924 and You Are There!, Play That Funky Baseball (Ball Nuts* in book form*), The Bragging Rights League,* and his most recent creation, *Dear Hank.* He is a lifelong Red Sox fan, resides with his wife and son in Culver City, CA, but is happy to report that the historic Double Play Bar and Grill in San Francisco is still right across the street from where Seals Stadium once stood—and serving a damn fine tuna melt.

Website: jeffpolman.com
Twitter: @jpballnut

Acknowledgments

First off, I can't thank my lovely and dear wife Carmen Patti enough for putting up with my constant Strat play and computer hogging. I also want to thank the sixteen "absentee managers" from around the Internet who provided me with lineups and rotations to help fuel my '58 season replay and inspire this book. They were:

CUBS: Scott Simkus, author of *Outsider Baseball*
REDS: Jimmy Moore, of *A Second Time Through the Order*
GIANTS: Daniel Day, Director of News & Editorial Services at
    Princeton University
DODGERS: Bill Miller, of *The On Deck Circle*
BRAVES: Larry Granillo, of *Wezen-Ball*
PIRATES: Pat Lackey, of *Where Have You Gone, Andy Van Slyke?*
CARDS: Daniel Shoptaw, of *C70 At the Bat*
PHILLIES: Max Gallner of *The Eric Bruntlett Fan Club* and
    Paul Dylan of *OneForFive.com*

RED SOX: Mike Lynch, of *Seamheads*
WHITE SOX: Rob Warmowski, of *Can't Stop the Bleeding*
INDIANS: Mike Bates (The Common Man) of *SB Nation*
TIGERS: Dan McCloskey, of *Left Field*
YANKEES: Kevin Graham, of *Baseball Revisited*
SENATORS: Ted Leavengood, author of *Clark Griffith: The Old
    Fox of Washington Baseball* and *Ted Williams and the 1969
    Washington Senators*
ORIOLES: T. J. Smith of *Eutaw Street Hooligans*
ATHLETICS: Aaron Stilley of *Royal Heritage*